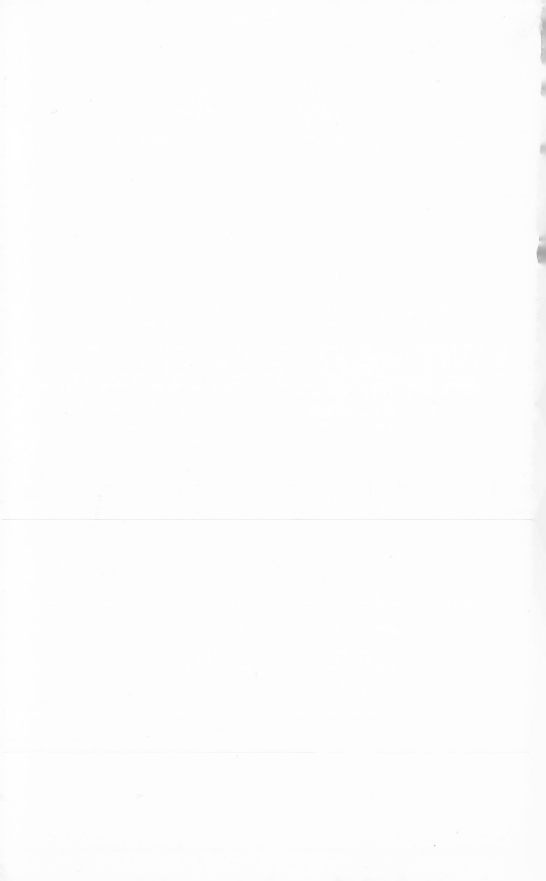

The Free Fall

of

Webster Cummings

Also by Tom Bodett

As Far As You Can Go Without a Passport

Small Comforts

The End of the Road

The Big Garage on Clear Shot

Tom Bodett

The Free Fall of Webster Cummings

HYPERION

NEW YORK

Library of Congress Cataloging-in-Publication Data

Bodett, Tom, 1955–
The free fall of Webster Cummings / by Tom Bodett.
p.   cm.
ISBN 0-7868-6209-2
1. Travelers—United States—Fiction.   2. Alaska—Fiction.
I. Title.
PS3552.0357F74   1996
813'.54—dc20   95-25694
CIP

Book design by Jennifer Ann Daddio

FIRST EDITION
1 3 5 7 9 10 8 6 4 2

To

Bill, Dick, Peg, Linda, *and* **Bob**

Thanks

Thanks a lot to a lot of people. It's said that writers use everything around them when they are writing. If I was smart enough to do that, this would be a better story. But I have at least been smart enough to use the good people I have around me. Sharon McKemie sat with me through every chapter of this story and through much of what inspired their moods. I could never exaggerate her importance to this book and I won't. I will just leave it like that.

Gary Thomas and Luana Stovel also were there as producers and as friends as we trudged through yet another ill-advised radio program designed for the distinct purpose of scaring me into writing. Thank you, good friends. It worked.

Thanks especially to Steve Saslow, June Brody, Beverly Padratzik, Allen Rosenberg, and all the other folks at SJS Entertainment for your confidence and, ultimately, your understanding. Thanks as well to Ben Manilla and Ben Manilla Productions of San Francisco.

I asked a lot of silly questions of a lot of people, but none more than farmer Dave Belzberg of Medford, Oregon, who showed me the poetry in peaches. I also want to thank my good friends Bob and Kay Dorris for putting me up and putting up with me on those grueling research trips to the Rogue Valley.

There are the names of many other people I have around me which I could list; but lists of names mean very little, and the people I would put on such a list mean tons to me. Truckloads. Whole ships. Fleets of them. So thanks to you all. We've seen each other through a lot, and we're all still here. That counts for everything.

I

The worst thing in the world is the homesickness that comes over a man occasionally when he is at home.

—E. W. Howe

There is a road that stretches from America all the way to the Last Frontier. The stories of hope and determination that have gone up this highway in the past fifty years are too many to be told: modern pioneers leaving convention and home behind to challenge their dreams.

Over-inflated gas prices, bent rims, loose gravel, and broken windshields aren't exactly the hazards that earlier pioneers might have faced, but it was enough to impress upon our pilgrims that there are dues to pay along the road to our dreams.

That road is paved now; the road to Alaska, that is. Almost any car with the gas money can make it to the Last Frontier with barely a scratch. The road to our desire is still a rough ride, and like all roads, it points in both directions at once.

Emily first came up this road with a master's degree in English Literature from Radcliffe College and a general disgust with an America swaggering into the *Me Decade*. As she nursed and nudged her beat-up old car along the Alcan Highway, she must have imagined every possible future for herself, each more perfect than the one before.

There is something about the landscape you cross to the Last Frontier that seems to summon every ounce of wishfulness a person holds. Whether it is the almost total absence of anything touched by human hands for as far as the eye can see—and the feeling of emptiness that accompanies it—or the brilliant panoramas of serpentine glaciers, sweeping forests, and great blue slopes of mountains that obliterate every horizon, it is hard to define.

But what is plain to any who have made the journey into this country is the sense that anything is possible, and that you can get what you deserve. Coming into Alaska is more than crossing a state line.

Emily thought about all that, this time on her way out. She considered what her efforts of the past fifteen years had wrought, and wondered if the promises of the land had been kept.

Looking around the car, she tried to recall what she'd come looking for those years ago, and although she couldn't bring anything in particular to mind, she was fairly certain they didn't include three kids and a one-armed man. Had she met them along the road then, she certainly wouldn't have recognized them as hers.

Ed Flannigan leaned his head against the window and pretended to be asleep. Through half-closed eyes he watched the dirty spring snow along the highway fly by. A hazy sky concealed anything beyond the most immediate horizon. The road ahead felt like empty mileage with nothing at the end of it. Behind him, a lifetime in Alaska and three gloomy children to show for it. Ed still couldn't believe how the past two years had conspired to place him in this situation.

It had all started with the accident at work that took his right arm and left him with a piece of hardware for a limb. It took almost a year of rehabilitation and physical therapy, but he got back on the job and into his road grader at the Highway Department just in time for the lay-offs. Because of his seniority he was only cut back to half-time at first. Then he was limited to emergency snow plowing, and finally, after putting twelve years and one good arm into his job, Ed was let go for good.

State budget cuts were responsible and Ed, being a lifelong Alaskan, was used to the comings and goings of an oil-fired economy. Things would turn around. They always did.

He tried his hand, so to speak, at being a deck-hand on a few of his friends' boats, but the sea water didn't agree with his prosthesis and tended to jam it up. He had the use of a clamp at the end of it which was connected to the muscles remaining in his upper arm and shoulder. He could grab hold and let go of things when he wanted to, except when the salt water made it sticky.

With as much line, netting, and anchors as can be pushed over the side of a fishing boat, one thing a guy better be able to do is let go of a thing when he wants to. When his friends started referring to him as "snap-on crab bait" Ed decided to stay on the beach and collect his unemployment.

Ed kept up hope of getting his old job back, but got pretty nervous when his unemployment benefits began running out. There were two weeks left on his final extension when Jack, his old boss, came by to tell him they were closing the maintenance garage at The End of the Road, and moving all the equipment up to Soldotna.

Jack said all the positions had been eliminated. Ed could reapply up the road, but he'd have to stand in line with everybody else. Ed thanked Jack for coming by and closed the door behind him, and the best heavy equipment operator north of the forty-second parallel sat down on his couch and cried. It had been the worst two years of his life.

Emily thought she heard Ed grumble something and it drew her out of her head into the car again. Ed sat slouched up against the window. She reached over and took his hand, but there was no response. *He must be asleep,* she thought, and checked out the kids in the rear-view mirror.

Ed Junior was staring deep into the abyss of his Gameboy, making little snorts and grunts as he tuned into yet another deadly battle concealed in his headphones. It relieved her to see him at least momentarily distracted from his whining. She couldn't decide who was taking the move harder, big Ed or little Ed.

Pulling the boy out of the sixth grade with just two months to go seemed incredibly cruel and unusual to Ed Junior. His dad thought no more of being separated from the land of his birth and the only place that ever made sense to him. Father and son's identical pouting methods pointed to genetics; or, Emily considered, there is not a great deal of difference between the sixth grade and Ed's Alaska.

Missy and Corey looked at the move as the adventure it was. "Will there be lots of girls to play with and not so many boys?" Missy would ask.

"Are you sure they have first grade in Oregon?" Corey worried.

The two of them were slumped bonelessly against their safety belts lost in the sleep of the innocent.

Emily checked her watch as she passed a mileage sign. They were making good time and would be out of Alaska by noon. At this pace they would reach their stop in the Yukon Territory for the night. Relieved, she took a deep breath, stretched her neck, and bent to the wheel.

With her thoughts miles behind her and her dream just days ahead, Emily drifted to the events that had brought them to this place and time. It had been the most exciting two years of her life.

When Ed had his accident she thought at first she would die. Watching his pain and his struggle with such a grave and permanent predicament was almost too much for her. She vacillated between rage and despair, mercy and revulsion.

But Ed had handled himself beautifully. His strength and good humor were so effervescent that Emily felt more comforted by Ed than anything she had to offer him. Emily looked at her husband as some heroic metaphor for the finest things a man could be.

Ed's one-armed-this-and-that jokes quickly became legend and he was quick to dismiss the whole subject. "Can't just stand around waitin' to grow a new one like a lizard. I got a family to feed."

The problem was he couldn't feed it. At least not right away. Ed stayed home with the kids while he recovered, and Emily went to work for the first time in their marriage. It was a heavenly experience in spite of the hellish circumstance that had brought it about.

The local college had written a grant and created a position, tailor-made, for Emily. She became the department head, instructor, administrator, and secretary of the Beluga Community College Department of English—and she had thrived.

After a dozen years resigned to her role as a wife and mother, it was exhilarating to have new things to think about. Instead of driving to town wondering how her food budget would be spent, she'd be pondering Milton's *When I Consider How My Light Is Spent*. She traded a pound of ground round for Ezra Pound. Defrosting freezers and baggy knees were replaced with Robert Frost and Sophocles. Shakespeare's limericks. Whitman's muse.

As a veteran Alaska housewife, Emily had a wardrobe that consisted pretty much of three pairs of sweatpants. As a teacher, she'd bought skirts and jackets, suits and heels. And she'd bought them with *her money*. It had been so long since Emily had earned a paycheck, she had the first one copied and stuck to the refrigerator.

As Emily drove her sleeping family southward she could hardly believe it had only been two years. So many things had changed; everything, really.

At first, Ed took deftly to the responsibilities of the home with his trademark good humor. There was an endless comedy series of *How does a one-armed man fold sheets?* or *How many arms does it take to screw in a lightbulb?* routines. He learned how to cook and would present his concoctions, which weren't half-bad, with great fanfare and bluster.

But the longer it went on, the less fun it became. After Ed's brief time back at work and then the permanent lay-off there seemed to be nothing left but the bitterness of it all. Emily herself was outraged over how a man could lose an arm in the course of his job, and then have that job taken away from him. She fed Ed's anger, and Ed's anger in return nurtured a simmering disgust in Emily for all things Alaskan.

"Short-sighted opportunists," she would rant. "All of us. We'll tear up anything to create these almighty *jobs*. Jobs are everything in this silly place. And if you don't have a job you're nothing. There's no substance here."

Ed didn't agree with Emily's view of his home state. He didn't think there was anything wrong with Alaska that wasn't twice as wrong everyplace else. He was comforted some by her anger on his behalf, but he'd heard it all before.

Emily had never taken to Alaska. She loved Ed and her family, and she loved their friends. But the rest of the place was lost on her. Whatever romantic element this land had once held for her—whatever it was that had drawn her up that highway and rooted her at The End of the Road—had long ago atrophied and was soon to perish.

Ed began to get sloppy about the household and spent less time there. He went off with his buddies a lot: fishing, bowling, shooting. And drinking. Always drinking. If Emily tried to say something, Ed would deflect it with an increasingly forced wit: "Hey, I never drink on a work night," or "I might be a drinker, but I'll never be a two-fisted one."

Ed's feats of strength and courage were so impressive that Ed began to be impressed with himself. A natural machismo that had always been bridled and made irresistible by a gentle manner began to come unharnessed. He talked louder, and rougher. Daring statements turned mean spirited.

"Don't let that wimp get ya!" he yelled at Ed Junior's Popeye Wrestling meet. And when his son was beaten he couldn't look his father in the face. Instead of *You'll get him next time,* it was *You should have had him.* Emily found herself following Ed around to smooth things over—with the kids, with their friends, and with each other.

His manner in bed went from masculine confidence to rough aggression. Ever so gradually Emily slid from being seduced to being subdued. The experience would leave her back turned to him listening to his snoring and wondering how Ed's irresistible boyish recklessness had simply turned thoughtless.

Ed was spending less time at home, but nobody really missed him. His mood had gone from playful self-degradation to defensive sarcasm. His gentle nature turned lifeless. It was as if he'd left his arm and his soul lying underneath the dump truck that day.

Emily looked again to Ed, still sleeping beside her, and shuddered at the thought of what her family had almost become. She offered up a little prayer of thanks, the latest in a series of thousands, for her friend Faye in Quartz Creek, Oregon.

Faye Bessett graduated from Radcliffe with Emily and was now Dean of Liberal Arts at Applegate College, one of the most progressive private schools in the West. She offered Emily an associate professorship with all the trimmings.

"But Faye," Emily had tried to warn, "until last year, I hadn't even been in a classroom in fifteen years. I'm not sure if reading John Donne to bored fishermen's wives really counts."

"You're exactly what I'm looking for," Faye had countered. "Remember, we're a progressive school down here. I'm sick of all the career academics we put in these positions. They're all in an intellectual lockstep that has nothing to do with the world anymore. I want to show the students a fresh point of view. You can do this, Emily."

And that was how it had happened. There really wasn't any choos-ing to the matter. Ed was unemployed and partially unemployable. The grant funding Emily's position at the college was running out. They were one month behind on the mortgage and two months on almost every-thing else. She was being offered a salary greater than Ed used to make in his best years with the road crew, and a chance at a real career.

There was a lot of kicking, screaming, and outright refusal from Ed at first, but in the end there was little he could do but pout and help the movers pack the van.

"We'll be back," he'd say, turning away any pitying farewells. "As soon as we get back on our feet and Emily gets this out of her system. Save my locker at the bowling alley. We won't be long at this Quartz Creek place."

Emily shifted her weight in the driver's seat and wondered if this was true. Ed suddenly stretched and spoke as if he'd been reading her thoughts. "Tell me about this Quartz Creek vibrator again."

Emily sighed, weary of this routine. "It's a vibration. Modern spirit-ualists believe there are certain power centers on the Earth formed by crystalline structures under the ground. Sante Fe, New Mexico, is one; Quartz Creek is another. These places radiate a great sense of healing and serenity. The energy draws spiritual people to it naturally.

"Quartz Creek is teeming with seers and healers, channelers and astral travelers. It's a virtual holy land, in a humanist sort of way. People actually make pilgrimages to it. Very exciting, don't you think?"

"I think I'll just throw myself out of the car now." Ed stared out the window. A sign reading *Canadian Customs, One Mile* swooped past.

"Oh, come on Ed." Emily wanted to be gentle with her man. She understood he was giving up a lot. "I know you hate all that stuff. And I know you're frustrated about not having a job, but there must be some-thing you're looking forward to."

Ed spoke without having to think. "I'm looking forward to coming home again. And golf. I might learn how to play golf." He held his clamp out in front of him. "Maybe I'll have this thing made into a putter."

Emily ignored it. "Ed, there's a lot of opportunity down there for all of us. You, too. Maybe you, especially, if you'd only give it a chance."

Emily expected something from Ed. When it did not come she asked, "Can I quote a poem of Shelley's?"

Ed groaned. Ever since Emily had gotten back into her books she wouldn't stop quoting poetry. "Shelly who?" he said, knowing darn well.

"Percy Bysshe Shelley," Emily said wearily. "The poem is *Ode to the West Wind* and one stanza really seems to fit. *Drive my dead thoughts over the Universe like withered leaves to quicken a new birth.*" She let the line hang in the car and waited for Ed's response.

"That Shelley. He's an English fella, isn't he?"

Emily was cautious. "Yes, he *was*."

"The English haven't gotten anything right since dry gin. I'll rake my own leaves if it's all the same to you."

Emily turned to Ed to implore him to work on his attitude, but she stopped. Ed's eyes fixed on another sign as it went past. His head followed it clear around; *Leaving Alaska* was all it said. Emily only caught a glimpse of it. She had to slow down for the customs gate.

As she brought the car to a stop she reached over and took her partner's good hand in hers. They both sat silent, trying to look past the wilds of the Yukon Territory and into the world beyond. Both squinted to see clearly—to see anything.

There is a road that stretches from America all the way to the Last Frontier. And it goes in both directions. Sometimes at once.

2

"**Four thousand feet** seems like a long way to fall, I know, Robert. But you'd be surprised how fast it moves along once you get started."

Robert, the cable television star and host of *Late Talk with Robert,* pushed a button under his desk engaging a foghorn downstage which shot confetti onto himself and Webster. The studio audience roared obediently and with his patented contempt Robert proceeded with the interview.

"Now let me get this straight, um, *Web.* Can I call you Web?"

Webster Cummings hated being called *Web.* He hated it more than anything. "Sure—*Bob.*"

The audience chuckled nervously, clearly annoying Robert, who pretended to ignore it and continued. "So—*Web,* you were sucked out of an airplane, fell 4,000 feet without a parachute," Robert paused to look at the camera indignantly, ". . . and you weren't even hurt?"

"Yes, Robert, that's true." Webster's lip got hung up on his teeth again. His media coach said he should put vaseline on his front teeth to keep them lubricated if his mouth went dry, but he kept forgetting to do it. Luckily this media tour was almost finished. "It's hard to believe, isn't it?"

"It sure as heck is," Robert insisted, looking at his producer. "And we're going to get to *the bottom of this*—no pun intended—after these messages." Robert grabbed a handful of crackers from a bowl on his desk and threw them at the camera, distracting *Bravo the Bubble-Eating Dog* who had been sitting quietly in the wings chewing on sound cables. Robert stalked off to complain about something while Webster sat alone on stage staring blankly at the dog lapping up pieces of cracker.

It *was* hard to believe, this whole business of celebrity. He'd been on the road for two weeks with a small gang of handlers from every network and tabloid promoting nothing but the fact that he'd had a near-death experience on a routine commuter flight into Bangor.

In the past two weeks he'd stammered with Jay Leno. Stuttered with Letterman. Bumbled with Larry King. Small-talked with Regis and Kathie Lee. Spilled coffee on Charles Gibson. Repeated himself to scores of radio hosts, local market coffee tables, and late-night call-ins. He'd been driven to airports in long black cars with reporters from *Newsweek*, *Newsday*, *Washington Times*, *High Times*, *USA Today*. His face was on the front page of three grocery store tabloids: *Fallen Passenger Says "Alien Saved My Life."* He had had to wear a disguise just to buy some lip balm and a soda in Cincinnati.

Prestigious legal firms had offered pro bono representation. But Webster, not having been injured in any way, could not understand what he would possibly want to sue about. There were tenuous offers for television movie deals from at least two networks and one cable syndicate, but they backed off when Webster explained that the whole story took place in less than thirty seconds.

He'd been on his way to Maine to conduct some field studies of the effect of Northeastern winters on the dish detergent buying habits of the rural consumer. Bittner Research & Rectification had assigned Webster the project because of his exemplary credentials.

After all, it was Webster who discovered the control error in the study that asked *What percentage of men wash their hands after using a public restroom?* He argued that most men will only wash their hands in a public restroom if someone is watching them. The study's claim that ninety-five percent of men wash their hands was debunked because the researchers were there to observe them.

Subsequent studies with hidden cameras in cooperating airport men's rooms revealed the much lower figure of twelve percent—and also resulted in several arrests on unrelated activities. Webster's careless colleagues were sent packing—and Webster became the golden boy of Bittner Research.

Webster had worked at BR&R for almost eight years, ever since graduating from college. It wasn't that he loved his job so much. It's just that he was good at it. Observing human behavior and writing it down was a whole lot easier than doing anything with it.

The Bittner mission was to observe and record raw data on human beings. They catalog it, store it, and wait to see if anybody ever wants to buy it. Psychiatrists, advertisers, and newspaper columnists looking to back up ridiculous premises were their most reliable customers. *What percentage of Americans fear danger? What percent fear things other than danger? What percent of those who admit to no fears fear fear?* It was all somewhere in the BR&R archives.

The dish detergent project was a paid assignment from a large soap concern, so the firm sent their very best: Webster Cummings.

They said later it was caused by an improperly installed window seal, but Webster knew it was complicated by a faulty memory and two pet goldfish. Webster had taken his seatbelt off to get into his pants pocket. He wanted to know if he'd remembered to leave his key for Mrs. Finster so she could feed the fish while he was gone. He had, and that relaxed him. He'd fallen asleep with his head against the window when the next thing he knew he was whirling around in thin air.

Webster had had falling dreams before, at home and on the road, and they'd stopped concerning him. He knew soon enough he'd wake up with a big twitch and either bang his head on the bed board or startle the person sitting in the seat beside him.

What he didn't know at the moment was that he'd already surprised her by disappearing through the empty window which was now trying to suck her wig off. She struggled with her hair, screaming *Sweet Lord have mercy* as the pilot dove for control, and Webster dove for New Hampshire.

The most immediate problem Webster faced upon awakening and coming to grips with the fact that he wasn't dreaming was getting his mouth closed. Free falling at thirty-two feet per second squared creates a heck of a wind—a wind which at that moment had Webster's cheeks puffed out like a face in a fun house mirror.

Webster squinted through his watering wind-blown eyes at the white New England landscape below him and got depressed. Thirty seconds—tops—he figured. Webster had a good head for numbers. He also had a good memory for them. At least a better memory than he had for keys and things. He remembered the pilot announcing their present altitude of four thousand feet, he remembered the formula for a free-falling object, and his mind did the rest. Thirty seconds—less now.

As anyone who has free-fallen four thousand feet and lived to tell about it will tell you, thirty seconds is a long time. Closing your mouth and doing a little arithmetic barely scratches the surface of what the human mind can accomplish in half a minute when faced with the challenges of becoming a grease mark on the New England countryside.

Webster managed to work his hand up in front of his face to block the wind a little. Once he could see what was coming, he wished he hadn't looked. There was a patchwork of dark green forest and white pastures of snow interrupted only by the abrupt dark lines of fence and road, field and window. He could see a small town off to his left, but nothing appeared to be much softer than the next in terms of a place to splat.

Then, up ahead of him, something caught his eye. Movement. Color. A break in the landscape. He leaned his body toward the area. He could sense his direction change to his whim; it was an awkward circumstance to be learning the rudiments of skydiving in, but Webster was enjoying it all the same.

He spread-eagled his entire body and felt his fall noticeably slow. When a person has less than thirty seconds to live, any impediment of progress is comforting. Webster grinned a sly grin, which was a mistake. As soon as his lips parted, the wind popped his mouth wide open again. This acted as a big air scoop that flipped him around upside down, helpless again in the wind of falling.

Having the cold air off his face felt good, almost warm in comparison. He could open his eyes and see clearly. There were blue skies, and white clouds, and the ever-shrinking silhouette of an airplane across a pale winter sun.

Why hadn't he taken an aisle seat? Why hadn't he fastened his seatbelt loosely around himself while seated, as the attendant had suggested? Why hadn't he made an extra key for Mrs. Finster to feed the fish? Why did he even have the stupid fish?

A falling body reaches the terminal velocity of a hundred twenty miles per hour pretty quickly and stays there. Thoughts in a person's head race at the speed of light, a hundred eighty-six thousand miles per second, and might even get faster when the body that holds them reaches terminal velocity.

So you can appreciate the confusion Webster felt as approximately twenty-six thoughts per second raced through a head that was about to be planted in the American Northeast.

Fish were quickly left behind, only to be replaced by the most mundane aspects of his life: a solid B average through school. Good personal hygiene. Very straight teeth. Regular bowels. Fair eating habits.

Of course the danger to counting your assets is that you will eventually discount them with liabilities, as Webster promptly did: He never really knew what kinds of clothes he looked best in. He couldn't ride a two-wheel bike until he was eight. He never learned to ski. He didn't have sex until he was twenty-three and he didn't like it much. His parents didn't think he was funny. He wasn't funny. His parents weren't his parents. Oh God, that's right—he was adopted.

All through Webster's life, whenever he remembered this glaring fact of his existence it would give him pause—but not in an unpleasant way. It was no more discomfiting than one remembering they were, say, born in Illinois.

But this time he fairly froze. Somehow, in these last precious moments, it meant something. Out of all his diligent studies of other people's behavior—who does what to whom, how often, and why—he'd never applied his formidable research skills into finding out who he was. Where did *Webster* come from? What was *his* heritage? Why didn't they want him? He could have known. He should have known. He always thought one day, when there was time, he would go to work on it.

However you might think you'd feel on the cusp of augering yourself into the landscape—it's probably not like that at all. You'd think that fear would play an important role. Downright panic, maybe. Reluctance, certainly. Beggarly pleas for mercy and forgiveness, probably. But none of that worked for Webster.

As he lay with his back to the wind, looking up into the great blue beyond, he felt only sadness. A sadness that his life was for nothing. A nameless child with somebody else's parents who spent his entire life figuring out how other people acted for still other people's benefit.

Webster stopped thinking at the speed of light and started feeling. Feelings have no speed. He had a great urge to know who he was, and as this occurred to him his body contracted into a little ball. His knees came up. His hands covered his face. It was a natural thing to do—go out the way he came in. A comfortable position to be in under the circumstances. Time, as Webster knew it, was up.

The Earth first touched Webster like a nudge from a close friend. It built from there into a heated embrace as the friction from his parka nestling into a steep snowy hillside at a hundred miles an hour built around him. Webster felt his internal organs band together in protest as he reached the bottom of the slope and swept up the opposing run of an extremely popular New Hampshire sledding hill. The pitch of his whining parka lowered, and Webster could do nothing but wait for the end to come.

He felt himself slow to a comprehensible speed; his body left the ground again, and as he unfolded in surrender, he met the world square on his feet.

There was a squadron of children gathered around him with a collection of sleds and toboggans under their arms, and one of them blurted out, "Are you the Second Coming?"

Webster wobbled on his pegs for a moment, looked out to the snowy bowl that saved his life, and answered. "No, this is my first time."

Analysts would speculate the odds against him the entire following week. CNN said it was a six hundred million chance in one that a person would live through such a thing. The networks didn't give him near as good a chance. Of course, Webster, being a scientist of sorts himself, was no less fascinated.

The odds of a person landing along the opposing face of a deep bowl with a gradual and nearly perfect parabolic curve up an elongated and polished sledding hill to be catapulted a few feet onto his legs were so fantastic that this person should be, well, on *Late Talk with Robert,* at least.

"That's right, Robert. I fell, I lived, I'm here." They were back from commercial. Robert was in a sour mood, but Webster didn't care. There comes a point in a man's life when he can't be intimidated anymore.

"So tell me, *Web,* did you have any *revelations* on the way down? Did you see, maybe, God?" Robert hammed to the camera, making a face to suggest that seeing God is akin to buying a mood ring.

"No, Robert, I didn't see God. But I got the picture, and I know what I'm supposed to do—and that's to apply my talents as a research analyst to recover the two people who gave me birth, and find out why they gave me away. And that's really all I have to say. Goodnight."

Webster walked off the set without gesturing to the audience or anybody. Robert looked helplessly to his producer who gave the signal for some segue music, but they had nothing to segue to. The producer finally pulled a jar of suds out of his jacket and *Bravo the Bubble-Eating Dog* rescued the remainder of the segment.

Scattered spottily across America, a tiny share of the late-night viewing audience wondered out loud why they were losing sleep over this. They switched off their sets and turned out their lights and rested comfortably knowing they had probably heard the last of Webster Cummings. *Late Talk with Robert* was every would-be celebrity's last stop before obscurity. And no one deserved obscurity more than this guy. But it would be nice, they thought, to see more of that dog.

3

Oliver had leaned in the kitchen door of the Merrimont Hotel the same as always. He stood in this door a couple hundred times a year and each time they'd hand him a loaf of bread and he'd leave. But this time he stayed and watched the television the room service waiters and kitchen help gathered around on their breaks.

"Hey, Oliver, you see that guy? Walked out on Robert. Fell out of an airplane and walked out on that twerp." Oliver's friend Buddy tossed him a loaf of the dining room bread and turned back to the set where a spotted dog chased and snapped at soap bubbles.

As the credits rolled, Oliver had slowly moved away from the door and made his way back down the alley. It was getting very late. Arthur would be hungry. John Doe and Ramona would be worried and frantic. It would take time to calm them so they all could sleep. And Oliver suddenly felt a great urge to sleep. Something weighty had just entered his thoughts without permission.

"And I stood under the big sky on the top of this huge white mountain that quivered under my feet like a living thing. The young man I saw on the TV was flying all around me in an airplane sticking his head in and out of the window and yelling my name at me. Another man—much older than me with white, white hair and eyes blue like jewelry you sometimes see—stood by me and just watched it all.

"It was cool and bright up on the mountain but below me was this thick dark jungly stuff so close I could see the snakes and there were fires and voices coming out of the bushes. Then, off in the distance, this was so beautiful, there were these lovely white trees all in rows and people I couldn't quite see, but I could see them moving, dancing I think, all around the trees and one by one they turned shiny green and alive. But not like the jungle trees. These trees looked like the good kind. Like I could just pick one and fall into it. Just fall down and live like that guy on TV did.

"The old man beside me pointed at it all and laughed. His white hair and white teeth turned into the snow of the mountain. His eyes were suddenly the blue sky and his laugh was the trembling I felt under my feet."

Oliver the Dreamer shrugged and shoved his hands down into the mass of wool he used as coat and bedding to signal that he was finished telling his dream.

Ramona Baggins' eyes darted randomly around the shadow of the highway abutment where they all lived. Nuts as she was, Oliver valued her opinion. He waited while her focus flipped from one thing to the next: A wax cup. A lost shoe. Arthur Tender's blanket roll. Her shopping cart. John Doe's sleeping bulk. The malignant blend of gravel, cigarette butts, dirt, bottle tops, bag scraps, and cement chips that was their floor. And finally, she settled on the propane burner, their communal pride and the focal point of these morning socials. Everyone knew Ramona was about to speak and they waited.

"At least you didn't dream me. I don't like it when you dream me." Ramona looked up at Oliver ferociously. "Especially if you dream me naked! And don't you do it no more!"

Ramona lurched to her feet, snatched her blanket, and scampered up to the far recesses of their hulking shelter. She began frantically arranging things in her little area as Oliver watched from below. He had great affection for Ramona, but sometimes he wished she wasn't so nuts.

Arthur P. Tender rose from his knees and methodically brushed the dirt from his impossibly filthy trousers. "Oliver, old friend, I must say it is a daily delight to listen to your visions of the night before. If you could market those dreams to the buying public you'd be as wealthy as I. Now, I must beg your leave as I believe there is a sermon and a bowl of hot oats down at the mission with my name on it—or my name isn't Arthur Prentice Tender III."

Arthur nudged the mound of blankets beside him with his foot. "Will you be joining me this morning, Mr. Doe?"

John Doe snarled and rose out of his wrapping like a ghoul and fell into step beside Arthur. It always amazed Oliver how quickly John Doe could shift from off to on and back again. They were the only two speeds he had. His *on* was a deliberately slow shuffle with dark brooding eyes following cracks in the sidewalk. His *off* was just off. Asleep. And John Doe could fall asleep anywhere, anytime, at will.

Oliver the Dreamer had interesting friends. And Oliver's interesting friends were all he had. With the exception of his dreams, his sleeping bag, a few clothes, and his leather cap, Oliver had nothing on this Earth but the people around him. For this reason they were all the more precious despite their glaring defects.

Ramona Baggins was a lunatic. She saw things that weren't there, talked to people who weren't there, shouted at people who were there, and wore more clothing than would adequately dress six like her.

"Why do you wear so many clothes?" Oliver asked.

Ramona barked back with a fierceness that was her nature. "Because I don't have a closet!"

There wasn't a lot about Ramona to love except that she was always there. Oliver couldn't remember a time when she wasn't around, and that added up to a steadfast companion no matter how obnoxious she was.

The same held true for Arthur P. Tender, a quiet soul and practiced gentleman. An engaging conversationalist and alleged philanthropist, he was probably every inch the fruitcake Ramona Baggins would ever be.

Arthur Prentice Tender III claimed to be a millionaire who was living on the streets at the suggestion of his therapist. His alleged counsel was that a few months of homelessness would put some stimulating experience back into his melancholy life as a pampered old industrial trustee with no real function but to entertain other pampered old industrial trustees.

Some of his story added up. He did talk like he had money or at least an education, and his bearing was that of a man of means. He carried himself erect and looked every person in the eye regardless of their station in life. The hunkered and shuffling posture so many men on the street carried to ward off the Seattle rains and the judging glances of shoppers and tourists on Pioneer Square was nowhere to be found on Arthur Tender.

But there were a few things that didn't wash about Arthur's millionaire story. For one, he was a drunk. For another, he ate garbage. There were all different classes of people living on the streets of Seattle. From folks with families and full-time jobs to yellow-eyed junkies with their heads in a dumpster and one foot in the grave. But one thing was for sure, if you ate other people's garbage you were gliding a lot closer to the ground than most. Even Oliver's dubious social circle doubted that scarfing a half-gone Big Mac from a public trash can was the therapeutic action of a displaced millionaire.

Arthur also tended to hold out on the others when it came time to pool their money for groceries. Or he'd claim to have fared poorly begging change on the street when in fact he'd drunk it all gone again. Not quite what you'd expect of a voluntary vagrant.

So, despite the fact that nobody quite knew exactly what Arthur P. Tender was, they felt for certain he was no millionaire. At least they hoped not. The thought of it was altogether too disgusting.

John Doe was another one nobody had quite figured. A menacing-looking character with an intense and bottomless gaze, he appeared to look right through a person. It seemed as if he were about to open his mouth and say your darkest secret right out loud. But he rarely spoke. He only threatened to.

Arthur lectured him endlessly on softening up a bit for the sake of business. "Begging is an act of *humility*, Mr. Doe. You really should try not to appear quite so, well, *homicidal*. And staying awake you'd find would help immensely."

John Doe would growl from beneath his blankets, and be asleep before another word could be said.

John Doe, he maintained, was his real name. He blamed his entire sorry lot in life on that one fact. "As soon as I tell people my name they don't believe another word I say. What's the use?"

Arthur Tender once pointed out that there were legions of John

Does in the phone book—all with phones and, presumably, homes to go with them.

John Doe would have none of it. "The only good thing about my name is that someday when they drag me off the road and slab me down at the morgue they'll get the name right on the toe tag."

As morbid a thought as this was, the fact that it was probably true made Oliver jealous. They wouldn't get the right name on his own toe tag even if he were still there to direct.

The only name he had was Oliver. Oliver the Dreamer to those who didn't know him well. The *Dreamer* part was meant, he supposed, to distinguish him from any other Olivers there might be wandering the area without names or clues to where they came from.

All Oliver remembered was a man in white clothes letting him out of a van. He handed him a twenty-dollar bill saying, "Take care of yourself, Oliver. I'm sorry we can't help you anymore."

That was five or eight or ten years ago. Oliver had no real way of knowing how long he'd been here. His days all blended together like smoke.

Most people dream in black and white. Their night landscapes hold none of the color and vibrancy of their lives. Oliver's worlds were just reversed. His days were filled with the gray and black of city streets. The brightest light was mostly from the damp pale northwestern sky. Even the cheer of a clear sky could be diffused to nothing by the time it reached Oliver's dim haunts. The verdant hills and parks of Seattle seemed sucked dry of their life and color by his circumstances.

But Oliver's dreams took him to the most amazing places. There were brilliant blue and impossibly turquoise waters with mountains that shone like crystals and smoked like gods. His dreams were filled with power and warmth and safety and voyages of such fantastic melodrama that he could no longer contain them, and he began telling them to people. The more Oliver told, the more he could remember until it seemed his dreams were as clear to him as his life was not.

Oliver's epic dreamscapes had become legendary among his small circle of intimates. Every morning they'd huddle around the propane burner heating water while Oliver told his dream of the night before.

He'd never not had a dream, and while some were certainly more entertaining than others, they were all more interesting than the hour at hand.

Arthur Tender pointed out some weeks ago that Oliver was getting a lot more of this jungle business in his dreams. "I don't like the sound of these places. Not as pleasant as your other adventures at all. There's something going on in those trees. I'd advise you to stay clear of them."

It had never occurred to Oliver to do anything with his dreams but dream them. But he had to admit that he did not like the look of some parts of them. If he could think in his dreams he would think to stay out of the jungles. He'd remind himself of this every night before sleeping and believe it worked every morning he woke without entering the dark places.

The best part of Oliver's dreams was that dark, scary, or otherwise, they were familiar. They were always filled with faces, sounds, smells, and senses that felt more his own than did the qualities of his days. Not that his days were all entirely without value.

Every morning after coffee Oliver and all his friends would stash their belongings up in the girders of the abutment and head off to work. Their *work* entailed a variety of activities.

For Ramona it meant a long day of rummaging. Mostly she was sensible about it, searching for the recyclables that could be converted into hard cash. But occasionally she'd go off on a *shopping jag,* as the boys called them, and come back in the evening piled high with junk: Broken toys. Solitary shoes. Unrecognizable parts to unknown pieces of discarded furniture.

Oliver and the others allowed Ramona this little eccentricity because she did contribute her fair share to the household and often she'd come in with something. Bringing back a working propane camp stove will keep her in good favor through barrels of trash she's yet to drag home.

Arthur P. Tender's day at work consisted of panhandling in the financial district. His proper manner and bearing made him quite successful. Somehow these bankers, brokers, and lawyers became blind to Arthur's generally ratty appearance and lack of personal hygiene when approached with, "Pardon me—oh, that's a stunning suit—Pierre Cardin, is it not? Exquisite. Say, could I burden you for a dollar for my meter? I'm totally strapped for cash this morning."

It worked often enough that Arthur Tender was usually half in the bag by noon. But the whole ruse broke down once he got liquor on his breath and by mid-afternoon he was back at the nest sleeping it off. He'd wake hungry and often broke and rather than beg the charity of his comrades, he'd sneak off for some late-night dumpster diving.

None of the others under the bridge drank, but no one held it against Arthur Tender. It was a part of him just like nuttiness was a part of Ramona and orneriness belonged to John Doe.

John Doe's day at work amounted to sitting next to a sign that read SICK AND TIRED OF BEING BROKE. It was everything that Arthur Tender's approach was not. That is to say, it was honest. He rarely looked at people except to intimidate them and often just dozed in and out of his day moving only when told to and never speaking. The crass sincerity of John Doe's enterprise usually filled his cup with sympathetic change, and he always had his fair share to contribute to the gang.

Oliver's workday was a lot different from the others' in that he actually worked. He had jobs going all over the downtown area. He swept the sidewalk in front of the outfitter's every day for two dollars from Frank. He washed the windows for Laundry Patty for a shower and a load of clothes every week.

Oliver always kept himself pretty well groomed for somebody who sleeps under a bridge, and that, along with his gentle nature, gained him positions that many of his friends could never achieve. His most prized daily task was organizing the milk crates and bottle cases in the alley behind The Merrimont, the finest hotel in the city. He'd taken the chore at the request of Buddy Bedinger, one of the young room service waiters at the hotel who resented the job. "I mean I'm a *waiter* here, man. I work with the guests, you see? I shouldn't be messin' in the alley with the trash. No offense."

Oliver took no offense. He rather enjoyed the job and he enjoyed listening to Buddy talk of all the things that went on with the elegant people in the rooms and how Buddy was going to be just like them one day when he finished school. But most of all Oliver enjoyed the loaf of dining room bread Buddy would give him for his labors—the finest, freshest, most exclusive bread in Seattle.

Buddy and the rest of the waiters and kitchen help hung around the alley door a lot. Some smoking, some watching a ball game on their little television inside, and all trading stories about the high-minded, gold-plated guests upstairs.

The boys in the kitchen were Oliver's friends just as everyone was Oliver's friend: Frank at the outfitter's. Patty at the laundry. Old Milton at the Crusader Arms where he occasionally cleaned rooms for a bed and a night out of the cold.

Oliver's back was bothering him again, and his knees a little bit. So he'd been grateful that afternoon when Milton told him, yes, he could have a bed tonight if he stripped the linen and swabbed out three recently vacated rooms.

"Take the sheets from 304 and put 'em right in the incinerator, young man. That fellah had more smells on him than a hound dog. 'Fact he reminded me of a dog I had once. Died of infections. The dog, I mean."

Old Milton always called Oliver *young man,* but he wasn't. Everyone seemed younger than Milton, though. Even Oliver's tired, late mid-aged bones were spry in comparison.

Oliver spent a lot of time wondering about his body. There was a great collection of scars, big and small, spread generously around him. The bones under the bigger scars on his back and legs gave him fits of severe discomfort. Especially when the weather changed, as it had that day.

A stretch of early spring warmth had turned to a steady and cold March drizzle which in this town could last for days, weeks, even months. For all its seaminess, Milton's rooming house was still a damn sight better on the bones than the hard ground of an underpass.

Wanting a spell from those raw surroundings and odd thoughts, Oliver rested that night on the uneven terrain of a Crusader Arms mattress. The harsh smells of commercial detergent and starch in the clean sheets stirred something down inside of him. A feeling of comfort and safety, so rare in his remembered life, came over him. A picture almost formed in his head. Windows. A white room. Metal gleaming. He strained against the fog. A memory came and went before he could capture it, flitting by like a phrase of a familiar melody.

Oliver lay and listened to the rhythm of a split rain gutter leaking two stories onto the lid of a dumpster in the alley below. *Bang. Bang. Bang.*

He thought of his friends under the road and knew they'd be waiting for him in the morning. He could count on that. That and his dreams.

Oliver rubbed one knee absently as he began to slip away. *Bang. Bang. Bang.* A black-and-white life became all color: green below and a rich blue beckoning ahead. Dark wet fronds grabbed at his legs and lunged from the jungle. And he was falling down into it as, *Bang, Bang, Bang,* bright orange balls of light sped toward him like fireflies.

He swatted at them and felt a scream come up in his throat as the green gnarled landscape below him gaped open to swallow him. Going in, he again saw the great white trees looking cold and warm at once, turning soft green and inviting him in.

He stretched himself toward them. Willing the direction of his fall away from the jungle. Straining against the inevitable. He could do it. He would do it. He would do anything to stay out of the jungle.

4

Lloyd and Evelyn Decker have been married for almost fifty years. They were just kids when they met and fell in love, and when they look at each other still, all they see is those two kids. It's a convenient hallucination that only old age and true love can induce. Younger adults might get the sensation by looking at pictures of their mothers or fathers when they were very young. It's the eyes. The eyes never change. Whether looking out from an old black-and-white photo with youthful intensity, or gleaming beneath the wrinkled faces of dear old Mom and Dad—it's the eyes that show the soul, and souls never age.

Lloyd and Evelyn are aware that they're not kids anymore. Lloyd's as bald as a rock and doesn't stand up as straight as he used to. And Evelyn more resembles something out of her garden than the girl in their wedding picture. But they laugh about it. Lloyd likes to say that they look like the bags those two wedding kids came in if kids had come in bags. But kids don't come in bags; they just grow into them.

Lloyd and Evelyn were pretty comfortable with their bags. No big problems so far. Evelyn had a little bit of arthritis in her hands, which was normal. Lloyd had some trouble with his knees from forty years as a plumber. But their tickers both ticked, their eyes weren't bad, and both of them could hear just about everything they wanted to.

By the looks of things, Lloyd and Evelyn weren't going to be folding it up anytime soon, but they could do the math. Seventy years is pushing right up against the big calendar and they knew that every day was a gift, not a gimme.

Mortality is like chocolate—impossible to describe to someone who's never tasted it, and just as difficult to forget for those who have. Once aware of it, Lloyd's mortality was never far from his thoughts, and everything he heard and saw seemed to be filtered through it.

Because of this Lloyd could not help but blurt out his mortal anxieties right in the middle of a Jacques Cousteau television special. "Ya know, Evy, I'd sure like to see the ocean before I go."

"Where do you think you're going?" was all Evelyn had replied, but she knew what he meant and Lloyd knew she knew.

Old friends as they were, it never took Lloyd and Evelyn very long to agree on something. What they both pretty much agreed on was that neither one of them had ever been anywhere to speak of. Born and raised in and around Avalon, Ohio, and being people of modest means and simple ambitions, they had gone beyond the Ohio state line only a handful of times.

Lloyd's first time even out of the county was when he was sent to basic training in Mississippi during World War II. He was never called to fight, and his only real memory of the experience was that it was a lot hotter in Mississippi than it usually was in Ohio.

Evelyn's only time away from home was on a field trip with the Ladies Auxiliary to Orlando when Disney World opened. She also thought it was hotter in Florida than it usually was in Ohio. Our pair had seen few exotic places or natural wonders outside of Niagara Falls, the Erie Canal, and a rock that looks like an Indian along the Ohio river basin.

It wasn't that the Deckers were bothered by their unworldliness so much as they were starting to notice it. Seeing the world is one of those things that we're always going to do later, and Lloyd and Evelyn were keenly alert to the fact that it *was* later.

Their lives hadn't been empty by any means. Lloyd had been a successful and sought-after plumber right up until his retirement ten years ago. He'd never left an unhappy customer, and just about everyone in Avalon had been a customer at one time or another.

"You wanna be popular—become a priest or a plumber," his dad had told him all those years ago when plumbing was pretty much a wide-open field, and only visionaries saw the future in it. In those pious days of old, the priesthood had a lot to recommend it as well, but a pipe wrench and a hot lead pot seemed less daunting to young Lloyd than the secrets of the blessed sacraments.

And Evelyn wouldn't have traded her life for the world. It was a thing of beauty by its very simplicity. She'd watched two fine children, children she never thought they'd have, grow up healthy enough to be gone.

Lloyd and Evelyn had tried to make a baby for fifteen years. They didn't suffer any for the practice, but it never worked and the doctors couldn't find anything wrong with either of them. It got harder and harder to keep the hope alive as they started to look middle-age in the face.

And then one day Evelyn just turned up pregnant—which led to Anthony. The Deckers felt as if they'd been given such Divine good fortune and were so grateful to their Lord that He must have decided to make up for all those years of distress by giving them Deirdre only a year later.

Evelyn threw herself at the task of motherhood with a relish few could know. She kept her house as she might tend to her own person— thoughtfully, lovingly, compulsively. Her Jello molds were masterpieces. Her floors were palace halls. And her windows shone like sheets of water. Even the bag lunches she sent out the door with Lloyd and the kids looked too good to be real. Although she insisted they re-use the bags and wax paper, she ironed them to make them flat and neat again.

Each day one of them would get a secret candy in the lunch bag. The practice was never spoken of and therefore each felt as if they were getting special treatment. They were a good family. A well-groomed and smiling household. The very picture of a loving home.

Although neither Anthony nor Deirdre was a particularly gifted child or high achiever, they had always been good kids and that was enough to keep the flame of parental pride burning in Lloyd and Evelyn.

Anthony decided at a very young age and for no clear reasons that he was going west to seek his fortune and future. Shortly after his graduation from high school that's exactly what he did. Unfortunately, his old Rambler station wagon made it only as far as Booder, Indiana. He worked at a gas station to pay for the repairs, started getting used to the place, and stayed. That was ten years ago, and as far west as he ever got. Not a high achiever, but still a good kid to a proud mom and pop.

It was easy for Lloyd and Evelyn to imagine that Anthony had made it Out West for as often as they saw him. Their son's life in Booder, Indiana, while maybe not a full one, was at least full of excuses. He couldn't make it home because his car was broken for about the first three years. He was shifted to working weekends at the gas station unless invited to come on a Wednesday, and then he would be capriciously shifted back by his unpredictable boss.

Ray apparently couldn't do a thing without Anthony. The notion that their son was indispensable to somebody partly swelled his parents and made up for the sad fact that he was headed toward his grand future at the speed of cement.

Deirdre, on the other hand, did manage to achieve escape velocity. After a stalled attempt at college she showed up on the front porch dressed like Calamity Jane, as Lloyd later put it, introduced her boyfriend, Buffalo Bill, and announced they were taking the buffalo's motorcycle all the way to Oregon to plant trees.

Evelyn packed them both lunches in pressed bags, slipped a secret candy in each one, and held Lloyd's arm as they waved them off down the street.

"Well, the babies are gone, Mother," Lloyd said.

"Yes, they are," Evelyn whispered, and they stood looking at the empty street for a long time.

Judging by the actions of the children, there certainly was some wanderlust in the Decker family fiber. Who's to say when and why these sorts of things will surface and change a person's ideas? These hereditary traits can lay dormant for years—whole lives even—then begin to percolate up out of a heart like a new spring.

It took most of the past ten years for Lloyd's first sensation of restlessness to erupt in front of the TV that night. It didn't end there, though, for him or for Evelyn. Sitting on the porch one warm still afternoon, Evelyn poured them each a cup of coffee and said almost dreamily, "They say you can smell the sea for miles and miles before you can even see it."

"Big deal," Lloyd said. "You can just about smell Lake Erie from here. Kinda reminds me of that fish stick you dropped behind the freezer last year."

"Don't kid, now. I'm being serious."

Lloyd held her hand on the arm of the rocker. "I know you are. I'm glad to hear it, too. I was looking at some of those old postcards Deirdre sent from Oregon. All those mountains and trees and rocks. Could you imagine just waking up in the morning and seeing that? I don't know how a fella'd get any of his work done."

"I suppose you'd get used to it."

"Sure like to have the chance." Lloyd looked through the porch screen and tried to turn the cars and houses into rivers and mountain peaks.

The seed of intention had been planted, and as it sprouted up day by day in conversation, the fear of the whole idea was falling away.

"Joey Benson down at the garage says no picture of the Grand Canyon does it justice. Biggest hole in the ground you ever saw."

"I heard there's a gas station in Wyoming with almost two hundred pumps. Can you believe it?"

"We've never even seen where our children live. I wonder if Anthony's as messy as he ever was. Deirdre was always so neat, but I don't know about her now that she's stopped shaving her legs."

Lloyd and Evelyn were being propelled down a path of action by the momentum of their own willingness. There was very little thought and no evident planning on either of their parts until one evening at the kitchen table. Evelyn was showing Lloyd some pictures of the Rocky Mountains in an old *National Geographic* when suddenly Lloyd put his hands flat on the table and leaned back in his chair. "Alright already. So—how we gonna get there?"

Evelyn fielded the question as easily as if he'd asked where the kitty litter was. "I suppose we'll have to drive," she said, and suddenly the whole thing became real.

"I agree. But not in that old beater of ours we ain't." Lloyd had no intention of becoming stranded in Indiana like his elder child. "Besides, where would we sleep at night?"

"Well, I'm sure there are places along the way with reasonable rates."

"Evy, we haven't slept away from home in fifty years. I like to sleep in my own bed at night."

Evelyn could see that Lloyd was up to something. "You can't have your cake and eat it too, Mr. Decker."

"The heck you can't." Lloyd pulled a wrinkled old photograph out of his pocket. "You can have this, bake your cake and eat it, and sleep in it too."

Lloyd turned the photo to reveal to Evelyn a spit-shined, baby-blue, chrome-grilled, sport-packaged-with-optional-awning thirty-two-foot Road Ranger motor home.

"What in heaven's name is that?"

"It's what they call a *RV*, a recreational vehicle. And boy-howdy, does this thing recreate." Lloyd was leaned over the picture like he could see right inside of it. His enthusiasm drew Evelyn in close as well. She hadn't seen the old man this excited since he won a game of Scrabble using only the names of plumbing fixtures.

"This rig's got a full kitchen with a refrigerator and everything. It's got a queen-size bed, a shower in the bathroom, a color TV, stereo, CB radio, and a Road Coaster No-Tip Cup Caddy built right into the console." Lloyd beamed at his wife.

Evelyn was intrigued by this exotic conveyance, for sure, but seventy years of living without in Avalon, Ohio, had somewhat tarnished her ability to desire or accept outrageous propositions.

"You've turned old and goofy on me, Lloyd Anthony Decker. We could never afford such a thing." She gathered up their coffee cups, dismissing the idea with a deliberate stride to the sink.

"Ben says he'll take ten thousand down and finance the rest until the house sells."

"What and who are you talking about?" Evelyn turned and stared at her man, who stood before her waving his hands in the air.

"Ben, Ben Puskins out on Puckerlevel Road. Him and Marlene bought this for themselves last year and can't use it. She won't travel without those stupid little dogs of hers, and they get car sick. It's never even been out of the state."

"You've been talking to him behind my back?"

"Well, no. Not really. Ben told me about it at the K of C meeting last week and we took a ride out to look at it afterward. I wanted to think it over a little bit before I sprung it on you." Lloyd put his hands together and held them at his belt line.

"You've been thinking alright." Evelyn looked over the tops of her bifocals at her husband. She could see the excitement of ten minutes earlier running right out of him. His frame began to sag even more than normal. It put years on him, she thought. Years neither one of them could afford.

"Who are we ever going to talk into buying this run-down old house from us?" Evelyn smiled as Lloyd inflated. The old man took both her hands in his. They stood that way and swayed on the linoleum to an unheard waltz looking into each other's eyes.

Letting go of their house and effects was easier than they'd imagined. Once it dawned on the Deckers how much of America there actually was to see, they didn't figure to live long enough to make their way back to Avalon. Nothing there had a value beyond nostalgia, and Lloyd and Evelyn saw few reasons to keep any of it. Most of the stuff of memories had turned to junk anyway, and with the exception of a few photo albums that fit neatly under the Road Ranger's extra bunk, it was all liquidated in a marathon of garage sales and flea markets.

"Six years easy." Lloyd had meticulously paged through a road atlas working a ruler and a pocket calculator. "And that's if we don't stop to pee."

Idling at the intersection of the Avalon interchange and the toll road waiting to make the turn, Lloyd and Evelyn had a moment to observe the other traffic before they entered it. Cars of all colors and constitutions. Buses, trucks, and tractor trailers roaring north and tearing south. Drivers bent to their wheels intent on their destinations, or slumped in their seats and conceded to theirs.

As they accelerated up the ramp and Lloyd brought the Road Ranger into pace with the flow, there was no sense of leaving. Like falling into a parade, there was more a rush of belonging, joining a community of vagabonds who had nothing in common but their motion and their path. A hundred thousand different places to go and the same way to get there.

It was a hazy midwestern spring evening that greeted them as they crossed the state line into the western wilds of Indiana. Lloyd and Evelyn traded smiles when they saw the sign welcoming them to a place they'd never been before.

Thunderstorms building on the horizon before them caused a thick black barrier in the western sky. As the sun slipped lower it cast a wide band of color across the flat territory ahead. It appeared for a moment as if a dark and heavy lid had been lifted for a look outside.

Lloyd hummed old themes from TV westerns to amuse his mate who sat her swivel bucket seat like royalty. She had a wide map on her lap and her bifocals tracked a bony finger across the page. There were the important-looking, deep yellow stains of great cities. The road-scarred vastness of the plains. There were towering peaks marked with black crosses, wide deserts named in red, and towns with names that spoke their places. *Boulder. Green Lake. Happy Valley.*

Evelyn looked down upon it all from her great scaled height and she followed her finger to a point on the other side of the page. She held it there on the edge of a great plot of blue named Pacific then looked to where Lloyd had them pointed. The same place. A place to smell the ocean from.

5

The hyphen was only the first thing to come between Richard Hoople and Katherine Bedinger when they became the Bedinger-Hooples. Soon enough an entire continent separated them. After less than four weeks of marriage and living together in their Manhattan flat, Katherine took an account supervisor's position at a Los Angeles advertising firm and moved to the West Coast.

Richard, who was perfectly satisfied with his career in publishing, remained in New York. He was assistant chief editor of the diet book division of a large publishing house, and—what with diet books being released almost twice a day—there wasn't time for Richard or Katherine to consider the consequences of becoming a bicoastal couple.

They readily agreed that the long distance calling should be kept to a minimum. Not for any lack of affection between them—or so they claimed—but because they figured out that if they kept the calls down to twice a month or so, they would save the price of a plane ticket one way or the other, every two months. Then they could be physically reunited on a regular basis. In the meantime, they would write letters.

> *My Dearest Katherine,*
> *Another long lonely week in the city without you. I managed to get through the new edition of* <u>The Improved Aluminum-Free Life Diet</u> *and it is finally off to the printers. It's about as interesting as reading—well—diet books. But they do sell well. It amazes me that I've been responsible for the sale of over three million diet books in the last five years, and I've yet to meet anybody who ever bought one. Are they all being sold out there?*
> *Oh, by the way—I had lunch with Betty Harper this week.*

She's with the Stonewall Press now. She said to say hello. She's gained at least fifteen pounds, and I'll bet it wasn't from eating aluminum.

Take care of yourself out there, Pumpkin. Don't breathe any air you can't see. Ha-ha.
Love, Richard

Richard didn't know why he always whined in his letters to Katherine, but he was aware that he did. If he mentioned a dinner he'd had with old friends, he'd also remember to complain about the food. If the weather was nice, the subway was late. A walk in the park would inevitably produce an errant dog or indecent pigeon. There were so many things to be miserable about in New York, Richard had no trouble at all fabricating suffering. He seldom had to be creative at all.

What all this was, of course, was guilt over the fact that he didn't really mind having Katherine gone. He was having a perfectly fine time of it without her, but didn't want her to think he was having too much fun and hurt her feelings. Really, the only honest bad news he kept from her at all was that the houseplants were all dying.

There may have been some sense of this across the continent.

Dear Richard,
How are my plants? I do miss having them to take care of. They are my little baby loves—along with you, of course. This apartment is simply barren, but there's just no point in buying things out here that I already own in New York even if I never do get to see them. Don't forget to leave a Mozart CD playing softly for the plants a few days a week. (The piano concertos, not the operas.) It comforts the philodendron. And remember to walk the kitty on Sundays.

Richard was only peripherally aware of the houseplants and had entirely forgotten they owned a cat. He suddenly realized he hadn't seen it in over two weeks. This was very bad news, and it cheered him to know what he could put in his next letter.

*It's been so lonely here since Muffin's terrible accident with—umm—
the incinerator shaft.*

Katherine, for her part, tried to exude resolve and accomplishment
in her letters. She hoped it would comfort poor Richard to know she
was taking care of herself and he needn't worry about her. Even though
she'd been feeling very strange since she arrived in L.A., and her biological clock seemed totally off schedule, she let none of these concerns into
her correspondence.

> *I made an announcement in staff meeting this morning that my last
> name is not Bedingerhoople, but Bedinger <u>hyphen</u> Hoople. The way
> everyone was saying Bedingerhoople it sounded like a Scandinavian
> pastry. Unfortunately they all took me literally and instead of being
> Katherine Bedinger (pause) Hoople, now I'm Katherine Bedinger-
> hyphenhoople. I haven't been here long enough to know if these people
> are really this stupid, or if they're just trying to annoy me. Anyway,
> it's working. If the rest of this year goes the way it's begun, it's going
> to be a long one.*
> *I remain your loving wife—Katherine*

Richard Hoople and Katherine Bedinger's marriage had little to do
with love. It had little to do with devotion. It certainly didn't have much
to do with convenience. If truth be told, Richard and Katherine were
married only because the institution of marriage had outsmarted them.
Caught them on a dull day. Blind-sided them. Sucker-punched them
both and stood laughing over their bloodied noses. Marriage can act that
way if you let it. And Richard and Katherine knew no better way to
act.

It wasn't entirely their fault. They just hadn't been paying attention.
Richard's father worked for the law firm that represented the interests of
Katherine's father's advertising firm. Katherine's sorority friend Betty
Harper knew Richard's fraternity brother Ken Henson. They'd met at a
messy ribs-and-beer dinner in the Village where everyone laughed a lot

and groped for more napkins. They started dating, traded laundry and stock information, and said "I do" before they even knew what they were I-do'ing.

I love you, Richard.

I love you, Katherine.

It was like saying thank you to the doorman in their building. Spontaneous. Unconscious. Unsolicited.

They never listened to what the other one was saying, but they never paid attention to each other long enough to notice that they didn't.

They went to Mexico for six days on their honeymoon. Richard spent the first three days on the toilet while Katherine scolded, "I told you not to eat the vegetables."

Katherine spent most of those early days searching the streets of Cabo San Lucas for a current *Wall Street Journal.* She eventually had to settle for *USA Today* and sat reading the blue-chip stock prices on the veranda. "I can't believe I'm reading this rag."

Richard read the food columns in the bathroom. "Did you find any more Kaopectate?"

Richard's condition improved and they had one very pleasant evening together at the local hot spots. The last club of the evening was very crowded and they both rotated their fanny packs around in front of them so the other dancers wouldn't bump their money. Katherine was getting drunk by this time and kept rubbing her pack against Richard's as she screamed over the music, "I think being married to you is going to be a lot of fun."

Richard was lost in his own notions and hadn't heard her. "I think they're overcharging us for these drinks. We should leave."

Katherine gave Richard a suggestive look that he missed because he was checking over the American Express slip. He hooked Katherine's arm in his own and suggested they walk the beach back to the hotel. Katherine warmed to the romantic idea and leaned against her man as he explained how he'd stepped on somebody's old burrito and needed to rinse his flip-flops in the surf.

.   .   .

The Bedinger-Hooples made it back to New York with only minor burns and scrapes. Katherine made some calls to her office from the airport while Richard found them a taxi. Their lives together started at a dead run in a cold November rain, outside Kennedy International Airport—one bag short of having had a great trip.

Actually there were few things that could benefit the Bedinger-Hooples more than separating them by nearly three thousand miles. They were both much too self-absorbed to live in the same few rooms. Katherine didn't stop making phone calls until nine o'clock in the evening—when the people in their California offices went home for the day. Richard had reams of manuscripts rubber-banded around the apartment—only half of them read at any one time. He read them constantly—making marginal notes with a red pen, and notes on his legal pad with the black pen Katherine's father had given as a wedding present. He hated switching pens, but he wanted to impress Katherine. Too bad she was too busy to notice.

Katherine spread her briefcase out on the kitchen table and talked into the phone crooked under her chin while eating take-out from a cardboard container.

"I don't care what his last supervisor told him. Remind him I'm his supervisor now, and I want that account moved out of his group tomorrow. They'll handle it in New York from now on. Oh, and fire that woman who voices the pasta commercials. She sounds like a hooker." Katherine hung up without saying goodbye, as was her habit.

Richard came in from the living room and went to the refrigerator while Katherine redialed. "Still talking to L.A.?"

"Just one more call. Still editing?"

"*Health on the Highway*—it's a naturalist cookbook for road kill. Disgusting. Hey, do we have any more of that pork sausage? I'm starved."

Katherine answered without looking up from her filofax. "On the bottom under the romaine. Oh, hi Suzy, Katherine. Is Frank still there?"

Richard closed the refrigerator and began to leave. "I love you."

"I love you, too." Katherine frowned at her phone. "What? Not you, Suzy. Just get me Frank."

Richard returned to his work in the living room and lost himself in his papers. Katherine emerged from the kitchen sometime later and headed for her nightly bath.

"Are you still at it?" she asked.

Richard fumbled with his pens. "Hey, it's my job."

"I understand," Katherine said, grabbing an issue of *AD WEEK* on the way past the coffee table.

Katherine did understand. It *was* their jobs. Everything was their jobs. It was their jobs that consumed them. It was their jobs that held their passions. And, inevitably, it was their jobs that separated them—and saved their marriage.

Katherine returned from her bath just as Richard was leafing through a fresh manuscript. She stood behind his chair and rubbed his shoulders. "I've been offered an account supervisor's position and a chance at a vice-presidency with our office in Los Angeles."

Richard turned a page on his lap. "That's nice, Pumpkin. Did you know that you burn more calories chewing a stalk of celery than you get from eating it?"

Katherine continued to massage her husband, but talked with her eyes focused out the window. "I'm looking at it as short term. I think as soon as I get the VP spot, I can manipulate my way back to New York."

Richard hadn't heard a word she'd said, but he looked up from his manuscript long enough to see that Katherine was troubled about something. He hadn't seen the look since the airline lost her bag, and it concerned him. "What is it, Pumpkin?"

"I'm moving to L.A. to keep my career on track."

It was a statement filled with resolve but also, Richard thought, sadness. He looked to the work in his hands and tried to offer something encouraging. "They say the mercury content in West Coast fish is much less than they thought it was, and that you can eat it almost without thinking about it."

Katherine looked nauseated. "I hate fish."

To recover, Richard pressed on. "For good reason, according to many authors I read. But then again, nobody recommends beef or pork these days either, and I know what the vegetables did to me in Mexico. I guess it doesn't matter anymore."

Katherine and Richard had a last few intimate evenings together, and took full advantage. It felt like a sacrament. A last rite. A rite of passage.

They did love each other. Didn't *this* prove it? Hey, it was the best thing for her, and if it was the best thing for her it was the best thing for her *and* him. It was selfless discipline at work, wasn't it? After all, unbridled sex was one of those kinds of things that were bringing this society to its knees anyway, wasn't it? How many couples loved each other so much that they could live a continent away and still keep the passion? The Bedinger-Hooples, that's who.

At least that's what they said that night. And that's what they said as they packed Katherine's essential things. And that's the way it was left at the airport.

"I'll see you for Valentine's Day, and I'll write every day." Katherine left one last peck on Richard's ear and walked up the ramp.

"I'll write every day, too."

And the most amazing part is that they did write every day. Every single day. Sunday to Saturday the last thing they'd do each evening was write their lives to each other. It started off as a promise which became an obligation, but ever so slowly it turned into a devotion.

The written word worked for each of them in different ways. Richard looked for rhythm and meaning in relatively inconsequential elements.

> *I was eating my corn flakes this morning and heard a man calling your name out on the street. Over and over. He sounded angry. I looked out and it was just some guy yelling at his partner to push harder on the washing machine they were packing up the stairs of the building across the street. It made me think of you.*

Katherine thought Richard was becoming quite sensitive in her absence. She was in advertising; she looked for meaning where there was none, or the hope of any.

> *I watched the sun set over the ocean tonight. I don't know why, but I had the thought that as I watched it fade into the west that somewhere across the water it was rising in the east for somebody. And I thought of you—and felt a world away.*

Now that Richard and Katherine didn't really have to deal with each other they were falling rapidly in love. Words of devotion—words of intimacy—poured out of them. It was so easy when the followthrough only meant licking a stamp.

A new honesty crept into their relationship. They shared their secrets and confided their doubts. It was so much easier to look into that envelope every day than to look into somebody's face. Their transcontinental partnership took on a quality that was rare in even the closest couples: They became each other's friend and confidant.

Richard confessed his professional insecurities:

> *I just finished reading a new author's first draft of a book called . What's Wrong with Everything You Eat. It's a virtual encyclopedia of bad news—depressing—boring, and it offers nothing but criticism. It'll probably be a bestseller in the spring, and I'll get my bonus. But I wonder sometimes if it's all worth it. I wonder if I should move on to cookbooks, or fitness. The change could do me good. Any news yet on your promotion?*

Katherine shared her true feelings about politically sensitive topics around the agency:

> *It's the stupidest advertising campaign ever conceived. Some guy from Alaska who talks like a garage mechanic on Thorazine going on about motel rooms. I don't get it. Probably rent a lot of beds to somebody,*

*though. If this one takes off I might be Vice President Bedingerhyphen-
hoople by the summer. But I'm not holding my breath.*

*I've been feeling sick ever since I got here. It must be the water,
or the smog—I don't know. It's worse in the morning. Maybe I
should lay off the espresso.*
Until tomorrow. I love you. I want you,
Katherine

Richard laid down his black pen. Katherine switched off her lap-
top computer. They both stared off into the night feeling lucky to be
alive. They had it all. Love, money, jobs they liked. They had each other,
and they didn't. It was a delightful mix of appetites.

"You either starve to death or you die from eating food," Richard
thought out loud watching a hard snow falling on the Upper West Side.

Katherine closed her curtains against the sprawling sparkling city
below. "I don't get it."

And Richard and Katherine Bedinger-Hoople, bless their hyphen-
ated hearts, each went to bed hungry—and satisfied.

6

Norman Tuttle sat in his bedroom window watching the darkness dwindle away in fits and starts, the same way the snow melts this time of year in this part of Alaska. It begins with dirty patches of gray wet grass pushing up through the seasoned snow; ever so gradually it becomes dirty patches of snow left scattered on the gray grass, and finally, it is all gray grass lying lifelessly, waiting for the sun.

Norman's head was filled with the electric mush that comes of a night without rest. Well beyond the urge for sleep, he could only stare at the world as it slowly brightened and the vague dark shapes in the twilight took form, assembling themselves into another day.

When the sun finally did show itself, Norman would find a world wholly unchanged from the day before, yet different in every way. He could feel the disparity in every taut fiber of his young body.

Norman still couldn't figure out how it happened. The *party*. The word held no celebration whatsoever. He shouldn't have let things get so out of hand. It wasn't like him. Of course, nothing was these days.

His dad had said, "Norman, I don't even know who you are anymore. Where's my boy?"

A small voice would shout from the back seat of Norman's head, *I'm here Dad. I'm way back here. Can't you see me?* But the surly driver would only shrug and flip his hair. A face like stone and a heart lost in traffic between boy and man.

The party hadn't been his fault. It just sort of happened to him like everything else these days. After all, it was his parents' dumb idea to take his brothers and sisters over to Valdez to visit with Grandma and Grandad. Norman had begged and stomped and pleaded and pouted not to go. "It's so *boring* at Grandma's house. They don't *do* anything."

"They're old and Grandad's not so well. There may not be a whole lot of opportunities left to see him." Norman's father had let the implication dangle, but Norman neglected to reach for it. At sixteen everything lives forever, and the universe orbits the day at hand.

"But I've got a date with Laura on Saturday night to the April Fool's dance."

The older Tuttle shook his head sadly and dismissed his son. "If it's a fool's dance, then I guess you'd better be there."

Norman's family left on Saturday morning. His father's silence rang in the empty house long after the car had disappeared down the road. His mother had left a kiss on his forehead and a three-page note on the refrigerator.

There are hot dogs and beans in the blue Tupperware. Pot pies are in the basement freezer. Don't forget to turn off the oven. Feed the cats. Lock the doors. Do your homework. No shoes in the house. Stay out of your Dad's candy bars. . . .

Norman flipped ahead through an endless list of chores and kitchen safety tips until on the last page a message in bold block letters seized his attention: *AND ABSOLUTELY NO FRIENDS IN THE HOUSE.* It closed with *We'll be home on Monday if the roads stay open—Love, Mom.*

Norman put the pages back up with a banana magnet and talked to himself. "Norman do this. Norman don't do that. They think I have to be told everything like a little kid!"

Norman rummaged around in the top cupboard for one of his dad's chocolate bars. Then, as he wandered into the living room to initiate spiritual contact with his Super Nintendo, he let his mind drift to where it always did if left unattended: Laura Magruder. Soft, white, fragrant Laura Magruder.

With most of Norman's thinking being done far south of his brains these days it was possible for his consciousness to linger in the limbo between Laura's warm embrace and the iron grip of a video game. That's where he stayed through most of the afternoon, emerging only long enough to shower, change, and meet his ride to the dance.

.   .   .

"So your parents are gone for the weekend?" Laura had said after their first dance of the evening.

"Uh, yea." Norman didn't trust the look on Laura's face, but it turned him completely to goo all the same. "The whole tribe went."

"I've never been alone with you in your parents' house before." Laura ran her hand up Norman's forearm and suddenly the temperature in the high school all-purpose room rose seventeen hundred degrees and turned into Norman's own personal hell—a hell that would last well into the next morning.

A fish burp in a rip tide has more control over its destiny than Norman Tuttle did in the clutches of Laura Magruder. Any suggestion that came out of Laura's mouth seemed ultimately doable. More than doable, actually, it became mandatory. And always there was her unspoken promise of something. Something undefined. Laura ran her finger around Norman's shirt collar. *That.*

"You can't tell anybody!" Norman whispered urgently to Laura.

"We have to tell Alex and Kathy, they're our ride."

Norman was freaked, but in a spineless sort of way. "Okay, but *they* can't tell anybody either."

"Don't worry," Laura said as she made her way into the throng of dancers to find their friends. It was the last encouraging thing Norman would hear for the rest of the night.

The foursome looked out Norman's front window uneasily. Alex was the first to speak. "I didn't tell anybody."

"I didn't tell anybody," Kathy said next. "Unless you count Jessica, but you can't count her because she's my best friend and she wouldn't tell anybody either, except for Jason, but they're going steady now so it's not like a big deal or anything."

"I hope your Dad paid his insurance," was all Laura had to offer as she settled into the cushions of Norman's father's favorite chair and stretched as if to go to sleep.

Norman could not summon a molecule of serenity from anywhere in his being. He paced back and forth in front of the window, watching the line of headlights making their way up the road. Even the closed doors could not protect him from the nauseating sound on the wind. Norman spun on his companions, wild-eyed. "Do you hear that?"

Everyone was quiet for a moment, then a chill swept over even the most seasoned teenagers in the room. Like the ancient cries of invaders designed to break the wills of the besieged, the evening breeze delivered a chant guaranteed to strike terror in the hearts of anyone left in charge of their parents' house. Dozens of eager young voices raised in unison. "Par-DEE. Par-DEE. Par-DEE."

In Norman's dilated eyes the headlights all became one large moving mass swirling light. An inferno. Out of control. Unpredictable. Dangerous. The party took off like flame before a wind with only Norman to fight the fire.

"You can't stay. You can't stay." Norman started his refrain while the herd of hormones was still pouring in the door. "You can't stay. We're not allowed. My parents will kill me and send you my head." Very quickly it just became a yammer. Background noise to the party's other interests, interests which gave Norman some opportunity for embellishment.

"That's my parents' bedroom. Don't go in there. Don't touch that. Don't eat those. You can't stay, you can't stay, you can't stay, you CAN'T STAY!"

For the first time in two years Norman forgot all about Laura. She was submerged somewhere in the throng which was continuing to move through the house like gremlins, picking things up, moving furniture, laughing at family portraits. Somebody put a thud rock tape on his parents' big console stereo and turned it up so loud that it sounded like the woofers were about to spit up blood.

Laura's older brother Burt, who had graduated the year before, showed up with his girlfriend Jackie, a vicious sneer, and a case of beer. They disappeared downstairs into the TV room with several other seniors whom Norman didn't even know by name.

Norman went through the house on a mad search for Laura. He

needed her help to plead with Burt to get the beer out of the house. It took him a good half-hour between clearing Alex and Kathy out of the master bedroom, breaking up a fight over the Nintendo, and hiding the whipped cream from the wrestling squad. Finally he found her, down with her brother's gang, sitting on the lap of a senior who was flipping his cigarette ash into Mrs. Tuttle's tomato starts.

That was it. Booze. Cigarettes. Promiscuity. *Infidelity*. This went beyond any worldly punishments his parents might serve upon him. He could be grounded until he reached retirement age or served up the death penalty and still not satisfy them on this one. It meant his eternal soul. He just knew it. There was only one thing left to do.

"I'm calling the cops," he said on the way up the stairs, noticing yet another car pulling in the driveway.

"What'd he say?" said Burt after him.

"He said he was calling the cops." The senior holding Laura looked at her and asked, "Is he serious?"

Laura bit her lip. "I think we'd all better get out of here."

"Cops!" The alarm went up.

"Cops!" somebody repeated upstairs.

Norman ignored the commotion and marched with grim intent to the phone in the kitchen. Everyone was at the kitchen door trying to get out all at once. Norman's best friend Stanley Bindel led the pack and struggled to pull the door open against the press of bodies behind him. When the door finally opened it was Stanley's voice that cut through the sound of breath being sucked into two dozen sets of teenage lungs at once. "Mr. Tuttle! What are *you* doing home."

Norman froze with the phone to his ear.

911 Emergency. Where is the location of your emergency?

The sea of heads parted between Norman and his father. The look on his dad's face was somewhere between tears and homicide. Norman felt his eternal soul burning through the bottoms of his shoes. "Never mind, operator." He let the phone fall to his side. "It's too late."

．　．　．

It had taken until nearly three o'clock in the morning to clean up the most major offenses. Norman's mother had put the kids to bed without a word and disappeared into her room. She emerged briefly, a few minutes later, ashen-faced, and dropped an empty beer can into the garbage.

Later, as he worked his way down the hall with a bucket and sponge, Norman thought he heard her crying through the closed door.

He cursed the avalanche in the pass that had closed the road and turned them back. He cursed his parents for not calling ahead. He cursed himself for living.

His father's silence was making him crazy. No yelling. No stomping around. He just sat at the kitchen table giving short quiet directions. "Vacuum the living room. Straighten the books. Get whatever that is off the wall." Between instructions an icy blaring quiet hung around Norman's dad like a force field, daring anyone to test it.

Norman went about his duties stunned and deliberate. What was it going to be? Military school? The Foreign Legion? Obedience school? Maybe they'd make him live in a damp hole out back dropping small bits of food through a metal grille. That would be okay. Anything would be better than this silent treatment. It made Norman want to run away.

Run away. Hey, that's what he could do! He could sneak away and go to Anchorage. Get a job bagging groceries until he had enough money to fly to Seattle, then work his way down the coast into Mexico where he could learn to speak Spanish, marry a señorita, have children, grow old and die, and then it would all be over with.

Norman fancied himself in a sombrero, and it was late enough that it was starting to look good on him. He was just getting into the wife and kids part when his dad finally interrupted.

"Norman, you can get the rest tomorrow. Sit down here a minute."

His father's voice did not sound angry, but not kind, either. Norman sat in the chair across the table and waited. There is no place in the world quieter than around a kitchen table with your father at three o'clock in the morning after a big party. Norman could hear the lightbulb above their heads ringing.

Eventually his dad began. "Norman, I want to tell you a story about my brother."

"Uncle Stu?" Norman said, immediately relieved they weren't talking about him.

"No, my older brother. He'd be your Uncle Oliver. That is, if he's still alive. Nobody's heard from him in over thirty years."

Norman was perplexed. "I thought it was just you and Uncle Stu."

"That's what Dad—Grandad—wanted everybody to think and that's why I need to tell you about Oliver tonight. It can't wait another day."

It never occurred to Norman to question what was being said. He could only rest his head on his hands and listen with an expression of intensity fashioned after his father's.

"Oliver was my big brother. Great guy. Took me hunting, taught me how to fish, mend net, pilot a boat. Stu was a little younger. I taught him, but Dad taught us all. Oliver and Dad were close. Dad was always telling him what a fine fisherman he made. Oliver was allowed to take the family boat out for trips on his own by the time he was your age. I think Dad had big plans for Oliver.

"But as good a fisherman as Oliver was, he had a lot of mischief in him. Just normal stuff for a boy that age—girls, pranks, a little drinking—but you know how tightly wound your grandad is about those kinds of things. And Oliver had a knack for letting it get out of hand. He was such a nice fella that he'd let his friends talk him into anything.

"Once they all got caught joyriding in Fritz Ferguson's truck. When the police brought Oliver up to the house Dad went berserk. He took out his Bible and beat Oliver with it until he cried—Dad cried, that is. Oliver just stood and took it. Didn't say a thing. He had bruises on him for weeks after. He'd look at them every night in our room before he went to sleep. He'd just sit in the lamplight touching those Bible bruises with his fingers and not say a word.

"I don't remember Oliver and Dad ever talking to each other again. Except one night. Oliver was about eighteen or so I guess, and he'd been living on the boat for awhile. I didn't know what he did with his time. He'd stopped paying attention to me along with everybody else. Well, then one night Oliver shows up at the door all sheepish and shuffling. The rest of us get scooted out of earshot while he and Dad sat down.

"Next thing we know all hell breaks loose out in the kitchen. Dad was just about choking on his tongue he was so mad. He was cussing a blue streak in between chapter and verse and poor mother didn't know whether to cover our ears or fall down and pray. Oliver finally blasted through the door and ran outside just ahead of Dad's Bible. We found it later layin' a good forty feet from the house. Dad had flung it right at him but missed. Good thing; it might have killed him."

Norman's dad took a breath. "He might as well have killed him. It was the last time we ever saw our brother. Dad never spoke of him again.

"Of course, as small as this town was, we didn't have too much trouble figuring out what had gone on. It seems Oliver had gotten a girl pregnant. Nobody even knew they were seeing each other, but that's because she was only sixteen and they were sneaky. Oliver was in a lot of trouble, but he loved the girl, and he'd come to ask Dad for help. The times being what they were, he had no other place to turn.

"Well, Oliver and this girl disappeared. It was a terrible scandal at church and all, and Dad moved us over to Valdez so he didn't have to face people. He still hates coming back here, as you know. The girl's family moved out too, and as far as this town goes those two kids never existed. Me and Stu were forbidden to ever mention our brother again. Mom must have been keeping some promise to Dad, because she wouldn't allow it either. He was just gone."

Norman stared at his father's whiskers. This was awesome. He couldn't believe, after all these years, that the Tuttle family history actually had some action in it. Between Grandad's preaching and his mom and dad trying to raise a sea-faring Walton family, Norman had given up all hope of ever relating to his relatives.

He had to chew the insides of his cheeks to keep from breaking into a grin. His dad obviously saw no fun in the story. He rubbed his face and looked directly into Norman's eyes.

"Dad's gonna die without knowing if his oldest boy is alive or dead himself. Oliver and your grandad forgot how to talk to each other. Just like a switch was thrown, it was over between them. That's why you don't have an Uncle Oliver."

Norman's father got up from his chair and stood over him. "I'm not going to let that happen to us, Normy. You've got to be able to bring your troubles to me, but half of that is up to you. Do you hear what I'm saying to you?"

Norman stood up and let his dad hold him by the shoulders. From the back seat of his head a voice cried *I hear you, Dad.* But the voice up front could think of nothing to say. Norman just shrugged and let his father finish.

"You go up to bed now and think about what we're going to do about this trouble tonight. We'll talk about it in the morning."

Norman sat in his bedroom window and watched the morning come. The sun behind the mountains across the bay brought a relief of color into the world, but it cast little light on Norman's gray mood. Everywhere he looked he saw his life, and it looked exactly like dirty snow and dead grass.

As the intensity of the dawn continued to brighten it became impossible for Norman to hold his attention within the confines of the dismal yard. Finally, he let his reluctant gaze travel across to the vista for the first time all night. He immediately felt more comfortable. It was good to be away from his sorry situation, if only in his head.

And while he was out there it occurred to Norman that somewhere beyond these mountains was an uncle he'd never met. And however far he'd gone and whether or not he lived or died, he was—for the moment—the closest person to Norman in the whole darned family.

Anthony Decker stood beside his pump watching the digits flip by as he listened to the gas gushing deep down inside his parents' motor home.

Anthony knew his mom and dad had bought a motor home and were stopping by on their way west. But this baby-blue, flashy chrome and classy camper was everything his folks were not, and one thing for sure Anthony knew Lloyd and Evelyn were not, was flashy. From its dual mounted air horns on top, to its barber-pole-striped curb feelers under the rear end, the Road Ranger could have belonged to anybody but his mom and dad.

But like it or not, beaming through the huge front windshield as it had swung over the curb was his mother's face capped by a pad of permanently molded bright white hair. And working the wheel for all his short stocky arms were worth was his father with his familiar bald dome gleaming like his puffy red cheeks, and the playful little grin that made Anthony cringe.

His dad only used that grin when he was about to do something goofy. When Anthony was a kid, Lloyd would grin like that, then tickle him. Or push him from a dock. Or he'd surprise him with some gift of such monumental and unexpected proportions, Anthony would become overwhelmed and cry. He still didn't like the looks of his father's grin.

Anthony had stood helplessly on the pump island watching his dad maneuver the RV back and forth across the apron attempting to attain some optimum placement that Anthony could only guess at. Every time Lloyd made another pass over the drive hose, the bell inside the station would ring.

Anthony cringed, knowing that his boss hated that bell. Ray took it as a personal insult and he'd yell mercilessly at kids who rode over the hose on their bikes and reprimand bored or mischievous customers who stomped on it. Anthony could see Ray peering out from underneath the hood of an Oldsmobile in the garage and wished his father would just park the damn thing.

Anthony and his mother looked at each other through the windshield as Lloyd persisted in his efforts to park. Their delighted smiles of a few minutes earlier had faded into frozen, almost pained grimaces as they continued to follow each other's eyes for fear of being the first to break it off.

Anthony became self-conscious and he lifted his right hand to his left breast to check that the duct tape was still in place. Printed on the tape in bold block letters was his name, ANTHONY. Underneath it, permanently embroidered in red letters into a white patch on his coveralls was TONY, the name he'd used since leaving home. He did it for his mother. Evelyn had always hated it when people called him Tony.

It has no dignity, she had told him many times. *Anthony commands respect.*

He was so glad he remembered to use the tape.

Evelyn watched the face of her son, paralyzed and pleasant, and she felt an old sorrow returning. The sadness of seeing her boy grow up out of touch. Out of touch and out of reach. All his life, it seemed, he'd stood there like that—smiling, waiting for something to happen to him, and hoping it wouldn't be too bad.

Lloyd and Evelyn moved from their seats and the side door facing Anthony burst open. His dad pressed a button on the bulkhead beside him, a servo motor droned somewhere, and a set of three chrome stairs began to unfold from beneath the door. As soon as they were fully extended and locked, Lloyd scampered down and grandly held his hand up for Evelyn to follow.

"Evelyn, Queen of the Turnpike, I present you Anthony, your young prince."

Evelyn started down the stairs playfully slapping Lloyd's hand away. "Oh, for crying out loud, Lloyd, cut it out." She looked to her son in mock exasperation. "He's been this way since we left town. I don't know what to do with him."

Lloyd raised his arms as if to dance and broke into song. "You could—*Fly me to the moon and let me play among the stars.*"

Evelyn giggled. Anthony couldn't believe his mother actually giggled. Then she gave him a big full-body mom hug while his dad clapped him on the back.

Anthony stepped back looking at the pair of people who brought him into the world, searching for the words. Finally he spoke. "Mom, Dad. Do you want regular or unleaded?"

Anthony watched the pump pass the thirty-gallon mark and appeared interested in its progress. Lloyd was up on Ray's stool with a squeegee cleaning the massive front windshield. Evelyn had walked across the street for some snacks.

Anthony stared at the State of Indiana weights and measures certification sticker while the gas ran. These were his parents. Mom and Dad. Those two in the white house on Center Street. The one with the hedges, and the tulips around the old wagon wheel out front. The mom who sat in the window cleaning beans waiting for the kids to come skipping up the driveway. The dad who came around the corner with two toots on his horn and a newspaper and a paycheck.

The times Anthony went back to visit, it was all still there. Two and a half hours and he was home. Just like he left it. Just where it should be. Just as it existed in his thoughts.

But where was it now? In the box of old books and photographs, ribbons and plastic models his mother had handed him?

These are the things out of your room, she'd said like she'd done him a favor, adding, *We had to get everything out of the house to sell it.*

Anthony watched the fortieth gallon go by and thought of some other family living in their house. Suddenly his heart was racing and he looked around the front of the gas station and across the street to the convenience store and video rental.

He turned and looked down the main street of a town he'd spent the past ten years of his life in, and it was as if he were seeing it for the first time. Like the sensation of looking up from a picnic in the woods and realizing you can't remember how you got there. Or how you were ever going to get back.

When your mother gets back you can show us all around! Lloyd's words left Anthony confused. Show what? The blinking light in the center of town that might keep two cars from smashing into each other if ever a time came where two cars came through at once? His house trailer blocked up in a bean field across from a cornfield?

Suddenly the sights and sounds of Booder, Indiana, closed in around Anthony as he gripped the pump handle for purpose. Anthony had arrived a decade ago in a robin's-egg-blue Rambler station wagon. He'd rattled into Ray's Garage in what was left of second gear and pleaded for some way to work for repairs.

Anthony had left home that June morning and pointed himself west just like he'd said he was going to do most of his life. He didn't know why west, only that it wasn't Avalon, Ohio. Since he was a child he'd kept his attention riveted on the horizon and grew determined to breach it. And that's just about as far as he had made it.

The momentum of his journey from Avalon began to ebb as soon as the town disappeared through the rear window. Anthony's determined jaw hung slack and lowered with every mile that came between him and the people he was leaving. Like an actor without an audience, suddenly his exit meant nothing. His movements and postures, his very thoughts, seemed baseless and contrived. It broke down completely, along with his transmission, just outside of Booder.

Ray was a fair man, but not a particularly charitable one. Anthony's car needed a new transmission, clutch, and linkage assembly. He estimated that the total repair, parts and labor, would come close to three hundred dollars. He would pay Anthony three dollars per hour to pump gas and clean up part-time, and the boy could pay room and board to stay in the extra room at his home until the repairs were paid for.

The old Rambler still sits next to Anthony's trailer and it still needs a transmission. It's not like Anthony's dream of going west died; it just sort of went into a coma. By the time he'd been in Booder long enough to notice his lack of progress he'd gotten used to the place.

He liked Ray, for one thing. Ray called him *Tony* right from the start. The fact that his mother wouldn't allow it, and the fact that his mother wasn't around to object, made the sound of it a delightful and devilish thing. A western sort of feeling all by itself.

Toward the end of that long hot summer, Ray's wife had finally gotten tired of having an extra face to look at every morning and an extra coverall to wash on Sunday. One day Ray offered Anthony a forty-hour week and a rent-to-own deal on a trailer and property out on Pilkington Road.

The momentary narcotic effect of being eighteen and having his own place drew Anthony's western horizons in a little closer. As close as Pilkington Road, which, actually, was a little north of there.

Anthony would never think of himself as stuck in Booder. He was still going Out West. Nothing had changed for him except he had a few commitments to clear up. He almost had the trailer paid off, which would free up some cash. Then he'd ask Melinda over at Big O Drugstore to go camping with him out to Yellowstone Park.

"I know she'd like that." Anthony explained it all to his parents who stood waiting for him to finish with the gas.

"We'd love to meet Melinda." Evelyn's interest was piqued. Anthony had never mentioned a girlfriend. Actually, Anthony had not gotten around to mentioning it to Melinda either. In fact, he wasn't sure she knew his name.

"She's off today and tomorrow." Anthony looked over his shoulder at the pump. "Fifty gallons. Holy smokes! This thing's got a hollow leg, don't it?"

Lloyd ignored his comment. "Maybe when we go out to see your place you could invite your girl over for dinner."

"No, we can't do that. The power's off at my place. They took it out with an irrigation pipe last night."

"Then you can eat with us."

"I'm eatin' at Ray's tonight."

"Oh." Lloyd and Evelyn finally got it.

The overflow safety switched the gas nozzle off with a clunk. Anthony pulled the nozzle out of the tank with a professional flourish.

Lloyd used the moment. "Well, we really oughta be gettin' on the road, anyhow." He looked to his wife for help.

Evelyn stepped beside Lloyd. "We've got reservations tonight at a park in Starved Rock, and then tomorrow we pass Chicago."

She stopped and squeezed Lloyd's arm with both her hands. "Can you believe it? Two states in one day and then Chicago! And then the Mississippi River!"

Lloyd patted Evelyn's hand. "That's right, son. Lots of places to go and not a lot of time to go there."

Ray had come out to gas up another customer while Anthony visited with his folks. Anthony noticed the Massachusetts plates when the car drove away and Ray walked over to them wiping his hands on a rag.

"You know who that was? That was the young fella who fell out of that airplane this winter. Remember? He was on the cover of *The National Interrogator,* and I saw him on *Good Morning Michiana.*" Ray was as excited as Anthony had ever seen him.

"Imagine that! A celebrity right here in Booder. I'll have to tell Shirley over at the *County Shopper.* She can put it in her 'Comin's and Goin's' column. He said he was headed all the way to Seattle, Washington. Maybe you folks'll run into him."

Ray looked at Lloyd and Evelyn and then at the total on the pump. "Tony, give your folks the employee discount." Ray chuckled. "They just about qualify for the bulk rate."

Anthony cringed at the sound of his nickname and looked expectantly at his mother, who seemed oblivious to it.

"We'd better git, Mother." Lloyd relieved Evelyn of a bag of groceries from the Quick Trip, placed them inside, then followed Ray and Anthony into the station. "We'll be back. You never know when, though. This beauty's the only home we got now and we plan to put some miles on it. After we go see your sister in Oregon we may turn right around and come back. You never know, you never know."

Anthony knew this wasn't true. They weren't coming back any more than he was going out. He took in this familiar and excited old man and he didn't know what to say. Just like he never knew what to say to his father. And rather than say the wrong thing, Anthony said nothing at all, as he always had. All he knew for sure was that the home he meant to leave behind was sitting out in the drive-through about to overtake him.

He looked at the cardboard box marked *Anthony* his mother had given him. It was filled with dog-eared westerns, a couple science fair ribbons, and an outfielder's mitt. It was all that was left of him.

Anthony returned Lloyd's credit card and followed it with a reflex banality worn into him by ten years of pumping gas. "Have a nice trip," he said and stopped cold at the sound of it, reaching for something more to say. He could only add, "Dad."

After a long hug Evelyn ascended the stairs one last time. Lloyd shook his son's hand and followed her. They stood grinning at Anthony as the steps folded out of view in front of them. Anthony swung the door into his mother's hand, and their eyes met.

"You'll be all right," she said, and Anthony couldn't tell if it was a statement or a question.

"Yes." He smiled weakly and the door clicked closed.

It took Lloyd just as long to get back on the road as it had to leave it. Anthony stood waving the whole time. The blood had about run completely out of his arm and just when he couldn't stand it one more second the Road Ranger stumbled off the curb. The torqued fiberglass shrieked in protest, then the beast found its footing and lumbered down the street to the blinking light.

Evelyn found her son in the huge side mirror and waved some more. "What just happened there, Daddy?"

Lloyd moved the RV slowly toward the corner. "Nothing happened, Evy. Absolutely nothing." The criticism in his voice did not hide Lloyd's sadness. "We made a good mix, Mother. The boy just never set up right."

Evelyn let her tears form but wiped them to get the last look of her son as they moved around the corner.

Not watching his parents anymore, Anthony reached up with his hand to tear the piece of tape from his chest. He did it with an over-calculated finality and the tape ripped the coverall half-way across his chest. His embroidered name badge dangled from the gray tape he held in total disbelief. Anthony looked down at himself as the motor home disappeared with two quick toots of the horn.

Lloyd and Evelyn had that pose to remember him by—standing beside the road, his good name in one hand and nothing in the other.

The pear orchards shrieked with color in the hot afternoon sun. *We are here and we are glad to be alive.* The peach trees, not far behind, tallied their fruit and dropped what they could not hold.

The valley spread out before Quartz Mountain like a party skirt. A patchwork cornucopia made of orchards and fields. The work of a hearty matron. The willows along the roaming drainages lay in feminine folds like the charms of a seductress.

A billion-year-old crystal rests deep in the heart of the mountain. With the size of a parlor piano and the harmonic of the spheres, it sings its serenity as it has for a million millenniums. A crystal of such size and clarity could only be formed of perfect and total solitude. Molten rock hardening to its finest form over millions of years of utter stillness. Tranquil cooling molecules free to join themselves like random words becoming poetry.

The song that radiates from a billion years of peace is as quiet as its source and as compelling as time: Regardless of your disposition on the matter, it moves you and brings you to it.

The long spring shadow of Quartz Mountain crept across the pool at the Ponderosa Motor Lodge. Ed Flannigan felt the air turn cooler and sat up in his lounge chair. Absently he tested his sunburned belly by pressing deep into the pink flesh with his hand, then removing it. He counted the seconds until the impression disappeared. "Mississippi One. Mississippi Two. Mississippi Three. Whoa! —Baked Alaskan."

It had been another busy day for Ed Flannigan. Since he and his family pulled into town last week, he'd done little but lay poolside and reflect on the wonder of sunbathing in April.

After a lifetime in Alaska, Ed had been entirely prepared, if not thoroughly rehearsed, to hate every single thing about moving to Quartz

Creek. Coming to the realization that April was not considered a winter month in most parts of the world was going a long way toward opening Ed's frozen shut mind to the possibilities of life in the lower forty-eight states.

Emily watched her husband's bitterness sweeten over the past few days and it calmed her. She was a bit perturbed that out of everything this glorious community had to offer, Ed would only be influenced by the weather, but she'd take what she could get. Living in two motel rooms with three kids and a whining husband was more than Emily could bear for even those few days. She was glad Ed had found something to do with himself during the day, even if it was just nothing.

To Ed's credit he had gotten the kids introduced to and enrolled in their respective schools for the remainder of the school year. Having them occupied throughout the day allowed Emily to devote her attention to getting oriented up at the college.

There were a lot of things about Applegate College that would take some getting used to. Being back in the academic world was difficult enough, but joining the faculty of the most progressive private college in the Northwest was requiring some gigantic leaps of intellect on Emily's part.

As open minded and worldly as she was, she'd spent the past twelve years as a housewife in Alaska and was unprepared for some of Applegate's peculiar ideas about higher education.

"We don't refer to it as education, but as consciousness raising. It's not a pass-or-fail program. Our evaluations are based on acceptance and denial." Zowat, the popular channeler and tenured spiritual adviser to the Applegate faculty, had given Emily a private orientation. "Don't think of yourself as a teacher, but as a conduit of truth and beauty."

Zowat had then performed a spiritual cleansing for Emily by burning some herbs on a flat rock in her office. It had clogged Emily's sinuses and she'd sneezed some truth and beauty onto Zowat's enormous paisley muumuu. It had been a powerful experience, nonetheless.

Zowat had a commanding personal energy. For Emily, there was an immediate sense of having known her. Emily had heard of her enlightening lectures as far away as Alaska and knew several people who subscribed to Zowat's audio-cassette series, *Circling the Light*. That notoriety, coupled with Zowat's stout physique and a wild mane of black-and-white streaked hair that flowed down around her, made any time spent in her presence seem valuable, whether it made any sense or not.

Emily also struggled with the daily flag ceremony at the college. Each morning selected students and faculty sat in a circle around seven brightly colored flags. The colors were said to represent the various energy chakras of the body and soul. What everyone was supposed to do was quietly meditate on a color until somebody got a clear notion to grab one and run it up the flagpole.

Emily had difficulty staying with it. One morning she'd let her mind drift to the night before with Ed—after the kids had gone to sleep. The head of the Biology Department ran the bright red flag up the pole and pointed it out as the sexual and creative energy chakra.

Something in the way Zowat turned to her with a knowing look made Emily blush as bright as the flag and consider skipping morning prayer for awhile. Maybe she would feel more sure of herself once the movers showed up with their things and they were settled into the new place.

They'd been offered a drop-dead deal on a farmhouse owned by the college just outside of town. It was surrounded by a few small fields and a peach orchard. None of it had been cultivated in years, but it retained a certain pastoral charm that was not lost even on Ed. *Pretty as a seed catalog,* he'd offered, which was as close to farming as he'd ever been.

The kids were thrilled with the place, too, and everyone was anxious to move in. The hold-up was that a departing professor of art therapy had painted murals on all the interior walls that depicted distressing episodes in his life.

"It was therapeutic for him to face his pain on a daily basis," the housing director had explained. "Unfortunately, he had a nervous breakdown and resigned."

"I can see why," Ed said, coming out of the bedroom. "There's a picture of an ice cream truck and a squashed dog in the hallway and you oughta see the bathroom! Keep the kids out of there until we get a few coats of latex on, okay?"

It was taking more than a few coats of paint as it turned out. The professor's bar mitzvah kept bleeding through in the dining room, and the morning light tended to draw his demonic ex-wife's face out of the kitchen ceiling. Two more coats would do it, the painters assured them. The Flannigans, in the meantime, just needed to keep busy.

The evenings posed some difficulty for the family because the list of available activities around Quartz Creek, Oregon, could be roughly divided into two unequal categories: things Ed would do and things Ed wouldn't do.

The vast majority of daily distractions fell into the latter category, and Ed would have been content to sit around the television channel-surfing with the kids if Emily didn't pressure them to get out and mix with the community.

Their first night out had been a disaster. Emily had heard about a performance art event up at the college and insisted they all attend. "C'mon Ed. We've been culturally starved for years. Please just give it a chance."

It turned out to be a spectral artist who asked for volunteers to sit quietly in chairs while their auras were allegedly sculpted into evocative shapes in her hands. Ed sat sideways in the audience with his arms folded tightly across his chest through the whole thing. When spontaneous applause broke out at one point he looked like he was either going to slap somebody or throw up. Unconsciously he let the clamp on his counterfeit limb open and close menacingly.

"I'm going to that bar I saw next door," he finally said, getting up to leave.

Emily touched his sleeve and whispered in his ear. "I was told it's a gay bar."

Ed puzzled for a moment. "I don't suppose that means everybody's just in a really good mood over there?"

Emily shook her head advisedly, and Ed sat back down more deter-mined than ever to hate this town.

"You can't even find any real ice cream around this place," he'd complained on the way back to the motel. "It's all frozen yogurt! What's the point? The only reason I can see to freeze yogurt is to keep it from stinkin'."

Emily had been unable to get Ed away from the television since. *Channeling Alaska style,* he called it. She'd just about given up on him altogether when a very fortunate thing happened on the way back from the farmhouse yesterday afternoon.

They were cruising down a country road admiring the orchards all abloom when suddenly a huge truck burgeoning with fresh-cut logs came roaring around them from behind and disappeared in a cloud of dust.

Ed lit up like a halogen work lamp. "Whoa! This place is looking downright civilized all of a sudden."

Emily looked at her husband, mystified.

Ed beamed with hope and mischief. "Hey, where there's logs, there's loggers. I knew the weather couldn't be the only friendly thing around here."

Like all birds of a feather, Ed had no trouble finding his flock. It turned out that while there wasn't a whole lot left of a full-scale lumber industry around the area, there was still some selective timber cutting going on here and there, so the presence and the tradition of logging remained an important, albeit diminished, part of the territory.

A few well-placed calls revealed the Logging Association's Annual Spring Jamboree was just winding down at the County Fairground and Emily was all too happy to let Ed go take a look.

"Take little Ed along with you. I'll walk with the kids to that Zowat workshop tonight. She's channeling for the spirit of her namesake that was revealed to her by an angel the day she first arrived. Zowat is a four-thousand-year-old Egyptian stone mason who was buried alive in King Tut's tomb. He has some hostility to work out about that."

"Try not to warp the children," Ed said cheerily, gathering eleven-year-old Ed under his good arm. "C'mon big guy, I'll show ya something real for a change."

Father and son stood in line at the food shack on the fairgrounds and took it all in. There were pole climbers bandy-legging around in their spurs. Young buck-rigging slingers strutted in their suspenders and Reeboks. They warmed up for the choker-setting competition by leaping over a six-foot ponderosa butt that laid in the dust and bright lights like an icon.

Potbellied old lumbermen with permanent grease fields on their shirt fronts ambled about telling old war stories of missing fingers and crushed bones like notches in a gun stock. Ed's mechanical appendage made him a bit of a curiosity. Men would pass by and notice it, then look to Ed with knowing approval. It made conversation easy and the jokes blasphemous.

One old timer, leaving with his order, turned to Ed. "What happened to you, Stumpy? Forget to let go?"

"Must have." Ed pointed at the man's food. "How's the chicken?" Ed asked. The man stopped, took an appreciative bite of a drumstick, and observed, "Oh, not bad. Somewhere between a condor and a spotted owl, I'd say."

After a pair of hamburgers, Ed ended up at the beer tent watching the contestants warming up for the log-rolling event. A single log floated like an alligator in a deep, muddy-watered trench.

It could have been the two beers, or it could have been all that testosterone in the air. But Ed couldn't stand it any longer. He was a natural competitor who commanded an athlete's dexterity in everything he did. A place like this was a playground to Ed Flannigan; at least it used to be. Since he lost the arm there weren't nearly as many games he was good at. Certainly not pole climbing or setting chokers. Axe throwing and whip sawing were out, too. But this log rolling—all it took was two legs, some good balance, and quick reflexes. All of which Ed Flannigan still retained.

Before Ed Junior even knew what was happening, his Dad was pulling him into the throng.

"Let's get your ol' man signed up here, buddy boy. I'm gonna show these Oregon timber snipes what an Alaskan man can do."

Ed's bluster was genuine. He had no trouble with his confidence. It was the first time since arriving in Quartz Creek that he'd felt at home. Hooting and hollering in the company of hard-working men. His oldest boy at his side. And a contest. That's the stuff.

Two men bellied out of the trench like drowned rats amidst a roar of good-hearted derision.

The referee shouted above it, "That's a draw. Next—Peidmont, Ammerman."

The two men faced each other shakily. The log moved back and forth beneath their feet like an anxious rodeo bronc waiting for the gate. One man had stripped down to his waist and had removed his boots. Ed thought that showed a great lack of conviction and said so. "Hey buddy, if you didn't want to get your shoes wet you shoulda stayed home."

As it happened, the bare-footed man was quick on his toes and he prevailed. While his opponent dragged himself out of the murky trench the referee checked his clipboard. "Ammerman up by one. Next challenge—Flannigan."

Ed took his end of the log and summoned his balance. It was there, like an old friend, holding him up on all sides. He shifted his feet, testing the weight of the log, the legs of his opponent. Ed's sureness of foot radiated from him like a good sunburn. A healthy glow. An aura of sureness. He held his competitor's eyes in his as they began. One way. The other. Back again. Ed let him move, followed him, felt the rhythm. One way. The other. Back again. Wait—Now!

A cheer went up. Ed could hear every voice, his ears drinking it up. "Way to go, Stumpy!" "Yeah—Dad!" Ed used it like fuel. It burned in every part left of him and focused his attention on the other end of the log like a high beam. Like driving at night, the only thing that mattered was in his headlights.

Challenger after challenger stepped into the wash of his lights and vanished again. *Flannigan up by three—Flannigan up by five—six—up by seven. Next!* It felt like it could never end. Ed stood his log as easily as a floor board. Total command. Total focus.

"Last challenge! Decker—you're up!"

Ed heard a wail of whistles and men barking and howling like dogs. "Give 'im hell, Deirdre."

Deirdre? Ed's balance momentarily faltered as she jumped onto the log. She wasn't much bigger than Ed Junior. She had bare feet and blue jeans cut off raggedly at mid-calf. She wore a torn sweatshirt and an intense blue gaze that said one word—*wild.*

"Don't let a lady dump you now, Stumpy."

The spectators continued their noisy ballyhoo, but Ed would not be distracted. Deirdre blew a thin wisp of hair out of her face and locked her eyes on Ed's.

Had the spectral artist of a few nights earlier been on hand she might have seen Ed's aura of sureness flicker for just an instant. But he relaxed his legs under him and let his unexpected little opponent begin.

She started with a jump. She was strong and quick, Ed could feel that. She pumped her feet and Ed let the log pick up speed. *She's nimble, alright,* Ed thought. *But she hasn't got the weight to shift this thing.* He knew this would be a contest of speed he might lose unless he could turn the log around without warning. There was going to be no wrestling with this gal. He'd have to let her get this log really humming, then stop it dead in the water. Ed got right up on his toes and bore down on her with his eyes, searching hers for any sign of weakness, fatigue, anticipation. He was going to dump her.

On three. Ed revealed nothing with his face. *Mississippi One—Mississippi Two—Mississippi . . .* Suddenly Deirdre's determined features melted into a coy smile.

What's she doing? Ed shifted his weight to brace for his move—and Deirdre beat him to it. Summoning all the power her hundred and ten pound being could muster, she winked at him.

· · ·

Ed had hit the water with his mouth wide open. He was still spitting grit out of his teeth halfway back to town as he leaned over the wheel and shivered.

"Maybe you should have taken your shirt and shoes off like that other guy." Ed Junior sat in the silence blaring from the driver's seat. "Second place isn't so bad, Dad."

The quiet continued in the car and became a noise of its own. It joined with the silent symphony of the moonlit landscape and it all turned into one thing. Quartz Mountain rose up before them, its granite outcroppings shining like diamonds, its crystal heart shivering a billion years of peace.

"You know what, little buddy?" Ed continued to look straight ahead speaking through clenched teeth. "There's something about this place that really bugs me."

9

The Hotel Merrimont rose above the business district with unrelenting self-importance. Its lofty profile bearing the pride of a hundred years of uncompromised service. The building itself dressed a person down with its very presence. Comfortable old shoes transformed themselves into public embarrassments; fine coats and hats became off the rack and threadbare in its shadow. Loud or playful voices were shushed by the cavernous lobby of chandeliers and ornament.

The arched Grand Entrance loomed at the end of the drive like destiny. Marion Michael Bedinger stepped out of the car, set down his case, and gathered himself to his full six feet two inches. His reflection shone in the gilded framework around the revolving door. He shot his cuffs and appraised the splendor before him.

Twin floral arrangements bracketed the plush red carpeting that reached to the curb like a coronation. Stiff-shouldered doormen stood white-gloved and attentive. Ready to anticipate the desires of any who crossed this portal.

A cab? A town car? Umbrella today, sir? A light for your cigarette, madam? Francis will see to your bags. Please follow me.

Marion Michael Bedinger basked in the accouterments of fortune. *Success is so very very sweet,* he thought.

"Have a nice day, Buddy. Get lots of tips." The voice from inside the car broke into his reverie. Buddy turned around and leaned in.

"Thanks, Sal, I better get inside before Willie sees I'm late again." Buddy Bedinger put a kiss on his fingertips, then placed it on the cheek of the young woman behind the wheel.

The failing exhaust system on the old car filled the great portico with an acrid blue smoke and an excruciating clatter. Buddy strutted up the red carpet as the stiff-shouldered doormen waved their white gloves in front of their faces. "If Willie ever catches you using the main entrance to sneak in late for work, you're going to get canned, Buddy. You better get your buns down to the kitchen. He's looking for you."

Buddy ducked down the service corridor next to the gift shop. He stashed his briefcase full of books behind the folding tables in the hall outside the employees' break room. Retrieving a serving tray from the same place, he balanced it on one hand and continued down the hall intently.

Buddy plucked two soiled plates from a cart piled with dirty breakfast dishes overflowing from the kitchen. He placed them on his tray and turned the corner just in time to introduce his alibi to the solar plexus of Willie Koontz, the room service manager. The two plates spilled to the floor and shattered dramatically at their feet.

"Oh geez! I'm sorry, Mr. Koontz!" Buddy stood looking at the pale face of his boss with great concern. "Are you okay? I'm really in a rush. We've got people waiting for their breakfast all over the hotel."

Buddy bolted down the hall leaving the broken dishes and an incredulous Willie Koontz in disarray behind him. He hit the kitchen at a full trot and headed right for the order line. Carlos, the head waiter, turned toward him with a tray of covered dishes.

"I lied for you again, man. But you gotta stop doing this. Willie is catching on to you."

"Thanks a lot, Carlos." Buddy noted the time on an order and pulled the tray toward him as he talked. "I was up late cramming for my bankruptcy law final."

Carlos plucked two yellow roses from a bucket next to the order board and placed one on each of their trays. "Yeah, well you keep this up and Willie's gonna bankrupt both of us. You're not even a lawyer yet and you're already causing nothing but trouble."

Buddy grinned at his reliable friend and headed for the service elevator. "You wait, Carlos. Someday, I won't be answering to anybody."

The elevator doors closed like a curtain on Buddy's big, affable face. Carlos shook his head and crossed himself before returning to his work. "We all answer to somebody," he mumbled, but Buddy was already on his way upstairs.

. . .

Buddy stepped onto the fourteenth floor and checked his tray. Coffee, mineral water, croissant. A simple working breakfast for a busy man, he thought. This was the Executive Floor of the hotel, private and privileged. Only the most distinguished and favored guests of the Merrimont held keys for the Executive Floor.

Buddy checked himself in the hall mirror. He straightened his tie with his free hand, tried his smile, then his thoughtful squint. The most successful business people in the world stayed here. Making impressions on this lot could serve Buddy well someday.

He knew that the corporate world existed not of companies, but of networks of individuals who banded together in unwritten lifelong associations for mutual advantage. Well-placed friends in a wide variety of industries would bode well for an ambitious corporate attorney. *Marion Michael Bedinger Esquire, Attorney at Law, at your service.*

Buddy could hear a man's voice through the door of 1416. He knocked sharply, pulled the pass key out of his pocket, and knocked again.

"Come in—come in!" The voice called out, impatient and distracted.

Buddy swept through the door, "Room Service," and headed directly for the table in the suite. He pulled up short when he saw that every available surface in the room was covered with file folders, documents, binders, and briefs. The man on the phone sat at the desk, fully dressed but coatless. A fax machine hummed on the floor dispensing a mass of curled pages at his impeccably shoed feet. The gentleman disconnected his call and immediately started dialing again. Buddy used the interruption. "Where would you like this, sir?"

The man continued to dial and looked at Buddy as if he had just become aware he was in the room. "Anywhere, anywhere," he said. He reached into his pocket, and without looking produced a five-dollar bill, then his attention returned to the phone. "Yes, this is Robert Pritchett, head of Legal Affairs for Principal Commodities Incorporated. Please put me through to the Senator."

Buddy cleared a space on the coffee table as his heart pumped in his chest. *Principal Commodities! PCI! The third largest company in the world! They were into everything! Shipping, Electronics, Insurance, Chemicals. They must get sued five times a minute. And this is their attorney!*

Buddy discreetly focused on some of the papers he was gently moving aside. Memos marked *Confidential.* Bound legal briefs bearing the commanding PCI logo. This was the pinnacle. Buddy poured a cup of coffee and set it next to the man at the desk, who took it and drank. He then dismissed Buddy with a gesture and the five-dollar tip, his mind on the phone.

"Senator Hoskins! Good morning, Sir. Bob Pritchett—Louise is fine, thank you. And your Abigail? Excellent. Listen, Phil, I've got a dicey situation here. Yes—that chemical leak—very unfortunate—yes. I just don't know what the other side is going to throw at us. Does your office have any history with . . ."

Buddy closed the door behind him. He might have listened further, but two men in suits were standing at the elevator. Buddy turned and headed to the service lift with a new spring in his step and excitement spilling from his lips. "Robert Pritchett. Gets through to a Senator on the first try! I've *gotta* get that guy's business card."

Buddy Bedinger's sister Katherine, who was in advertising, had counseled Buddy to collect as many business cards from as many important people as he could before he entered the job market. She claimed that business people don't remember the circumstances of half the people they meet. A well-placed call and a little finesse could open a lot of doors someday.

Buddy fantasized on the way down to the kitchen. *Hello, Robert? Marion M. Bedinger, attorney at law. We met a few years back when you were on that dicey business in Seattle. How is Louise?*

Carlos was still at his station on the order line when Buddy stepped off the elevator. "Better hustle, Buddy Boy. We've got cold eggs waiting."

"Room service eggs are always cold. They expect it." Buddy

grabbed the next tray in line, destined for 1123, and swept past Carlos for a fresh rose and ice water. "Oh, Carlos. Save anything from 1416 for me."

Buddy's head waiter smiled. "Who is it this time—Lee Ioccoca?"

"Better'n that! He's a lawyer. A real bigshot too. You'll do it?" Buddy got back in the elevator and turned with the question on his face.

Carlos lifted a thumb as the doors again closed on his determined friend. "I'll do it," he said sadly to the cold eggs, "if you want it that bad."

Buddy looked over the tray for 1123. A pitcher of coffee. Three donuts. Two Cokes. *Junkfood,* thought Buddy. *Tourists with kids.* Buddy stepped onto the eleventh floor and walked down the hall unenthusiastically, his mind still up on the fourteenth.

He found the door to 1123 propped open with a shoe. Again Buddy heard a man talking on the phone. He stopped at the open door and knocked discreetly.

"Just a minute, please!" he heard a polite voice say. *Tourist,* thought Buddy with some contempt. Only the tourists were polite to the hired help.

"Room service!" Buddy said patiently and waited for the man to get off the phone.

"Sorry, Paul, my breakfast is here. Yeah, that's right, room service. Can you believe it? You oughta try it sometime. Hold on." The man cupped the phone and called again to the door. "Come on in. Set it down anywhere."

Buddy pushed through the door with his tray and took in the small room, the hotel's basic tourist single. There were clothes hung on the backs of chairs, and the bed was covered with a mixture of neckties, underwear, file folders, and legal pads.

The man stood at the desk behind a pile of bulging expansion folders in sweatpants and a tee shirt. Buddy shuddered and looked for an empty space for his tray. There was a half-eaten pizza in a box draped over the television. A briefcase spilled its guts on the dresser. Even the vanity in the bathroom was strewn with sections of the morning newspaper and bits of take-out food. This guy is a pig, Buddy thought, shrugging helplessly. The man saw the predicament and spoke again into the phone.

"Paul, I gotta go right now, but believe me, Pritchett over at PCI doesn't have a clue we've got the Rodriguez family set to give their depositions. It's one they missed when they tried to settle all this out of court. They won't know what hit 'em. I'll call you back."

Buddy was accustomed to the hotel guests speaking freely on the phone or to each other in his presence. People tended to think of room service waiters as beneath concern, part of the furniture. It was amazing, sometimes alarming, what people said and did in front of the room waiters.

Buddy effortlessly masked his interest in the man's conversation. "Where would you like this, sir?"

The man looked around, perplexed. "Boy, this place is a mess, isn't it?" He cleared a corner of the bed by pushing things toward the center in a heap. "I've been working in here for two solid days. I haven't even let the maids in. I'm not used to these fancy places. I guess I'm still living like a public defender. I don't know why the firm puts me in these darn castles. They make me nervous."

Buddy set the tray down on the bed and handed the man his bill. He thought he'd better get a signature for charges by the looks of this guy. "You're a lawyer?" Buddy said, trying not to sound skeptical.

"Yes, I'm afraid that's true," the man said absently, looking over his check before signing.

Buddy wanted to know more. "I'm in my first year of law school right now. What sort of case are you working on?"

The man handed back the bill—Buddy noticed a tip was not written in—and spoke easily. "We've got a big class-action suit against a large chemical company. They had a leak out in one of the neighborhoods a year ago. Hurt a bunch of people. You probably read about it. Anyway, I'm with Weiderby-Klugh, a public service law firm. We have a grant to go to bat for the folks with sustaining injuries. They have no resources of their own."

Buddy's smile was frozen in place thinking, *a bleeding heart liberal do-good lawyer.*

"I'm going into corporate law," he said importantly. "That's where the real action is."

"I wish you luck, son. I hope you're a good one. We need all the good ones we can get in this profession." The man scratched his belly through his tee shirt and handed Buddy the cold box of pizza on his way out. "Would you mind taking this with you? It's starting to smell up my bed sheets."

"Certainly," Buddy said, not breaking his face or stride. He held the box far out in front of himself and walked quickly for the elevator before anyone might see him.

"Why do they let these people in the hotel?" he said out loud to himself while safely on his way down. "Why do they let these people practice law?" Buddy's ambition was exceeded only by his naiveté.

"Digging up victims to harass respectable corporations for ridiculous sums of money. It's lawyers like him giving us all a bad name. What did he say that family was? Ramerez? Rodriguez? Yeah—I bet 1416 would be happy to hear about that."

Buddy stopped as if somebody else had said it. "Heeey. I bet 1416 would be very happy to hear about that. Happy enough to remember one young law student named Marion Michael Bedinger."

Buddy was grinning like he swallowed a rat when the doors opened on the kitchen. Carlos immediately came over to him with a large coffee decanter. He took the pizza box and put the coffee in Buddy's hands. "There's your 1416—counselor. You better hustle. He called twice while I held it for you."

Buddy didn't even have time to thank him. Carlos punched the button on the wall and sent Buddy on his way up. The sensation of ascending was not lost on Buddy as he groomed his expressions in the grainy reflection of the stainless steel door. "The gods are lookin' after the Budman today."

Once again the man called through the door and Buddy entered with his pass key. "Sorry to keep you waiting, Mr. Pritchett."

"All right. Just set it down." The lawyer stayed completely engrossed in the papers before him. Buddy poured a fresh cup of coffee and set the pitcher down. He hesitated for a moment, and the guest looked up impatiently. "Yes?"

Buddy was caught off-guard. "Oh! Umm. Well. You're a lawyer."

The man closed his eyes slowly and opened them again. "I know."

Buddy tried to recover some composure. "I'm studying for the bar. Well, I have a ways to go, but I want to pursue corporate law. Maybe even with a company like PCI."

The mention of the name caused the man to narrow his gaze and calmly close the brief in front of him. He took the resigned breath of someone who was about to be solicited for a favor and waited.

Buddy pressed on. "I was wondering if the firm of Weiderby-Klugh had any significance for you."

The man stood up with his arms behind his back and walked slowly forward, putting himself between Buddy and the papers on his desk. "I've heard of the firm. Why do you ask?"

Buddy summoned a full air of confidence. "Let's just say that there's a certain *Rodriguez family* that is also familiar with this firm. I thought you might find this information useful."

The man displayed no reaction at all. He slowly let his eyes look down and back up the young waiter in front of him. "How did you come by this information, might I ask?"

Buddy executed his best interpretation of an in-the-know corporate lawyer grin. "Let's just say I was a fly on the wall."

The man stood and held Buddy's eyes for a long time. Then he looked to Buddy's nametag and spoke. "Marion Michael. Is that your whole name, son?"

Buddy was totally relaxed now. "Marion Michael *Bedinger,* Mr. Pritchett. Glad to make your acquaintance." Buddy held his hand out in front of him, but the lawyer kept his arms behind his back.

"Marion Michael Bedinger," he repeated. "I'll have to remember that name." He looked at Buddy, who was positively glowing.

"Yes, I'll certainly have to remember that because I hope I never find myself across a boardroom table or in a courtroom with a lawyer named Marion—Michael—Bedinger."

The space left between the words gave the name a grave and vital sound. Buddy stood silent.

Robert Pritchett turned his back on Buddy and looked out the window to Puget Sound. In the distance a ship made its way carefully up the channel to port, its horn sounding importantly.

"You see, Mr. Bedinger, the law is a profession of ethics. Without our ethics, without our integrity, we are nothing. And if we become nothing, so do our laws. I don't know what they're teaching in the law schools these days, but I do know we already have enough lawyers like you."

Pritchett turned and again faced the bellboy. Buddy felt like vapor. A mere projection of himself in the room. The rest of him was somewhere else watching and listening, but not believing. The man's lips moved and the words passed right through Buddy taking pieces of his soul along with them.

"I suggest you find another career you're more suited for. Even your present job appears to tax your scruples. Now please leave before I report you to the management."

Marion Michael Bedinger sat in the alley on the back kitchen stairs. Twenty floors of the grandest hotel in the Northwest towered behind him in service to some of the most elegant and prestigious clientele in the world. A ship's horn sounded and barely made its way around the corner of the building before dying in the alley.

Buddy watched Oliver, who was whistling a tuneless melody as he organized the bottles and crates piled around the alley.

Buddy's briefcase laid open at his feet mounded with textbooks and notes. *Constitutional Law* . . . *Forensics* . . . *Comparative Ethics*. The titles made him cringe, and he kicked the lid shut. "Damn!"

Oliver looked up from his work.

"Nothing, Oliver. Nothing," Buddy said.

Oliver was always interested in his young friend's exciting life. "How's your studies comin', Buddy?"

"I'm learning a lot," Buddy said. "I'm learning a whole lot."

Carlos stuck his head out the door and handed Buddy a stained and wrinkled hotel envelope. "This came down on the tray from 1123. That guy's a pig, man. And hey, your 1416 is asking for his lunch."

"Give it to someone else," Buddy said. "I'm done with that."

Carlos shrugged and disappeared inside. Buddy read the envelope, *Marion, the room service guy,* it said. He opened it and inside there was a five-dollar bill and a business card from Weiderby-Klugh. On the back of the card was a scrawled note: *Didn't mean to stiff you. If you ever change your mind about corporate law, we're always looking for good guys.*

Buddy let the business card fall out of his hands while he wadded up the bill. "Hey, Oliver," he called out, pitching the money across the alley and hitting the man's pants leg.

Oliver bent slowly and grabbed the bill. "What's this?" he said. "I don't take money for this."

Buddy stood up with his briefcase and turned to go inside. "Somebody upstairs sent money down by mistake. Keep it, they're gone."

As Buddy withered into the kitchen clatter and confusion, Oliver tipped his head to look up at the hotel looming over Seattle like a rich uncle. He pocketed the five-dollar bill, waved to the empty doorway, and moved on, grateful to have friends in such high places.

10

Lloyd breathed and cradled his cup of coffee nervously. There was not a hint of a new day in the world. The generator under the motor home gratefully quit, allowing the pre-dawn stillness in the RV park to resume. A dog barked far away to the east. A car started. But all of Lloyd's attention was in front of him. To the West.

The lawn chair shifted in the stones beneath him. He waited, not taking his eyes from the blank black scene before him. Lloyd reached back and rapped his knuckles on the side of the RV. "Better get out here, Evy. This is what we've been driving for."

Lloyd heard Evelyn stir through the thin wall. He followed her movement through their house and home as it creaked on its springs. The door opened and she stuck her head out clutching her robe around her neck with one hand. "Lloyd Decker, it's the middle of the night! The sun won't be up for hours yet."

" 'Bout an hour and a half, I figure, Mother. I don't want to miss even a peep of them mountains." Lloyd pulled his wool coat closer around himself. "Dress warm. It's a might chilly yet this morning."

"I'll be out in a little bit," Evelyn said. After looking at the pitch black void beyond the lights of Boulder she added dryly, "Tell me if I miss anything."

Lloyd sat his vigil in the dark quietly, almost reverently. He tried to penetrate the vacant landscape with his most deliberate scrutiny. *I know you're out there. I can feel you. Show yourself.*

The foothills of the Rocky Mountains sat patiently in the darkness. Going nowhere. Feeling none of Lloyd's suspense. Some things just are. And there are few things like the Rocky Mountains.

The biggest thing Lloyd and Evelyn had seen in their whole lives was the Chicago skyline, and that was just two weeks ago. The idea of mountains was just an abstract at this point. They'd looked at reams of pictures, but nothing had gotten through. It was like looking at pictures of men on the moon. It appears plausible and interesting, but how could you ever really know what it's like, if it's even real, until you get there yourself?

Lloyd and Evelyn had driven up from the plains after dark the night before. Even though they couldn't see anything, they could feel the mountains all around them. The air was cooler. The sky was blacker, and each star seemed distinct and alone. The motor home struggled up some of the grades coming into Denver, and Lloyd couldn't seem to find his breath. "I think I left a lung in Ogallala," he joked on the way to bed.

Evelyn was pleased to see Lloyd so excited. The last week or so of their journey had begun to get monotonous for them both.

Lloyd thought crossing the Mississippi River was the most be-witching thing he had ever experienced—the first time, anyway. The spell had worn off by the fifth or sixth time across. It had taken them weeks to get past the Mississippi.

Lloyd pulled over and parked just before the first crossing at the Quad Cities. He made Evelyn take a picture of him. He stood smiling, half-sideways to the camera, pointing at the river.

"What in the world are you pointing at?" Evelyn had asked.

"The river! The by-gosh Mississippi River!" He pointed even more intensely, and spoke carefully to the camera, "Mis-sis-sip-pi," as Evelyn snapped the picture. The camera froze Lloyd's mouth in a most ridiculous shape, and the picture made no sense at all: a grimacing old man pointing across an expressway, and some water.

They followed the gentle, powerful waters down, never venturing too far from its banks, crossing again and again. Rock Island. Burlington. Quincy. Following the Great River Road. Down to St. Louis.

"Let's go into Illinois again," Lloyd had said after looking over Mark Twain's hometown of Hannibal, Missouri. "I want to come into St. Louis from the east, like the pioneers did."

Evelyn was just as impressed, but less expressive about it, at least out in the open. She tried to keep a daily journal at the start of their trek and saved most of her remarks for that nightly ritual. That and the letters to her children. It was impossible to come from Avalon, Ohio, and not find almost everything remarkable. Even the diagonal downtown parking in one small Illinois town had fascinated her enough to take a picture of it. *Darndest thing I ever saw,* she wrote to Deirdre that evening. *You just never know what kind of things there are in the world until you go out and meet them.*

As unworldly as Lloyd and Evelyn might be, they were also keenly aware of and interested in every new sight they saw along the river. They soon noticed they were seeing many of the same things over and over.

Even the power of one of the greatest rivers on earth could not entirely mask the redundancy of the roads that intersected it. Every new town had the same strip of fast-food franchises in a fluorescent row of painfully lighted parking lots and price wars. *Biggest burger. Best Buy. Double dippers. Triple toppers. Super Doopers.*

It began to feel to Lloyd and Evelyn like their big journey to discover America was becoming just an endless series of left and right turns prompted by the signs they read. *RV Dump Station One Mile. Camping Next Right. Don't Miss Ottumwa, Iowa—Adventure Land.*

Every night it was the same thing: back into another vacancy in yet another roadside RV park. Roll out the awning, set up the lawn chairs, meet the neighbors.

"Where from?"

"Ohio. You?"

"Michigan."

"Nice weather we're havin'."

"Sure is."

Then there was the endless RV talk. The men compared holding tank capacities while the women talked closet space. Lloyd and Evelyn's Road Ranger was top of the line and quite a conversation piece. The Deckers never had been very social animals, though, and quickly grew weary of the attention.

Occasionally they'd round up a pinochle game, but Lloyd and Evelyn were most comfortable with themselves. They closed their shades early and sat at the dinette. Lloyd would leaf through maps and tourist brochures, sharing interesting ideas for the days ahead. "We could go to Keokuk and drive through three states in ten miles."

Evelyn would write in her journal. *The trip has been very pleasant, but I think we've seen enough of this area. No matter how great a river might be, after awhile it's just a lot of water moving by.*

What Lloyd and Evelyn were unaware of is that they had run up against more than a river when they reached the Mississippi. They had come to an invisible but mighty boundary. From right down in the heart of their primordial selves, possibly imprinted on the very DNA that determined who they were, came an instinctual hesitancy to move forward. Like animals in the wild, people, too, can sense the outer reaches of their natural habitat. Some, like their son Anthony, are unable to move further. Others, like themselves, need some time to think about it.

Lloyd and Evelyn's lumbering excursion up and down the Mississippi River gorge, in thirty-two feet of fiberglass, formica, and tunafish salad, was more than two old people buying postcards. It was a primeval dance—akin to the ancient Eskimos who paced at the Asian foot of the Bering Land Bridge. Watching. Waiting. Stalling. Promise spread before them. Everything they know left behind.

The first steps are tentative—suspicious and short. Soon, the ground underfoot becomes agreeable. New terrain is considered and adapted to. We bring the familiar with us: the sun, the rain—our thoughts. Soon we feel like we belong, and we move on more quickly, not satisfied again until we reach the next border.

Lloyd and Evelyn could feel the grip of the river loosen as they drifted toward Des Moines. As the Great Plains flattened out before them, Lloyd felt his foot getting heavy on the gas pedal. The smell of the freshly plowed earth that lined the highway for as far as they could see was tempting. Roadside distractions beckoned. *Seashell City. Live Buffalo. Free Dumping with Fill-up.* But the Deckers pressed on.

They crossed the Missouri River at Omaha with scarcely a sideways look. By the time they cleared Lincoln the plains seemed to rise before them like a challenge to move onward and upward to the backbone of

America—where all rivers chose their direction once and for all. To the Continental Divide.

Evelyn pulled her lawn chair up beside Lloyd. The sound of the metal legs in the gravel made them both wince. It was like banging a kneeler in church. The anticipation of the light of day was commanding the Deckers' highest regard and reverence.

Lloyd looked over his shoulder to the east and south. The faintest glow seemed visible out beyond the gleam of Denver. He looked to the stars overhead. There were fewer than there had been a moment ago. "Here we go, Mother." Lloyd took Evelyn's hand in his as they both stared into the vacant West.

There is no way to describe the surprise you feel when seeing mountains for the first time. Some people grow up around mountains, but never have the privilege of meeting them. Others live out their whole lives with nothing on the horizon bigger than what was built there by human hands.

People's senses of perspective and scale are imprinted on them by their surroundings. The tallest point of reference in Avalon, Ohio, was the water tower. It could be seen from anyplace Lloyd and Evelyn needed to go for over seventy years. So it was with more than a small sense of wonder that the Deckers had witnessed the high-rise buildings of Chicago for the first time.

Still, they were buildings. Straight lines and points in the sky. There was height, but no depth. Size without density. Forms without soul. Tall buildings can be accurately represented on a postcard. Mountain ranges cannot be mailed home or sold to magazines. Mountains cannot be looked at; they must be felt.

Lloyd sat breathing and watched the sky slowly lighten, black edging barely to blue. His soul sank as a bank of clouds appeared to form before them. A distinct dark line in the sky that stretched like heartbreak from north to south. Lloyd turned to Evelyn and opened his mouth to speak his disappointment, but Evelyn spoke first.

"Oh, my Lord," she said squeezing his hand hard. "It's them."

Lloyd looked back at the clouds. It *was* them. The clouds were the mountains, or the mountains were the clouds. It was a dizzying change of perspective that caused Lloyd to sit bolt upright in his chair puffing for air like he'd just dodged a bus. And that's exactly what it felt like: a bus, where there should have been a bicycle. Due to an eye trained to look for nothing on the horizon higher than the Avalon municipal water tower, the outline of the mountains that loomed before Lloyd was a full twenty measures higher than where he'd been looking for it.

"My God," Lloyd said, letting himself relax again into the chair. "They're— ." Lloyd searched through his low-profiled midwestern vocabulary for a word, but found none and simply let the mountain fill his empty statement.

The dawn was on its stride, and the Rocky Mountains appeared to march forward in their rising clarity. The faces of the Flat Irons absolutely gleamed beneath the rosy mantle of late spring frost.

When the sun broke free behind them, the mountains took their final form. Lloyd and Evelyn just sat quietly and watched as if they had box seats for the third day of Creation.

Evelyn's camera, which had not seen an hour's rest since Indiana, dangled by its strap from the arm of her aluminum lawn chair. She knew this could not be captured by a lens. A camera gathers only light. A mountain puts out light *and* mass. Mass is something you have to be involved with to appreciate. Like feeling the Earth under your feet. Really seeing a mountain is to feel it on your face.

Lloyd and Evelyn sat with the mountain on their faces and the sun on their backs, and for a moment they were suspended in time and space between the two. Lloyd's lawn chair shifted in the stones tenuously. Evelyn eased her grip on his hand and let the warmth of the sun into her.

There must have been a similar moment long ago for the spring that flows from the top of the Great Divide. Just an instant when it could have flowed in either direction. Why it chose the way it did was a function of physics. Some invisible influence of nature gave it a course.

Lloyd and Evelyn stood and breathed and held each other by the waist. The sun was high above the horizon now. They could have turned around and seen the great golden plains of half a continent rolling off to the east and beyond to everything they had ever known.

But they held their faces to the mountain and allowed their desires to roam up the draws and through the foothills to the summit—where everything changes course.

Ed heard the creak of hinges and the screen door spring tightening. The metal stretched, singing low and sweet like a cello. It strained and dug into the wooden jamb with a final painful rasp—then it was still. Ed buried his head deeper in the pillows. He hated that quiet empty time before the door slammed shut.

"Ed, we're leaving." Emily stood in the bedroom doorway frowning at the mound in the center of the bed. She sounded all business. "Try to get the rest of the boxes in the dining room unpacked, and get the legs screwed back on the sofa. Everybody's getting used to having it on the floor and I don't like it."

"Mmmmmmm." Ed tried successfully to sound half as awake as he was.

"It's a half-day at school for the kids. I'll bring them up to the college with me for a little while, then we'll be home."

"Mmmmmmm."

Emily started down the hall. "Try to get out of the house. It's a beautiful day."

"Mmmmmmm." Ed again heard the creak of the screen door hinges and the twang of the spring tightening this time with a vindictive force. *Bang.*

Ed's feet hit the bedroom floor.

It had been getting harder and harder to pull himself out of the sack in the morning. There was even less to do here than there was at the motel. At least there they had cable TV and a pool. This old farm had nothing but weeds and grass and broken fences. Ten acres of it.

Whatever charisma the farm had held on a first meeting had vanished for Ed as soon as they moved in last week. The place seemed dead inside and Ed easily embraced it. The various farm implements and antiquated tools left lying around no longer looked rustic and provincial, but pitiful and useless.

Even the flower boxes under the windows were full of nothing but long grass. It trembled through the panes of glass in the breeze giving the impression the house had sunk partly under ground. The clean fresh paint on the walls could not hide the simple truth that no one had called this house a home in a long, long time.

For years the property was used as housing for academics in residence and other transient faculty at the college. These people were not typically predisposed to the trappings of a rural lifestyle. In fact, it seemed as if they had hardly looked at the place.

Ed ate his breakfast of cold cereal and looked out the kitchen window. The orchard that appeared to cover about four acres was choked with underbrush and sagging. It was difficult to determine the orderly rows of trees for all the collapsed branches and thick deciduous growth underneath. The leaves were yellow and twisted, sickly looking. The woman from the college had said they were peach trees, but Ed wouldn't have known a peach tree from a Presto Log, or given either much thought. It wasn't Alaska. That's all he knew.

To the west of the orchard, another four or five acres was defined by a broken wood rail fence. It was a small sea of knee-high grass that fell back and forth in the slight morning breeze like a horse flops its tail. In the middle of the forgotten field was a battered wagon left pointing futilely toward the barn, which leaned precariously away.

The kids loved the wagon and the barn. Their shrieks of fantasy and discovery could be heard throughout each evening until Emily called them in from the back door. "Yoo-hoo, Eddie, Missy, Corey. Time to come in."

"Yoo-hoo?" Ed had mocked last night. "The perfesser says *yoo-hoo?* What's this, a Lassie re-run?"

Emily looked at her cynical husband and scowled. "Cheer up, Ed."

Thoughts of the night before made Ed shake his head to clear them. The kids, Emily, everybody was so damned exuberant. You'd think this broken old farm was Disneyland the way they carried on. They'd stampede into the house breathlessly recounting all that they'd found on their latest foray.

"The neighbor kids say the barn is haunted and there's ghosts in the trees!"

"There's frogs in the creek! Real frogs!"

"We saw a snake! We never saw snakes in Alaska! Weird!"

Ed could not share their enthusiasm. He could barely listen to it. He hadn't even been out to look at the field or orchard. It all seemed foreign and impenetrable to him. Everything else around this place looked like work. Ed Flannigan was no stranger to work, but being a human weed whacker was not what he had in mind.

He needed a job. A real job. If they had any around this candy-ass town. But the hope of finding one was fading with every passing day. Heavy-equipment operators were twenty to the job around the area. With logging all but shut down and construction at a standstill, there were men with families standing in line for hippie-dip tree planting jobs. Ed scoffed at the very idea, never admitting he wouldn't have been able to manage it without two good arms, anyway.

Even if there had been plenty of jobs to go around, Ed might have run into difficulty convincing people of his prowess on machinery because of his artificial limb. Ed did not have the advantage of the reputation he left in Alaska alongside his joy. To the people around Quartz Creek he was becoming *Emily's husband, that one-armed guy with an attitude.*

The one-armed guy with an attitude sat in the dining room and sliced open another box with the tip of his prosthesis. The breeze brushed aside the grass in the window for a moment and Ed thought he saw something move out in the orchard. He stood to look, but there was only the barren grass.

Returning to the task at hand he pulled back the flaps on the box between his knees.

"More books," he said out loud, and began unpacking them, announcing as he went: "*The Experience of Literature. The Norton Anthology of Poetry. The Pocket Faulkner. A Farewell to Arms.* Hey, my life story." Ed jammed the books into the shelf without care or humor.

Ed resented Emily's rediscovered career at the college more than he dared admit even to himself, and especially not to Emily.

"It's not your job," he'd say. "It's that flaky college, and this flaky town. Everything around this freaking place has to *mean* something. These new friends of yours got crystals around their necks and they all walk like they're on pain killers. Nobody just talks to each other. They keep trying to figure it all out all the time."

"It sounds like you're holding onto a lot of hostility, Ed."

It was hopeless and Ed knew it. Every day Emily would come home a little worse. First it was her aura. Now her chakras. She keeps talking about *getting Rolfed,* but Ed's not letting her near that until he finds out who Rolf is.

Ed always knew that Emily leaned toward the mystical waters, but now it appeared she'd fallen completely into the pool. She didn't even try to keep it away from the kids anymore. Last night at dinner she'd held forth with her latest.

"Zowat told me today that she's communicating with angels. She says this area is full of them—there's something about the Quartz Mountain vibration that attracts them."

Ed thought that Zowat was a quack of increasingly dangerous influence on Emily. He could never leave a Zowat observation alone. "You see, kids, angels have wings like bugs, and just like bugs fly up to lightbulbs these angels fly to Quartz Mountain. Only problem is if they get too close they get stuck, then their butts swell up and pop."

The kids all laughed, but Emily was not amused. "Ed, there are worse things than angels for the kids to believe in."

"And just what are these swarms of angels supposed to do for my kids?" Ed challenged.

Emily got up from the table and began gathering dishes. The kids sat still, eyes down, ears wide. "I don't know, Ed. But I know it wouldn't hurt for them to believe in something. It wouldn't hurt any of us."

Ed had let Emily's implication alone last night, but the memory of it tweaked his temper. He needed a beer. He checked his watch and saw it was only ten-thirty. *Better not,* he thought. *Can't be drinking before lunch.*

He started to slice at another box, then thought better of it and went into the kitchen to see what might be around for an early lunch.

Ed grabbed a bowl of cold macaroni salad out of the refrigerator and counted four beers. Pulling one free of the plastic retainer, he was struggling to get the point of his clamp under the pop ring when something caught the corner of his eye through the screen door. Looking out, he thought he saw the back of a man in a white shirt disappear into the orchard.

Ed absently ate the salad while he stood in the doorway wondering what anybody would be doing in the orchard. He couldn't be sure he'd even seen him. Ed finished the last bites and was about to turn away when the man came through the trees. He stood twenty steps away on the edge of the undergrowth with his hands on his hips. He was looking right at Ed and Ed was looking right back.

He was a small man and dark skinned, but with a brilliant white mane of hair that grew in all directions. A mustache and eyebrows just as white described his upper lip and eyes, which all appeared to be twisted in thought.

Ed took him for a worker from one of the neighboring farms. But what he couldn't figure out was why this guy was standing out in the orchard sizing him up like this. Ed became even more bewildered when the little man began waving for him to come out.

Ed went out on the porch, set the unopened beer on the railing, and waded out into the grass. "Can I help you?"

The man stood right where he was and watched Ed come. "I doubt it."

"I'm sorry?" Ed now stood looking down on the little man whose intense turquoise-colored eyes gleamed as he spoke.

"You're not as sorry as some I've seen."

Ed let out a disbelieving chuckle and tried another tack. He offered the man his good hand, the left one, and said, "The name's Flannigan, Ed Flannigan."

The visitor made no effort to take Ed's hand. He only turned and started walking toward the open field. "I know. I know all about you. Come 'ere, I wanna show you something."

The man moved much more swiftly and easily than his apparent years might allow. Ed galloped to keep up. "What do you want?"

The man never broke stride. "Me? I don't want anything. What do you want? Never mind, here we are." He stood again with his knotty little hands on his hips and a ponderous look on his face. He pointed out into the field.

"Right along here would be your tomatoes and eggplants. Cantaloupe and watermelons would do best out that way. All that out there beyond the wagon to the fence is for your sweet corn. Then peppers, lettuce, and peas. Do just a row of basil, cilantro, and dill. It spices up the stand."

Ed was completely lost now. "What stand?"

The peculiar visitor walked out into the grass as he continued. "Your vegetable stand. You got about two weeks to plant, so get this bunch grass turned over right away." The man bent down and came back up with a large rusted sickle. "Now, let's go look at your peaches."

"I don't have peaches." Ed once again loped alongside the chattering old man feeling no will to stay behind.

"No, you don't have peaches, and you won't either if you don't take care of these trees. Look at this." The man reached out and touched some golf-ball-sized fruit on the first tree they came to. His manner suddenly changed, softening slightly.

"You see, the beautiful thing about a peach tree is that they know how much fruit their branches can bear. See these little shriveled things?"

The man fingered a wrinkled cluster of the fruit and one fell off into his hand. "Smart trees. They know not to take on any more than they can handle. Ya know how?"

Ed just shrugged.

"Of course you don't. You're not a tree. But as smart as these trees are about some things they're pretty helpless about others, and these trees need lots of help." He jumped easily up onto the lower limbs and continued his lecture to a dumbfounded Ed Flannigan.

"You've got to cut all this old deadwood out of here and leave just the healthy scaffold branches. The fruiting wood needs to be helped out some, it's confused. I'd say no more than three peaches to a branch this year. You've got leaf curl bad in the whole orchard—everything's turned yellow, but you can get rid of it. Don't worry about that. Yank all those dead trees out of here. I counted forty-three of them. And you've got to clear all these weeds away from the bottoms."

The man swung down from the tree and handed Ed the sickle. "Get after those weeds now. That hawthorne and cottonwood's the worst. Those blackberries, take it all out."

Ed looked at the man's eyes and never considered not doing what he said. He gathered a grip on the handle of the sickle with his hand and clamp. Ed started swinging and big clumps of twisted undergrowth fell down with each effort. The little man went back to work on the tree, taking out dead limbs, pinching and plucking at the little fruit, and never taking his eyes off Ed.

Ed felt the sweat building up on his forehead and stopped to take a breather. Holding the sickle out in front of him, he looked to the man in the tree sheepishly, not understanding exactly why he was doing this. The picture of himself holding the sickle lay in the shadow at his feet.

"I feel like the Grim Reaper," Ed said to break the awkward silence.

The little man cocked one eye and spoke. "I knew the Grim Reaper. I've worked with the Grim Reaper. And believe me, you're no Grim Reaper. Be grateful. He's a creep."

Ed laughed and went back to his chore, feeling the rhythm of it, forgetting the point of it. He just knew he liked this little guy, whoever he was.

The fresh-cut weeds filled his head with their musky essence. His sneakers were coated with a thick brown dust that continued up his pants legs. He felt a blister raising on the butt of his hand. His heart tromped in his chest with the effort.

When Ed had cleared the entire area under the tree, the little man jumped down and started dragging all the brush and branches away. Ed helped, and before long the one peach tree stood apart from the rest of the orchard like a trophy. The odd pair of men admired their work.

The noon sun beat down through the branches which were now serving a higher function. With the deadwood and debris gone, the tree took on the qualities of well-being. The peaches, thinned of the overburden, no longer appeared atrophied and doomed, but fresh and expectant. A fruit tree bearing fruit—no more, no less.

The old man looked into the rest of the twisted orchard. "You've got your work cut out for you. But you'll do it." He scratched his chin and then appeared to think of something. "I gotta go, but you know enough to finish the job, and you'll learn what you don't know."

The man turned to head into the trees, but Ed stopped him. "Wait!" The little visitor turned back and fixed his deep eyes on Ed's. Suddenly Ed could not think of anything to say except, "What's your name, anyway?"

The man bent his brow again and said cheerfully. "My name's Ed. What do you think of that? Lotta Eds on this farm. So, if you ever need anything, just ask for Ed." And he was gone.

Ed rocked in the porch swing enjoying his beer and admiring his possibilities. The sight of the lone peach tree and the little old man had infected the entire farm with the fever of potential. His body thanked him for the work as he eased himself back into the wooden slats and let the warm afternoon sun put him to sleep.

Ed heard the creak of hinges and the screen door spring tightening. The spring met the door jamb with the sound of a jew's-harp. It gouged itself into the wood, then was silent. Ed woke up.

Emily stood by the porch door frowning. "Another busy day on the farm, huh?"

Ed stood up unsteadily. His forgotten beer spilled from his hand and splattered on the porch. Emily said nothing, just looked at him pitifully. "Did you do *anything* today?"

Ed, fully awake now, recovered himself. "Well, as a matter of fact. I did do a little work around the ol' farm today. Just take a look at that orchard." Ed turned to his peach tree and dropped the empty can on the porch.

In front of him, where his solitary tree had stood so proudly less than an hour ago, was the same old sick and gnarly peach tree that had been there before. No different from the rest of the overgrown orchard.

"It can't be," Ed mumbled as he talked his way across the yard. "We trimmed this thing. I beat the weeds back. It was beautiful. Have you seen that motormouth little old guy who lives around here? We did it."

Emily stood on the porch with her arms folded across her chest. Her pitying look turned to genuine concern. Ed turned away and looked helplessly at the tree. It hadn't been touched. The deadwood. The wrinkled little fruit. The weeds. It was all there.

Ed saw something lying in the thick undergrowth and bent to it, pulling up a large rusted sickle. Holding the tool, he turned in time to see Emily walk back into the house letting the screen door go behind her.

Ed cursed and took a swipe at the weeds. The slash of the tool landed on the growth with a satisfying hacking sound—loud enough to obscure the remark of the slamming door. He looked at the weeds he'd laid down and lifted the sickle again, feeling his tired muscles begging for an explanation.

12

The hoedag hit the powdery turf with a dull thud. Deirdre opened a narrow slit in the earth with the tool and whipped a seedling from her bag in one smooth motion. She snapped the tree into the ground, careful that the roots were aimed downward, before removing the blade and closing the hole with a stomp of her boot.

"Grow," she said out loud as she had a thousand times already that day.

Deirdre took three steps and raised her hoedag, a cross between a pick-axe and a garden spade, totally aware of her father's eyes on her. Her one-handed swing struck with such force that the hoe sunk into the ground all the way and refused to release after she'd planted her tree. Deirdre cursed and yanked again, angry that she'd lost her stride. She stomped the tree too hard, folding it over into the dirt.

"Grow," she said again, but she knew it wouldn't.

Young trees need to be put into the earth with care in order to grow. If the roots aren't handled just right, the seedling would never be strong enough to compete with the forest around it. It would end up stunted—or dead, thinned by nature. If it grows to maturity, however, it might become something magnificent—like plywood or toilet paper.

Cynical thoughts clouded Deirdre's mind as they had all day. Everything seemed preposterous with her parents around. She tried not to, but couldn't keep from looking up to the road again. There they sat, like they had since dawn, beside the dusty Road Ranger.

Lloyd and Evelyn had arrived with their ridiculous RV at Deirdre's little house the night before, just after Deirdre had turned in for the night. "Hi Mom, Hi Dad. You're a little late. I've gotta get up at four in the

morning to drive the crummy—the crew bus—so don't block the driveway with your wiener wagon."

Deirdre hadn't seen her parents since she had left home. Seven years
ago she'd waved goodbye from the back of Nick's Harley as he gunned
the throttle and they roared off all leather and indignation.

She never looked back. Nick was long gone. Her mother and father
looked older—but the same. "You go on back to bed now, Precious,
we'll be fine."

Deirdre had hardly slept, listening to the puttering of the generator
on the motor home outside. Her conflicting emotions battled through
the night. The terror of them being here. The distracting and curious
comfort of having them nearby. They'd gotten up with Deirdre in the
morning and followed the crummy out to the job.

Deirdre's mother waved from her lawn chair and raised an Instamatic
to her face. Her father leaned forward with his hands on his knees like a
hometown ball fan in a tight inning—not wanting to miss a trick. Deirdre
wiped the hair and sweat from her face with the back of a grimy work
glove, pretending not to see them, and planted on. *Why did they have to
be here?*

Deirdre thought of all the times she had fantasized about her father
watching her work. So often she'd picture him just beside her, stumbling
along, seeing the sweat come through her shirt—the veins in her arms
tight against the skin, swelled with the force of hard work. Her dad would
be appalled. Reprimanding her as he always had for engaging in such
unladylike pursuits.

*Precious, you'll be filthy! Precious, you'll ruin your dress! What will your
mother say? Be a good little pearl girl, Precious, and just bring your Daddy his
iced tea.*

Deirdre had been building fantasies out of the memories of her dad
for so long that the inventions became as potent as the experiences. This
one clearer than the one before, the next one just like truth.

Deirdre drew her strength from these fantasies. Sometimes it seemed
as if her entire life was designed to horrify her father if only he were

there to witness it. And here he was in the big pink flesh with mother and her hairdo, watching Deirdre lead a ragged crew of twenty young men across a steep unit.

Deirdre could outplant most men two to one with a seemingly effortless grace and rhythm. Brandishing her hoedag in one hand, methodically plucking tree after tree from the bags at her waist with the other, she plugged away like a mechanical dancer: *Swing, plant, step—"grow." Swing, plant, step—"grow."*

Nobody messed with Deirdre, not even Chuck Blaze, the marine-like foreman who messed with everybody. Deirdre called him "CB," which his ego allowed him to take as a term of endearment. In time everyone began calling Chuck by his initials and his real name was left behind—gone with the people who had been fired, or quit and simply walked off—which happened almost daily.

Occasionally a new planter would ask what the *CB* stood for and Deirdre would exact her revenge. "It's short for *Cheese Ball,*" she would say.

Addressing Chuck Blaze by his initials was one of the few pleasures the planters on his crew enjoyed. The rest of the job was a totally unrewarding experience punctuated by frequent episodes of utter misery.

From the freezing two-hour pre-dawn ride in the battered old crummy to the stifling hot, dusty afternoons, the agony flowed from one end of the spectrum to the other. Lunch break provided a thirty-minute lapse in the day's journey from bad to worse. But today, Deirdre would rather have eaten her tree bag than climb back up to the landing for lunch.

Lloyd and Evelyn had unfurled their red-and-white-striped awning and rolled out a little piece of green plastic carpet under their lawn chairs. Cheese Ball stood off to the side with his tin hat and fatigues waiting for Deirdre. "What's with the geezers?"

"They wanted to watch," Deirdre said, dropping her bags and trudging by, not the least bit inclined to either apologize for or defend her parents. Lloyd and Evelyn stood expectantly beside a folding table that was covered with a red-checkered plastic sheet and plates of food.

"We made lunch for you and your friends," Evelyn said setting down a foot-and-a-half-high mound of meticulously stacked sandwich halves. "I have tuna fish, carrot sticks, Pringles, and Kool-Aid."

"These aren't my friends," Deirdre said, mortified.

The crew was roughly divided into three factions and Deirdre was sure they would be offended by Evelyn's little buffet in three distinct ways.

Latinos made up a full half of the outfit. They spoke no English for the most part and stayed to themselves, eating in a tight knot around a communal meal of beans and tortillas. They talked about their families back home and hoped to get paid before the immigration agents ran them off again.

The second part of the crew was made up of locals, out-of-work loggers mostly, who resented this dirt-head work and everybody who did it. They'd eat with the foreman, aloof with their black lunch boxes, steel thermoses, and dented tin hats—making crude and loud jokes about the rest of the crew.

The third part of the ensemble was made up of vegetarian vagrants and failed college kids. They ate tofu and sprouts and whined about their feet. Most of them had no experience with hard work and few of them lasted their first week.

Deirdre preferred the Latinos to any of them. They were hard workers and they rarely griped. Miguel, their leadman, was the next one up the hill for lunch.

"¿Cómo está?" he said pleasantly.

"Eh, bueno." Deirdre tried to sound as put-out as possible, rolling her eyes toward her parents and their absurd lunch.

Miguel tipped his hat respectfully and grabbed a sandwich without flinching. Manuel and Esteven came next and helped themselves. They were holding out their dixie cups while Evelyn poured Kool-Aid by the time the rest of the crew marched in wondering what the big deal was.

Deirdre stood back amazed and horrified. The loggers were passing the Pringles. Chuck the Cheese Ball munched carrot sticks and chatted up her dad like it was a church potluck. Miguel let Evelyn brush some dirt off the front of his shirt before handing him another sandwich. Deirdre couldn't believe it. All her mom and dad had to do was show up and everybody turns into Wally Cleaver.

Chuck glanced over to her a couple of times as he talked to Lloyd. Deirdre could tell they were talking about her. She glared at the side of her father's head until he turned to her. Lloyd and Deirdre's attentions met and froze them in their places, the sentiment gushing loosely and silently between them.

It hung in the middle of them both like a piñata turning in the breeze, waiting for the fortunate swing that would burst it open to rain treasure on all the players. Lloyd took his best shot.

Deirdre watched the corners of her father's mouth turn up and spread into that wide grin she hadn't seen in years. She felt those years falling away, taking pieces of her with them. All the distance she'd come. All the ordeals. All that she'd made of herself slipped away and left her standing there pigeon-toed and red-faced—Lloyd's precious little girl. It felt like home. It felt like hell.

The piñata dangled, burgeoning with prizes. Deirdre snatched herself back and bolted toward the crummy. Lloyd looked helplessly after her, then returned to his conversation with Deirdre's foreman.

"She's the best planter on the unit," Chuck was saying. "You raised a real wildcat there."

The piñata with all its promising spoils vanished like yesterday.

"I know," Lloyd said, sad and proud and distant.

Evelyn looked on from the food table absently wringing her hands.

The scene at lunch put Deirdre on a slow burn that smoldered dangerously into the afternoon. As the sun grew hotter so did she, and the closer to quitting time it got the closer Deirdre came to her kindling point.

She stormed through the dusty brush slamming tree after tree into the ground with no joy. She put as much distance between herself and the rest of the crew as her strength would allow her. Miguel's crew stayed a good hundred paces behind Deirdre, not needing to be told to leave some space.

Deirdre didn't know what it was all about. It couldn't be the embarrassment of having them on the job like this. The crew adored them. They wouldn't shut up about it. It couldn't be having them around at all. She was happy for them—glad they were getting out and seeing the world. Especially glad they were seeing her world. A world she'd created for herself.

And that's what it was. That's what was bugging her. Because while creating this world around herself she had systematically denied and disposed of just about everything she was raised to be. Now, all that she had so painstakingly left behind had caught up with her, and was sitting in lawn chairs at the top of the hill. On the power of her father's loving smile she'd been transformed across the years and miles to a baffled little girl in Avalon.

Her father's plumbing business had lived mostly in their garage. Deirdre was fascinated with all the pipes and fittings and the heavy black tools and cases.

"I'll help, Daddy," she would say, little hands clutching a wrench as big as her leg.

"No, no, Precious, let your big brother get that. You go see if mother has my lunch packed, okay?"

Her brother Anthony never cared about the work. He would whine and grumble, helping in the most ineffective ways possible, until Lloyd would give up and do it himself. All the while, there would be Deirdre, ever-present, ever under foot. Wanting so badly to help. Wanting so badly for her father to notice.

Sometimes Evelyn would intervene weakly on Deirdre's behalf. "I think Deirdre would like to ride along to the job today."

Lloyd would crack that wide warm smile and tilt his head toward his daughter. "Precious, this job is no place for a lady. It's noisy and dangerous. Besides, there's no little girls to play with, and you'll get filthy."

Deirdre would stand helpless and red-faced watching her father pull away with Anthony slumped beside him on the seat of the pick-up truck.

"You'll get filthy," Deirdre mocked the memory out loud as she slammed the hoedag into the ground again. The sweat trailed down her face in long dark streams. "I'll show you filthy." She stomped the ground hard beside her tree and raked her foot through the dust raising a thick brown cloud around herself.

Deirdre Decker could show her father filthy. After a single foolhardy year at Ohio State, she had climbed on the back of a motorcycle with the first outlaw she met and come to Oregon. Actually, she hadn't come to Oregon so much as she'd left Ohio.

But what she'd found in Oregon was everything she was looking for, which is to say, nothing she'd ever seen or heard of before. Picking in the orchards, thinning in the new-growth forests, slash piling, tree planting. They were the kind of jobs and these were the kind of people that would allow a woman to do her work.

Deirdre had thrown herself at hard labor with a great lightness of spirit. She could pick fruit beside the most seasoned farm hands. She could fix a chain saw and pull her own weight in brush out of the creek beds. She was a rare tree planter—one who returned season after season.

Determined and reliable, Deirdre was a welcome addition to any crew, no matter what the task. The fact that she was also very beautiful presented her with few difficulties. She kept a running order of boyfriends, all of whom would claim her, none of whom could have her. Men were her friends, her spark, her inspiration—but they were not to be taken seriously.

Deirdre glanced up the hill to the landing. Her folks had taken down the awning and folded up the table. Evelyn was out of sight. *Probably baking cookies,* she thought. Lloyd sat wiping his brow in the hot sun. He hadn't taken his eyes off her all day long.

He still leaned forward as if to relax would mean the whole job might come to a halt. Whenever Chuck walked near, Lloyd would stop him. They would stand there, talking and pointing down the hill, and out across the barren clear-cut valley.

Deirdre knew what was going on. Lloyd was asking questions. He'd have to know everything about what was going on. He'd want to know what his little girl was doing, and where his little girl was going, and who was she going with—just like he'd never stopped doing it.

The thought of her father probing the Cheese Ball about her well-being finally put Deirdre over the edge. Who in the hell did he think he was after all these years to come out here and question her life? Couldn't he see she was fine? Couldn't he see what she could do? Couldn't he see her?

The foreman blew the horn in his pick-up truck to signal quitting time. Deirdre ignited up the hill like a burning fuse. The seedling left in her hand dropped to the ground. She threw the hoedag over her shoulder and felt her legs pumping a beeline up to her father.

Lloyd stood watching, waiting, a wide warm grin on his face, his head moving back and forth in wonder and appreciation. But Deirdre did not see wonder and appreciation. All she saw was disbelief and patronage.

The rage Deirdre felt drew tears that mixed with the dirt and sweat on her face, becoming one mask of fury that met her father and stole his smile.

"Yes, Daddy. This is your precious little girl under all this dirt. Do you see me? Do you see me in here?"

Lloyd opened his mouth to speak, but nothing came out. Whatever words he might have found would have been said years ago if he knew them. But he did not. He could only stand in disbelief as his daughter went on.

"You and Mother parade out here in that duffer bus and you don't know anything about anything. You sit here all day watching me like this was some freak show. You wave and take pictures and serve your little sandwiches. This isn't a Sunday picnic! This is my job! This is my life! It's none of your business! What are you doing here?"

A hot afternoon breeze moved in and out of Lloyd's mouth. "We just came to see you," he finally said, but Deirdre was gone by then, storming toward the crew bus for the second time that day.

Evelyn stood in the door of the motor home wiping her hands on a dish towel. Deirdre spoke to her on the way past. "The dust is bad on the way out, Mother. You two follow close."

. . .

Deirdre let the heat inside the bus draw her sweat to hide the tears. The last of the crew stumbled aboard, and she checked the side mirror while dropping the bus into gear. Lloyd's face shone like stone through the windshield of the motor home behind her.

"Nice family," one of the loggers said.

"Oh, shut up and sit down." Deirdre popped the clutch and put everyone in their seats.

She put all her weight behind the big steering wheel, guiding the busload of men along the twisted road. A thick cloud of dust billowed behind them. Deirdre peered intently into the mirror, trying to penetrate the cloud, totally aware of her father following her—not wanting to lose him.

II

Home is the place where, when you have to go there, they have to take you in.

—Robert Frost

13

"Would you like some more peas, Norman?" Emily Flannigan held a steaming bowl with both hands. She smiled, her eyebrows raised to the query.

Norman looked at her from across the table and thought it over. It was a fair question. Straightforward. To the point. That's why he couldn't think of an answer right off the bat.

Back home with his family Norman would have had all kinds of clues and intimations to sort through with a simple question like that. His mother might have said, *Would you like some more peas, Norman?* but she'd have meant, *You should eat some more peas; they're good for you.*

His dad would have sat at the other end of the table, saying nothing, but meaning, *Your mother worked hard on this meal. You should show some appreciation.* His little brothers and sisters would sit quietly concentrating on their own food thinking, *How come Norman gets so many peas?*

Norman's knee bounced wildly under the table. He glanced anxiously around the kitchen before hazarding his reply. "Um—no, I don't think so, Mrs. Flannigan. I'm full."

"Okay." Emily set the bowl down again and went back to her own meal. Ed looked out the window chewing absently. The three younger Flannigans passively ate their dinners, oblivious to the exchange.

Norman felt the strain ease out of his frame. He stabbed another piece of pork on his plate and breathed again. Being away from his family was going to take some getting used to.

Norman's exile had begun less than twenty-four hours ago. His dad had driven him to Anchorage for the flight to Portland only this morning. Ed Flannigan had met his plane and driven him down to Quartz Creek just in time for dinner. Norman was still fairly staggered over the whole ordeal.

He'd never been out of the state of Alaska in his life. He'd never flown on an airplane. He'd never been this far from home. And he'd never been this far from Laura Magruder.

The sudden thought of Laura caught Norman by surprise. It had been a full ten minutes since the last time he'd thought of her. The pork in his mouth turned to paste. The sadness made a lump in his throat, and the combination of the two threatened to gag him. He didn't think throwing up his first dinner at the Flannigans' was the way to start his summer in Oregon, however awful it promised to be in every other regard, and he quickly excused himself to the bathroom.

"What was that all about?" Ed said, looking after him.

Emily just shrugged, "He's had a long day," and spooned herself some more peas.

Some things happen by design. Some things happen by accident. And some things just happen. Norman looked at his reflection in the bathroom mirror and wondered why it all happened to him. The past six weeks had gotten completely out of control.

Ever since he'd been busted for the party, Norman's world had become a very unfriendly place. His mom and dad had been pretty calm about it at first. Norman thought there would probably be a week or so of lectures and those interminable heart-to-heart talks to endure and then it would be business as usual. But that didn't happen.

His parents' immediate calm at finding two dozen of Norman's friends drinking, smoking, and carrying on in their house had only been shock. By the following morning they had regained control of their faculties and were acting more like themselves.

The first thing to go was Norman's car privileges. Since the Tuttles lived up on Flat Back Ridge, several miles from town, this effectively grounded him. Then to be on the safe side, they grounded him, anyway.

Every day after school Norman was given another endless and grizzly chore to perform around the house, and by far the grizzliest and most interminable chore of all was cleaning up the yard.

Springtime in Alaska resembles less a changing of the seasons than it does the peeling back of the tarp on a compost pile. With winter comprising a very generous portion of an Alaskan year, fully half of everything that hits the ground in Alaska hits it in the wintertime and reveals itself all at once in the spring. It is a disheartening sight to see.

Norman stood out in his parents' yard picking trash, sticks, toys, and tools out of the mud. There was the end of a broken snow shovel. A metal toy dumptruck which had been mangled by the snowblower. A petrified mitten. He could feel the still-thawing ground squeeze and give under his feet.

Norman worked his way out to the farthest corner of the yard. Pushing the limits of his restriction. Sizing up the parameters of his universe. Norman's universe was less of a lawn than it was a reclaimed field. The size of the yard varied from year to year depending on the ambition of the person behind the lawnmower. In Alaska, you could mow anything twice and call it a yard.

Norman sighed at the pointlessness of it all. The greening of the landscape did nothing to recover his spirits. There are only about six things that grow in Alaska in the spring; five of them are worthless and the other one is a weed. Norman had seen it all before.

The budding alder, sprouting dandelions, and greening willow were all lost on Norman. As he looked around the bench land that their parcel of land was carved from, and beyond to the greater panorama ringed by mountains, his thoughts were narrow and sardonic. Everything before him could be described with one of three words: trees, weeds, or rocks.

Looking back toward his corner of the world, Norman noticed his father standing in the kitchen window watching, and he mocked him. "Can't you work any faster than that? You missed a stick. Let's at least get it to look like somebody lives here. Sometime today, okay, Norman?"

Norman bent over for a stick and looked at his father through his legs. "Hey, Dad, look, it's a full moon!"

Norman was still laughing at his own cleverness when his dad started motioning through the window for him to come into the house. The blood ran from Norman's head for just a moment before realizing his father couldn't possibly have heard him. He dropped everything where he stood and headed for the back door still talking to himself. "It's lecture time, boys and girls. What's it going to be today? The *You're never going to amount to anything if you don't change your attitude* rant? How 'bout the *When I was your age we didn't have time for girls* sermon? Or perhaps today's special, *If you want us to trust you again you'll have to start showing more responsibility around here first.*"

Once or twice a week his dad would call him to the kitchen before the rest of the family had gathered for dinner, and they'd *talk*. The talk amounted to the recitation of one of the aforementioned lectures while Norman picked at his face and studied the pattern in the formica until his father got exasperated enough to send him away.

Norman dropped his coat and kicked off his muddy boots inside the kitchen door. He walked over to the table without looking up and took a seat. His dad was at the counter. "Cup of coffee, Normy? Kind of damp out there this afternoon."

His father hadn't offered him anything but advice for as long as he could remember. The only time he ever served him coffee was when they were gillnetting salmon in the summer, and Norman figured that was just so he'd work faster.

Norman looked at his dad skeptically, but welcomed the coffee all the same. Regardless of the motive, drinking coffee with his dad was irresistible even in the worst of times. Norman relaxed a little with the hot mug, thinking things couldn't possibly get any worse than they already were. But, of course, Norman had been wrong about a lot of things lately.

Norman's dad sat down looking satisfied with himself. Norman's stomach turned sour. "Norman," he began, "your mother and I have had a couple real nice chats with the Flannigans this week. They're getting settled down in Oregon, you know."

Norman could hardly hear his dad over all the danger bells going off in his head. His dad was way too calm. This was a set-up. Norman's knees were bouncing at about ten kilohertz under the table as his father went on.

"Well, it seems they've moved onto an old farm and Ed has taken it upon himself to get it going. Ed says there's no work around there and he might as well do something useful with his time. So, as it turns out, he's getting kind of a late start and could use some good help."

Norman was staring at one of the hairs coming out of his father's nose—numb and waiting.

"So, your mother and I talked about it and decided there was nothing for you around here this summer but more trouble. Me and your Uncle Stu can handle one salmon season without you. So, what do you think of sunny Oregon for the summer?" Norman's father took a long sip of his coffee and looked at Norman through the steam. The look on his dad's face seemed to beg for a reaction, but Norman was stunned. It was as if someone had come bounding up and said, *We're going to shoot you in the morning. What do you think?*

Norman wasn't thinking. He was just sitting there bouncing his knees and staring at his dad's nostrils and letting everything drain away. Every last vestige of control over his own life melted down out of him and left one singular concern emblazoned across his face. *Laura Magruder.*

His father read it perfectly. "The girl is nothing but trouble for you, Norman. That hare-brained party of yours was the last straw. I've talked to the Magruders about this and they think it's for the best. A little time apart will be good for both of you. Cool you down. Get your heads screwed back on straight. You haven't thought past your next date with that girl in a year. There's a whole great big world out there, Norman, and you're getting stuck. You'll leave the day after school is out. Ed's waiting for you."

Norman laid on his back on the Flannigans' hide-a-bed. Tears of helpless rage came from deep inside him and found their way down the sides of his face to his ears. It tickled, and he had to wipe them.

Something happens when you wipe your tears. The act of wiping tears sends a signal that the crying is finished, so the tears stop. It's best that people don't touch their own tears until they've cried them all.

Norman laid in the discontented daze that is left of an incompleted cry, his mind two thousand miles to the north. He was oblivious to the sounds of a foreign night going about its business around him. A chorus of bullfrogs gulped in the distance. Crickets creaked in a rhythm of disarray near and far. A breeze scented with the sweet smell of fallen peaches out in the orchard moved the curtains in the window.

Norman's eyelids bounced twice and stuck. The unfamiliar night crept up on him: the air, the sounds, the smells—all worked to smooth the creases on his forehead and draw his mind across the miles. When all of Norman was finally present, his jaw slacked and a deep rush of air poured from him—as if his entire soul was stepping out to stretch and look around. *Where are we? What is this place? Where do we begin?*

The morning came like a good idea—slow, clear, and divine—pushing everything else out of the way. Norman sat up, surprised, suddenly not being able to remember where he thought he was, but it wasn't here. The light coming through the window was warm and full—not the clean white light of Alaska, but a light with something else in it.

Looking out the window, all that Norman could see was green and unidentifiable. The grass, the trees, the bushes along the driveway—all were polished with the morning dew. Madrone, manzanita, holly, and pear trees glimmered in the rising light with an almost artificial quality. They were nothing he had ever seen before. They looked like houseplants.

Nobody else in the house appeared to be awake. The quiet and the light and the view all lent an other-worldly quality to the morning. It was as if Norman had woken up in another star system. He pulled on his clothes and slipped out the back door.

The tall grass rolled and did slow swirls in the barely moving air. A squirrel sat criticizing Norman in a tall stout oak beside the house. A robin hunted worms in the freshly mowed grass between the house and an old barn. Norman saw movement in the barn's long shadow, then saw that he wasn't alone.

Ed Flannigan pulled his head out of the middle of an old yellow tractor Norman had taken for junk. Ed noticed Norman standing on the porch and called to him. "Hey, there's my helper. C'mere, Norm, I could use your two good hands."

Norman stepped off the porch, aware of the ground under his feet as he walked out toward the tractor. Ed stood with a screwdriver in his good hand and a wrench dangling from the clamp on his metal limb. "Up with the chickens, eh, buckaroo?"

Norman rolled his eyes but couldn't hold the corners of his mouth down. Ed had the Flannigan smile smeared all over his big face—the smile that said a shucks and a shrug and a how-do-you-do—and he aimed it full at Norman.

"What a pair of farmers we're gonna make! Climb on up in the driver's seat there. I just got new plugs in 'er. She should purr like a kitten if she don't swallow 'er tongue."

Norman did as he was told, cautious, but willing to be a part of Ed's morning. Ed leaned across the axle and pointed at the array of controls screwed to or hanging out of the tractor console. "Choke. Throttle. Starter," he said without explanation, assuming correctly that Norman knew what to do with them.

Ed leaned into the engine to fidget something with the screwdriver. "Okay, choke it, give it about half a throttle, and turn it over."

Norman quickly found the choke and throttle, held his finger to the starter button, and looked to Ed. "Ready?"

"Fire away, buckaroo."

Norman pressed the button; the engine struggled for several revolutions and then erupted with a bellow of black smoke. Ed stood watching something inside the engine compartment for a bit, then looked up to Norman gamely. "Let's take 'er for a spin."

Ed jumped up on the axle behind Norman and leaned forward onto the seat and the boy's back. The closeness was easy, and good. "You're going to be the official tractor man, Norm. The thing's set up backwards for my arms, besides I got lots of work to do in the peach orchard. Now, the pattern's on top of the stick there, and watch the clutch, it's pretty sticky."

Norman found first gear with a guess and a grind, and tried to ease the clutch out. It grabbed suddenly and jerked the tractor to life, lifting the front end slightly off the ground. Ed almost fell, and then laughed. "We got a hot rod. Grabbed air on his first start. Take us out around the barn, Lead Foot, I'll show ya the field."

Ed directed Norman out to what looked like four acres of tall grass. There were already swatches torn out and tractor marks criss-crossing it in all directions. An old wagon and other piles of junk, rocks, and debris lay piled along one fence.

"I've already cleaned 'er out," Ed said over Norman's shoulder. "All we gotta do is plow this under and we're in business."

Ed motioned for Norman to continue, so he grabbed another gear and pointed them out into the sea of grass. He felt the vibration of the engine rattling his hands and coming up through the seat. The stiff old tractor's bones complained and creaked and popped across the rough ground. When they were deep into the field, Ed touched Norman's shoulder. "Hold up once, Norm."

Norman idled the tractor down and put it in neutral. Ed stood tall on the axle and pointed expansively. "We're in the middle of your sweet corn here. All the way back to that fence'll be corn. Over that way's your tomatoes, peppers, lettuce, and peas. I was going to do eggplant, too, but I couldn't sell anything I wouldn't eat myself. And over there along that back fence you'll never guess what you have."

Ed waited for Norman to guess. Norman didn't have a clue.

"Watermelons," Ed said reverently. "Watermelons and cantaloupes. Can you believe it? I tell you, Norm, you can grow just about anything in this country. Back home it seems like only six things can grow. Five of 'em are worthless and the other one's a weed."

Norman looked back at Ed, surprised, and the two men shared one of those flashes of recognition that feels like a compliment.

The mention of Alaska changed something on Norman's face, and Ed suddenly turned serious. "I didn't wanna come down here either, Norm. I had no choice. Neither do you. It's a crummy deal, I know, but let's have some fun with it, okay?"

Ed held out his left hand to shake. Norman took it with his right and the embrace was awkward. Ed held on long enough to make it seem untroubled, and Norman felt a friend forming in his hand. "We gotta get this planted first. Let's get this bucket of junk back over to the barn and see if we can put that plow on it," Ed said.

As Norman steered back toward the barn and house, he saw Emily come out on the porch. She waved big, and they both waved back. Norman sat up, aware of his one hand on the wheel and the other on the shift lever. For all its rattling and popping, the tractor moved with sureness through the field. Norman was driving it. He was in control. Ed stood holding on behind him.

When they got to the barn, Norman switched off the tractor and they could hear Emily scolding kindly from the porch. "As long as you have everybody awake around here, you might as well come in and eat something. Norman, do want some waffles?"

Norman could still feel the tractor resonating in his bones. He jumped down and felt the earth solid under his feet. "I'd love some waffles, Mrs. Flannigan," he said, not thinking of anything for the first time in a long while. "I'm *really* hungry."

14

A ship's horn blew long and expectant out in the fog and drizzle. The ship plowed through the black night waters of Puget Sound like a two-hundred-ton goose searching for its mate. The horn blew again, ending with a question mark, and the ship sailed on, guided on its course by some invisible hand.

Webster walked up the stairs of the rooming house, stopping to peek in his mailbox window. He was surprised to find something, and struggled with the combination for lack of practice. The first piece of mail was a notice of hearing from the court system.

"Finally," Webster said out loud, ripping open the envelope and then groaning. "June 30? Another whole month?"

Webster refolded the notice and trudged up the stairs. He glanced absently at the other pieces: a sale booklet from a discount drugstore and a letter from Boston. It was from his mother—his second mother. *M-2* was the code he used for his adoptive mother to distinguish her from his real mother, or *M-1*. His adoptive mom would have resented being given the second billing, but Webster knew no other way to organize them except chronologically.

Webster could see that M-2's letter was actually a greeting card. The outlines of the embossed face showed through the envelope. It was for his birthday, it was expected, and it was of little interest to Webster at the moment.

He'd been waiting weeks to get this hearing date. Without a court order, the hospital would not open their records to him. Without the records, he was at a dead end in his attempt to locate the identity of M-1.

The certificate of birth would be optimal, but almost anything would help. All he had was a date—May 27, 1964—and a city—Seattle,

Washington. It had been thirty years ago to the day that Webster was born. Now it would be another thirty days before he'd know anything more than that—if then.

Webster switched on the lamp in his room and closed the door behind him. It was less a place to live than it was a command post. Photocopies of newsprint, scraps of paper, and long lists of names covered every wall. Some things were crossed out. Others were circled. The sight of it all made Webster tired.

He eased himself onto the bed, sinking in deeper than the night before, a sensation he'd had nearly every night for two months. He looked at the card from the only mother he knew for sure, then set it aside unopened. He needed to eat something before he could face another letter from M-2. She became increasingly peculiar the closer he appeared to get to M-1.

Webster switched on the hotplate and opened a can. "One more month," he said to himself. "One more month."

He was a tireless professional researcher with eight years' experience, and flagging spirits under pressure were a new sensation. Webster Cummings was born to investigate. Finding things out was his purpose, his drive, his very reason for breathing. He had been that way since he was a child.

He used to compile data on the people around him simply for the joy of it. At the age of seven he had completed a milk-consumption study for their household which showed glasses consumed per capita and had designed a flowchart illustrating rate of consumption as it pertained to the day of the week and the age of the household member.

It was just Webster and his mom and dad, so it was completely useless information. Like the great ones in every field, Webster was born to his work.

Webster did not have any childhood friends. He would drive them away by insisting on telling them about the things they did. *Do you know you picked your nose seventeen times in home room? That's down from yesterday, but still high. You were five minutes late for baseball practice today. That brings your tardiness total to fifty-eight minutes, or nearly one entire practice.*

Webster did not do it to be malicious. He was personally fascinated with the things people did, and assumed everybody was. Upon graduating from high school he presented the senior class with mimeographed copies of *The Statistical Abstract of the Class of 1982.*

He'd worked on it for months. It included grade point average by race, religion, sex, and ethnic background; school lunches purchased per student; and rest room use by sex in gallons of water per hour. Nearly every copy was abandoned under the chairs at the graduation assembly. Webster was not particularly offended. He simply made a note of it.

Webster had a natural curiosity about the world, which he didn't apply to himself. He was a boring person. There just wasn't anything about Webster that interested Webster. He was aware of his adoption, and that had intrigued him from time to time, but his mother had always discouraged too many questions about it.

She had first told him he was adopted after his dad's funeral when Webster was ten. "We lived in Seattle and you were less than a year old when you came to us."

Webster was immediately fascinated. "Where did you find me? Who were my real parents? Why didn't they want me?"

His mother had dismissed the probes early and firmly. "None of that matters. You're with me." She'd given Webster a huge and uncomfortable hug. "It's just us two now. That's all that matters."

Whenever it came up, Webster would get the same thing: "It doesn't matter." For Webster it seemed to matter, but then, it didn't matter a whole lot. And here was his mother, at least the only mother he ever knew, telling him it didn't matter. Nothing else mattered about Webster. Why should this?

Webster carried on. He graduated from college at the top of his statistics class and was recruited by Bittner Research & Rectification, the premiere information-gathering agency in the known universe, according to their own statistics.

He started on the basic stuff: national soy bean consumption, the average life span of hamsters. But then he was put on more challenging projects and was really able to shine. When assigned to determine the amount of money Americans spent in the past twenty years on products for the nose and ears in constant U.S. dollars, Webster produced results so thorough and surprising that the face of the nose and ear product marketing industry will be changed for years to come.

Webster Cummings attained early notoriety in the hard-hitting world of statisticians, and settled into his life. He took an apartment in the same Boston suburb as his mother. He'd have remained living with her, but his propensity for bringing his work home and tacking it up around the house was becoming too much.

Webster ate dinner at his mother's several times a week, walked to the library on weekends, and in the evenings read survey results out loud to his pet goldfish to help him focus.

Webster was a drag, but he didn't mind. He didn't know it, really. He probably couldn't even have told you what he looked like. The mirror in his bathroom had computer lists taped over it that Webster would study as he brushed his teeth. He would go to bed at night with the *Gross National Product of Borneo* dancing in his head; wake to the *Mean High Temperatures of the Corn-Producing States* in the morning. Webster never looked at himself. It didn't matter.

All that changed, of course, after his fall. As reclusive and peculiar as Webster was, he was not made of wood. Even he could not unexpectedly fall four thousand feet to a certain death, be spared even a scratch, and not be moved by the experience.

The night of the fall they'd kept him in the hospital for observation. His mother had come and gone. Webster just lay there, unable to sleep—looking at himself. The amount of adrenalin Webster's glands secreted during his thirty-second free fall would take days, possibly weeks, to entirely leave his system. Webster was wired.

He pulled back the sheets and let the sight of his naked form capture all his attention. He raised one leg and then the other. He tightened the muscles in them and watched their shape change. He looked at his hips and up to the skin of his belly and his chest. He turned his arms around and felt his hands, one to the other.

The revelations he'd experienced that afternoon were indelibly printed on his every thought. At the moment when his will collapsed and he surrendered to the inevitable, Webster had the most intense and frightening episode of his rapidly departing life.

Other survivors of near-death experiences have described this experience as having your life pass before your eyes. What this is, actually, is the soul preparing to abandon ship. It does so with a powerful and indignant cry, the indomitable human spirit expressing itself one last time.

That day when Webster's spirit conjured its final epitaph, it was not a statement, but a question. He felt a hole open up inside of him, all the way through his being, and out rushed a low empty wail.

The hole snatched closed again. Webster's spirit remained in this world. His impact with the ground left not a mark on Earth or man, but Webster will never again be able to ignore the crater he found in his soul.

Webster's mother drove him back to Boston the next day. He was strangely quiet. He was always quiet in one way or another, but never strangely.

"Is something bothering you, Webster?" she asked, perhaps forgetting he'd fallen out of an airplane only the day before.

"Yeah," Webster said, full of purpose. "I want to know about my real mother and father. Who are they? Where are they? I realized last night laying in bed that I don't know a thing about myself. I don't look like you or dad. I don't look like anybody I know. I want to know who I look like. I want to know who I am."

Webster's mother reached over and patted his knee. "Now, now, Webster, you're just upset. You'll feel better in a few days, and none of that is going to matter anymore. You're safe. You're with me. That's all that matters."

"I'm going to find them." Webster looked straight at his mother as he never had. "Can you tell me anything more about it all?"

Webster's mother looked back to the road and gripped the wheel with both hands. "No," she said, finally, "I can't."

.   .   .

The media attention and brief celebrity that accompanied Webster's brush with fate invigorated him even further. People, important people like Bryant Gumbel and Geraldo, had looked him right in the eye and said, "You're a very lucky man."

Several people had called in to Larry King and asked if Webster thought he had a mission from God to fulfill. Regis Philbin had misted up as Webster explained to him and Kathie Lee how his only wish was to find his real mother and father.

Celebrity in America passes as quickly and easily as it comes. After he'd walked out on *Late Talk with Robert* the invitations for appearances stopped coming in, and Webster's acclaim was reduced to the tabloid back pages with the two-headed dogs and ninety-seven-year-old Olympic hopefuls.

Webster was soon left alone to his quest. He bid his mother farewell and opened file *M-2/D-2* on her and his dead dad. Tracing their whereabouts in Seattle in the early sixties could lead him somewhere.

She would offer no information herself except to say, "I've forgotten so much of it. None of it matters anymore."

It mattered to Webster more than anything. He secured an open-ended leave of absence from BR&R and left Massachusetts a driven man, driving from coast to coast with the adrenalin still coursing through his veins and his eyes set straight down the road. He entered the city of Seattle at a comfortable fifty-five miles per hour and had no sensation of running dead into a brick wall.

For all his experience with research, Webster had no idea that finding out what two hundred million people do with their ears and noses is easier than finding two people and a baby thirty years ago.

The first day he secured a room at an inexpensive residence hotel and set about his endeavor on the balls of his feet. He stood on the steps of his first stop and grinned. When the chief troubleshooter from Bittner Research walks upon the bricks of the Office of Vital Statistics, the bells of destiny ring somewhere.

But that had only been the first day, and the day that his confidence peaked. He ran into one obstacle after another. In one whole week of footwork, he discovered the address of M-2/D-2 while his adoptive dad was going to college. He rushed to the neighborhood only to find it had been turned into a hundred-and-eighty-store shopping mall.

Every day Webster would return to his room a little lower to the ground than the day before. About once a week there would be a letter from M-2 fanning the coals of despair: *I hope you find what you're looking for without spending all of your hard-earned savings. Thirty years is a long time. A lot of things change. Don't be disappointed if you fail. It doesn't matter, really.*

Perhaps the adrenalin from his fall was finally retreating. Perhaps it really was a hopeless enterprise. Perhaps it *didn't* matter, really.

Webster sat on his bed with a spoon absently searching for Waldo in his Spaghetti-Os. He looked at the unopened card from M-2 and felt his spirits sag. Never had he felt this kind of discouragement. It was going slow, for sure, but it wasn't like he was at a dead end. He'd found out many things including a list of five hundred unwed mothers from 1964.

That list was taped over the bathroom mirror. He changed the page every day to look at new names. He thought maybe there would be some kind of genetic recognition if he saw the right name, like a salmon catching a scent of its home stream a thousand miles away.

This was just going to take time. He knew that. He was a scientist. He must have patience. Where was his professionalism? He was getting closer gradually, by degrees.

What Webster was not aware of was that this process of getting closer is what was wearing him down. He was getting too close. Too close for comfort, anyway. For the first time in a lifetime of research, Webster, at some level, was grappling with the consequences of his investigation. He was facing the difference between wanting to find out about something and wanting to know something.

He'd always wanted to find out about people. He never wanted to know about them, though. Knowing people changes everything. They may not be what they seem, and then what are we left with?

When and if Webster found his real parents he was going to be faced with the answer to one terrifying question: *Why didn't they want him?* There was a large part of Webster Cummings that didn't really want to know.

It was the weight of this part that pulled him down into that crater in his soul. It's what made the next thirty days look like thirty years, and not worth the wait.

Thirty years ago, not far from where Webster sat, a woman gave birth to a little baby boy and made an important decision. A decision that changed the lives of many people in ways they'll never fully know. Who was Webster Cummings to mess with this? Falling four thousand feet without a parachute did not make him God.

Webster felt a sense of relief and exhaled. It was nowhere near the huff of accomplishment. It was the grave breath of resignation. He reached for the birthday card from the only mother he ever knew.

Webster did not read the sentiment emblazoned on the front of the card in gold sparkle. There was a drawing of balloons and a boy, and when he opened it a paper birthday cake popped up from the crease. It dislodged a yellowed envelope with a folded note paperclipped to it.

The handwriting on the note was his mother's. He didn't recognize the hand of the person on the envelope. It was one word written in tight little cursive letters—*Webster.*

Dear Son: You are my son, and this is the most difficult thing I've ever done. I don't know if it is harder to give this to you, or to face you again after having kept it from you all these years. Your mother told me to give this to you when I was ready. I'm still not ready, but it seems you are. Please forgive me. I remain, as Always, Your Mother.

Webster looked at the writing on the face of the envelope again, and a current passed through him. He carefully tore the brittle end from the envelope and slid the contents into his hand. There was a tiny note in the same cramped hand, and a document folded in halves.

Dear Son. You are my son, and this is the hardest thing I'll ever do. I don't know if you'll ever want to know me, but I am no good for you now. Please forgive me. With Love, Your Mother.

Webster unfolded the document and his heart gave one mighty heave. The official words embossed across the top rushed up and pounded him: *State of Washington Certificate of Live Birth.*

He read every single letter of it:

Sex: Male
Weight: 7 pounds, 11 ounces
Length: 22"
Date: May 27, 1964
Time: 12:05 pm
Child's Name: Flannigan, Webster

Webster's hands shook as he continued.

Mother of Child: Amanda Margaret Flannigan, Age: 17
Father of Child: PFC Oliver Francis Tuttle, Age: 19

He lay back on the bed, the notes and lists on the walls moving in the draft from the window, one at a time. The moist evening air coming from the sea brought a chill with it. Webster pulled his legs up and held his arms close around himself—drifting.

A ship's whistle blew out in the night, one long, low, empty wail coming to a crisp and conclusive end. A vessel making port. Somewhere on the docks sailors passed stout lines to longshoremen. Winches rattled and cleats strained their bolts against the timbers. The engines stopped, and the ship was secured.

15

Anthony sipped his Ovaltine and stared out across the field of beans to the line of willow trees on the other side. The trees followed a creek that described the far edge of the field. But Anthony only believed the creek was there. In ten years of looking across this field, he'd never gone over to see the other side of it.

The field was owned and farmed by Anthony's neighbor, Dirk Miller. Some years Dirk grew soy beans, other years corn. Field corn, usually; seed corn, sometimes. But never anything Anthony cared to eat. He liked it better when Dirk grew beans. Anthony didn't eat beans, either, but corn grew too high. By the beginning of August Anthony would barely be able to see beyond his yard, which was a small and perplexing plot of grass and weeds notched out of an entire section of working fields.

The years Dirk grew corn, Anthony would bring out the towtruck from work, hook up the house trailer, and spin it around so the big windows faced out toward the road. He would feel less hemmed in that way.

Anthony Decker's perpetually farmed-around patch of land held an abandoned and dilapidated corn crib, his small aluminum house trailer, a blocked-up blue Rambler station wagon, and a galvanized mailbox which stood on the road with most of his last name emblazoned on the sides in big stick-on reflective letters.

On the side facing town the *D* had fallen off. On the inbound side the *R* had somehow disappeared. People heading out Pilkington Road passed the *ecker* place, while those coming in went by the *Decke* residence. Anthony often thought of combining the letters to have at least one complete side, but could never choose which way to present it. It didn't matter to him that anybody coming from town would know who lived there anyway, and that nobody came from the other way except people who had already come from town and were on their way back. But it gave Anthony something to think about when he wasn't thinking about the view.

This year Anthony would leave the trailer facing the beans, ankle-high and thickening by the day. A deep green carpet spread all the way to the lazy willows along the other side. An occasional whiff of air would tease their long tendril branches. Anthony could sit at the table for hours staring off across the beans without a thought in his head.

Anthony heard the brakes on the mail carrier's car squeaking out on the road. *It's time Wilma came in for new linings before she scores the drums,* he thought. It wasn't Anthony's intention to know a little something about every single car and truck in Booder, Indiana, but he did. Working ten years at the only full-service filling station in town made it inevitable.

Anthony waved to Wilma from the trailer door and headed out to the mailbox. He watched the tail of dust rising behind her as she roared down the shoulder of the road. Anthony loved his Mondays off from work. It was a great day to be home. It seemed like everybody else in the world was working except him. Anthony had Sundays off too, but *everybody* had Sundays off. Mondays were all his own—not that Anthony had a huge press of people to escape on any day of the week. In Anthony's social life, less was more.

Sunday was certainly the center of Anthony's weekly events calendar. He'd go to late Mass at Saint Bernard's, stay for coffee and donuts, then come home and change for softball. Sometimes he played, sometimes he sat in his truck and listened to the Tigers game on the radio.

Actually, he played on two teams, St. Barney's and Ray's Full-Service. When his teams played each other Anthony would forfeit his batting privileges and play right field the whole time. He loved the games where he didn't have to hit. He'd pace boldly around beyond the first baseman and pester every hitter who came to the plate. *Hey batter, hey batter—swing!* Anthony was louder and more persistent than the other fielders, comfortable knowing that there would be no retaliation.

. . .

Anthony could see Dirk Miller's pick-up turning out of his farm down the road. Dirk always stopped to visit if Anthony was around, so he leaned against the mailbox and pawed through the small stack of mail, waiting.

There was about half a pound of catalogs and solicitations which would not make it past the burning barrel, and another thick letter from his parents. More specifically, from his mother, who had been writing weekly letters of epic proportions recounting their continuing adventures on the road. This one bore a Cheyenne, Wyoming, postmark.

Anthony was stuffing the fat envelope into the pocket of his tee shirt when Dirk pulled over from the opposite lane, already leaning out of his window. "Good mornin', Mr. Decke-ecker." Dirk Miller never failed to point out the flaw of Anthony's mailbox. "Have you seen that silly horse of hers this morning?"

The *her* in *hers* referred to Dirk's new wife Charmaine. Dirk's first wife, Rhonda, had died two years earlier of various complications from the fact that she never stopped eating even for a minute. Rhonda wasn't in the ground two months before Dirk came back from Fort Wayne with Charmaine on his arm.

Charmaine was everything Rhonda was not: trim, attractive, sophisticated—and she hated farming. In fact, she disliked everything about living in the country except horses, and it didn't take her long to get one out of Dirk.

By the end of last summer a graceful white fence had sprung up beside Dirk's equipment shop. It contained a stunningly beautiful and utterly useless Arabian show horse—thousands of dollars' worth of quivering muscle and nerves.

Charmaine and a few of her flashy friends from Fort Wayne would cart their horses around to shows and come back with hangovers, stories, and the fancy trailer—which had cost Dirk nearly as much as the horse—kicked to pieces.

Charmaine's horse also kicked its stall down at least twice a month and Dirk spent a good deal of his time driving around the fields looking for it. Anthony had helped Dirk corral his wife's high-strung horse a dozen times in the past year, and every time he wondered why Dirk tolerated the whole business.

Dirk wondered too, out loud, to almost anybody who'd listen, but his complaints were without conviction. He was painfully aware of the extravagance of it all. He knew what people were saying behind his back. *Anybody who'd own a horse has too much time and too much money.* Dirk had too much of neither, but he loved Charmaine and he would continue to chase the horse for her for as long as he had to.

"Sorry, Dirk," Anthony said. "Haven't seen it today, but I'll keep my eyes open."

"Thanks, Tony." Dirk wore the nettled face that came over him whenever he did his dear wife's bidding. He wished to escape it all for a minute, and pointed to the letter in Anthony's pocket.

"That from your folks again?"

Anthony patted the letter. "Yep."

"Where they at this week?"

"Looks like Wyoming."

"Wyoming," Dirk repeated wondrously. He followed the thought for a moment, then slowly pulled away like he was driving there. "I can't imagine."

Anthony felt sorry for Dirk. Unlike Anthony, Dirk never thought beyond his life in Booder. Distant places eluded Dirk's sense of possibility. He was here. They were way out there someplace.

Anthony didn't have this problem. His whole life was consumed with the potential of distant places. It was all he thought about for as long as he could remember. His ten years in Booder were just the means to an ultimate end Out West. Once things were settled up around here he'd be gone. It's just the way Anthony was. Or at least the way he thought he was.

Anthony returned to his seat at the table and tore the end off the envelope. There was a six-page letter in his mother's tidy pen, and three postcards. He laid the letter aside for the moment.

His mother's letters were getting tedious. She wasn't content just to relate the sights and sensations of seeing the West; Evelyn also had to include the day-by-day weather report, the names and biographies of nearly everyone they met, as well as the prices of things they bought along the way. The cost of their tuna fish and mayonnaise varied wildly, as did gas and oil. Anything above or below the standard price indexing of the Thrifty Shopper in Avalon, Ohio, was worthy of a mention from his mother. Evelyn's letters made Anthony's eyes cross, and he would save this one for bedtime.

The postcards were much more interesting, although a bit unsettling. Having his mom and dad sending him postcards from places he'd left home to see ten years ago and never reached yet felt odd to Anthony. He still wasn't used to the fact that they weren't in Avalon anymore.

The first card was a bad composite photograph of a jackrabbit with some sort of antlers attached to its head. *Greetings from Jackalope Land,* it read in bright yellow cursive letters across the face. Another one was an aerial view of a huge truck stop: *Little America, the World's Largest Filling Station,* read the caption. There was a brief note scrawled on the back in his father's rough hand: *They have over two hundred pumps here. I thought you could appreciate this.*

Anthony could, and it suddenly made the three pumps down at Ray's seem pretty ineffectual.

The third card was a very fetching photo of some jagged white-capped mountains. He looked into the photo for a long time before turning it over. *The Grand Tetons,* it said.

This is the most amazing country we've seen yet. I now understand how a guy like you would be drawn to this.

Anthony turned the card over again and squinted hard into the picture. He tried to pull himself into it and imagine being surrounded by such enormous sights. He thought of his father's words and he felt himself falling inward.

Anthony had been a Boy Scout, and not a very good one. His troop had spent their entire two weeks at camp constructing a rope bridge over the river. The project utilized just about every single kind of knot ever devised, of which Anthony knew approximately two. He'd barely made Tenderfoot in time to qualify for camp, and from the moment he arrived he regretted ever coming.

He'd marched directly off the bus and into a patch of poison oak. That was followed by seven bee stings, countless mosquito bites, and several large red welts from some kind of bed spider. Anthony had so much calamine lotion on he glowed in the dark. He said very little, did very little, and bided his time like any good prisoner until it was time to go home.

The second to the last day the bridge was completed. The troop was ceremoniously lined up for the maiden crossing. It was a handsome and complicated webwork of ropes which slung low across a particularly swift part of the river. The added drama of the current was not lost on the assembly, particularly not on one young tenderfoot who knew for sure that the knots he was responsible for couldn't be trusted.

The boys were told to go in pairs. They made their way across two by two with Anthony and Richard Flowers vying for last place. Richard, like Anthony, was a miserable coward of a Scout, and an extremely over-weight one, to boot. Anthony tried to muster the courage to team up with a leaner scout further up the line, but failed. He could only watch forlornly as each pair of boys staggered across the lurching hemp construction hooting and cheering an inflated pride in their work.

When it was Anthony's turn he forced Richard ahead of him and clutched the sides of the walkway so hard it puckered his underpants. As his pudgy partner neared the center of the bridge it dipped dangerously close to the swirling green water below and rolled absurdly to one side.

Richard, sensing that the point of no return had been breached, produced a sudden burst of effort and tried to scamper to the other side with Anthony close behind. The bridge rocked wildly. Anthony lost his grip on the ropes and lunged at the empty air. His hands found Richard's shirt collar just as the bridge beneath them gave one grand elastic heave and pitched them both into the water.

Swimming was just one of a great number of Boy Scout skills Anthony had failed to master. The river was deep and overwhelming. Anthony had nothing on his mind but holding on. His hands would've required surgery to release them from Richard Flowers's collar at this point in their ordeal. Richard thrashed savagely, screaming for help between large gulps of water, while Anthony rode along welded to his shirt.

While Richard flopped uselessly around on the surface Anthony felt himself sinking under the current. Just at the moment he was about to expel his final, the Earth brushed by his feet. He stretched his heels downward, where they bounced twice and slid to a stop in the mud bottom. The current tilted his head and shoulders out of the water and into the air. He stood there blinking, and breathing, and gaping at Richard Flowers, who was still firmly in his grip.

Richard coughed twice, hacked up a portion of river, and looked at Anthony reverently.

"You saved my life," he said just as two counselors reached them.

"Good work, Decker. You can let go now."

Anthony relaxed his grip as he watched a film of calomine lotion oozing from beneath his clothes and finding its way downstream.

That night at the closing jamboree Anthony was awarded a special commendation for courage and quick thinking. The conversations around the campfire were buzzing with the eyewitness accounts of the amazing rescue. "The bridge gave way under ol' pork butt Flowers. Decker jumped in, grabbed him, and never let go. It was awesome!"

The next day when Anthony's dad arrived to pick him up, the scoutmaster came over to shake his hand. "Quite a boy you've raised there, Mr. Decker."

The scoutmaster turned to Anthony, and right in front of his father said, "A guy like you will really go places in the world. Congratulations."

All Anthony could do was watch himself fade away. The Anthony Decker he'd known for the first ten years of his life was suddenly and permanently replaced with this mysterious *guy like him.*

It never occurred to Anthony to contradict this legend. How could he? Everybody treated the *guy like him* a whole lot better than they'd ever treated *him*. Anthony felt like a freshly painted house, only one thin coat of new color between him and the same old place.

Anthony never returned to the Boy Scouts, but he was forgiven. Never again was his courage, ambition, or integrity questioned. Everything he did was praised. Everything he failed to do was dismissed. "The Scouts probably seem a little tame to a guy like you."

Later, when Anthony stopped applying himself in high school, his parents understood. "We didn't think our little town could hold your attention for long. A guy like you needs to get the heck out of here, isn't that right? Go make his mark in the world. Well, you just bide your time. You'll be out of here soon enough, Tiger."

It all sounded just fine to Anthony, and he was able to postpone just about everything that came along until this mythical day that he would go make his mark in the world. He followed his own saga through to graduation and out the door. He packed up his Rambler and headed off into the sunset just like a *guy like him* would do.

The downfall of any hero comes when he starts buying his own PR. Anthony actually believed that Avalon, Ohio, was not big enough or worthy enough for him. It was more than a matter of faith that Out West was the only place he could thrive: It was the truth on which he based his life. He felt it with such an intensity that no amount of information to the contrary would ever persuade him otherwise. Not even ten years of a contrary existence.

The momentum of his journey from Avalon began to ebb as soon as the town disappeared behind the old Rambler station wagon. Anthony's set jaw slackened and hung lower with every mile that came between him and the people who knew him. Like an actor without an audience, suddenly his movements and postures—his very thoughts—seemed baseless and contrived. It had broken down completely, along with his transmission, just outside of Booder, Indiana, ten years ago.

. . .

Anthony came back to himself still staring at the mountains on the postcard. He could scarcely muster the strength to be in his trailer. Ray's Garage, Saint Bernard's, corn, soy beans—what did it matter? It was all temporary.

There's just no sense getting too close to the things we're bound to leave behind. Anthony hadn't held onto anything since he'd let go of that fat boy's shirt twenty years ago. Guys like him just couldn't afford to. They were ramblers, free spirits. That's just the way it was.

It was the movement that caught Anthony's attention at first, a graceful distraction at the periphery of his vision. He raised his head in time to see, perfectly framed in his window, the glistening flanks of Dirk Miller's horse caught in mid-air, profiled against the rich field of green. The athletic beast landed like a dancer, spun, and reared her head before bounding off across the beans toward the line of willow trees.

Anthony was frozen for the moment. Then Dirk came into the frame, arms raised, a rope in one hand, a fist in the other.

"Here we go again," Anthony said as he bolted from the table and out the door.

Anthony caught up with Dirk at the far edge of the field, where Dirk stood frowning into the willows. "I think she jumped the creek," he said breathlessly. "God love 'er, I don't know why I chase after this horse. She's just a damn show piece. *Worthless*. Tony, tell me why I keep chasing this horse."

"Because you can't let it go," Anthony said lamely, and stepped up to the creek bank. The water barely moved and it looked black and bottomless under the canopy of the willow trees. "I suppose we'd better get after it."

Dirk fretted up and down the bank, looking for a place to cross. The rope dangled futilely at his side. Anthony felt sorry for Dirk. He looked so tired and bothered—searching for a way over a creek he didn't want to cross.

Anthony, seeing the creek for the first time, judged it to be three paces wide. He counted ten strides back into the beans and turned. Pulling in a deep breath, he set his gaze on the opposite bank and took off.

When the creek was just two strides away Anthony mustered everything he had and drove it into his legs. He felt the young bean plants nipping at his shoes and slapping him in the ankles, tangling slightly, slowing him just barely—just enough.

He left the ground still looking across the creek, his anemic trajectory pointing him far short of the other side. He caught just a glimpse of the Arabian's tail through the willow trees before looking down.

Something on the surface of the smooth dark water looked up at him in total astonishment. Anthony's own face could wear no other expression. And that's the way he hit the water: looking right into the eyes of a guy like him.

16

Zowat stepped out of the van and took a moment to allow her garments to catch up with her. Her paisley print muumuu and accompanying ensemble of silk-screened veils and wrappings cascaded off the seat and reassembled themselves around her. It was difficult to determine how much woman there was beneath all those clothes, but her bearing made it clear there was plenty, and that she was in command of every bit of it.

Zowat gathered herself together and looked around, appearing to approve of the Flannigans' farm and the small knot of familiar people behind the house. With a jangle of bracelets and chains, she ran one hand through her long exotically graying hair, then extended her arm out from her side—as if she'd been there all along and it was the other guests who'd just arrived.

Emily Flannigan, Faye Bessett, and a dozen other faculty members from the college rose from their places and swept across the grass to receive their spiritual mentor and friend.

Ed Flannigan held his position at the grill, looking levelly at Zowat. "What a freak."

Although well out of earshot, Zowat fixed her look on Ed as if she'd heard. He shrank as what appeared to be the tiniest of smiles passed across her face. The depth and intensity of her gaze was offensive and alluring at the same time. Her eyes remained with Ed even as her head began to turn to her approaching friends. Then she broke off coyly, evidently energized by the encounter.

Ed finished the beer in his hand, suddenly feeling like he wanted to take a shower. He turned to the grill and lifted the lid. A hot cloud of dark smoke swallowed him for a moment, choking his breath and burning his eyes. Ed Flannigan: Alaskan expatriate and accidental farmer—and Zowat: born again and again and again spiritual crusader—had finally met.

Ed had been looking forward to Emily's year-end faculty party like one anticipates a creeping skin rash. No matter how good your attitude, you know it's not going to be any fun.

Ed had been feeling less and less a part of Emily's life for the past two months. She had immersed herself in academics, the politics of the moment, and the bewildering spiritual influences of Zowat: all things which Ed either didn't understand, refused to embrace, or just flat-out despised. Everything he knew about Zowat, not surprisingly, fell into this final category.

Ed resented the sway Zowat was developing over Emily. Zowat had given Emily a small rock as a *healing stone* and she'd begun sleeping with it on her chest at night. It wasn't the idea of it that bothered Ed so much; it was that Emily's metaphysical bond with the rock deteriorated as soon as she dozed off, leaving the stone to wander loose around the bed looking to bond in some painful way with part of Ed's anatomy, which it invariably did.

Emily was also working on locating her aura. Every night she'd stand in front of the bathroom mirror looking sideways out of her eye sockets. "They say you can see your aura if you try not to look right at it."

"I think the same thing works with Elvis sightings." Ed was totally convinced his wife was losing her grip.

Emily had stacks of books beside the bed. They were full of how-to information about life, and truth, and happiness. She often would read passages out loud that particularly interested her. Ed, glad to be included, sat still for it until one evening when he asked who had authored one engaging excerpt about raising children.

"The book was channeled through a woman in New Mexico from a three-thousand-year-old Mesopotamian warrior."

Emily said it so offhandedly Ed thought she was joking and asked, "Is this an old friend of Zowat's?"

Emily, still dead serious, said, "Of course not, Zowat is an Egyptian stone mason from an entirely different era."

Amazed, Ed was beginning to understand that Emily was in earnest about the whole business. "And tell me, please, what a mess-o-potatoes warrior and a dead bricklayer know about raising kids in Oregon?"

After that, whenever Emily read to Ed, he would interrupt her. "Before you go on, tell me, does this author have a body?" And there would be silence in the Flannigan master bedroom, as there had been for some time now.

Emily watched carefully as Zowat made her way across the yard toward Ed. She moved with a natural agility that belied her middle age and aging middle. Her eyes and arms were in constant motion: touching and assuring, always making contact with the people around her. When Zowat looked at a person, even for an instant, it would feel as if he or she were all alone in the universe with her. She was magic. She was wonderful.

Emily just knew that Ed would love her, too, if he would give her a chance. You couldn't really tell anybody about Zowat. She had to be experienced. Ed was like that himself: a greater whole than the sum of his parts would imply.

He was an over-opinionated, one-armed redneck who smelled like beer and dirt and tractor gas. But he worked and sweated and laughed and played and loved, and when it was all mixed up together you got Edward Campbell Flannigan.

It wasn't so much what you saw and heard with Ed or Zowat; it was what you couldn't quite see. As infuriating as it could be for Emily, there were parts to Ed she could never get close to. It was the push and the pull of it for her. Always knowing there was more. Always wondering what it was. Loving either of these two was like standing at the edge of a deep dark pool, wanting to take the plunge and afraid of falling in at once.

Emily stood outside the edge of the gathering and watched as Zowat approached her husband. Zowat held out her hand. Ed set down his can of beer and they shook like men do. He said something and Zowat laughed.

They both have it, Emily thought, that insufferable charm, and the ability to pour it on in a pinch. Emily watched Ed's face fold into that irresistible grin—all teeth and good will. And she watched as Zowat effortlessly emulated it—a nearly perfect parody.

Emily decided to join her two favorite studies before the moment deteriorated. "Well, it looks as though you two have met."

Zowat used the interruption to release Ed's hand. "Yes, Ed was just asking me if I was still angry about being buried alive in King Tut's tomb."

Emily looked at Ed ominously. "What did you tell him?"

"I told him, no, I wasn't mad about that anymore. It bothered me for awhile but you can get over a lot of things after a few thousand years of therapy."

Zowat laughed again and looked to involve the other people in the group. It was the catalyst for a general discussion of past lives and Emily used it as her exit to get the food from the kitchen. Ed remained, one eye on the burgers and the other one on the stone mason.

Zowat selected a lawn chair, which she sat on like a throne. The others pulled up close and revealed to each other, one by one, their past life experiences. The Art History professor claimed to have commanded a Bulgarian regiment in the eighth-century siege on Constantinople. The Environmental Economics department head said she was a live Aztec sacrifice during a lunar eclipse. The Yoga-aerobics instructor said he was an ancient Eskimo medicine man.

Emily brought the food out and offered a Babylonian alchemist some sushi. The Etruscan sailor went for the tofu and tabouli salad. The hummus was a big hit with everybody except the Phoenician helmsman, who was fasting.

The sailor, not being preoccupied with food at the moment, noticed Ed standing off by himself and tried to include him. "Ed, you seem like you've got the spirit of exploration about you. Do you suppose you were ever a Phoenician?"

"No, I've never even been to Arizona." Ed turned the last burger onto a platter. "Okay, who wants a burger?"

Ed held up the plate of patties, but it might as well have been a dead rat. Emily had tried to talk Ed out of the burgers, but he wouldn't hear of it. *Nobody can resist a grilled Burger El Flannigan.*

But Ed's confidence hung slack as a visible wave of nausea swept through the group. None of these digestive systems had worked red meat in twenty years. Ed held the plate motionlessly in the air and the lethal silence threatened to derail the whole picnic. It was Zowat who saved the moment.

"Sure, I'll try one of your burgers, Ed. A little red meat can't hurt. It'll just make you die early."

Ed scooped up a patty, relieved. "Well, you folks seem to bounce right back from that."

"Precisely." Zowat accepted a plate of burger and bun which she held at a comfortable distance to her while Ed feasted on his own. "Ed, do you ever get a sense of what you were in other lives?"

Ed squinted thoughtfully, and swallowed his bite. "Nope."

"Don't you ever dream about your other lives?" Zowat held Ed's eyes with the force of her penetrating gaze. Ed gave it right back.

"No, I don't dream about other lives, and I don't believe all of you kooks were ever crustacean generals and human sacrifices, either. I mean, where did all the normal people go when they died? How come none of you were dirt farmers or blanket weavers? Everybody was great and wise and gladiators and wizards. I think it's a little fishy that the only people who come back to life can find themselves in a storybook. I think you're all hallucinating."

Zowat's composure did not falter. She tilted her head slightly to one side and reached out to Ed's good arm. "Do you believe in anything, Ed?"

"Yes." Ed pulled away. "I believe I'll have another beer."

Ed spent the rest of the afternoon on the porch swing, watching. The sheen on his special Burgers El Flannigan congealed at his feet. The transient souls of Applegate College clustered around Zowat, listening, asking questions, laughing.

Ed couldn't hear what was being said, but he could see what was happening. He watched Zowat as she held the attention of the group. She would look expectantly over to Ed, trying to draw him in, but Ed wasn't buying it. No one could pour on the charm like Ed, and nobody understood better than Ed how counterfeit it could be. It was all just a light show designed to keep people from noticing the big dark spot in the middle of it all. Ed saw straight through to the middle of Zowat.

She was a charlatan, Ed was sure of it, and possibly a dangerous one. Maybe one of those God-gabbers who can sweet talk innocent people out of their homes and families. Get them living in the woods eating beans and waiting for the end of the world—and then making it happen.

Ed watched Zowat stand and start toward him. Emily followed, grabbing up an armload of dishes along the way. The party was breaking up and Ed was pleased. Norman would have the kids back from swimming anytime now, and Ed would just as soon have the place cleared of these fruitcakes.

Zowat reached the porch hiking up her wraps to climb the stairs. "Ed—Emily told us about all the work you've put into the farm. I was thinking I could come back and do an Earth healing for you. We could make a prayer circle and call upon the power of the mountain."

Ed didn't miss a beat. "I appreciate it, Zo, but what I could really use is some help brushin' out the orchard and powerin' through the weeds in the vegetable patch."

"You're impossible." Zowat tried to soften the charge between them.

"No." Ed looked at her even harder. "I'm very possible, even likely. *You're* impossible."

Zowat stopped and the two just looked at each other. Ed saw beyond the cool smile and unflappable poise, and he thought he detected something shudder. Zowat's smile widened and the moment passed. The fortress stood, but there was definitely a chink in the wall. "May I use your bathroom?"

Ed stepped aside and let her pass. Emily was close behind and Ed followed her into the kitchen. As Zowat disappeared down the hall Ed helped Emily load the dishes into the sink, but she showed no appreciation. "You're really annoying me, Ed."

"Well, I can't help it. There's more going on with that freak than she's letting on. I don't know what it is, but I don't like it."

Emily aggressively rinsed dishes as she spoke. "You don't like any- thing you don't understand, and that's most everything. Zowat is a kind soul, and she's very important to me. She's a little flaky, sometimes, but that's the mystery of her. That's her gift."

Ed was about to respond when he noticed that Zowat had not made it to the bathroom. She was standing in the hallway looking at their family photographs along the wall. She must have heard everything said, but she made no indication of it. All her attention was riveted on the photos.

Ed joined her, a little embarrassed. "Recognize anybody from an- other life?"

He hoped to rekindle the comic rapport from earlier, but the ques- tion seemed to startle Zowat. Nervously, she pointed to a picture in front of her.

"Who is this?"

Ed was glad to move on, and Emily joined them as he toured through the frames. "That's Emily's folks there, and this is mine. These are all the kids as babies—Little Ed, Missy, Corey. This is Grandpa Flan- nigan with my dad and these are Grandpa and Grandma Campbell, my mom's folks. They were great."

"Campbell Gramps and Ma." Zowat spoke matter-of-factly. Then she blanched and turned to Ed and Emily, wide-eyed, who stared back, no less startled.

Emily was the first to speak. "Yes, Campbell Gramps and Ma. That's what Ed always called them. It's a nickname from the time Ed was a little boy. How did you know that?"

Ed was silent. Struck dumb. He looked at Zowat in total wonder, not having an opinion for the first time all day.

Zowat reached in and found herself. She covered her own surprise by raking a hand through her hair, allowing her to close her eyes for a moment. When she opened them again, she was back, all serenity and poise.

"I pick up things like that from people all the time. The words we speak are only a small part of what we say to each other. Our souls hear everything. Now if you'll excuse me," Zowat turned down the hall, "I have to pee."

Ed stood quietly squinting at the photo of his grandparents, as if an explanation might appear. Emily looked at the side of his puzzled face, satisfied. "She's magic. You see?"

"You set this up."

"I didn't. You have to believe me."

Ed looked at Emily and knew he could believe her. But if he believed Emily, he'd have to believe in Zowat, and if he believed in Zowat, then he'd have to believe in what Zowat believed in. And if he believed in what Zowat believed in, then . . .

Ed felt himself slipping, careening through the middle of himself reaching for a handhold. Then suddenly, just before he lost his grip, he was snatched back to Earth by the sound of a three-thousand-year-old stone mason in a giant paisley muumuu flushing a toilet in the next room.

Zowat appeared again in the hallway. Ed looked at her as if he was sighting down a board looking for the warp. She was in turn the picture of serenity.

Who are you? Ed said without speaking.

Zowat heard and her face shone like Mona Lisa's secret. *It's me,* she said, not sure if Ed could hear her.

Emily shifted her weight and gave a dry little cough, suddenly nervous in a weird new way.

17

Senior Account Supervisor Katherine Bedinger-Hoople squatted and dropped the box of books onto the kitchen table. "I'm going to murder you, Richard," she said, returning to the door for her briefcase and purse. She wiped the sweat from her neck with the back of her fingers. "I'm going to murder you in six creative ways, including dropping each of these books on your head from a great height. Then I'm going to put different parts of you in boxes and mail them postage due to Drs. Brazelton, Spock, and Suess *and* Mr. Rogers."

Katherine had been a little edgy lately. Actually she'd been this way for almost five months, ever since this "baby thing" started.

It began pleasurably enough—the farewell dinner with Richard at the Rainbow Room, dancing. Home to the flannel sheets and Sarah Vaughan on the stereo. It had been a grand departure and Katherine had ridden the noon flight out of JFK with a dreamy look on her face, a houseplant on her lap, and some rapidly developing cells somewhere south of her solar plexus.

It had taken her awhile to figure out that throwing up wasn't how most people started the day in Los Angeles. Initially Katherine had attributed it to some cross between jet lag and culture shock. Moving to L.A. affects people in a lot of different ways including, but not always, severe indigestion. So it required an inspired dose of suspicion, a careful look at the calendar, and a home pregnancy test to finally determine that she was not merely adjusting to a hostile environment, but that she had in fact entered a new and very unanticipated stage in her life.

Katherine had immediately called her husband with the disturbing news. "Richard, I'm reproducing."

"What?" Richard had no context for the statement. "Oh, wait a minute, Pumpkin, I'll turn on the fax machine."

"I'm not reproducing *papers*. I'm reproducing people—you and me—breeding. Richard, I'm pregnant."

Richard Hoople sat on the Upper West Side of New York listening to the empty phone. He looked around his bedroom. He looked down to the street he'd called home for eight years, and he saw nothing familiar. Suddenly, eerily, everything had changed.

Katherine stood on the balcony of her apartment overlooking Universal City and waited for her partner to respond. To clarify, give it a perspective, or at least some fortification. They needed to face this situation square-on together. The Bedinger-Hooples could make the best of this situation if anyone could.

"So," Richard finally said, his voice relaxed and warm. "This is great news for our ninety-five taxes."

"Richard, the tax advantages of this are the last thing on my mind. I haven't got time to be pregnant right now."

"How much time is actually involved?" Richard's brain was already at work on the problem. "I mean—I know it's nine months, but can't you, like, do other things in the meantime?"

Katherine was pacing the balcony with her cellular phone. "Of course I can do other things. According to the doctor I mostly need to eat all the time, get more sleep, and grow out of all my clothes."

Richard poured himself a cognac in New York. "So what's the problem?"

"Richard! The problem is that in seven and a half months we're going to have a time management crisis on our hands! We need to get ready!"

There was a long pause on the line. Katherine paged through her filofax as if she might turn up a solution. Then she heard her husband's calm, confident voice on the line. "I'll handle it."

"What?"

"I said, I'll handle it. We've got a lot of friends with kids back here. I'll ask around, get some answers, and make the arrangements."

"What arrangements?" Katherine was suspicious, but she could feel the first waves of relief washing ashore.

"I'll find out, and I'll make them."

Richard's solid assurance seduced Katherine in her panicked state and she fell into his arms—in a cellular sort of way. "Richard, you're wonderful."

"So are you, Pumpkin."

And Richard did exactly what he'd said. He handled it. He made lists of pertinent questions, gathered answers, compiled some action charts—and got to the business of having a baby.

Richard's job editing diet books used up less and less of his brain capacity with every passing year. Sometimes he didn't even remember what a book was about only minutes after finishing it.

Richard needed a challenge, and there was no challenge more complicated or righteous than children. Katherine was at a crucial place in her career. She needed more than a partner right now, she needed a guide, a handler, a full-time birthing consultant. She needed him.

Richard became so competent and so encouraging in such a short amount of time that Katherine was finally able to relax with the situation. In Katherine's world the "baby thing" was a nine-month-long physical challenge followed by a childcare problem. Nothing that couldn't be handled with Richard's help and the proper amount of preparation and scheduling. After all, she oversaw three of the largest accounts of the western division of the twenty-seventh largest advertising agency in America. Everybody has babies. How much trouble could they be?

Katherine sprawled in a chair beside the box of books and caught her breath. It was another load of baby books her darling consultant had put together for her required reading. Being in the publishing business, Richard had an annoyingly vast access to published material on the art and science of having babies. Taped to the side was an envelope marked, importantly, *Development Report*.

Richard thought this was fascinating and essential information. The *Report* was Richard's weekly memo on exactly where the fetus was on

the road to becoming an actual biped. The refrigerator was already covered with them. Richard had taken a yellow highlighter to the really
important events just in case Katherine should skim and miss them: *Fingers
fully formed. Liver and kidneys functioning. Eyes open and close.*

The information interested Katherine, but she was not overly af-
fected by it. It was like watching her holdings on the stock exchange rise
and fall: When you're in for the long haul, what can you really do?
Katherine thought it was bad enough being pregnant in the first place
without having to think about it all the time. She left that to Richard.
He seemed to be interested.

Katherine's interests were at the agency; this baby thing could really
ball up her plans. Somebody was going to get that vice-presidency, and
it had better be her. If she got the VP spot she could write her own
ticket. She could transfer back to New York with Richard and they'd
settle into the day-to-day routine of juggling two careers and a baby in
the second-most-uninhabitable city on the continent. If she didn't get the
promotion before the baby came, then Richard would have to move out
with her to the most uninhabitable city on the continent until something
changed. No problem.

Katherine rubbed her swollen ankles and felt the tears coming. *Oh
God, not again.* She'd been crying at just about everything lately. She had
to get this under control.

This morning at the agency while test pitching a new campaign for
Little Darlings Dog Food she had to leave the room—twice. The art
director had created a video that depicted a woman feeding creamed dog
food to her puppy while a string quartet played a compelling theme in
the background. The close-up of the woman's hand and the puppy's face
cross-faded into the scene of a mother nursing her child while an off-
camera announcer read the tag line: *Little Darlings, for the ones you really
love.* The baby's face crossed back into the puppy's who gave two satisfied
little barks. Katherine burst into tears and left.

Although she was genuinely moved by the presentation, the creative
people took her reaction as negative, and when Katherine returned they
immediately launched into an alternate pitch. This one showed a man
spoonfeeding the same puppy a mud-colored gruel then taking a taste of

it himself. As he looked into the camera, delighted with the experience, the announcer said, *Little Darlings, looks so good you'll be tempted to eat it yourself.* Katherine made for the door again, this time green with both hands clasped over her mouth, while a very dejected creative department returned to the drawing board.

Katherine's notoriety as a hard-edged supervisor and domineering manager of people had preceded her to the Los Angeles office along with her nickname, "Mother Superior." After becoming aware of her condition in recent weeks, Katherine's minions had adjusted the moniker to "Mommy Dearest."

Katherine was aware of her nicknames and her reputation around the agency. It didn't bother her for the most part. She felt that good leadership always incorporated a certain element of fear, and fear naturally bred resentments. As long as it was kept under control, Katherine merely considered it a cost of success. One overheard conversation in the executive women's room last week did finally touch her, though. Katherine was in a stall while two women from Accounting chatted at the sinks.

"It looks like Mommy Dearest is really packing on the pounds."

"I saw her eat three buttered croissants at the senior staff meeting this morning."

"She'll gain forty pounds at this rate."

"On her it'll look good."

"You're mean."

"I'm mean!? Can you imagine having that woman for a mother? I'd rather be raised by wolves."

The remarks about her weight gain didn't bother Katherine much. She was a pragmatist above all. Her doctor had predicted she'd gain twenty to thirty pounds. Her pregnancy-obsessed husband verified this every time he called: *Get on the scales, Pumpkin, so I can fill in that growth chart. You should be gaining about a pound a week right now.* Richard was filling in a weekly graph of her ups and downs, then faxing the results to her on Saturdays.

According to the information at hand, Katherine was just as heavy as she should be. No, what was bothering Katherine was not the petty insults about her appearance, but the brutal remarks about her mothering capabilities.

It hurt because she had her own doubts about it. In fact, if truth be known, Katherine was ninety-five percent convinced she was incapable of motherhood. Not even her rapidly expanding belt line gave her the assurance that this whole baby thing was actually going to happen.

She'd shop, attempting to initiate the process of motherhood. It seemed as if entire sections of malls and shopping districts were devoted to maternity needs and children's necessities. From designer stretch pants to pre-school word processors, there was nothing that the eager parent couldn't find to rub a credit card against.

But Katherine could only stand helplessly at the front windows. The drool bibs and nap-sacks, papooses and snugglies might as well have been plumbing supplies for all the allure they held for her. She'd watch as the other bulging young mothers-in-training sniffed, purred, and sighed, then waddled out the door with armloads of necessities they hadn't known existed a few short months before.

Katherine had finally made one purchase on the way home that afternoon. She'd wandered into a children's department store, which appeared to be a solid acre of unspeakably cute things. She'd hoped that a closer proximity to the paraphernalia of motherhood might trigger a compulsive purchasing instinct, a kind of nesting impulse with a gold card and frequent flier miles.

She stopped in one aisle absently fingering some infant toys. One, a rubber-coated jumbo pretzel, issued a peculiar and peaceful chiming sound when moved. She was tipping the toy back and forth, listening and wondering what was making the lovely sound, when a humorless matron in a clerk's apron approached her. "Can I help you with something today?" She eyed Katherine suspiciously, sensing an imposter.

"No," Katherine said, caught off-guard. "I was just looking at these chew toys."

The clerk narrowed her gaze. "Chew toys are for pets. These are teething products."

"Of course they are," Katherine said, reflexively putting the rubber pretzel in her mouth and giving it a thoughtful bite. "This will do fine."

She handed the toy to the clerk who carried it to the cash register with two fingers, leaving a trail of tiny musical notes. Katherine followed at a chilly distance.

The phone rang and Katherine checked her watch before answering: *seven-thirty*. "Hello, Richard."

"Hi, Pumpkin, you sound tired. Hard day on Mommy-kins?"

"Don't start, Richard, I'm tired." Katherine tucked the phone under her chin and opened the refrigerator to graze. "The air conditioner in the Beemer quit. I was stuck in traffic for two hours, and I almost had a miscarriage packing your stupid box around."

Richard was unfazed. "There are some great books in there. Have you opened it? I put one right on top that I found fascinating. It's by a Dr. Ralph Bonner called *The Causes of Pain during Childbirth*. Very informative."

Katherine snorted, nearly passing some cold pizza through her nose. Recovering, she bore down on the phone. "Leave it to a doctor named Ralph to write a book about what causes pain during childbirth, and leave it to you to read it! Figure it out, Richard! It's not that difficult to understand!"

"I'm sorry, Pumpkin."

"And stop calling me Pumpkin! If you're going to call me a vegetable, pick one that isn't so round and fat! Okay?"

Richard didn't say anything for a moment. He was getting used to his dear wife's outbursts. "You're just tired, Pumpk— Katherine."

"Richard, I'm not just tired. I'm not just anything. I'm pregnant!"

The anxiety in Katherine's voice surprised even her. For one small moment all the implications of her condition seemed to descend upon her. She set her pizza crust on the counter and slumped against the fridge, feeling the cool metal door through her blouse.

She looked at the box of books on the table next to three days of unopened mail. Her briefcase laid open on the floor, spilling her account reports, cellular phone, candy wrappers, and Kleenex onto the dusty floor. Everywhere she looked something needed to be done. She felt like she'd gained a hundred pounds in the past five minutes. Her legs folded as she slid down the cool metal to the floor pulling six weeks' worth of *Development Reports* down with her.

"Richard? What am I going to do?"

Richard had been waiting for this. He stood in the doorway of Katherine's former study overlooking West 92nd Street, which was now covered floor to ceiling with unspeakably cute things he'd never known existed.

"You don't have to do a thing, Katherine. I'm taking care of it. The nursery is all set up. We're on standby for the best diaper service on the West Side. Mom sent a baby quilt she and the church ladies made, and Aunt Evelyn knitted booties. I've got a Lamaze Video Training series coming with duplicates being sent to you. We can practice over the phone. Also, in that box are a dozen or so books of baby names—I took the liberty to highlight some of my favorites. There's also some enrollment forms for the three best pre-schools in Manhattan. There's a four-year wait-list, you know.

"Anyway, you don't have to do anything. Just look this stuff over, get your promotion, and have a baby. I'll do everything else. It's a little slow at the office right now. Diet book submissions are way down since the Republicans took over."

Sitting spread-eagle on the cool floor listening to her husband's bumbling assurances, Katherine let herself be calmed. "You're wonderful," she said, meaning it for the moment.

Richard closed the door to the nursery in New York. "Everything's going to be fine. You just take good care of yourself—Pumpkin."

After her bath Katherine stood looking at herself naked in front of the bedroom mirror. She turned sideways and patted her hands on her belly. "This is getting weird," she said, holding the roundness that was such a part of her and so hard to comprehend. "I hope you know what you're doing, Richard."

She patted herself again in good-humored disbelief, and suddenly she was patted back. The pumpkin bumped. The hump jumped. The bulge budged.

Katherine sat down on the bed looking down at herself. Her baby had kicked her in the ribs. She felt like she needed to get out of its way, but there was no place to go. She stood and walked into the kitchen holding her belly as if it needed separate handling.

She went to the box on the table, almost frantic, her eyes scanning book titles for some assistance: *Diapers and the Environment. Raising Happy Children in an Economic Downturn.* As Katherine stood still she felt the movement inside her. She spotted the blue rubber pretzel sticking out of her purse and, desperate, she stroked her belly with it.

She returned to the bedroom pacing nervously to the hidden musical chime. Richard and the nursery suddenly felt every single inch of the three thousand miles distant that they were. She was alone with her baby, and her baby was so close she couldn't tell its movements from her own.

And Senior Account Supervisor Katherine Bedinger-Hoople, *Mother Superior,* had no way of knowing it would be this way for the rest of her life.

18

Ed held the main trunk of the tree with his hand and pushed his way up through the branches. The step ladder teetered beneath him. When he looked down he noticed the manufacturer's warning sticker on the top—*This Is Not a Step*.

Ed surveyed the young peaches. There were too many of them, he could see that, but how many too many? The little old man told him to leave no more than two or three to a branch. There were close to a dozen of the fuzzy white fruits on every branch at every level. Ed estimated there were a thousand peaches on this tree alone; he'd have to clear seven or eight hundred of them to do what the man said.

It seemed totally excessive to Ed, but he couldn't be sure. Ed understood that these peaches would all shrivel and drop if they weren't picked back. The tree was interested in seeding itself, not feeding peaches to people. To get the good fruit, Ed would have to leave a selected few on each branch. But which few?

Ed started counting the number of peaches on the uppermost branch because maybe having an actual number would provide some answers.

"One-two-three-four," Ed counted out loud, and the ladder shifted beneath his feet. He swooned and plunged, all the way to the bottom— to yesterday afternoon, where he stood again beside his overturned pickup truck.

"·five·six·seven·eight." Ed was on one foot, arms wide, counting to fifteen. An Oregon State Patrolman was in his face. The officer watched as Ed's balance shifted and he put his foot back down.

"Would you care to try that again, Mr. Flannigan?"

Ed rubbed the tender spot on his forehead and looked at his son standing beside the road like somebody's orphan. The boy jabbed his shoes into the soft shoulder—digging a hole to hide in. Norman Tuttle leaned against the truck, spinning one rear wheel.

A shudder went through Ed when he looked at the cab of the truck again, windows broken, roof crushed. The blood in his veins ran like cold chowder and his head rang with consequences. "No," he said looking once again at the policeman. "Let's just get on with it."

"You are under arrest for suspicion of driving under the influence of alcohol."

The patrolman was decent enough to put Ed in the car, out of earshot of the boys, before reading him his Miranda rights. A second patrol car pulled up.

"Mr. Flannigan, Officer Gowan will take the boys home. Is there someone there to be with them? They both seem a little shaken up."

Yes." Ed thought of Emily and felt like throwing up.

Ed rode silently to the police station looking through the black wire-mesh barrier at Quartz Mountain looming ahead like judgment. He watched the world outside, how changed it looked to him, and wondered how such a perfect afternoon could have gone so wrong.

"Don't drink any more beer, okay, Ed?" Emily had left the picnic at the lake early with the sunburned little kids. Ed was in the middle of a rowdy horseshoe marathon with some other men who were taking full advantage of a hot Fourth of July weekend and several coolers full of beer.

"Yeah, yeah." Ed had dismissed her. He'd become fast friends with the other men and, as usual, Ed was the life of the party and the center of attention. He hurled ringer after left-hand ringer, and everyone was naturally drawn to this one-armed man from Alaska with the easy laugh and steady hand. No amount of beer appeared to faze him. If anything, his game just got stronger as the afternoon wore on.

"Let Norman drive you home."

"Yeah, yeah."

Emily knew she was talking to herself, but she felt better for having said it and left while the boys gathered the inner tubes, air mattresses, and barbecue into the truck.

Norman had heard what Emily said and when Ed was finally ready to leave he started the truck and hovered around the driver's door hopefully. Norman had only had his license for a few months, and any opportunity to drive felt better than sex to him, even if sex was mostly speculation at this point in Norman's career.

Ed finished his beer with a big gulp and dropped the bottle into the bed of the truck. He noted the look on Norman's face and grinned down at him. "Sorry, Norman. Not today. This old beater ain't safe for you to drive."

Ed was right. It wasn't safe for anybody to drive. He'd paid less than five hundred dollars for the truck, intended to be strictly a workhorse around the farm. It barely shifted gears, barely steered, and barely held itself together. The safest thing about it was that it also barely ran and there was some question whether it could go fast enough to hurt anybody.

"But I drive it around the farm," Norman had argued.

"Not today, buckaroo," Ed said, taking the door handle. "I could never face your parents again if something happened to you."

Ed sat in the holding cell at the police station and thought he would die. He'd flunked the breathalyser by one-tenth of a percent and they'd formally arrested him for drunk driving. They'd allowed Ed a phone call and he'd asked Emily to come and get him.

"I'll be there in awhile," she'd said, her voice as cold and distant as the cooler full of trouble that got him here. Ed stared at the creeping mildew in the corner of the cell and began to appreciate why they'd insisted on taking his belt and shoelaces.

Ed wasn't convinced it was his drinking that put him in the ditch, but he couldn't be sure it wasn't, either. With only about four teeth left on its steering gear, the old truck wandered down the road like a drunk. There was enough play in the wheel that it felt, at times, as if it wasn't connected to anything. This truck wasn't driven so much as herded down the road.

Ed didn't know how he'd let the truck slip off the pavement onto the soft shoulder that day, or why he'd whipped the wheel so hard to compensate. All Ed knew for sure was that before he could do another thing they were upside down in the ditch. Ed had banged his head on the steering wheel and the boys had to help him free his shoulder harness. When he finally squeezed through the window into the ditch weed, the first thing he saw was a pair of shiny black Oregon State patrol boots straddling an empty beer bottle.

By the time Emily got to the police station Ed had rationalized that it could have happened to anybody. But as soon as he saw the look on Emily's face he knew it hadn't: It had happened to him.

"I'm through with this, Ed." Emily didn't even wait to clear the front door. "You lost your arm and that was an excuse to drink. I understood. You lost your job and that was an excuse to drink. I understood. You had to leave your almighty Alaska and that was an excuse to drink. I understood."

Emily stopped in front of the car and turned to Ed. "You could have killed those boys today!" She noticed the swollen black-and-blue spot on her husband's forehead and reflexively reached out to examine it. "You could have killed yourself! And I don't understand anymore! You can't drink yourself a new arm, Ed, and this has got to stop."

Emily looked as if she were about to weep. Steeling herself, she rapped her knuckles against Ed's lump and ordered him into the car.

"I'm taking you to a recovery group," she said, turning the key with purpose.

Ed gingerly probed the knot on his head. "Recovery from what? It's just a bump. Some witch hazel and a cold cloth should do it. If you'll stop thumpin' on it."

"I'm talking about an alcohol recovery group. I've spent the last hour and a half on the phone, and I've found you a good men's group that meets every night. For one thing you can get out of a lot of trouble in Oregon with your DWI if you go into a recovery program, and for another thing . . . " Emily paused to breathe and gather herself. ". . . and for another thing—if you don't stop drinking I'm leaving you."

Ed felt for the second time that day like he'd rolled a truck onto himself. "I'm sorry," he said, meaning it.

"Yes, you are." Emily's conviction would not soften. "I want my husband back." She said it as if the man beside her was somehow responsible for the disappearance of her mate. Ed sat quietly fingering his lump, feeling guilty of the crime.

"My name is Roger and I'm a happy, grateful alcoholic, addict, co-dependent, abuse survivor. Welcome to the regular Saturday night meeting of the Quartz Creek Men's Recovery Group. I see we have a new face or two in the group tonight, so let's start by going around and introducing ourselves by our first names only and say why we're here."

The new face in the group sat with his arms locked so tight across his chest he could hardly breathe. Ed couldn't bear to even look at the shiny faces around the circle of chairs. They all acted as if they had nothing they'd rather be doing on a Saturday night other than drinking weak coffee out of Styrofoam cups in a musty church basement having a contest to see who was the biggest mess.

"Hi, my name is Trevor and I'm an alcoholic coke-head bulimic prescription drug abuser. I'm here for today and happy to be here. I'm happy to be anywhere."

"Hi, Trevor," the group sang.

By the time it came around to Ed, he had his face completely hidden by his good hand and his artificial limb lay in his lap fairly snapping from the tension in his shoulder. He slumped further in his chair and addressed his belt buckle.

"My name is Ed, and I'm here because my beat-up truck rolled itself into the ditch and my wife thinks I'm a drunk."

Hi, Ed.

Ed wanted to get up and slap every cheerful face in the room. But he held fast. For one interminable hour he sat and listened to story after story from men he'd never seen before. Stories about the way their parents mistreated them. Stories about the way they'd mistreated their own kids. Stories of drunken debauchery, financial destitution, moral turpitude, and shameful obsession.

Ed squirmed in his chair like someone was holding a match underneath. He had never heard these kinds of confessions even from his best buddies, let alone total strangers. He had no idea what he was doing here. All he'd done was roll his truck after a few beers. It was bad luck, that's all. He wasn't like these guys.

The group adjourned by standing in a circle holding hands while the one named Roger said a prayer. The two things that kept Ed from hurling himself through the nearest window were thoughts of his dear wife Emily, and the sad fact that they were in a basement.

After the circle broke up Ed made a beeline for the door only to be intercepted by Roger. He offered a wide smile and an extended hand. "Ed," he said, standing too close. "There's an old saying around here I want to share with you—*denial* is not just a river in Egypt."

Roger stood beaming at Ed with a satisfied grin, which Ed might have tolerated had Roger not leaned forward and given him a great big hug.

"AAAaaaa."

The thought of it jerked Ed back to his orchard and he lost his balance, barely catching himself by the branches of the peach tree.

"Watch what you're doing' there. You could break that tree."

Ed looked down to see the little dark-skinned, white-haired man looking up at him with piercing turquoise eyes. He held the base of Ed's ladder and shook his head. "You reach too far and you'll break your fool neck!"

Ed started down the ladder, startled and pleased to see his mysterious little friend. "Are you really here?"

"You see me standin' here, don'tcha?"

"I saw you standing here once before, too, and we pruned a tree together and the next thing I knew you were gone and the tree hadn't been touched."

The little man tangled his brilliant white eyebrows together with a puzzled expression. He glanced down the row of peach trees to the end. "Looks done to me."

Ed was getting riled. "Of course it's done. I did it. I did the whole damn orchard, and I planted all those vegetables you told me about, too."

"I know." The man obviously wanted Ed's point.

"How could you know? You haven't been around. I needed you. You told me you'd be around."

"What I told you was that if you needed anything to ask for Ed."

"But you're Ed!"

"I know. How come you keep telling me things I know? Tell me something I don't know."

Ed took a frustrated breath, opened his mouth to speak, then stopped and let his face fold into a smile. "It's good to see you."

The man's eyes softened. "I know."

The silence left between them created a vacuum that seemed to pull the words from Ed before he knew what he was saying. "I'm in trouble."

"I know." The little man scratched his head and relaxed a hip and looked right into Ed Flannigan in a way that drew the story right out of him. The picnic. The wreck. The jail. Emily. His marriage and the meeting.

He paced when he talked about the meeting, and kicked a young fallen peach when he got to Roger.

"And he hugged me! I just about belted him."

"Why didn't ya?" The way it was asked, Ed knew he wasn't being goaded. He was expected to give an honest answer.

"I don't know why I didn't." Ed looked at his shoes. "I just don't understand those guys. How can they sit there and tell all those things to total strangers?"

The odd little man shifted and started to move. Attentive to Ed's story, but not seeming particularly interested in the subject. "Maybe it makes them feel better. Maybe it makes you feel better. I don't know about that stuff. All I know about is farming, and you got some farming to do in this orchard—look at this."

The man was up the ladder before Ed knew it, pinching the peaches off the middle branches almost frantically. One after another came raining down around Ed, who had to dance out of their way.

"You've got four times as many peaches here as this tree will support. These others gotta go. Dump 'em."

Ed looked up from the ground. "But how do you know which ones to save?"

"Save the big ones. Save the pretty ones. Save your favorite ones. It doesn't matter. You'll know; just get rid of the overburden. Take this one and this one and this one and this one and this one."

The little white fruits came down so thick Ed had to move completely away from the tree. He stood and watched, fascinated, as the other Ed moved effortlessly through the tree with a running monologue. ". . . and this one goes and this one and this one . . . you can't keep it all . . . can only carry so much. If mosta these don't go then nothing will be fit to eat. You want healthy fruit you gotta dump what you can't take care of . . . this one and this one and this one."

When the little man was satisfied he stepped back down the ladder and stood with Ed. There were hundreds of peaches laying on the ground in a circle around the tree.

"Two or three to a branch. That's all you can handle this year. If you're lucky you'll get a hundred good peaches to a tree. You'll do better next year, and the year after that, but you'll be happy with your hundred."

Ed looked up and down the four-acre orchard and felt himself droop. The little man noticed. "It's a lot of work, but you've got a good start."

Ed looked at him, suspicious. "Are these all going to fly back on the tree when I turn my back?"

The man's face revealed nothing. "You do your work right, it stays done."

"Are you going to be around?"

"If you need anything just . . . "

"Ask for Ed." Ed finished the little man's sentence and it seemed to finish his visit as well.

"Well, you've got lots to do." The man rose up on the balls of his feet as if to take off. Ed looked into the wise old eyes and felt a sudden compulsion to reach out and hug the little guy. A caution flickered across the man's face as he clumped back down on his heels.

"Not me you don't. Save it for Roger and that bunch. I'm liable to belt ya." With that he laughed and bounded down the orchard out of sight.

Ed watched after him for a long time before turning to face the thinned tree. It branches were visibly lighter and loftier than they'd been. The rest of the orchard looked despondent in comparison. Stumbling and sliding on the discarded peaches, he grapped the ladder and moved it to the next tree.

Ed checked his watch and then scrambled up the steps trying to imitate the enthusiasm of his strange adviser. If he really pushed it, he could get another tree thinned before the meeting. Committing himself to the task, Ed steadied his legs against the ladder at his head filled with the sweet smell of raw and broken fruit.

19

The sun made its methodical way across Montana. Sweeping the plains from the east at a thousand miles per hour, its sure clear light saturates everything in its path, never missing a spot until it reaches the foothills. There it splits, its longest fingers leaping freely westward from mountaintop to mountaintop, its heart and soul left to seep down into the valleys, filling in every feature. The long shadows lose their daring and creep beneath the nearest things standing. There they wait out the day, plotting their return.

Lloyd leaned into the utility compartment in the rear of the motor home and quietly cursed to himself. A couple things were bothering him this morning. The first thing was that the water line had rattled off the pump housing again and they were losing time on their early start. Lloyd felt for the loose end with his hand and swore again. The other thing bothering him was that he was dying.

"Is everything okay down there?" Evelyn's voice came filtered through the rear bench seat inside the camper.

"Same trouble we had in Pocatello. You'd think we could go two hundred miles in this thing without something falling off. We're wasting a lot of time lately."

"What's the hurry?" You got a date or something?" Evelyn focused on the plaid seat cushions, not expecting an answer, but wanting one. Lloyd had been like this lately—restless and cranky.

Lloyd held the loose pipe in his hand and caught his breath. He hadn't felt like he'd really caught his breath in weeks. Evelyn didn't know Lloyd was dying. Actually Lloyd didn't *know* he was dying. It wasn't like a doctor had said, *Lloyd, you're dying.* He just knew, like sometimes you know if a growling dog is going to jump up and bite you. You don't know how you know, but you know.

He'd lay in bed at night listening to his heart beating. The more he heard it beat the more he thought it wouldn't, and the more he thought it wouldn't the harder it would beat until he'd nearly give himself a heart attack waiting to have one.

He hadn't told Evelyn anything about it. She seemed to be enjoying herself so much he didn't want to worry her. She'd probably make them both go home. Calling the trip off was out of the question even if their quest of a lifetime had lost much of its luster for Lloyd in recent weeks.

It started heading downhill after their visit with Deirdre. Hard as she tried to be pleasant and interested, Deirdre remained unreachable. She was determined to be obstinate and was cool to the point of disrespect. What friends she had introduced them to were appallingly dirty and crude, or deliberately foreign. Lloyd grew annoyed enough to feel that Deirdre's Mexican friends were speaking Spanish on purpose just to exclude him.

It was hard for Lloyd and Evelyn to admit, once they realized it, that a big part of their trip was reclaiming their children. It was even harder to admit that they could not. It amazed Lloyd how his kids had grown up and baffled him. Whatever he'd done wrong was still wrong and not about to be undone. It was nice to see them. It was just as nice to leave again.

See you later, Princess. She wouldn't even hold her old Dad when he left.

The ruined expectations of the reunion with their daughter seemed to cast a pall over everything. All the really big deals were over with. They'd met the mountains and moved through them. They'd gambled under the lights of Las Vegas, gaped at the Grand Canyon, circumnavigated the smog monster over L.A. They'd smelled the Pacific Ocean and craned their necks at the redwood forests.

The pictures of these highlights were scotch-taped on all the cupboard fronts; two white-haired old people standing slump-shouldered in front of scenic overlooks—smiling. What were they smiling at? The other white-haired old people they'd pestered to take the pictures? The young park volunteers with their scrubbed faces and ardent nature sermons? The red blinking light on the auto timer? Lloyd had lost track of the point to it all.

The point had been to get their sorry old stay-at-home selves out of Avalon and see some of the world. Good enough, that's what they were doing—wandering around every crooked line on the map looking for gas, water, and a place to park.

Every time the motor home crested a hill, another blue mountain ringed with dark green trees would come into view. Lloyd would go *Ooo,* Evelyn would go *Aah,* and then she'd snap a picture to add to their *Blue Mountain through Buggy Windshield* collection which was now taking up more room in the closet than Evelyn's support sneakers.

Lloyd was getting impatient with the routine. Every evening was the same thing. It didn't matter how far they drove that day, at the end of it they'd pull into what looked like the RV park from the night before. The same old duffers would already be there in lawn chairs circled around the mosquito coils. They'd be telling flat-tire stories, or passing on road construction warnings.

Lloyd started calling them *D.O.A. Campgrounds.*

Evelyn would cluck. "Don't be so ornery, Lloyd Decker. They're nice folks, just like us."

"That's the problem. Everybody's nice like us. Everybody's just like us. We've been in Montana for two weeks and we haven't talked to anybody who actually lives here. The only people we ever meet are geezers in Winnebagos. I've met more people from Ohio out here than I ever knew back home."

Evelyn didn't share Lloyd's frustration. The familiar routine of their trip thus far was fine with her—comforting, actually. Everything in the motor home had a place. She was proud of her little kitchen and cooked the same things they always had at home: toast and jam with coffee for breakfast. Tuna salad or thuringer sandwiches with carrot sticks and chips for lunch.

If they were staying in a campground for several nights Evelyn would cook nice dinners: pot roast, oven-fried chicken, mashed potatoes, and corn. She'd bought two artichokes in Oregon at Deirdre's suggestion, but had given up before she even got them in the pot. "You peel and peel these things and never get to the purpose of them!"

They ate out regularly, but when they did Evelyn preferred the name-brand franchises to the local fare. *The restrooms are clean, and you always know what you're getting.* Evelyn found a sense of peace in the notion that a McDonald's fish sandwich tasted the same in Spokane as it did in Flagstaff. And there was always plenty of room to park.

Lloyd pulled his head out of the utility box to straighten his back. He peered around at the wide valley that was beginning to fill with the long light of day. He noticed, for the first time, the tumbledown cafe across a weed-patched dirt parking lot.

They'd been up before the sun and on their way into Livingston. Evelyn was hoping to find a Burger King there—she liked their coffee. Lloyd was just happy to be moving. Evelyn had spotted the water leaking from under the cupboards and Lloyd had pulled over at the first wide spot on the road.

The main sign on the building spelled out the word *BAR* in mostly broken lightbulbs. Underneath was a smaller plywood sign with the spray-painted footnote, *AND BREAKFAST.* Smoke rose from a crooked roof stack. Lloyd could see lights and movement through the grimy front window.

Quite a place, Lloyd thought, looking up to see Evelyn looking back at him through the rear window. She smiled and waved. Lloyd waved, too; unable to grin at his wife any longer, he leaned back in to finish his repair.

Lloyd cursed again. Evelyn had that look of fret and fuss on her face she always wore when something wasn't just the way it ought to be. It was the same way she'd stand in the front window back home if there were strange kids playing in the yard, or if the neighbors had the nerve to paint their house without consulting her about the color. And what made Lloyd maddest of all was that he'd be standing right there beside her.

They'd spent the first seventy years of their lives peeking out from the safety of their little home and family in Avalon. Whether it was looking through the front window or into the TV screen, the outside world stayed at a sanitary glass-lined distance. And now here they were at the grand finale of their lives and they were still looking at the world through a window pane.

The Road Ranger was painstakingly designed to be maneuvered past huge expanses of the world without the occupants' ever having to get any of it on them. Their home on the road was weather-sealed, climatrolled, cruise-controlled, and shock-absorbed. The windows were tinted for the daylight, blinded for the night, and sealed for protection. The power plant was self-contained, the drive train self-propelled, and the residents self-possessed.

Lloyd pulled his head out of the back of the motor home and slammed the hatch shut. His hands were covered with grease and road dirt and he held them out away from himself. He looked up at Evelyn who made a face over the mess and then turned pale as Lloyd proceeded to wipe them on the front of his shirt.

"Lloyd Anthony Decker," Evelyn's outrage passed impotently through the glass window. "I'll never get that out. What do you think you're doing?"

Lloyd finished wiping his mitts and turned toward the cafe. "I think I'll go have a cup of coffee."

"In there?" Evelyn lost sight of her husband and she scrambled to the door. By the time she undid the latch and got it opened, Lloyd was half-way across the parking lot. "Lloyd Decker, we can't go in that greasy spoon. If it's coffee you're after I'll make us some instant."

"I want to taste the coffee in Montana," Lloyd said without breaking stride while his bewildered traveling companion went for her sweater.

Lloyd was already sipping his coffee at the front table by the time Evelyn dithered in the door. The woman behind the counter smoked her cigarette, not looking up.

Evelyn checked the seat of the chair opposite Lloyd, then sat down with her arms folded. She looked sternly at Lloyd, about to speak, when the proprietor clunked down a heavy coffee mug and filled it.

"Is that decaffeinated?" Evelyn asked.

The woman only laughed as she went back about her business behind the counter. Evelyn was mystified. "Do you have any Sweet n' Low?"

The woman laughed louder, then broke off into a hacking cough. Evelyn appeared ill for a moment and shot a hard look at Lloyd. "What are you grinning about, mister?"

Lloyd sipped his coffee, satisfied. "Life," he said.

Evelyn took a breath, about to get to the bottom of her husband's peculiar deportment, but was diverted by a frightening sight streaking across the parking lot directly toward them.

Raising a rooster tail of brown dirt behind it flew a partly blue and mostly rusted pick-up truck which left the factory sometime before the Korean war and hadn't seen a carwash since Truman fired MacArthur.

The fenders continued flapping a good while after the truck had stopped just inches from the front window. Evelyn had already abandoned her position, but Lloyd just sat grinning out at the cloud of dust.

The driver's door fell open and flopped from one hinge. One cowboy boot with a toe worn through appeared first, then a whiskey bottle fell to the ground, another boot much like the first came next, and finally a long, knob-kneed man pulled himself out into the day.

His face was the color of burlap and the texture of a dried apple. His eyes were as dark and wet as Lloyd's coffee, and there were barely any whites to them—just shiny dark places where the parchment of his face quit. He adjusted the hat which was as much a part of him as his face, leaned over, and spit an impossibly long dark stream of tobacco juice, not quite clearing his own feet.

"Look at that, Evy, a real cowboy."

Evelyn said nothing. The man came in the door still trying to stomp the bad aim off his boots. He appeared unsteady on his feet, but not uncomfortable with the condition. An invisible haze of sweat, cigarette smoke, liquor, leather, gunpowder, cows, and horse hair billowed through the room.

"Mornin', Gert." He tipped his hat to the woman, his voice clear and strong. He turned his watery eyes on Lloyd and Evelyn. "Good mornin', folks."

Lloyd looked straight into his eyes, eyes that had seen it all set in a face that had been rubbed right up against the world. This was the face of a man who'd lived. Lloyd took him to be about his own age, but in his presence Lloyd felt absolutely fresh and pink. He rubbed his hands together nervously, grateful for the grease on them and the mess on his shirt. "Good morning," Lloyd said. "Fine day."

"Zat so." The man sat down to a waiting cup of coffee at the counter.

"I've got postcards to write," Evelyn said curtly, getting up to leave. She didn't need to see any more of this nonsense. "I'll be waiting in the camper," she said as if there were a variety of places to wait.

Lloyd was not at all apologetic. "I'll be out after awhile."

He watched Evelyn pucker up her face and fold her sweater tightly against the dust that still lingered in the parking lot. The proprietor filled his cup and as Lloyd looked up to thank her he saw the cowboy coming over to his table.

The big man held out a hand the size and look of a gardening spade. "Sid Winston," he said.

"Lloyd Decker." Lloyd straightened in his chair as the man sat down.

"I see you're from Ohio."

"Yes, that's right." Lloyd couldn't imagine how the man noticed their license plate at the speed he came by it. "You from around here?"

"You seen what I drove up in. I can't have come from too far off."

Despite what his appearance might indicate, Lloyd could see that Sid was fully in command of himself. This relaxed him. "Are you a cowboy?"

Sid looked at Lloyd through the steam from his coffee. "More cow than boy these days."

The rock-solid calm in Sid's eyes made it impossible to be uneasy in his company. Lloyd wanted to know more about him.

"So, what are you doing now?"

Sid looked out the window. "I'm dyin'," he said not sadly.

"Me, too." It came out so easily, Lloyd wasn't sure he'd said it.

Sid looked full at Lloyd again. "What you dyin' from?"

"I'm not sure." Lloyd brushed at the morning whiskers on his chin, thinking of letting it grow. "How 'bout you?"

Sid massaged one of his hands with the other as he spoke. "I'm not sure, either. It might be the whiskey. Or the tobacco. It could be the four horses that fell on me. Or the three wives who walked out on me. Or the bullet in my neck. It's hard to tell some days."

Lloyd didn't feel like mentioning his shortness of breath. He didn't say anything. The cowboy looked out at the Road Ranger.

"You must have seen and done just about everything."

"Hardly." Lloyd laughed.

"You seen the Grand Canyon?"

"Well, yes."

"How is it?"

Lloyd thought, *How is the Grand Canyon?* "Fine," he said.

"You seen the Pacific Ocean?"

"Yeah"

"Howzat?"

"Good."

"Seen the Atlantic?"

"No."

"Me, either. 'Course I ain't seen anything. I was to Wyoming once, but I got in a fight and never went back. Where you go from here?"

Lloyd smiled. "We were thinking about Wyoming."

"Don't worry," Sid dead-panned. "I started that fight."

Lloyd leaned forward. "Where would you go if you could?"

The cowboy didn't even stop to think. "New York City."

"New York City? What on Earth for?" It was the last place Lloyd would have featured a broken-down Montana cowboy.

"Because it's like nothing around here. Everything here's those blue mountains. I've spent my whole life lookin' at blue mountains. I whisht I'd seen more people and places."

Lloyd was off in his head for a moment. "Me, too. You know, I've got a nephew in New York."

The cowboy took a last long gulp of coffee, swallowed, and pulled a round snoose can out of his shirt pocket and scooped a wad under his lip. "I hear it's against the law to spit on the sidewalks in New York. Can you imagine? Gittin' arrested for spittin'?"

Lloyd couldn't.

The cowboy took a last long gulp of coffee, swallowed, then spit a noisy stream into the cup. He considered the can of chew in his hand and slid it across the table to Lloyd. "If you ever go to see that New York nephew, give a big spit for Sid Winston. Now, go back out to that wife of yours before she drives off and leaves you talkin' to a drunk old cowboy. It happened to me three times, ya know."

Sid stood to leave and Lloyd got up to shake his hand. "It's been real nice talking to you, Sid. I've never met anybody quite like you."

"Most like me is already dead." Sid's face bunched up around his eyes as he shook Lloyd's hand goodbye. "All except you maybe."

Lloyd somehow understood it as a compliment. "I'm gald you stopped by, Sid." He let go of the old cowboy's hand, who used it to tip his hat.

"And I'm glad *you* stopped by, Lloyd."

The two men stood there like day and night looking at each other. Nothing in common except where they meet—at dawn and at dusk.

The proprietor was nowhere to be seen, so Lloyd left a five-dollar bill on the counter, pocketed the snoose can, and walked out the door. The dust behind Sid's departing truck rolled across the lot toward the motor home. Lloyd could make out Evelyn in the rear window. She waved tentatively. Lloyd waved back and picked up his pace, trying to catch his breath. His long shadow rushed ahead of him to the camper as the sun cleared the rim of the valley filling it with the luster it had lost since the day before.

20

Webster felt his knees starting to buckle as he made his way up the gangway. This was to be his first time on an airplane since being sucked out the window of one five months ago, and he hadn't been able to get an aisle seat.

"Maybe you can trade with somebody once you get on board," the disinterested ticket agent had told him. "But don't bet on it. Window seats on the left side of the plane aren't very popular on the Alaska flight. All the scenery is on the right."

Webster was the last one aboard. Pale and wobbly-legged, he found his row and eyed his potential trading partners. An older woman whose face appeared to be constructed entirely of make-up sat on the aisle holding the hand of a man already sleeping with his mouth open in the middle seat.

Webster glanced to his ticket stub like it was a bad check before he spoke. "Excuse me, but I seem to have been given the window by mistake. Would you mind switching? I'm sure you'll enjoy the view."

"Keep the view, there's nothing to see. I have a bladder condition and I get up a lot. My husband took a pill. We won't hear from him until we land." The woman's eyes seemed to be the only thing capable of moving on her and the man combined. Webster noticed that not only did he have a window seat, but also an exit row. There was a large handle on the wall with a big red arrow that read *OPEN*.

Being on an airplane was one thing; being near a window was another. Being near a window that opened was something else entirely. A tremor passed through Webster's entire skeleton as he grasped at straws. "I have a weak kidney and a nervous stomach."

The woman seemed encouraged by this. "I've just had my gall bladder removed and I get dizzy spells."

Webster, an experienced flier, rose to the challenge. "I get claustrophobic and am prone to panic attacks."

The woman sat forward in her chair. "I've had my varicose veins stripped and my feet swell."

Webster could see he was working with a pro, and when he saw the flight attendant coming toward him he panicked. "I'm, umm, allergic to bees." He shrunk, knowing he'd been beaten.

"We can't leave the gate until you take your seat, sir. Please sit down."

Webster felt the urging eyes of the other passengers on him. The woman on the aisle rooted herself smugly into the seat. "I'm just getting warmed up, sonny. You better sit down."

Webster climbed over the woman and her corpse-like husband feeling like a dead man himself. After sitting down and tightening his seatbelt until it made him light-headed, he looked at his comatose seat mate wondering if he had any of those pills to spare.

The plane broke away from the gate with a lurch and Webster knew he should have taken a bus to Alaska. It was only a fifteen-hundred-mile drive. A person could do that in a week, tops. What was the big hurry?

Webster closed his eyes and tried to recapture the phone conversation the day before with his Uncle Frank. What a strange notion. *Uncle Frank.* He had an Uncle Frank in Alaska, an Uncle Stu, too, and who knows what else he might find on the trail to his father?

Webster had found him, or at least what was left of him. It didn't take long for U.S. Army Private First Class Oliver Tuttle, the father listed on his birth certificate, to become U.S. Army *Missing and Presumed Dead* Private First Class Oliver Tuttle.

A couple of telephone calls to the proper military channels and that was that. Dear old Dad was dead. Easy come, easy go. Having known him less than twenty-four hours, and then only as a name on a piece of paper, that was pretty much the beginning, middle, and end of Webster's relationship with his biological father.

At least it would have been except for one thing—two, actually. Webster learned that notice of Private Tuttle's sad status in July of 1964 was sent by the Army to two addresses: his mother, Amanda Flannigan's, at a Seattle location which is now a shopping center—and to a Mr. and Mrs. Grover Tuttle at The End of the Road, Alaska.

Determined to leave no stone unturned on the gravel bed of his past, Webster summoned every bit of his considerable research capability and went to work. Actually, he just got on the phone and called information for The End of the Road, an unlikely but accurately named community on Alaska's southern coast. He was given the numbers for two Tuttles: Frank and Stuart.

Webster counted four rings before an answer. "Hello?"

The voice sounded far away. It was far away, Webster reminded himself. But closer than he'd expected to get so easily. "This is Webster Cummings calling for a Frank Tuttle."

"Speaking."

"Does the name Oliver Tuttle mean anything to you?"

There was a long silence that filled with the ghosts of other conversations going on in the phone cable. Finally, Webster heard the voice he was waiting for. "Yes. I used to have a brother by that name. What do you know about him?"

Webster had not prepared for this. "Umm—I used to have a father by that name. I'd like to talk to you about him."

As the plane left the ground Webster became grateful the man beside him was so heavily medicated. It allowed him to put as much distance as possible between himself and the window while still maintaining his seatbelt at maximum tension. To distract himself from his terror and his discomfort, he pulled out his calculator.

In the wake of his accident the airlines had scrambled to minimize the risk of such a thing happening again. He remembered a fairly widely known statistician at MIT alleging in an article for the *New York Times* that it was a one in two and a half billion chance that a person would get sucked out of an airplane on any given day.

Factoring in that, as far as Webster knew, nobody else had been sucked from an airplane in the one hundred and thirty-three days since he had been increased the odds of its happening again to almost one in nineteen million. Considering the huge number of people who flew on airplanes worldwide on any given days raised the odds of someone's being sucked out into thin air today uncomfortably high. Fortunately Webster's seatbelt was so tight he passed out before he could generate those figures.

Webster had to stop the car when he got to the top of Flatback Ridge. The view of the mountain-rimmed bay was too much to ignore. Like some fabled sanctuary, the jagged tops of knife-backed ridges with glaciers gleaming lent a quality of mysticism to the tiny little community that sat in the center of it all like an offering.

Webster had never found himself particularly interested in scenery until he'd begun the drive down from Anchorage to The End of the Road that afternoon. He was aware that he was returning to the land of his seed. He couldn't be sure if the weight he was feeling from his surroundings was just his imagination, or if there was some kind of inherited memory at play. A vague impression left in the gene pool so we can always identify our ancestral territory. It is a trick the mind plays when we really believe in something.

Webster followed the directions Frank Tuttle had given him on the phone and found the house described—a plain, neatly trimmed gray ranch-style home with a yard full of bicycles, bats, and frisbees. Webster knew it must be the work of his cousins and the idea warmed him. He felt the earth solid under his feet as he made his way to the front door.

One man stood framed by the doorway. Another stood just behind him. Their faces were friendly, but there was a caution about the place— a tension in the way they held their places at the door before giving way.

"Hello, Webster, I'm Frank Tuttle and this is Stu. From what you told us, we're your uncles."

The three men shook hands while Webster was shown through the door. They sat down at the dining room table where two cups of coffee were already in progress. A shredded napkin lay beside one. Webster could see the men had been sitting here for some time.

"I'll get us a fresh pot." Stu went into the kitchen.

Frank returned to fingering his napkin and Webster looked around the house. The place was clean, but things were not put away so much as straightened up and piled out of sight. Undoubtedly a house of children. Webster used it as his opening. "You have kids?'"

"Four. Their mother took them to the movie." Frank placed the balled-up napkin scraps into a neat line in front of him.

"Four," Webster repeated, unsettled by this cool reception and searching for another starting place. His Uncle Frank took a deep breath and saved him the trouble.

"Listen, Webster. We're a simple family of simple means. Stu and I own a fishing boat together and we feed both of our families with it. We have enough, but just enough. What is it that you want from us?"

Webster felt shock and relief. Shock that these men would think he'd come with some claim of rightful inheritance, relieved that's all this was about.

Stu came back into the room with a steaming pot of coffee and another cup for Webster. As his Uncle Stu poured, Webster looked at his Uncle Frank and decided to start at the only place he could think of, at the beginning. "Maybe you remember the story of that guy who fell out of an airplane in New Hampshire this winter?"

"Yeah." It was Stu who answered. "That was on the news a lot for awhile. A real lucky young fellah."

"Yes, I am," Webster said looking at the only relatives he had at the moment.

Frank squinted back at him. "That's why you look so familiar. I thought it was the family I was seeing in you, but it was from those magazines." Frank looked at his brother, acknowledging that they had a genuine celebrity in their midst, if not in their tribe. "Of course the family is there, too, but you appear to resemble the Flannigan side way more than the Tuttles."

"You knew of Amanda Flannigan?" Webster pushed forward and knocked his cup over with an elbow. The stream of coffee made its way across the table and thwarted the neat line of napkin balls between Webster and his uncle. Frank captured the spill with another napkin, never taking his eyes off Webster.

"I haven't heard that name in thirty years, or Oliver's either, for that matter." Frank and Stu sat still in what was clearly new territory, or perhaps native territory long forgotten. Webster, too, seemed momentarily immobilized by the mention of these mythical and vital people. Then they all found their voices together. "Tell me what you know about them," they said at once, as the family got down to business.

Webster went first. He had the least to tell. All he'd been able to find out thus far was that Oliver Tuttle and Amanda Flannigan were not married at the time of his birth. The Army was not forthcoming on any information other than that Oliver was listed missing in action in May of 1964 and changed to *presumed killed* a short time later. His file was permanently closed in 1986. Webster had gotten nowhere on locating his mother. The address that the Army corresponded with no longer existed.

"I was hoping that this Grover Tuttle who the Army also notified of Oliver's MIA status might know something of her. Who is he?"

Webster noticed a shift in his two uncles. A little bit of a return to the chilly climate of awhile ago.

"Grover Tuttle is your grandfather. He probably never received that notice. Or if he did, it was tossed out unopened. He moved us all over to Valdez shortly after Oliver and Mandy left town. Oliver was dead to him already, and Dad never knew the Flannigan girl."

Frank Tuttle considered the lost look on his newest nephew's face and decided for the second time this year to divulge the Tuttle family secret.

Webster sat dispassionately while Frank detailed how Webster's mother and father were teenaged lovers who made a mistake and found themselves trapped outside of two intolerant families. Their love for one another was genuine, but their situation hopeless. It was a tight-knit little community with rear-ends to match.

The Tuttles moved to Valdez to avoid the scandal. The Flannigans eventually left, too, for Fairbanks. The younger brother, Ed, returned as an adult, but never mentioned Mandy. He was only in the first grade at the time, so either he'd put the whole thing out of his memory or he was keeping the same code of silence as the Tuttles had for the past thirty years in deference to their father's notions of sin and damnation.

"I always thought Oliver would come back and make things right with the ol' man." Frank looked at his brother Stu. "I guess now we know why he never did."

Webster let the respectful silence rest for a moment, then pressed for more. "Tell me about the Flannigans. Maybe they've heard from my mother. Where can I find them?"

Stu answered, "The parents are both dead. Grandparents too. Ed's the only one left far as I know. He just moved his family down to Oregon. Norman, Frank's oldest, happens to be spending the summer down there. But I'm sure Ed doesn't have anything for you. We've known him for years. He'd have said something by now."

Webster was taking only mental notes. He'd fill in the details later. For now he added Uncle Ed Flannigan to his list of new relatives. "How about Grover Tuttle? What happened to my grandparents?"

"Mom and Dad are still with us. They're over in Valdez." Frank spoke it sadly, thinking of something.

Webster brightened. "I can't wait to see them! How do you get to Valdez from here?"

Stu Tuttle picked up the coffee pot, shook it empty, and disappeared with it into the kitchen again. Frank resumed ripping and balling his napkin. Webster, beginning to understand his family a little better, waited.

Frank put a fourth little ball in a row and then spoke. "I called Dad yesterday as soon as I hung up with you. I told him Oliver was dead and that you were coming up to meet us."

Webster was delighted. *His grandfather knew about him!*

"What did he say?"

Frank didn't look at Webster when he continued. "He said that Oliver died a long time ago, so what was the big news?"

Webster waited for his uncle to continue, but he didn't. He just seemed to slide backwards into a more distant place. Distant and comfortable. A position made familiar by thirty years of hard use.

Webster didn't like the look of it. "Well, what did he say about me?"

Webster noticed Stu hanging back in the kitchen as Frank struggled to find the words. "He said that you were from a bad seed and didn't belong to us."

Webster sat staring down the aisle barely aware of the plane lifting off the runway. Alaska fell away beneath him, but the loss of it meant nothing. He reached in his jacket and produced a notebook. Opening it, he absently glanced through the scrawl of notes. There were names of dozens of cousins, and uncles and aunts that would all have to be organized and compiled into a readable family tree.

He was really making progress. Far more in the past two days than in the whole previous five months. He now not only knew who his parents were, but his grandparents and their other children and all their names and ages and places of birth and current residences.

This was what he's been after, he told himself. So why did he feel like this? He'd set out to find out who his father and mother were, and he'd done it. What did he expect these people to do, buy him new shoes and show him to his room? The file on the search for his father could almost be closed. He'd go to Quartz Creek to see one last lost uncle. He'd go to Fort Lewis one more time to see if he could learn how his father was actually killed, and he'd put this project to bed and get back to his life, such as it was. Some people spend their whole lives avoiding their relatives; he sure wasn't going to spend the rest of his looking for every last one of them.

Webster returned the notebook to his pocket and had just closed his eyes when the captain's voice blared out of the speaker overhead.

"Ladies and Gentlemen, we are approaching our cruising altitude of twenty-seven thousand feet. We expect a smooth ride today and clear skies as we pass along the southern coast of Alaska on our way down to Seattle. For those of you on the left side of the aircraft, we're presently passing directly over the city and port of Valdez, the southern terminus of the great Trans-Alaska Pipeline and site of the world's largest oil spill. Have a pleasant trip."

Webster looked toward the window. A man in a business suit read a paperback with the shade closed. Webster leaned across the empty seat between them and touched his arm. "Excuse me, but I seem to have been given the aisle seat by mistake. Would you mind trading?"

"Not a bit," the man said immediately, getting up. "I've seen it all before."

Webster sucked in his breath and opened the shade. The brightness momentarily blinded him, and then he was able to focus on an endless world of mountains—grim, gray faces and white peaks. They stretched to the horizon and ended below only where the deep green water of Prince William Sound began.

The town passed by almost directly beneath them. Just as interruption in the coastline from this altitude, but the most significant thing on the landscape to Webster.

Webster's seatbelt dangled uselessly as he leaned into the window for a better view. The gulf of altitude between him and the town of Valdez had no effect. Fears of falling never occurred to him. He felt no sensation of sucking. He felt no sense of gravity. He felt no pull from the ground at all. He only pressed his face tighter to the cool window and wished that he did.

21

Buddy sat on the stairs behind the kitchen and watched Oliver stacking crates and organizing boxes in the alley. Oliver hummed quietly to himself as he worked. He stacked three wire milk cases and stood back to appraise them. Not satisfied, he nudged the whole collection to align more evenly with the wall.

Buddy shook his head and wandered across to his vagrant friend. It was the mid-afternoon room service lull. Most of the well-heeled guests were either out shopping and dropping piles of money, or were up in tall buildings at meetings making piles of money to replace what they'd dropped shopping.

Buddy hated when it slowed down in the afternoon. It was no way to pay the bills, but he did enjoy talking with Oliver during his down time.

"Oliver, you do nice work." There was an edge of sarcasm in Buddy's voice, but none that Oliver detected. Oliver's world was what it was and the people in it meant all the things they said.

"Thank you, Buddy. If you're going to do a job you should try to do your best." Oliver made his point by trapping a passing candy wrapper under his foot and picking it up.

"I agree," Buddy said, and he did. But he didn't understand. "Oliver, how is it that you can do this day after day?"

Oliver said nothing while he walked to the dumpster with the piece of captured litter. On the way back, appearing to have sufficiently thought it over, he asked as if to answer, "How do you do what you do day after day?"

Buddy knew what he was talking about. "I do what I do to get ahead."

"Same with me," Oliver said, bending to another stack of crates. "I straighten up the alley, you give me a loaf of bread, and I'm ahead."

Buddy shook his head and brushed a dusty spot on his black linen pants. "No, you don't understand, Oliver. I'm working to get ahead in the world. I'm just waiting on rooms here for the money to get me through law school. Five years from now I'll be in the big bucks. Tell me, Oliver, what do you think you'll be doing five years from now?"

Oliver thought for a moment and smiled. "Buddy, I can't tell you for sure what I was doing five years *ago*."

Buddy stood, confounded. "Oliver, you just care about today, don't you?"

Oliver looked up, surprised. "Don't you?"

"Of course I do. But there's more to life than just getting through a day."

Oliver stopped what he was doing and looked up, intrigued by the notion. "Like what?"

"Like getting an education and a good job. Making something of yourself. Put your mark on the world. Get married. Have some kids."

Oliver's interest was piqued by the last two items on Buddy's list. "Are you going to get married, Buddy?"

"Sure. I want to."

"Are you going to marry Sally?" Oliver knew Buddy's companion who often drove through the alley when she fetched Buddy after work.

Buddy made a hard, sure face. "No, I don't think so. Sally has her sights set too low. She wants a life in the country somewhere with two kids and a cat. She doesn't really appreciate what the world has to offer if you really go after it."

Oliver could only repeat himself. "Like what?"

"Like money and respect. Good cars. Fine homes. Like being able to walk into the nicest restaurants in the country and get a table. Like having the doormen at joints like this know you by name."

Buddy stopped and gestured up to the great presence of the hotel beside them, as if Oliver might have forgotten it was there. "Like being able to stay for a week in the Merrimont Hotel while people like me wait on you hand and foot. I want a woman who appreciates that, and wants to help me get after it."

Oliver thought for awhile about everything Buddy had said, but only one thing seemed important. "I like Sally," he said quietly.

Buddy's next thought was interrupted by Carlos in the kitchen doorway. "Order up, Buddy. Hey, Oliver, do you mind hanging around awhile longer? I've got a bunch of trash coming out as soon as the guys finish mopping the cooler. There's two extra loaves in it for you."

Oliver nodded, pleased. He grabbed his ragged broom and started to sweep around his feet, a habit he had whenever there was time to kill.

Buddy dashed through the kitchen doorway brushing at pieces of dust on his uniform. He prided himself on being the most efficient, well-groomed, and articulate waiter on the hotel staff. It wasn't that he liked his job. He hated it. But it was great for tips. Buddy always got the most tips. He grabbed the tray in one motion on the way to the service elevator.

Once inside he assumed his waiter's air—head up, chest broad. He checked the corners of his mouth with a finger, and examined the tray. He always enjoyed sizing up a guest by their order.

This tray held a single service of iced tea which sweated seductively in a crystal pitcher. There was a tiny bowl of fresh strawberries and a single cut rose which Carlos had added.

All class, Buddy thought: a rich wife back from shopping on a muggy day. She'd be in the bathtub when he arrived and tell him to leave it on the dresser. The wealthy were so predictable.

Buddy took a last look at himself in the hallway mirror across from 1512 before knocking on the door. He held his pass key, waiting to hear the order to enter, and was surprised when the door opened.

Standing before Buddy in walking shorts and a tank top was a strikingly beautiful woman only a few years older than himself. Her long dark hair was tied back with a silk scarf. Buddy let his waiter's bearing fail as his eyes tracked her back across the room. She retrieved the phone left laying on the bed amidst a head of shopping bags.

"Please put it on the desk." Speaking to Buddy without looking at him, she returned to her conversation.

Buddy cleared a spot on the glass-topped writing desk and began setting up the tea service, acquiring the invisible qualities of a good room service waiter. The young woman returned freely to her conversation even though Buddy was less than ten feet away.

"I'm incredibly bored, Janice. Bill has been in meetings all day yesterday and today, and then he makes me go to these indescribably dull dinners with his clients." The woman pushed some of the boxes and bags aside with a leg and continued.

"I've spent about all the money I can stand. I don't know what I'm going to do all day tomorrow. Bill's got a stag dinner tonight, so I'm on my own. What? You dirty girl. Yes, Danny's still out here. He's managing a rock club about six blocks away." The woman shifted her position and appeared to notice Buddy for the first time. Buddy stood passively holding the check for her signature.

"Hold on, Janice, I've got to take care of room service." The woman set the phone down, briefly glanced at the bill, and signed, writing in a tip equal to the charges.

"Why, thank you, madam," Buddy said enthusiastically.

"My husband's a big tipper," she said, dismissing the gesture and turning to her phone once again.

As Buddy headed for the door he heard her voice turn slightly conspiratory. "Yes, I called him. Can you believe it? Well, he's still single. I know, I know I'm a married woman, but what good is being married if I don't have a husband around? One little drink can't hurt anything."

Buddy closed the door behind him and spoke quietly to himself. "Bill, if I was you I'd stay home tonight."

Buddy had completely forgotten the incident by the time he reached the kitchen. He'd gained so many revealing glimpses into the guests' personal lives, they were hardly worth thinking about. All he'd brought back with him from the fifteenth floor was the memory of the woman's shape walking to the phone.

Back in the alley, as if Buddy's face revealed his thoughts, Oliver spoke directly to them. "So Buddy, after you get a lot of money and a wife—what are you going to do then?"

Buddy was aware that Oliver was still with their earlier conversation. Buddy and Oliver would often string a dialogue across an entire afternoon of interruptions. Still, it took Buddy a moment to gather his thoughts and reply.

"Well, Oliver, after I start to make my pile and find a good wife, I'm going to have a couple kids, raise them to be smart and responsible. I want a boy and a girl. A lawyer and a banker. That's my retirement plan." Buddy laughed as if he were kidding, although he wasn't.

Oliver leaned on his broom with a wistful look. "I sure like children. I like to make them laugh. Sometimes I do tricks for them, but mothers don't let their kids too near me. I don't blame them. . . . " Oliver beat some dust out of one shirt sleeve to make the point.

Buddy tried to bolster his friend. "You'd make a fine grandpa, Oliver."

Oliver thought about this. "You have to be a father first, don't you?"

The melancholy in Oliver's voice made Buddy uncomfortable and he was grateful that Carlos appeared again in the doorway. "Order up, Buddy."

Buddy fell in step beside Carlos who handed him the bill. "Double dry Martini. It's her fourth since lunch. Make sure she's okay—okay?"

"Okay." Buddy turned serious with his boss. Carlos didn't like the guests getting drunk. They made messes and burned holes in things. He was always afraid they would hurt themselves or burn the whole place down.

"I watered the gin," Carlos said, handing Buddy the tray covered with cut crystal decanters for the gin, vermouth, and ice. "She's probably too far gone to notice, but be prepared."

Buddy stood outside 1157 and gathered himself together. He didn't like these calls. Rich alcoholic women in the middle of their lives getting drunk in the middle of the day and making passes at the room service help.

"Come in, please." Buddy heard the surprisingly alert-sounding voice as soon as he knocked.

He opened the door with his pass key and saw a woman in her late forties or so sitting in the armchair by the window. Silhouetted against the lace curtains she looked remarkably erect and composed.

"Please set it down here." She indicated the table at her elbow which held a spent cocktail glass and decanter. As Buddy cleared and wiped the table, the woman looked up at him. "How old are you?"

Oh, boy—here it comes. Buddy assumed his most distant air. "I'm twenty-three, madam."

"Twenty-three," the woman repeated and she smiled at him. But Buddy could see this was not a pass. This was something else. "I have a son your age. Somewhere."

"Somewhere?" Buddy couldn't stop the question.

The woman poured herself a fresh drink. "He went off to college with a thousand dollars in his pocket four years ago and that was the last we ever heard from him. He never showed up at school, and he never came home again."

The woman took a sip of her drink and made a face. "This gin is watered."

Buddy opened his mouth to object, but she stopped him. "No matter. You were right to do it. I've had quite too much already."

The woman turned her attention back toward the window and her thought. "The boy had no father," she said to the curtains.

"I'm sorry." Buddy moved the check in his hands, anxious to have it signed and be gone. "Is he dead?"

"Golfing," the woman said without humor. "He was golfing with his cronies the day Matthew was born. He was golfing with the same men the day he left. He's golfing right now. I'm not sure he knew he had a son except for the one disastrous time Matt tried to caddy for him."

She paused to take another sip of her drink and noticed Buddy anew. Grabbing the bill and pen from his hand she said, "But you've got more important things to do than listen to a drunken golf widow."

Buddy took the check and turned to leave. The woman spoke again. "Do you have a mother and father?"

Buddy stopped and turned. "Of course."

"Go call them," she said and turned back to her curtains and her drink.

.   .   .

"Buddy, I don't understand." Oliver was back to stacking crates.

Buddy sat on the steps reading through his notes for a term paper. "What's that you don't understand?"

Oliver picked up two more crates and stood with them in his hands. "I don't understand this retirement thing you talk about. I mean, you say you want this good law job and all this money, and then you talk about quitting like that's what you're doing everything for in the first place."

Buddy smiled. "It is."

"What is?"

"We find a job we really like and work it so hard we can't wait to quit, and then we do."

Oliver set the crates on the ground again and chose two others. "And then what do you do after you retire?"

Buddy put his notes down and looked off into thin air. "That's when you play. Travel. Maybe a yacht on the Baja or a villa in the South of France. Tropical cruises. Slow dancing under the Southern Cross. That's when I'm going to see the world and enjoy my money."

Carlos appeared once again in the doorway. "Got one more before you punch out, Buddy."

Buddy spoke to Oliver as he turned to leave. "The world's full of opportunity, Oliver. All you gotta do is look around. Everything you need to know is there."

Buddy felt energized by his own sermon and strutted into the kitchen leaving the perplexed Oliver looking around the alley. Buddy hit the elevator at a trot and checked his watch. Sal would be coming to pick him up in ten minutes.

The tray in his hand held a service of hot tea and a bran muffin. *An aging matron up from her nap,* Buddy thought, and his spirits sank a little. The old matriarchs were the worst tippers. It didn't matter how rich they were, they still thought a quarter was a lot of money.

Buddy knocked on the door of the suite at the end of the hall on fourteen. He waited and was about to knock a second time when the door opened. A handsome white-haired woman in a loose cotton house-dress stood apologetically arranging her hair with the palm of a hand.

"Come in, dear. Please forgive me. I'm not quite awake from my nap."

Buddy smiled to himself as he swept past her. With the curtains closed the sitting room of the suite looked lifeless and unusable. Like a window display at a furniture store. The woman, apparently having a similar sense, walked to the corner and drew the drapes open as Buddy set up her service on the coffee table.

The woman appraised herself unhappily in the mirror over the bar. "Good Lord, I'm a total wreck. I just arrived from Singapore this morning. These old bones are not quite sure what time zone we're in yet."

Buddy was always willing to hold up his end of an empty conversation. "You've been traveling a lot, then?"

"Oh, yes," she said wearily. "Tons. Herbert and I were always going to see the world. As soon as he retired his partnership. Which he did. We spent two whole years planning our adventures, and then, ten days before we were to leave, the old fool thoughtlessly dropped dead of a heart attack at the breakfast table."

"I'm sorry," Buddy said, awkwardly holding out the bill and a pen.

"So was he," she said, taking the bill and signing without looking at it, or adding anything to the charges. "He laid on the kitchen tile, and the last words he spoke to me were *Go—have some fun.*" She handed the bill back to Buddy with a sardonic smile. "So here I am, having fun."

"Enjoy your stay, madam." Buddy turned to leave and had almost made the door when the woman addressed him again.

"Excuse me, dear." Buddy saw a shred of panic cross the woman's face as she spoke. "I am in Seattle, aren't I?"

"Yes, ma'am," Buddy said, amused.

"I'm glad," she said sitting down to her tea. "Herbert always loved Seattle."

"So do I," Buddy offered helplessly. After rocking on his heels for a moment, he left.

.   .   .

Sally was leaning out the window of her dilapidated old car talking to Oliver when Buddy came into the alley. He handed Oliver three loaves of fresh-baked dining room bread wrapped in a clean white towel. "Don't tell Carlos about the towel, okay?"

"Okay, Buddy." Oliver stepped back from the car to stuff the bundle into his sack. "Two extra loaves and a fresh towel. This was a big day. Is this what you mean by opportunity?"

Buddy smiled as he slid in beside his girlfriend and took the wheel from her. "That's right, Oliver. Everything you need to get ahead is right at your fingertips."

Buddy dropped the car in gear and winced as the broken exhaust pipe bellowed against the alley walls. Steering to negotiate the obstacles of crates and dumpsters, he felt Sally's familiar hand on his leg.

"Aren't you even going to say hello?"

"Oh, sorry, Sal." Buddy turned and gave her a quick peck on the lips as he pulled up to the street end of the alley. "I was just thinking about Oliver. Life could be so much easier for him if he'd just get a clue. You know what I mean?"

Sally said nothing as she eyed the heavy late-afternoon traffic and cringed at the way Buddy always nosed out of this blind alley.

22

As the airliner banked south for its final approach, the clouds scattered and the city of Seattle presented itself like a show piece. The plane had been in clouds all the way from Portland, so Norman was somewhat startled by the view. A quiet gasp fogged the window and he wiped it clear again with his sleeve.

Norman could pick out the Space Needle and the King Dome. His eyes tracked the endless grid of streets and highways teeming with the mid-day traffic. Whoever they were and wherever they were going, Norman was certain it was a thousand times more interesting than what he was doing. He was going home. His family and friends were waiting for him. It was time to resume his life among the people who knew and cared about him in Alaska. It was time to be real again. Norman Tuttle would rather eat rocks.

Going home meant going back to school with all his dorky never-been-anywhere-never-done-anything friends with their noogies and jock-strap jokes. It meant sharing a house with his demented younger siblings. It meant living under the tyranny of his parents' rules again. After a summer of being treated like a worthy and mature human being by the Flannigans, returning home meant going back to a place he could no longer abide.

Even thoughts of Laura Magruder did little to brighten his journey home. And that might be the most aggravating development of Norman's over-developing summer: His parents had banished him to Oregon to get Norman away from Laura Magruder and her bad influence. They hoped that a little distance would allow Norman to forget about her.

Being manipulated like that in the first place had Norman on a slow boil for two months, but what really had his kettle hooting lately was that it seems to have worked. He looked forward to seeing Laura again with about the same enthusiasm he anticipated his mother's meatloaf. Filling and familiar, but from Norman's aloof vantage, still a part of that same dull bill of fare that was his home.

Norman looked down at the city below and wished it belonged to him. Every face a stranger, and everything under the sun at his fingertips. Ed Flannigan had given him his last pay all in cash and Norman felt the weight of the five hundred dollars in his pocket as he came within range of the shops and malls spreading forth on the ground.

Boy, what I wouldn't do to lose myself in Seattle, Norman was thinking as his heart descended with the landing gear. He rode the plane down, unaware that boys' wishes are often granted just to spite them.

"I'm sorry, but Flight 188 has been canceled due to mechanical problems. The next flight to Anchorage will be departing at seven P.M."

Norman looked at the clock on the wall behind the ticket agent. "That's six whole hours!"

"That is correct." The agent glanced up at the long line of disgruntled passengers behind Norman. "Shall I confirm you on that flight?"

Norman nodded, handing the woman his ticket and wondering how to burn up six hours riding around on the shuttle train and escalators. Like a horse left in the corral too long, Norman had forgotten what to do when the gate is finally left open. He failed to comprehend the open range at all until the woman handed him back his ticket.

"There are regular shuttle buses to downtown if you'd like to see some sights and do some shopping." She said it with such a straight and confident face that Norman thought it sounded much like permission, if not an out and out order to do so.

"Thank you," Norman said, suddenly flush with capability. "I might do that."

Norman bought his round-trip ticket for downtown and stood in line with the other stranded passengers who sought distraction and distance from the airport. Norman, for his part, sought one thing: clothes. Real clothes. Not those things his mother ordered from J. C. Penney's, or nabbed three-for-one from the Back-to-School sale tables at Anchorage strip malls. Not the tractor-stained, high-wader jeans from his summer on the farm. Not the dusty no-name sneakers on his feet. And not the Applegate College *Fighting Pharaohs* recyclable volleyball jersey.

Norman was sixteen years old and he knew it was time he found a style. Back home in Alaska, a sharp dresser was a person who was still warm and dry at the end of the day. Norman knew it was time to move beyond cotton-wool layering and get into some clothes that made sense.

And here he was on a bus into Seattle, Washington, world head-quarters of the nasty, nerve-damaging grunge rock music scene. Fashion center for a new generation of truly hip impresarios who haven't gotten their hormones under control.

Norman gaped at the gradual build-up of the city scene on the way in from Sea-Tac Airport. Grunge rock might well be founded on the beat of a young man's heart in a situation like this. To go where no Tuttle had gone before. To go where no Tuttle had even wanted to go before. His parents would have a whale when they found out. This was great.

When the bus nudged itself into the surface traffic between the tall buildings downtown, Norman nearly swooned. The amounts of vehicles, stores, restaurants, and people were incomprehensible to a kid from The End of the Road whose biggest adventure in life to date was spending a summer on a small farm in Oregon.

Norman Tuttle was aware that his life story would not be appearing on the Discovery Channel anytime soon, but he felt things were defi-nitely looking more interesting as he was taken into the heart of the city. There were Music Lands, Leather Lands, hot tacos, Chinese and Cantonese—whatever that was—cuisine. There were five-story depart-ment stores, mega-plex movie houses, and dancing bare-naked lady places. There was more to a city block of Seattle than the entire commu-nity at The End of the Road had in its most pretentious aspirations.

Norman was swept into the pedestrian flow before he had a chance to hesitate. The swift human current dashed down the sidewalk carrying Norman with it. He brushed against buildings and parking meters. A street musician sang in his face one instant, a panhandler put an open hand in it the next. Barely aware of his legs moving, Norman let himself be swept along until he was finally deposited at the mouth of Pike Street's teeming open-air market and merchant gauntlet.

Scarcely pausing for breath, Norman plunged in. He made his way past the taunting fish mongers without temptation. He'd seen a lifetime of fish in his sixteen years in Alaska. He barely looked at the produce stands. A summer spent growing vegetables and peaches will take the luster off an apple no matter how hard it's polished.

But when Norman finally got past the edibles the merchandise began to get more inviting. There was jewelry, and leather, and tee shirts with things written on them that Norman wasn't even allowed to say. He sorted through some of these just for sport, then his eye was captured by a large silver cross on a thick black cord. The styling suggested Madonna, the Pope, and the Red Baron all dangling from the same string. It was blasphemous, ostentatious, and expensive. It was perfect.

The woman behind the table was an utter pincushion of fashion jewelry. Every hole or fold of skin on her face had a piece of hardware screwed into it. She wore fingerless black leather gloves with studs on the knuckles, and she had the complexion of a person who sleeps under a car. "That's forty-five dollars," she said skeptically.

Norman tugged at the wad in his pocket, anxious to show off his buying power. It seemed to have taken root there and when the ball of money finally cleared his pants it exploded in a shower of greenbacks. Twenty- and fifty-dollar bills scattered at Norman's feet.

Abandoning any shred of composure he had, Norman threw himself on the pavement groping for the loose bills. A passerby, unaware of what was going on, scuffed a fifty with his foot and sent it skidding out of Norman's reach. Still on his knees, Norman hustled after, but just as he was upon it, a foot came down hard on the bill stopping it dead in its tracks.

"That's mine!" Norman said to the foot.

A voice from overhead spoke calmly. "I saved it for you."

Norman looked up and met the eyes of a boy about his own age who smiled at Norman and shook his head. "Man, you really shouldn't be flashing your dough. There's bad people around this place." The boy lifted his foot and Norman recovered the money.

"Thanks." Norman stood and took a good look at his ally. The boy had long straight black hair on one side of his head. The other side of his scalp had a pattern shaved in it that looked something like a fish or a hot dog bun, maybe. His leather jacket had white paint splashed on it and a piece of steel cable draped around the collar. His tee shirt was about a foot too long and sported the image of a maniacal-looking man shrieking with his tongue hanging an impossible distance out of his face. His black jeans looked to have been removed from the victim of a car accident, and his enormous sneakers flopped wide open with the laces trailing behind them.

Norman knew a sharp dresser when he saw one and extended his hand in friendship. "I'm Norman. Norman Tuttle. I'm from Alaska."

The boy responded with a choreographed street shake losing Norman on the second twist. "My name's Tango. What are you doing here with those big Alaska bucks?"

Norman finished his transaction for the cross and put it around his neck. "I'm buying some new clothes to take home."

Tango appraised Norman's purchase and approved. "But that ain't going to keep you warm in no Alaska."

"No, I know." Norman was looking at Tango's jacket. "I want a leather coat, too."

"You do now?" Tango put a friendly arm on Norman's shoulder as the two new pals wandered away from the commotion inside the market.

"Yeah, and I want some pump-up shoes like those."

Tango stopped and looked at his own feet, feigning a little soft shoe. "Now you're talkin' big big bucks, Norman of Alaska."

"I've got almost five hundred dollars." Norman patted his roll of bills. "But I don't have much time. Where can I find this stuff around here?"

Tango narrowed his gaze at Norman, sizing him up. He appeared to think something over, then put his arm once again on Norman's shoulder. "I tell you what, Norman Tuttle. I like you, and I know a lot of people in the wholesale clothing business that like me. I get all my styles from them at half-price."

"Half-price?" Norman's first thought was that his dad would be proud of him—which was incredible considering that his father would probably not even let these clothes in the house—but Norman hadn't been swinging on all his hinges the whole day. "How can I find these friends of yours?"

Tango pulled up his sleeve to look at a watch that wasn't there and started walking again. "Well, I've got time and I'm going that way. C'mon, Norman Tuttle. You'll be glad you ran into me."

Norman fell in with Tango's jaunty gait. Tango was a real city kid and Norman was soaking up the genre. Tango carved a path down the center of the sidewalk. He seemed to enjoy bouncing shoulders with the people who passed the other way, and answered their insults with those of his own. Some good ones, too. Norman stayed silent and just tried to keep up.

They turned onto a quieter street leading down to the waterfront. Norman was relieved to be away from the crowds. "What kind of name is Tango?"

"It's the name my ga—my group gave me. It's like a stage name."

"Stage name? You're in a band?"

"Sort of." Tango seemed anxious to change the subject. "What sort of name is Tuttle?"

Norman was unimpressed by the query. "I don't know. It's my dad's name. Some dumb thing from Germany or England or someplace like that."

"Oh." Tango wasn't listening. He had his eyes locked on a graying vagrant who was polishing a parking meter with a rag. "Look at that crazy old man. These bums are making this city a bad place to live. Watch this."

As they walked by Tango reached out and roughly snatched the man's hat, a well-worn leather driving cap, and took off.

"Hey, that's my good cap."

Norman heard the man calling behind him as he ran to keep up with his confederate, not sure why. Tango darted into an alley with Norman nearly stepping on his shoelaces. "Why'd you do that?"

Tango plopped the cap on Norman's head. "Why not? It's free, man. Throw it away if you don't like it."

Tango continued down the alley and Norman followed more slowly. Tango's mean spirit had caught Norman by surprise. He pulled the hat from his head and finally looked at what he was doing.

He'd told a total stranger he had five hundred dollars in his pocket and then followed him into a dim alley of a huge city Norman didn't know from Mars. The danger in the situation dawned on him just about the time it happened to him.

Suddenly, where just moments ago were shadows and doorways, there was company. Several boys the same age as Tango, and a few older ones, were standing around him in the alley with coyote grins. In the middle of them, with the coyote-est grin of all, stood Tango. "I told you, Norman of Alaska, there's bad people around here."

It just goes to show, thought Norman, *you can't judge a man by his clothes.*

"Tuttle, Tuttle, Tuttle. Tuttle—comma—Norman—comma—Tuttle, Tuttle, Tuttle."

Norman woke to the sound of his name. A blurry silhouette of a man moved in front of him as Norman's mind tried to make reality out of a fragmented scene. His face lay against the damp bricks, and his head throbbed to a grunge rock beat. When he moved, the silhouette stopped suddenly.

"What have we here? A boy! Are you hurt?" The man squatted down and put his face right in Norman's.

Norman smelled the breath of a dog, but through his hazy vision and scrambled judgment he saw the face of his father. "Dad—help me." The words sounded muffled and far away, his tongue like fried liver.

The shadowy man pulled Norman up by his shoulders and leaned him against the wall. He took off his coat, put it behind Norman's head, and spoke in a kind voice, like a child to a troubled pet. "I'm not your dad, I'm a friend. My name is Oliver. Do you know who you are?"

Sitting upright, Norman felt his head begin to clear, and his sight returned enough to see the man from the street whom Tango had harassed. "My name in Norman. Norman Tuttle."

"Oh, what luck!" The man held up Norman's ticket envelope. "I just found these." Oliver spread the envelope to show Norman's plane ticket and the bus pass to the airport, and pointed with a grubby finger. "See, Tuttle—comma—Norman. Tuttle, Tuttle, Tuttle. What a fine name. Too good to lose."

Oliver pressed the tickets into Norman's hand, then noticed something on the ground beside him. "My hat! Oh, this is a lucky day! I thought it was gone for good."

Norman's head was fully awake now, just slightly clouded with the aching throb. He patted his empty pocket, checked for the missing necklace, and slumped against the wall again. "You didn't lose your hat. It was stolen by the same guys who took my money—Tango and his gang of friends."

"Tango." Oliver nodded sadly. "I know that bunch, and they're no friends. Bad eggs, every one of 'em. Come on, Norman Tuttle, get up off that damp ground."

Norman stood with the man's help. He seemed to be alright. Rubbing a fist-sized knot on the back of his head, he looked around the alley in awe.

"Wow. I got mugged!" Norman was impressed and partly pleased with the idea, already thinking of telling the story back home. The thought of home brought a sudden panic across his face. "What time is it?"

The older man dug deep and methodically inside his layers of clothes, finally producing a cheap pocket watch with a cracked face. "It's nearly five o'clock."

"I have to get back to the airport! I'll miss my plane!" Norman started one way down the alley then stopped and went the other, then stopped altogether. "Where is my bus? Where am I?"

"This way, Norman Tuttle." The man steered Norman by one arm toward the light end of the alley. "I know that bus. I got on it once by mistake and spent a month at the airport. Didn't like it much. Too noisy to sleep."

Norman had never been in the company of a genuine homeless person before. "Do you really sleep on the streets?"

Oliver looked at him, astonished, as they turned up the hill toward the busy intersection. "Of course not! I sleep under them! It's much safer."

Oliver was speaking literally of his home under the bridge abutment, but Norman took it as a joke and laughed. Oliver laughed too, just to be agreeable, and they continued in silence to the corner.

"Your bus should be leaving that hotel there in a few minutes. Can you make it alone, Norman Tuttle?" Oliver stood looking carefully at Norman. Watching for any unsteadiness, or an unwillingness to part ways.

"I'm alright. Thanks for your help, umm, Oliver?"

"That's right. Plain ol' Oliver." Oliver shook Norman's hand and pointed him across the street. "You go ahead. I've got more work to do, Norman Tuttle-tuttle-tuttle."

Oliver turned and walked down the street making a song of Norman's name. "Tuttle-tuttle-tuttle-tuttle—now I know a boy named Norman Tuttle."

Norman reached the other side of the street and turned to see Oliver moving slowly along, a red rag in his hand, wiping parking meters as he sang quietly to himself. Norman let out a heavy breath. Still dazed, he watched Oliver work his way down the sidewalk to eventually disappear into the press of shoppers.

In a few hours Norman would be a thousand miles away in a warm house with a loving family. Oliver would be a few blocks away sleeping in the rain with nothing to show for his good will but the name of a lost and beaten boy. Norman moved to the bus and wished there was something he could have done for this crazy old man. Something he could have given him.

23

'I'm Ed and I'm a —. Ed sat within the circle of light the fire maintained in the night and was drawn back to the circle of men at his recovery meeting the night before. "I'm a—I'm an alcoholic."

Hi, Ed.

The group sat grinning at him, and Ed wasn't sure where to go next. He couldn't believe he'd actually said it. He'd come to twenty meetings in as many days and not uttered a word, particularly not this obnoxiously repetitive greeting, the ticket of entry to any recovery group address. But somehow, having that out of the way, the rest came easier.

"I got a call today from a guy who said he was the son of an older sister I haven't seen since I was six. He's coming down tomorrow. This hit me like a big rock. I haven't talked about my sister in thirty years. I wasn't allowed to. This is all pretty weird for me and my wife and everybody. Emily didn't know I ever had a sister until now. I can't tell if she's excited or scared. I can't tell what I am. Anyway, I thought I'd take him out to the river to camp, just him and me, see if we can sort through it all. I don't know why I brought it up. Thanks for listening."

Ed looked around the circle of faces when he was done talking. They were all looking back, and they seemed to care. Ed didn't know why they cared, but it warmed him all the same. He allowed himself to relax, and he stretched in the stiff folding chair and let his thoughts drift away to what tomorrow would bring.

A log popped like a gunshot and Ed snapped back to the fire. Through the hail of sparks rising he saw the features of the face across from him and marveled again. This Webster was a Flannigan, no doubt about that.

You two could be brothers! Emily had said as she saw the two of them side by side at the farm this morning.

Emily was right. They were only eight years apart in age and their features were unmistakably turned on the same lathe. But the cut of their faces is where the similarities ended. If for every action in nature there is an equal and opposite reaction, for every Ed Flannigan there is a Webster Cummings.

The differences immediately told in the two men's postures. A fairly accurate sketch of Ed Flannigan could be drawn with a ruler. Back straight. Shoulders square. Eyes level. Webster would have to be done free-hand with a rock tied to your wrist.

Webster's shoulders fell around in front of him. They nearly formed the basket his head would fall in if it ever came loose from sticking so far out in front of him. He'd be a full two inches taller if he'd put his chest out where it belonged, and his eyes never stayed put long enough to consider anything. They skittered around like a runaway surveillance camera filming data faster than anyone could ever read it.

For a moment, Ed's eyes met with Webster's through the fire. Ed could see that his new nephew was ready to talk and he was glad. The awkward silence was about to kill them both. As Webster opened his mouth to speak, a loud crescendo of laughter and clatter came from the campsite next door. There were several people with a rusty van and three large black motorcycles having a party that had gotten progressively louder since Webster and Ed arrived.

Without a thought Ed turned to them. "Hey! Shut up! We're tryin' to talk here!"

The noise stopped like a lid had been slammed on it. There were a couple rebellious grumbles, but the commanding nature of Ed's voice did not invite any real debate. Webster shrunk down around himself like it had been him causing the trouble.

"Maybe we should go to a motel or something. We could talk over coffee in the morning."

"Don't worry about those greaseballs," Ed said. Webster had his arms wrapped around his knees and was trying to make himself as small as possible on the camp stool. His face would never leave the fire, but occasionally his eyes would venture out into the darkness and dart back.

Ed took a lucky guess. "You've never been camping before, have you, Webster?"

"Once," Webster said, "but I didn't get out of the car. My parents, well, my *adopted* parents tried to take me camping in the Berkshires when I was a boy. It didn't work."

The mention of Webster's adopted parents caused Ed to lose interest in the subject of Webster's camping experiences. "Tell me what you know about my sister."

Webster was mostly unprepared for the question. He'd come to learn more about his mother, not tell what he knew about her. But Webster also didn't know how to avoid a direct question—especially a direct question from a one-armed man who yells at drunken bikers in the dark. Webster pulled his knees closer together with his arms and spoke directly to a rock at his feet.

"I was born Webster Flannigan in Seattle on May 27, 1964, to your sister Amanda and Oliver Tuttle. They were not married at the time."

Ed listened intently as Webster outlined what he knew of Oliver and Mandy's disappearance from The End of the Road in that long-ago stifling autumn of 1963. How the shame of their families drove them out into the world to survive.

Oliver, for unknown reasons, enlisted in the Army and died. Amanda had her baby, gave it up for adoption, and vanished into an uncertain and unknown future. Webster's mother in Boston finally told him how Amanda had simply walked away one afternoon. She left a baby and a note and nothing else. She'd taken less than that.

Ed leaned forward with his hands steepled under his nose. He stared into the flames and said nothing. Webster let his eyes be captured by the fire as well, and the two surviving Flannigans sat that way for a long time.

"That's all I know," Webster finally said, not moving any part of him.

Ed's eyes seemed focused a thousand miles away. "It's funny. I can remember her not being there anymore, but I can't remember her leaving. I don't remember what her face looked like. I can't see it."

Webster concentrated on one small coal burning brighter than the others. Suddenly it exploded with a resonant pop. "What do you remember of her?"

Ed kept his attention on the fire. Blue flame squirted from the cracks in the wood. There was an invisible gap from the even blue burn to the shredded yellow flames that rolled and danced about the pile of split pine. It seemed to put a spell on Ed, as campfires often will to any who let them, and he was able to speak of things he didn't know he still knew.

"She used to read to me. She would sit on my bed and read books to me." Ed squinted in at the glistening coals. Webster leaned closer to hear him over the fire.

"She had long dark hair in a pony tail and a flannel nightgown with little round flowers on it. If I was being punished by Mom and Dad, which seemed to happen a lot, Mandy would sneak into my room and read to me in a whisper. Her eyes were full of fun."

Ed stopped and chuckled to himself. "She would pretend to point at something on the front of me and when I looked down she'd flick my nose with her finger. I could never keep from looking where she pointed."

Webster's attention remained fixed in the flames, his mind conjuring images of the girl who was his mother laughing and flicking the end of a little boy's nose. Ed sat high on his stool now, animated and expansive.

"She took me for walks on the beach. She knew the names of everything—all the plants and seaweed and shells and bugs and birds. She'd point and talk, and I'd listen and follow her in these big black rubber boots I could barely walk in.

"I don't remember the name of a single thing she pointed at, but I remember one thing she said a lot. She'd roll rocks over to show me what was underneath, or she'd squat right down in tall grass to see the little plants near the ground and she'd say, *There's more to the world than you can always see.*" Ed regarded the fire again and repeated it.

Webster's eyes were now fixed solidly on Ed. He was seeing him as the boy on the beach, with Amanda Flannigan. He felt himself in those big black boots, his arm stretched up to a warm hand and a wise adviser.

Webster was fascinated with the idea that Ed had known his mother, had spoken to her, and actually remembered things she said. He was barely in his stool now, his hands pushed his knees wide apart, and he spoke up. "What else?"

Ed continued to look into the flame that formed pictures in front of his face. He appeared to sort through them—rejecting some, smiling at others as they went by, then going back for another look.

"We went sledding one day, the whole family. I got soaking wet somehow and I was shivering and crying on the way home in the back seat of Dad's car. Dad was in a bad mood about something and said *Amanda, do something about your brother.*

"Amanda slid over and opened her coat and I climbed inside. She held me like that all the way home—our two heads coming out the top of her coat—not saying anything. Nobody said anything."

The fire in Ed's eyes died a little as he appeared to realize something. "You know, that's the last time I can remember seeing her."

The party in the next campsite flared up again with the breaking of glass and a burst of rowdy laughter. Ed looked to the sound but made no move to say anything. Webster ignored it altogether, still totally absorbed by Ed's reminiscences, still shivering in his mother's coat. "What did your parents tell you when she left?"

Ed returned to the fire for the answer. Webster watched his uncle struggle once again through the landscape of his recollections. Ed shook his head occasionally as if rejecting cuts of meat at a butcher counter. He dug his heels into the dirt around the fire, worked some phlegm up from his throat, and spit it on a rock. As it bubbled and hissed Ed's gaze narrowed and the muscles in his jaw quivered.

Webster watched the angles of Ed's face change in the firelight. As they went from the shape of concentration to that of studied anger, Webster shifted on his stool. He tried to see into Ed's eyes for some clue, but the eyes were closed. Wearily at first, then they drew tighter and became just deep slits on his face.

Ed opened his mouth to say something but instead of words coming from his lips, drops of water formed in his eyes. Ed tried to speak again and the tears dropped straight and fast, leaving two brilliant lines shining in the firelight.

The party through the dark rumbled again and Webster leaned forward, annoyed. "Did you say something, Ed?"

Ed opened his eyes and looked at his nephew, not conscious of the radiance of his own tears. "I said, when Mandy left they told me she didn't love us anymore and she wouldn't be coming home ever again. They never let me talk about her."

Ed closed his eyes to the fire and felt himself plummet into the uncharted, untouched depths inside of him. The bitter juices of a lifetime of deception and broken trust spewed out.

The party next door murmured in his ears. A bottle broke. The top to a beer can cracked and whiffed. Ed wanted a drink so badly. His body ached for it. From the bottom of a pitch-black hole anything looks like a ladder.

A loud chorus of laughter brought Ed to the world again. He turned to the noise of the party in the darkness and was about to move when an oddly familiar voice seized the night.

"Hey! Shut up! We're tryin' to talk here! Okay?"

Ed swung to face his nephew, who sat tall in his stool. Webster pitched a hard scowl at the shadowy group next door. There were a few poorly phrased insults tossed back, but no one there seemed willing to challenge the command in the voice.

Ed's eyes froze in disbelief. Webster put a hand to his mouth, not believing it either. "Well, we *were* trying to talk," he said apologetically.

Ed's face curled in at its edges and he could feel the stiff places on his cheeks where the fire had dried his tears. A low snort bubbled out and stood there between Ed and Webster. The two men looked at each other and knew what was coming.

The first good belly laugh ever to erupt had to have taken place all those millennia ago around a fire much like Ed and Webster's. That original laughter may even have been a frightening thing: Fear through the mirth. Fear even through the joy. Sometimes it happens all at once and all you can do is laugh until you cry and cry until you laugh again.

The men who looked like brothers and laughed like the originals clapped their hands on their knees and teetered on their stools and the fire burned on. Streaks of red trailed the sparks flying into the night as the hottest coals—those in the heart of the fire where nothing lasts for long—finally exploded from the heat.

24

Ed Flannigan was vaguely aware of someone watching him from the bottom of the ladder. He figured it was another person looking for the hired-hand job, and decided to ignore him for the moment. He really felt the absence of Norman around the farm, both his good help and his good company. It had been bad timing for him to leave for the start of the school year right before the harvest.

The ad Ed had put in the paper for Norman's replacement had received a tremendous response, but nobody who'd answered it so far met Ed's exacting standards. Those exacting standards pretty much boiled down to being able to speak English.

At the dinner table the night before, Emily Flannigan observed her husband's scorn for the large numbers of Latinos applying for the job, and offered her counsel.

"You're a racist pig, Ed. Give one of them a chance. Just because they can't speak English doesn't mean they're stupid, and it certainly doesn't mean they can't work. It's just picking fruit. How much is there to say?"

"It makes me nervous that I can't talk to them. And I don't know what they're saying. How do I know they're not sayin' terrible things about me when they talk so fast like that?"

Emily got up from the table, disgusted. "They probably are."

Emily had taught Ed how to tell the job hopefuls in their own language that he couldn't speak Spanish in hopes of at least leaving them with a civil explanation, but that hadn't made the process any smoother so far.

No hablo español had somehow become "No Hobble a Spaniel" by the time Ed got to it. He'd repeat it over and over, louder each time, until the befuddled applicant would throw up his hands and leave mumbling terrible things about Ed in Spanish.

Ed reached high into the uppermost branch and snagged a plump, succulent peach. He was holding it in his hand, turning it in admiration, when the person on the ground finally spoke up.

"I woulda had that tree picked and be on the next one by now."

The English startled Ed nearly as much as the sound of a woman speaking it. Ed swayed on the ladder, reaching for his balance and dropping the peach in the process. It plummeted into the agile grasp of Deirdre Decker, who snatched it out of the air with a neat smack to her palm.

As Ed made his way down the ladder Deirdre appraised the fruit in her hand. "You grow a nice peach, Stumpy."

Ed bristled and whirled to face down this insulting reference to his disability, but contained himself when he recognized Deirdre as the young woman who had bested him in the log-rolling competition after he had first arrived.

"Not you again," he said, feeling his temper cool.

Deirdre lifted the peach to her mouth and took a big, ravenous bite, the juice splashing down her chin. As she leaned forward to keep it off her shirt, Ed used the distraction to give her a quick once-over.

Deirdre's lifestyle of hard outdoor work kept her in a shape that was considerably fetching to a man's eye. She anticipated Ed's scrutiny and looked up from her peach. Deirdre trapped his examining eyes in her sharp focus, then deliberately looked Ed down and slowly up again in perfect mockery of his own leer.

Ed flushed as Deirdre took command. "My friend Miguel said you were a jerk. Your wife just told me you were a racist pig. Are you a sexist pig, too?"

"No!" Ed said, not altogether sure he wasn't.

"Then you'd have no trouble hiring a woman for this job?"

"Absolutely not!"

"Good, I'll be here when the sun comes up in the morning." Deirdre turned without waiting for a response and strolled indifferently out of the orchard.

Ed looked after her for a long time, waiting for Deirdre to turn around and receive some acknowledgment that she was in fact hired. She never did.

The next day Ed stood in the gathering light and inhaled the sweet aroma of damp soil and ripe peaches. The farm looked like a dream in the morning mist. The corn had easily outgrown his kids, and then Ed himself. The stalks were heavy with crop. The huge ripe tomatoes hung with effort, appearing to defy gravity by their weight and girth. The lettuce and cabbages flickered in the dew.

Today would be the grand opening of *Ed's Vegetables and Fruits*. Ed Junior would man the roadside stand while Ed and his hired hand harvested. The freshly painted plywood booth stood prominently at the end of the driveway with Emily's hand-lettered sign proudly hanging from the awning. Emily had wanted to call it *Flannigan Farms Organic Veggies*.

"I'd rather be stoned to death with hacky sacks," Ed had said.

"But you've grown everything organically, Ed."

"I know, but I'd rather not advertise it, okay? People might get the wrong idea."

"What, that you're a sensitive and environmentally responsible farmer?"

"Exactly." Ed had closed the discussion and insisted on *Ed's Vegetables*. Guys don't grown veggies.

"You're burnin' daylight standin' there dreamin', Stumpy."

Deirdre's voice just about put Ed on top of the vegetable stand. He stood speechless for a moment, catching up with his racing heart, then his surprised face gave way to indignation. He placed his one hand on a hip and pointed his menacing metal arm at Deirdre's face. "Listen, little girl, you better watch how you talk to people. If you ever call me *Stumpy* again I'll throw you off this farm by the scruff of your neck."

Deirdre moved to push the arm out of her face, took stock of Ed's expression, and thought better of it. Instead, she pulled herself up to her full height and peered over the top of it. "You ever call me a *little girl* again, I'll pull your ears down under your nose."

Ed's mouth was warped in frustration and disbelief. He was so mad he could spit. He felt the urge to haul off and kick dirt at her, then he caught a grip and took a breath. "Okay, we've got a deal then. Let's get to work."

Deirdre needed no instruction. She had her first wooden box harnessed and was up a ladder before Ed could even begin to tell her what to do. Instead of offering her any instruction, he stood and watched her expertly plucking the peaches from the high branches.

The first picking was a sparse one with only one in ten peaches fully ripe, and all of those in the very highest places. This pick would produce only a few peaches per tree. After a couple days the others would ripen until they could take up to three in ten, and then after another few days they could clean them up. This first picking would be tedious.

Ed had only one hand to pick with, so Deirdre filled her boxes much faster. She wasn't twice as fast, though, so she didn't gloat. Ed worked his trees and Deirdre worked hers. They watched each other closely, but if their eyes accidentally met they would simply return to their labors without expression.

As they leap-frogged through the orchard Ed moved the old pickup along the row of trees. When each box was full of the delicate ripe peaches they carefully added it to the stacks in the truck, then replaced them in their harness with an empty one. Ed Junior came out with a handcart at one point and took several boxes out to the roadside stand hoping to entice the morning commuters.

Nothing was said between Ed and Deirdre until nearly noon. The day had heated up into the nineties and there was no ignoring the sun. Deirdre changed into cut-offs behind the barn and tied her tee shirt up over her midriff. Ed took his shirt off entirely and wore it around his head like a turban. The sweat poured off them both.

At the back of the truck the two finally met and broke their silence. Ed took a giant gulp from the three-gallon plastic water can and handed it to Deirdre. She drank without hesitation and then set it down again.

Then Deirdre spoke. "You don't like me, do you?"

Ed was not fazed by the question. "I don't like the way you come on."

"You just don't like aggressive women." Deirdre was fastening another box to her harness.

Ed grabbed one himself and fumbled the straps with his clamp. "I don't like rude people. I don't care if they're men or women. If you'd been a man I think I would've punched you out by now."

"Why haven't you?" Deirdre reached over and snapped Ed's right-hand strap into place for him.

"I nearly did this morning." Ed looked at Deirdre, almost smiling.

"I know." Deirdre almost smiled back, and the two returned to the harvest.

By mid-day the heat had become intolerable, and it was almost all Ed and Deirdre could do to climb up into the last two trees. After they'd hefted their boxes onto the tall stacks in the truck bed they drained the water jug and leaned heavily on the tailgate. With a final gasp of air, Deirdre handed Ed the jug and brushed the loose hair out of her face. "Well, I'll see you in a couple days, Ed."

"Wednesday, sun-up." Ed spoke with only token authority watching Deirdre walk away and making no effort to control what his eyes followed out of the orchard.

Ed wasn't totally concentrating on the corn and tomato harvest over the next two days. The peaches were ripening at a good pace and would be ready for picking again, as scheduled. As much work as it was, Ed found himself looking forward to the second peach harvest with strange anticipation.

"How's that Deirdre working out for you?" Emily had asked one night.

"She's a good worker," was all Ed would allow himself.

"Good morning, Ed." Deirdre came around the side of the truck bed where Ed sat sipping his morning coffee. He sloshed some out of the thermos cup onto his pants leg.

"You've got a habit of sneaking up on people, don't you?"

"Did I scare you? They say that's a sign of a guilty conscience." Deirdre wore none of her confrontation of the other day. She smiled pleasantly, if not a little mischievously. Ed felt at a loss for words and looked to the trees for help.

"They're really taking off. We could fill this truck a couple times today if we get on it."

Deirdre seemed as awkward as Ed. "How's the vegetable stand doing?"

Ed lit up at the question. "Unbelievable! Emily had to stay home yesterday to help Ed Junior. We've got all the college traffic into Quartz Creek goin' one way and the mill traffic headed the other. We've been selling out of everything, and they're really asking for the peaches. You'd think people around here would be used to peaches."

"You never get used to a good peach. You just want more." Deirdre grabbed a harness out of the truck and headed for her ladder. "So, let's get some."

The sun peered through the haze of humidity hanging in the valley and watched the golden peaches disappear one by one from the orchard. Through the tops of the trees there was the occasional glint of a metal arm or the flash of damp skin as the two harvesters gathered the yield.

As the color vanished from the trees it accumulated in the hot moist air beneath the orchard's canopy where Deirdre and Ed worked quietly and quickly. The fleshy seasoned peaches lay like treasure neatly and tenderly stacked in the bed of the truck in their uniform wooden boxes.

Ed and Deirdre approached their work the same way—full throttle. There was joy to the rhythm of it for each of them, and they shared that joy in the occasional glance through the peach leaves, or the satisfied smile after a welcome gulp of water. Little was said and volumes were spoken.

Deirdre, abandoning modesty in the heat of the day and the fever of the workpace, changed into her shorts beside the truck. Ed happened to see a glimpse of her through the leaves and it may have meant nothing, but Deirdre glimpsed the glimpse and the moment was made eternal.

At the end of the day's work the truck squatted right down on its axle, loaded over Ed and Deirdre's heads literally with the fruit of their labors.

"That's a lot of peaches," Deirdre said picking the earwigs and spiders from the trees off her shirt and out of her hair. She looked up at Ed, who leaned against the truck toweling himself off with his own shirt, and she said, "Can I buy you a beer?"

Ed smiled and reached over to pick a spider from the top of Deirdre's head. "Sorry, I don't use it anymore."

Deirdre glanced at the crushed cab on the pick-up. "I heard about that. So you're giving up on drinking altogether?"

"I hope so."

"Well, if you ever change your mind . . ." Deirdre left the invitation dangling like a baited hook as she turned to go.

"I won't." Ed said it with authority, but his conviction dogged Deirdre's form out of the trees, leaving him alone with his thoughts, his appetites, and a truckload of peaches.

He watched Deirdre's canary yellow '53 Ford pick-up until it shrank from view and clanked out of earshot, and wondered how it was he never heard it coming.

Two days later, Ed worked in his tomato patch carefully placing tomatoes in cartons for the stand. The stand on the road was bringing in a thousand dollars a day. The word had spread about Ed's Vegetables and Fruits. A state patrolman stopped to warn him about people parking along the shoulder, but ended up carrying a bushel of produce back to the patrol car with him.

Ed's vegetables and fruits were first-rate. The tomatoes were as red as a dancing dress, and dangerously ripe. The sweet corn when peeled open almost cast its own light it was so healthy and yellow. The lettuce and carrots, cabbages and cauliflower all stood up and demanded to be taken home. And the peaches—the peaches needed no introduction.

People would often pull a peach from a box and bite into it before they'd think what they were doing. They would close their eyes, savoring every nuance of the sweet-tasting meat. Inevitably two more cases would be carried down the road.

Ed didn't know why his produce had turned out so well; beginner's luck, he figured. He had never grown anything more substantial than a toenail in his life, but now the process of farming became filled with mystery and magic for Ed. He came out to his vegetables and his trees each morning and felt more than pride of ownership. There was something stronger—a sense of having caused it. Possibly a taste of what God feels like some days.

But Ed's thoughts were not with God or down on the farm today. They were across the orchard peeking through the leaves of a tree at a long flowing leg. Not even the two passing days had diminished the sharpness or the impact of that image.

"Nice peaches."

Ed felt for a moment like his thoughts had been read, and he blushed as bright as his tomatoes. Then he turned to see the little man whose uncanny visits Ed had grown to expect, but never to anticipate. He stood over Ed Flannigan with his hair as white as rice paper and with eyes that could not be avoided. Ed looked into those remarkable eyes and blushed even brighter knowing that his thoughts had been read.

"Why does everybody have to sneak up on a person around here?" Ed stood and looked down at his odd little friend.

"The best and worst things happen when you least expect them."

Ed smiled, always glad to see him. "Which are you?"

True to form, the man tangled his white eyebrows together in thought and ignored the question. "Your peaches will all be ready to pick tomorrow."

"I know." The thought of another long day in the orchard with Deirdre had not left his head since dawn.

"You've got some beautiful peaches there."

"I got lucky."

"Yes, you did, but you don't know how lucky, and you don't know how beautiful they really are. And I came to tell you that you shouldn't know."

Ed Flannigan's blank expression begged for more.

The little man turned toward the orchard. "Somewhere in there is a magnificent peach. The best of your crop. When you see that peach you are going to want it. You're going to want to pop it right in your mouth and swallow it down." The man turned back to Ed, looked at him for several heartbeats, then cocked an eyebrow over one eye. "Don't do it."

"Don't do what?" Ed felt accused of something he wasn't even sure he understood.

"Don't eat that peach. Leave it. You need to wonder what that one tastes like. That wonder will keep the orchard alive for you year after year. Once you taste it, it's just a peach. You understand?"

"No," Ed said.

"Get some more help. You'll have to pick the whole thing clean tomorrow, and it's more than you can handle alone."

"I won't be alone."

The little man nodded his head. "That's what you can't handle."

Ed stood in the spare morning light and marveled at the orchard emerging from the night and sweeping into view. The trees appeared to curtsy, the branches slung low with the weight of thriving fruit.

"My God, they're beautiful."

The sound of Deirdre's voice neither startled nor distracted Ed. He stood looking at his orchard saying nothing. Simply admiring it and gauging the work ahead. Deirdre walked up to the nearest tree and plucked a peach from the lowest branch. The branch moved slowly up and down, searching for its balance again as Deirdre returned to Ed with the peach.

"Have you ever seen one so perfect?" Deirdre presented the peach in her open palm, but Ed did not receive it.

"There's lots of nice peaches here," he said.

"Not like this one." Deirdre pulled the peach to her mouth and bit into it. She kept her eyes on Ed, and he felt her pleasure as she tasted the sweetness of it.

Again she held the peach out to Ed to share. "Maybe it's just because I skipped breakfast, but I tell you, Ed Flannigan, I've never tasted a peach this good. Try it."

Ed looked at the fruit before him. Its orange radiance and the rich yellow hue seemed like the only thing of color in the dim black-and-white dawn. Ed looked at Deirdre's hopeful face and felt his hand rising to the peach. It was the most magnificent piece of fruit he'd ever seen.

"Buenos dias, Señor Ed." The sound of the voice and the three approaching figures startled Deirdre and the peach fell to the ground between her and Ed.

"Miguel!" Deirdre recognized her old tree-planting friend as he walked out of the shadows. "What are you doing here?"

"They came to pick peaches," Ed said bending to the fallen one at his feet. He glanced briefly at the peach which was now furry with dirt and dried bits of leaf, then side-armed it into the tall grass at the end of the orchard. Deirdre looked after the peach for a moment, then to Ed.

Ed could not quite conceal the depths of his appetite or emptiness it held before he turned his eyes toward the orchard and walked inside the brightening shadows between the trees.

"Deirdre, tell these guys where they can find the ladders. We've got a lot of peaches to pick."

25

"Progressive absentmindedness," her husband had been saying on the phone the night before.

"What? I'm sorry, Richard, I was drifting." It was getting harder and harder for Katherine to keep her mind on Richard's transcontinental pregnancy lectures.

Richard, for his part, was ultimately patient and understanding. "I said, you should beware of this progressive absentmindedness I've been reading about. Have you been particularly forgetful, or noticed any difficulty concentrating lately?"

"I don't think so," Katherine had said looking at the kitchen curtains. *They need washing,* she thought.

"How about nesting? Are you doing any nest-building types of things?"

"I'm not a bird, Richard, I'm an advertising executive. And advertising executives, pregnant or otherwise, don't build nests."

"Just curious." Richard took some notes on his end of the line. He was fascinated with the psychology of pregnant women. Even though he had taken on all the classic *nesting* or home-preparation responsibilities himself, the books he'd been reading had him convinced Katherine would be experiencing many of these things in spite of herself.

"I told you, Richard, all I'm concentrating on right now is the Bramble account. If I bring in Bramble, I'll be vice-president before my first contraction." Katherine looked at the clock on the stove: *nine o'clock.* "Richard, I have to go. If I don't get to bed, I'll be wasted in the morning."

"It's awfully early, Pumpkin. Aren't you sleeping well?"

"Sleep is a theory at this point, Richard. My bladder is the size of a grape. Watching a Pepsi commercial on TV is enough to send me to the bathroom."

Katherine stretched herself in the chair and rubbed her extended middle. "And by the way, Richard. If you call me Pumpkin one more time, I'm getting an unlisted phone number."

"At least you haven't lost your sense of humor. You go to beddy-bye now, and Daddy will call you again tomorrow."

"Good night, Richard." Katherine let her cellular phone fall back into her briefcase on the table.

She drew a manilla folder from a flap in the case and opened it. It was an eighteen-month cost projection of the Bramble account. Just as she was lowering herself into its intoxicating grip she felt a sharp pain in the arch of her foot.

She bent to rub it, but couldn't reach that particular extremity over her newest extremity and leaned over to one side. As she did, she noticed the bathroom light reflecting off the vinyl flooring and saw it needed waxing. *I'm out of Mop n' Glo,* she remembered, and pulled out her organizer to make a note.

Katherine closed the briefcase on the open cost report, then headed for her bedroom massaging the small of her back with both hands. She stopped to straighten a picture in the hallway, mumbling to herself. "Nesting. Absentmindedness. Give me a break."

Katherine rolled herself into bed and began arranging her pillows. This was becoming a fifteen-minute nightly ritual. She had two pillows between her knees, one under the baby, one behind her, and two for her head. That would be comfortable for about ten minutes and then she'd have to put the harder pillow behind her back and lay her head on the softer one, eliminate one of the knee pillows and stuff it under her belly. This would be okay for twenty minutes or so, then she'd have to pee.

The night rattled past in a series of fragmented dreamscapes alternating between suffocation and clear images of being a whale lost at sea. Katherine looked forward to the morning knowing she could stand up and stretch. Then she would spend her entire day wishing she could lay down again.

Katherine hurried down the stairs to the parking garage as fast as her condition would allow her. The door at the bottom of the stairs opened and she shuddered at the sight of her next-door neighbor, Mrs. Freeland. *Uh-oh,* she thought. *Here it comes again.*

"Oooooohhh. Theeere you arrre. You shouldn't be running up and down the stairs. You'll upset your baby." The elderly Mrs. Freeland put both her hands on Katherine's baby without any acknowledgment that it was still inside Katherine.

"I don't have a baby to upset yet, Mrs. Freeland. And I'm late for work." Katherine gave her neighbor a pinched smile as she continued past, Mrs. Freeland's words echoing through the stairwell.

"You'll really have your work cut out for you in a few weeks. You just wait and see."

Katherine growled as she entered the garage. This woman made her crazy. Once Katherine had begun to display her advancing pregnancy, Mrs. Freeland had taken a proprietary interest in her.

She was a widow and a card-carrying alumna of the *Old School*. The school that taught us women had the babies, men had the jobs, and the Americans won the war because of it.

"What's your first name, Mrs. Freeland?" Katherine had once asked to distract the conversation away from childbearing for an instant.

"Oh, how rude of me," the woman had replied extending her hand. "I'm Mrs. Andrew Freeland. I'm a widow."

A woman who thinks her name is Mrs. Andrew is destined to get on the wrong side of a woman like Katherine Bedinger-Hoople who negotiated the terms of her own marriage contract.

Between her husband Richard, with his nightly lectures from New York, her neighbor with her endless pregnancy prattle, and every second person she met—from the security guard to her hair stylist—Katherine was absolutely filled to the gills with baby talk. She felt the advice building inside her like retained water, and like her weight, she was bound and determined to ignore it.

You'll really have your work cut out for you in a few weeks. Forgetfulness. Nesting. Get me out of here!

On the way out of the garage Katherine noticed that the old clothes she'd left beside the trashcans the day before were gone. Two nights ago she'd gotten the impulse to sort through her closet and throw out all her old clothes. None of the clothes were all *that* old and they were much too good to throw away, so she'd packed them down to the trashcans in hopes someone in need might find them.

Who there might be in need, in a four-thousand-dollar-a-month apartment complex, was unclear, but it had made perfect sense to Katherine that night. Right now the only thing that made sense was getting back to her natural habitat. Katherine breathed a sigh of relief as she pulled out of the parking ramp into traffic and the smog-shrouded, workaday world of Los Angeles.

Senior Account Supervisor Katherine Bedinger-Hoople braced herself for the walk past the Accounting department. The elevator doors opened and a dozen faces, perpetually frozen in knowing smiles, turned on her. The women in Accounting were the worst. It was like having an entire room full of Mrs. Freelands.

Denise, the payroll clerk, always spoke first. "You haven't had that baby yet?" Denise had been saying this every single morning for a month and Katherine fantasized about pulling an Uzi out from under her maternity jumper to put an end to it.

Eileen in Payables, with four children of her own, would peer over her divider and nod. "You're carrying pretty low. It's going to be a girl. You wait and see."

Amy, the expense account auditor with one monster of a two-year-old at home, would sit at her desk looking gray and ominous. "You think this is bad, wait until next month."

Motherhood courts misery and Katherine could hear the women of Accounting recounting their birthing nightmares long after she'd gone by.

I was in labor for thirty-six hours.

That's nothing—I had a forty-hour labor, then a c-section.

I had a "c" with my first, and had my second one at home. They said it couldn't be done.

Katherine's daily gauntlet through Accounting added a whole new dimension to the term *morning sickness,* and her condescending male counterparts in Management were the final straw.

The men would greet Katherine with these saccharine smiles, heads tilted in adoration, then they'd pull a chair out for her to sit in. "How are you *feeling?*" they'd say, as if they really wanted to know.

If she was on one of their cases over the way an account was being handled, which was quite regularly, they would dismiss her crankiness as part of her condition.

Before she was pregnant they dismissed Katherine's crankiness as PMS. It infuriated her beyond words that it never occurred to these men she might be angry because they didn't know what they were doing. To Katherine they were just a gang of incompetent schmooze captains whose only job skills were sucking up to their immediate supervisors.

Katherine's immediate supervisor was the company president in New York. She wasn't required to please anybody, and she didn't. She did her job, and she did it well. PMS, pregnancy, or Armageddon itself could not keep her from doing her job.

"We've got to lock this Bramble account up tomorrow. We'll present our marketing strategy and cost analysis at the nine o'clock meeting." Katherine paced back and forth in front of the window in the executive boardroom.

It had always been her strategy at meetings to keep moving. It commanded everyone's attention, and if she remained in front of the windows it kept her in silhouette—lending an empowering presence to her authority.

But that was before her silhouette resembled Orson Welles in his easy chair. Also, her pacing was less the pensive movements of a secured commander than it was a sort of authoritative waddle. Mother Goose with an attitude.

Katherine looked at the half-dozen young men who sat trying to keep their attention on her face and off of her outline. She could see they were not taking her totally seriously. Men thought pregnant women were precious, adorable—entertaining even—but certainly not intimidating. Katherine wouldn't have it.

"I'll be frank with you, gentlemen. I want this Bramble account more than I want anything in the world right now. I'll make this simple for you. . . ." Katherine spread her fingers in ten points on the table and leaned in over the group for emphasis, nearly tipping over the creative director's coffee with her substantial frontage in the process.

She ignored the small commotion of scrambling hands and continued. ". . . If we get Bramble, I get the VP job back in New York, and one of you takes my place."

This kind of candor was rare and unsettling in the world of advertising. The men shifted in their chairs, some cleared their throats, and all groped for a place to focus their attention besides on each other. They finally and unanimously settled on staring at the most prominent feature in the room, which was Katherine's belly resting on the end of the conference table.

"You all know what you have to do, and you've got until five o'clock to do it."

Katherine's lieutenants scrambled out of the room as she stood smiling after them. She loved her job, and as soon as she finished eating the rest of the donuts, she was going to do it.

It was a long day of number crunching, concept testing, and best guessing. One by one the department heads had brought their finished reports, story boards, and sketches to Katherine. She'd chided them, praised them, picked lint off their sweaters, and by six o'clock she was dragging the weight of the presentation up the stairs from the parking garage.

Mrs. Andrew Freeland stood at the top of the stairs clucking her tongue. Katherine braced for her with a vacant smile and a preemptive strike. "I know, Mrs. Freeland, I shouldn't be carrying this heavy case in my condition."

The older woman reached for Katherine's load and helped her lug it down the hall. When she spoke she sounded changed, almost sad. "It's not my place to tell you what to do. You'll just be the kind of mother you are. Nobody can tell you very much at this point. You're all on instincts now." It wasn't meant to be a put-down, but when the apartment door closed behind her, Katherine suddenly felt lower than her fallen arches.

Mrs. Freeland had incidentally hit upon Katherine's chief concern over her pregnancy—she didn't think she had any instincts for motherhood at all. This thing growing in her belly felt more like a science project than anything else. Her husband had made all the preparations in New York. The nursery, the nanny, the pre-school tutor all waited back there.

Richard had taken care of everything. All she'd accomplished on her own was to grow fat, and tired, and miserable. *Having the baby,* to Katherine, was more about not being pregnant any more than it was bringing a human being into the world.

Every time the baby kicked Katherine thought they could both use a little more room to breathe. Motherhood was for the Mrs. Freelands of the world. Katherine had more important things on her mind.

Katherine was surrounded by the women in Accounting. They were all pointing and screaming obscenities at her in impossibly high, squeaky voices. Mrs. Freeland stepped forward out of the group with an Uzi and took aim as the women taunted and shrieked.

Katherine woke up, confused, her cellular phone beeping right beside her ear. She'd fallen asleep with her head in the open briefcase. As she unfolded the phone she could see the make-up image of her own face smeared on the Bramble project file.

"Hello?"

"Hi, Pumpkin, it's Daddy. Were you asleep already?"

"Um—no, I just had my face in some work." Katherine began gathering up the paperwork and piling it into the large case. Noticing the time, she spoke before her husband had a chance to build any momentum with his nightly epic prenatal nattering. "Richard, it's after ten o'clock and I've got the Bramble presentation first thing tomorrow. I really have to go to bed."

"Alrighty, you're the mommy, you know what's best. Nighty-night. Don't let the bed bugs . . ." Katherine hung up before she threw up. If Richard didn't stop reading children's books, she was never going to be able to live with him again.

Katherine set the case down next to the front door where she wouldn't forget it in the morning. She went to the refrigerator for a last bite of leftover take-out Szechuan and a Dove bar, fought back an urge to defrost the freezer—and dragged herself to bed.

She was surrounded by soft white clouds, and all around her tiny yellow flowers fell making the sounds of bells and harps when they landed at her feet. Off through the falling flowers sat Katherine's mother cradling a bundle in her arms and beckoning her to come see. Katherine padded barefoot through the flowers; the sound of bells got louder as she reached out for her mother's hand.

The sun coming in the bedroom window blinded her as soon as she opened her eyes. The doorbell was ringing.

"Who is that at this time of the morning?" Katherine searched around the room for her clock realizing she didn't know what time of morning this was for sure. The clock read eight-thirty and Katherine felt relief. "Thank God, I finally got a decent night's sleep."

She answered the door in her housecoat and was surprised to see Mrs. Freeland standing there with a bundle in her arms. "Oh, I didn't think I'd wake you! I know you usually leave about this time, and I had a little something I wanted to give you and the baby."

Katherine allowed herself a glance at the bundle. It looked vaguely familiar to her, but she was still too groggy to comprehend. "It's alright. I slept in. Please come in."

Mrs. Freeland crossed to the kitchen table and held the bundle in her lap excitedly. "You're going to love this," she said, beckoning with a hand to Katherine.

Katherine came closer and Mrs. Freeland let the bundle unfold down her legs and onto the floor. It was a beautifully stitched, brightly colored baby quilt made with what Katherine recognized as her own old clothes.

"I saw you put these out the other night and had the idea. I did this for all my daughters and, well, I'm just an old lady with nothing to do."

Katherine stood, speechless. She took one corner of the quilt and tried to say something. She recognized her old jeans, and her favorite blouse that had gotten red wine on the front, and her friendly old walking shorts that had worn too thin in the stern.

All were cut into perfect little shapes, pieced together, and bordered in such a way that Katherine was powerless before it. She held it up to her cheek and the words gushed out of her before she knew what she was saying. "It's so *cute!*"

"I just knew you'd like it. All my girls did." Mrs. Freeland sat in victory at the table as Katherine spent a few moments appreciating the work in the quilt.

"This is so nice, thank you. Can I make you some coffee?"

"Oh, I know you're very busy. I don't want to keep you from your important things."

Katherine crossed the kitchen to the coffee maker. "Nonsense. There's nothing that important going on." She laid the quilt down on the heavy black case by the door and began filling the coffee pot with a little chuckle. "Unless I'm forgetting something. I sure have been feeling spacy lately."

"Oh, that's natural." Mrs. Freeland leaned into the table, warming to the conversation at hand. "Everything from here on in comes pretty natural if you let it."

Katherine let her weight rest against the counter as the water climbed up the pot and the sun filled the kitchen. She'd awakened with the sense that this was going to be an important day. She was glad she'd slept so well. She hadn't felt this good in the morning in a long time.

26

Anthony leaned into the aisle to see out the front of the bus. Indiana unfolded before him like a dream; he recognized everything he laid eyes on knowing he'd experienced it before. It was all exactly as it should be. In Indiana everything is in its place, and that's the nice thing about it.

Anthony checked his watch. If there were no more delays they would make Booder before six. Big O Drugstore would still be open and Melinda would be working. He pictured her behind the counter, pricing lipsticks and Baby Wipes with the labeling machine. She wouldn't see him come in, and he'd stand there watching her for a minute before going to tell her he was home.

Anthony remained leaning into the aisle, his elbows on his knees and his eyes down the road, urging the bus along with every bit of will he had.

The ride through the mountains early the night before had been uncomfortable. A large man in a cowboy hat boarded in Pendleton and made himself at home beside Anthony. He took out a paperback, plugged himself into a Walkman, and fell sound asleep. Every time the bus swept to the right on the winding mountain route, the man would lean dangerously out into the aisle. Anthony felt obliged to salvage him by clutching his jacket sleeve.

Whenever it lurched left Anthony would be pressed helplessly into the window with the full weight of the stranger. On one particularly sharp turn the view out of Anthony's window was of a thousand feet of thin air and a dry craggy river bed. The force of the man leaning against Anthony felt as if he was punching him right through the side of the bus.

Anthony mustered all the strength he had and heaved against the snoozing dead-weight just as the bus followed the mountain switchback to the right. The combined forces pitched the man out into the aisle where he knocked his face on an armrest.

The resulting shiner doubled in size approximately every thirty miles, and the man's good humor diminished proportionally. Every time he turned his face to Anthony, he looked meaner and uglier. If the cowboy hadn't left the bus in Cheyenne, Anthony surely would have.

Anthony was grateful for the flatlands—the long straight roads that made sense and behaved themselves. Once they got to Nebraska, the bus pointed straight at the rising sun and didn't turn away again. You could never tell which way you were going in the mountains. Mountains were much more trouble than they were worth by Anthony's estimation, and so was everything on the other side of them.

Four days ago Anthony had stepped off the bus in Quartz Creek. His sister Deirdre walked up behind him and slapped him on the back hard enough to cut his wind off for a moment.

"Hey, Big Brother."

Anthony sucked for breath and turned to face his sister for the first time in seven years. He hardly recognized her. The pale, sullen, barely-a-woman sister who'd torn through Ray's service station on the back of a chopped Harley was gone. The last thing Anthony remembered her saying was *Goodbye and good riddance to you and this whole sorry place.* Then her boyfriend had gunned the throttle and off they roared—all leather and indignation—on their way west.

Now, here she stood—a solid, brown, straight-up-and-down woman—and she was smiling at him.

"Hi, Deirdre. You've really changed." Anthony awkwardly held out a hand. Deirdre pushed it aside and stepped forward.

"Hi, Anthony," she spoke over his shoulder as she held him stiffly. "You haven't changed at all."

Since Anthony had only given a few days' notice of his arrival,

Deirdre had other commitments. "I'm helping a neighbor jerk the dead trees out of his peach orchard this week. You're welcome to hang around and help us, or you can take the truck and explore if you want."

Explore—the word scared Anthony nearly as much as the dilapidated old truck did. Deirdre's classic '53 Ford had a striking canary yellow paint job. Besides the paint job, nothing seemed to be holding the rig together except Deirdre's good faith—a faith which her brother could not embrace.

Everything that was supposed to be in the dashboard was either dangling out of it or stuffed under what was left of the seat. The gear pattern on the transmission was just about out of reach. Second gear was two feet south of first and reverse was over near where the glove box used to be. The stick shift knob constantly unscrewed itself from the vibration of the four mismatched tires.

Deirdre's hands were a blur of activity: tightening the gear knob one instant, checking the ignition wire the next. Reaching to pull her door closed again after a turn as casually as some people turn off their blinkers.

As Deirdre wove her way confidently through the rolling hills and down between the orchards Anthony knew he was on totally foreign ground. He pulled his arms across himself and sank quietly into the bare springs.

It wasn't supposed to be like this. The roads went every which way. He couldn't identify a tenth of what grew along the road: manzanita, madrone, ponderosa, holly. People's houses weren't lined up evenly with the road; they were turned any way they wanted them. There'd be a flat place with farms and fields in it and then it would get all hilly and broken up again. You couldn't really see from one place to the next. It was weird. Even the license plates looked funny. Not like Indiana plates at all.

Whatever Anthony's visions of the West might have been, the scenes going by the cracked windshield matched none of them. It was plain to see that going Out West was a whole lot different from being Out West. Going there was a great idea; being there was weird.

Deirdre took a sudden right at a plywood produce stand labeled *Ed's Fruits and Vegetables*. "This is the job. I gotta finish out the day. You can stay or leave. Up to you."

The time was just past noon and Anthony became anxious. "Aren't we going to eat somewhere?"

Deirdre swung the truck in behind the vegetable stand and killed the engine with the clutch. "The best lunch in the valley's right here. Sun-ripe tomatoes and carrots, chased by the sweetest peaches you ever tasted."

Anthony wore his opinion on his wrinkled nose as they went to the back of the stand. "I don't usually eat a lot of vegetables and stuff."

Deirdre looked at her brother, slightly inflamed. "Vegetables and *stuff*. What do you mean? What do you eat?"

Anthony was not the slightest bit defensive with his answer. "Well, usually I walk over to the Quick Trip across from the garage and eat a microwave ham and cheese with a Big Slurp. That's real good. At home I eat Hungry Man dinners mostly. Salisbury steak is my favorite, but I never eat the vegetables in 'em."

Deirdre looked at her brother in amazement, then handed him a tomato. "There's a 7-11 ten miles down the road, or you can eat this. Be careful. It's fresh and it's organic. It might be a shock to your system."

Deirdre said hello to Ed Flannigan's son, who was minding the stand, but she didn't introduce him to Anthony. "Where's your dad?"

"In the orchard with Miguel," the boy said without looking up from his Gameboy.

Deirdre grabbed a tomato and a peach for herself, and strode through the door. Anthony followed uncertainly behind feeling about as welcome as a sore foot.

Deirdre led him toward a commotion happening on the other side of the orchard. There was the roar of a sick motor and the squealing of metal on metal, some unintelligible cursing—then a lull, which Deirdre and Anthony walked into.

Deirdre saw that Ed Flannigan had just pulled another dead tree down with his tractor. Miguel was chopping the last of the roots free of the dirt so they could cut up the tree and add the stump to the smoldering pile beyond them.

Anthony saw a very bizarre scene. A one-armed man with no shirt was at the controls of a rusted old tractor that made more noise than Judgment Day. A dark-skinned man in a straw hat hacked savagely at a tree root, taunting it the entire time in some strange tongue.

Ed shut the tractor off when he saw Deirdre, and the dark-skinned man removed his hat. "Hey, Miguel, our good helper's back and she's brought reinforcements."

Ed jumped off the tractor and joined Miguel, who moved away from the root wad and approached with the axe still in his hand. Anthony saw the metal clamp on the end of Ed's artificial limb working open and closed as the edge of the other man's axe glinted in the sun. He couldn't help but slide behind Deirdre as she tried to introduce him.

"Ed, this is my brother, Anthony."

Ed stuck his left hand out beside Deirdre. She stepped aside and Anthony stood facing Ed and his extended hand. Anthony, confused and hesitant over shaking left-handed, undershot the mark and ended up grasping just Ed's fingers. It felt feeble and unsatisfying for them both, so Ed tried to make up for it by clapping Anthony on the shoulder when they were through.

"Nice to see you, Anthony."

The nudge caught Anthony by surprise and rocked him off his planted heels, sending him a half-step sideways. "Pleased to meet you, too," he said, wondering why everybody Out West kept hitting him.

"And this is Miguel," Deirdre continued, inviting Miguel forward with her hand. Miguel smiled broadly as he tipped his hat. "Buenos dias, Señor."

Anthony didn't know what to do with his hands since none was offered him, so he leaned forward and spoke too loudly, "NICE-TO-MEET-YOU."

"He's Mexican, not deaf." Deirdre had finished eating her peach. She whipped the pit into the burning pile of stumps and slash, then pulled a pair of worn work gloves from her back pocket. "I've got work to do. You can help, you can watch, or you can go."

Ed returned to the tractor while Deirdre unhooked a steel cable from the uprooted tree. Anthony watched as she dragged the heavy cable toward another dead standing tree with the tractor dogging her heels. Miguel started a chainsaw and began bucking up the heavier branches and the trunk of the tree into firewood size.

Anthony felt excluded by the barrier of sound that came from all the commotion. He stood in the hot mid-day sun, his stomach growling loud enough to be heard over the chainsaw, and wondered why Deirdre was still so angry.

The Deirdre he saw throwing a cable strap around the tree in front of him was the same little sister in the ponytail who would open her bedroom door when she heard Anthony walking by just to tell him he could not come into her room.

"But I don't want to come in your room," he'd say.

"You do, too!" Deirdre would scrunch up her little mouth, flip her ponytail as she turned, and slam the door in his face.

Anthony watched the cable tightening. The top of the doomed tree swooned and shook. Ed gunned the engine and through the clamor Anthony could hear the roots tearing and popping under the ground. He could feel it through his shoes and the sensation carried up through his legs and into his chest, where it seemed to tug on his own heart.

There was a last yielding crack and the tree toppled over. All resistance was gone as the tree moved away from the hole, any connections with the ground severed. All that was left of its former self was a big empty place in the orchard. In this empty place stood his sister watching the tree skidding behind the tractor. It left a trail of straight lines in the dirt where the broken roots dragged their feet.

Anthony watched Ed pull the tree over to the Mexican man and his chainsaw. Putting his hands in his pockets, Anthony kicked at a shriveled peach at his feet. Suddenly Deirdre was standing on his short shadow speaking his thoughts. "Anthony, what are you doing here, anyway?"

Anthony looked at her, and to the hole in the ground, and to the two men disassembling trees, and back to Deirdre again. "I guess I don't really know."

Deirdre scrunched up her face. "You do, too!" she said spinning in the dirt, and Anthony could have sworn he heard a door slam.

Coming up the eastern side of the Rockies on the way to see Deirdre, Anthony's heart raced with the thrill of it. This was Out West. Incredible. The familiar plains and their endless crops gave way quickly to rocks and scrub brush, leaning pines and lean livestock. It was like nothing Anthony had ever seen.

The bus began to sway back and forth as it wound up the steepening grade, dropping to lower and lower gears until the engine settled into one high determined groan to the crest.

As the bus started down from the summit it picked up speed and descended into a bank of fog. Anthony's first sensations of the West included only the solid white line flying by the side of the bus, the mist floating past, and the sound of the driver grabbing another gear.

Anthony rode the bus like a passenger on an amusement park roller coaster that had reached its highest vantage. The real ride was just beginning. It's the place where everybody screams and wishes they hadn't come.

Out West was where he was supposed to be. Anthony had been telling people that since he could remember. Booder, Indiana, was a point on the way West. He'd killed about all the time he could there, and it was starting to look pretty bad.

First his little sister Deirdre had beat him to the West by about seven years. That didn't look good, being that he had a year headstart on her. But what really took the cake was when his going-nowhere-special-today-thank-you parents packed up and went West.

Reading his mom and dad's reports from the big country Out West put Anthony over the proverbial edge. His friends and neighbors around Booder knew what was going on, and they'd ask Anthony about it.

Dirk Miller, his neighbor, wanted to see all the postcards his folks sent him. "You're a lucky man, Anthony Decker," he'd say and curse his small life among the beanfields of Booder.

What finally sent Anthony for the bus ticket, though, was Melinda at Big O Drugs. Anthony had gone in during his lunch break one day. As usual, he feigned interest in the toenail clipper keychains next to the register hoping Melinda might notice him and marry him and have his children or something.

"I hear you're heading Out West pretty soon," she spoke matter-of-factly while straightening a container of ten-cent pocket combs.

"Yes, that's right," Anthony answered, not wanting to appear in any way contrary.

"That's exciting."

"Yes," he said, infinitely more excited about the conversation than with what the conversation was about.

"When are you going?"

"I'm not sure, I have to check with Ray for some time off first—go see my sister in Oregon—check it out, you know. Then come back for my stuff."

Then the young woman behind the counter had done a remarkable thing. She put the container of combs aside, leaned forward onto the counter letting her face into her hands, and smiled at Anthony. It was a smile like he hadn't seen in the whole five years she'd been working there—not through probably six hundred superfluous purchases of nail clippers, pocket combs, or Tic Tacs.

"We're going to miss you around here," she said. As simple as that.

"Well," Anthony had intoned courageously, "a guy's gotta do what he's gotta do."

"I'm happy for you," Melinda said. "I can't wait to hear all about it when you come back."

"It'll be quite a story by the time this trip is done." Anthony edged himself toward the door. Melinda looked after him with her smile mounted between her hands like a trophy.

Anthony trotted down the hot summer sidewalks of Booder, Indiana, already imagining the stories he would tell. He turned into the Quick Trip for a ham-and-cheese sandwich, a Big Slurp, and a bus schedule—not realizing how often these kinds of stories end exactly where they begin.

Seeing the Manhattan skyline for the first time excites a delightful mix of nerves and comfort. There is something unsettling in the dense concentration of human beings settled there, yet there is consolation by how surprisingly familiar it all seems. Probably the most filmed, photographed, and talked about place on Earth, New York City feels like destiny at first glance. And for some people, it is.

There was a tense calm in the cab of the Road Ranger rolling steadily toward the west end of the Lincoln Tunnel. The traffic around New York City flows into it the way a bathtub empties: The closer one got to the drain, the faster the water moved, and the more turbulent it became. Lloyd and Evelyn, negotiating the white-water rapids of Highway 495, silently accepted the gravitational forces of the city.

Evelyn gripped the knitting in her hands and pulled her knees together as if making room for the determined cars and trucks joining the river of eastbound traffic and squeezing dangerously close in beside them. She checked on her husband at the wheel—his face was tight, beads of sweat formed on his temples.

"How are you doing, Pop?"

"Fine. I'm fine." Lloyd straightened and put a game smile across his distress. "You got some more of those antacids on you? I keep tasting that tunafish salad of yours."

Evelyn dug in the console and produced a cellophane pack holding two tablets. "You've had indigestion ever since Ohio. Are you sure you're okay?"

"I've been eating your tunafish since Ohio." Lloyd took the tablets and several deep breaths.

Evelyn did not like the feel of any of this. She'd been feeding Lloyd tunafish for half a century and he never minded it. She tried to get Lloyd to see their old family doctor when they passed by Avalon, but he wouldn't hear of it. *The old coot's half-dead himself. There's nothing wrong with me that won't kill him first. We gotta get to the Big Apple before some lunatic blows it up.*

Lloyd had been this way since Montana—this urgency about things, especially getting to New York—and a single-mindedness that was totally unlike him. Evelyn had always been fifty percent of every decision the Deckers ever made, but her stock had seemed to fall.

"One dirty cowboy mentions New York and you have to drop everything and go. Thank goodness he didn't say anything about Timbuktu!"

"He wasn't dirty."

"He was filthy! Disgusting! Tobacco juice and whiskey all over him. Honestly, Lloyd, I still can't believe you took coffee with the man."

Lloyd reached out to the can of snoose on the console between them and patted it like the butt of a loaded gun.

"Lloyd Decker, don't you dare!"

Lloyd had laughed and Evelyn had eventually caved in to the idea of New York.

Evelyn had called her nephew Richard in New York to tell him they were coming. Richard told her not to even think of bringing the motor home into Manhattan, "Find a convenient place outside of the city, then take the train in."

"Where would be convenient?" she'd asked.

In all seriousness Richard had told her, "New Jersey would be good. Pennsylvania would be even better."

But Lloyd would have no part of it. Studying a map of Manhattan one night in a campground not fifty miles from their hometown, he'd made up his mind.

"We've driven this road barn through every kind of wilderness and wayside. I'm not leaving it behind on account of one nervous travel agent. Besides, look—there's this Central Park right in the middle of New York. There's gotta be an RV camp in there somewhere."

Evelyn's anxiety built as they plunged under the Hudson River into the deafening roar of the Lincoln Tunnel. It doubled again as they emerged into the light of day and the perilous concrete-and-glass gorges of New York City. Evelyn grew deadly serious and studied the map in her hands.

"You'll need to take a left on Eighth Avenue, so get over." The urgency in her voice confirmed for Lloyd that missing your turn in New York City was probably a fatal mistake. There was no such thing as just finding the next driveway and turning around in Manhattan. The next driveway was in Connecticut—if they made it that far.

The traffic in New York moves slow but with an eerie precision, the cars like stealthy predators. They move in packs, signaling each other like bats with blasts of their horns. A short blast simply means *See me*. A long blast: *Look at me, you idiot!* Silence is deadly on the streets of New York. The town feeds on the weak and the sick, ravages the naive, and scorns the well-intended.

Lloyd had the quarry's sense of predicament. Abandoning all humility, he nosed out into the intersection against the light to make his turn. The traffic cop on the corner froze. The whistle in his lips grew silent and fell to his chest, dangling from a leather cord. His eyes filled with the dubious profile of the powder-blue power cottage that rolled through his domain.

He trained his official scrutiny on the collapsible television aerial, the red-and-white striped rolled awning, the matching lawn chairs secured to the rear ladder with bungee cords next to the hand-lettered spare tire shroud proudly declaring *Spending Our Children's Inheritance*. And he did what any conscientious Manhattan street cop would do. He threw his hands to his knees and laughed so hard his hat fell off.

"Boy, he's sure in a good mood," Lloyd said, relieved to see the long straight boulevard that lay before them. The buildings stood in orderly rows and the cross streets interrupted in predictable intervals.

It is the most logically laid-out city in the world. Lloyd immediately felt more comfortable. Taking a deep easy breath he dared a glance at his navigator. "So far, so good. What's next, Evy?"

Evelyn's total attention was out her window. She couldn't stop looking at the sheer mass of humanity moving down the sidewalks. And the humanity looked back. The Road Ranger was a curiosity even by

New York's jaded standards. But New Yorkers have a curious way of showing their curiosity, which is to say, they don't.

You could drag a Saturn rocket down Fifth Avenue and people would look at it like it was the third time that day they'd had to see a three-stage booster go by. They'd each have a comment on its relative condition to the last one they saw and it would be forgotten five minutes after it passed unless it exploded.

This was the treatment that Lloyd and Evelyn and their powder-blue booster received. The people on the sidewalk would look up and Evelyn would look back. The pedestrians would then shake their heads, or smile, or laugh, or mumble something to themselves, and then they would go back to their newspapers or cellular phones or Walkmans or whatever it was that they were doing because New Yorkers were always doing two things at once, only one of them being walking.

Evelyn could scarcely pry her eyes from the sidewalk scenery to read the map, but she managed. "Get over. We need to stay on this street. Don't let yourself get cut off here."

Evelyn's warning was of no use. There was some herd instinct that turned the snarled traffic to the left, sweeping Lloyd along with it. "They don't even use their turn signals around here!"

Lloyd gave a blast of the air horns, but the once-potent hoot was swallowed whole by the din. Evelyn let the map slide from her hands and said nothing. The feeling of being inside something much more powerful than they was so strong that Lloyd and Evelyn could only submit with quiet dignity.

The pack led them deeper into the heart of the Upper West Side and the Road Ranger became funneled down the increasingly narrower streets. Cars were double- and triple-parked in places, leaving barely enough room for the most average of autos, let alone a fully furnished home.

"I think you'll clear over here," Evelyn hollered with her head out the window as Lloyd tried to negotiate between two parked cars in the single lane down the middle of a two-way street.

"If somebody comes from the other direction, Evy, just pack up our clothes. We'll sell this thing for the price of a train ticket out of here."

Evelyn couldn't tell if Lloyd's good humor was genuine or just masking a panic attack, but he was doing a superb job of driving nonetheless.

Things were going pretty well under the circumstances until the corner of Broadway and a cross street in the low nineties; they never would know for sure because Lloyd took the street sign out when he cut the turn too close. He wasn't so concerned about that, though, after he knocked over a newspaper vending machine trying to back off the curb. And he even lost interest in that when the crate of grapefruit from the grocery on the corner spilled over after being jostled by an elderly lady and her two dogs, which had bolted.

"Oops." Lloyd checked his mirror and saw only the face of a frantic Korean grocer who Lloyd figured was explaining in perfect Korean how he felt about having a motor home with two very white people in it docked at his pier.

Evelyn watched the faces of the inquisitive and well-dressed diners at a stylish seafood restaurant named Francoise next to the grocery. The restaurant had several tables under the awning in front and as Lloyd maneuvered their road barn back and forth on the sidewalk the diners' faces turned from curiosity to concern.

"Lloyd, you're making this worse." Evelyn looked at her husband, who was desperately spinning the wheel from one side to the other and thrusting the gear lever forward and back.

"I'm all jammed up against a light pole over here. I'll just have to drive forward a ways. I'm not going to hit any of those tables, am I?"

"No," Evelyn said, trying to smile nonchalantly at the ever-more-attentive lunch customers at Francoise.

What Evelyn couldn't see from her perch was the sandwich board advertising the day's lunch special directly in front of their massive grill. When Lloyd drove forward it toppled over, dragging under the chassis until it caught on the outfall for the sewage holding tank and neatly clipped the valve end open.

An immediate blue pool of chemicals and unspeakables formed around the lunch special billboard which quite despicably proclaimed *Blue*

Point Oysters, only eight ninety-five, and sent most of the lunch crowd into a clutch with their linen napkins.

"What was that?" Lloyd said, all his calm gone now.

"I don't know, but we're sure making the natives jumpy. Maybe we should get out and take a look." Evelyn looked at her husband, who was suddenly pale and drawn. All concerns over their cornering situation vanished. "Lloyd Decker, are you alright?"

Lloyd swallowed and took a couple careful breaths. "Yeah, it's just that darn indigestion again."

Evelyn watched Lloyd down two more antacids then pat himself reassuringly on the breastbone, and she knew they never should have come to New York. "Why don't you stay put, Pop, I'll handle these people. They look pretty surly."

"Nonsense," Lloyd said, looking out the window at all the faces looking in. "They're just honest Americans like us. They'll help us out of this jam if we just ask them. How hard can it be?"

Lloyd's question was answered when the door swung back and the barrage of sound from the gathering crowd thumped him on the chest. There was a man in a turban shaking a newspaper and barking in some incomprehensible tongue over the head of a boiling maitre d' from Francoise who strung more French curses together than Lloyd had ever heard. Actually, Lloyd had never heard a French curse in his life, but he felt the meaning of every one of them. The Korean grocer wagged two grapefruits stained blue and lectured with a tone reminiscent of a fork caught in a garbage disposal.

Lloyd saw the creeping blue stain making its way across the hot city sidewalk and realized what had happened. He backed away from the door and took his seat, embarrassed and overwhelmed.

Out the window he saw a student in running clothes trying to scrape something off her Reebok with a bagel. Another woman in a business suit stood on a chair breathing through her silk scarf.

Then he heard an aggressive and alarming knocking on the front window. Lloyd's attention snapped to the gleaming badge of a New York policeman who was rapping on the nose of the Road Ranger with his nightstick, shouting through the windshield and the clamor of the mob outside the door.

"Get this circus wagon off my sidewalk, Gomer."

The club hit the camper again and Lloyd saw a piece of paint flip away. The cop looked straight at Lloyd.

"Sometime today, Goober. It's against the law to have this thing here."

Against the law. Lloyd stared out at the irate cop, the angry mob, and distressed diners and he felt their anger and their stress. Reaching out for the can of chew he said to no one but himself, "I've never broken a law in my life."

Lloyd stuffed an indignant wad of the furry-looking snuff in his red face while Evelyn sat gaping. "What in heaven's name do you think you're doing?"

Lloyd worked the tobacco in his mouth with false satisfaction and headed for the door. "I'm gonna straighten this mess up once and for all."

He stood in the door and the rowdy gathering made way. Lloyd took an exaggerated and indignant chew on his plug. The juices came down his throat and the rush of it entered his system without warning. As Lloyd's feet touched the ground his head seemed to float above the throng and he thought he saw Evelyn reaching up to catch him hollering, *Lloyd Decker, don't you go out there!*

A half block west and three stories up, Richard Hoople looked up from his magazine. Like the sailor who wakes when the wind shifts in the night, he turned to the open kitchen window, suddenly mindful of the noise outside.

He'd lived in this neighborhood, on this street, in this apartment for six years. He knew the sounds and rhythms of the city like his own heartbeat. It ebbed and flowed with the time of day and the day of week, but it was all familiar. Horns honked, sirens wailed, bike bells clanged, buses growled, lunatics ranted, conversations drifted, boom boxes boomed, and it all blended together into an everyday symphony of white noise that was changed only by the most impressive calamities.

There were accidents sometimes—robberies, or fires—and the pitch would change or the volume rise or fall. Special events like visiting presidents or mass marches would alter the chorus for awhile, but these thing were well-promoted and anticipated.

Richard knew of nothing that would explain what he heard through his window—the unmistakable tenor of gridlock on the Upper West Side. He put his head out into the day, joining five hundred others on the block, but unlike his neighbors, Richard's face went white at the sight of the problem. The problem was that big things happen in big cities all the time—and a person gets used to them—but it isn't very often that the big things happening are centered around a relative of yours.

Richard blinked and checked again. Sure as bad weather, it said *Lloyd and Evy* on the back of the blue camper which was lamely lurched over the curb in front of his favorite restaurant—half in the street, half in Korea—and oozing some sort of toxic waste that was probably backing up traffic all the way to the UN.

Richard hit the street trying to summon some composure. *Well, Aunt Evelyn—Uncle Lloyd, how nice to see you again. So, this is your camper.*

Aunt Evelyn, what a surprise. Just park anywhere, I'll take your bags upstairs. Uncle Lloyd, don't worry about that mess right now. Somebody will sue us and it will probably be tied up in court for years.

Richard tied the sleeves of his sweater around his shoulders and watched the scene across the street for a moment before crossing. Guillaum, the maitre d' at Francoise, looked apoplectic. Richard kissed window table goodbye. He saw Michelle, the girl across the hall, trying to clean something off her shoes. Mrs. Krenshaw, the admissions director of the preparatory pre-school where they'd applied, stood on a chair in front of Francoise breathing through her hands.

I'm ruined, Richard thought crossing the street. *Socially dead in the neighborhood.* Then he saw the policeman and the ambulance lights flashing and the EMTs rushing through the crowd with their gurney and cases.

Oh, no, Richard thought trying to remember his lawyer's name. *Somebody is injured.*

Richard came around the corner of the motor home just as the paramedics reached the scene and he froze for an instant. Although he hadn't seen her in several years, he immediately recognized his white-haired old Aunt Evelyn who was sitting on an overturned news box cradling the head of his Uncle Lloyd. He could hear her talking to him.

"Lloyd Anthony Decker, don't you try to leave me alone in this city. Coming to New York was your bright idea, so stay with it, Buster. The ambulance is here." Lloyd could see his wife's face right in front of his, but her voice sounded like it was across the street. The other faces were above hers in a big circle. They all looked down with blank expressions. The sidewalk felt hot and wet on his back.

Another face dipped close. Someone grabbed his wrist. Someone else pulled at his shirt. "This man is having a heart attack. Stand back, please."

The higher faces moved off and Lloyd saw the ambulance lights flashing and another EMT rushing through the crowd with a gurney and cases.

Lloyd was taken from Evelyn's arms, and she stood and watched helplessly as the medics stripped open Lloyd's shirt, attached their monitors, and covered his face with an oxygen mask.

The policeman pushed through the onlookers and told Evelyn, "Don't disappear until you get this thing off the sidewalk, lady."

Evelyn ignored the policeman and turned to her nephew. "Thank God you're here, Richard." She handed him a set of keys on a rabbit's-foot chain. "I'm going with Lloyd. Please find someplace safe to park our home."

Evelyn didn't say another word. As the gurney with her mate on it started down the walk she caught up with it. She found her husband's hand, and Lloyd found hers, and their wide eyes saw nothing but each other's as the medics opened the doors to the ambulance. As the gurney was hefted, Lloyd lifted his oxygen mask and leaned over sideways. A thick dark stream of tobacco slipped from between his lips, landing with a satisfying splat on the hot sidewalk.

"That's for Sid Winston," he mumbled before they put the mask back over his mouth, cinched his chest strap tight, and rolled him hacking into the back of the van.

Richard looked at the mess drying up in huge blue patches at his feet and at the feet of a New York cop nearing the end of his patience. He saw the crowd of people thinning and the neighbors beginning to notice him. The maitre d' took a step toward Richard, a man in a turban right behind him, and the grocer was gathering momentum on his flank. Gripping the rabbit's foot, Richard stepped up into the thirty-two-foot Road Ranger and found the bolt on the door.

In New York City, calamity passes as quickly as it arrives. There is no time to notice the things that happen for very long because new things keep happening. Tragedy in New York flares like a match that will not light. Nothing bad can last for long in a city with so much life. It moves steadily and brilliantly on, dragging everyone along with it.

An ambulance blaring down Broadway draws the interest of nobody—the misfortune aboard is a mystery no one cares to solve. A huge blue recreational vehicle leaks a thin trail of wetness. It inspires only brief speculation before disappearing beneath the river heading uncertainly for New Jersey.

28

Buddy felt the sidewalk lurch suddenly to the right and he staggered sideways into the granite face of a bank. He stayed still a moment, mustering his equilibrium. The rows of streetlights continued to twist and spin down the avenue. Buddy felt sick again and gulped for air.

He could hear the hoots and laughter of the men of the Pessimists echoing off the tall dark empty buildings. He couldn't tell where they were anymore. He'd lost them. They'd lost him. He was too drunk to tell which it was.

They'd been drinking since early that evening. The Pessimists were a group of finishing law students that met in a tavern every Friday afternoon. The foundation of the group was an allegiance to help one another find their maximum potential in the world of business once they cleared law school and began their careers. If you can't be in the *Good Old Boy* network, then start your own.

The name of the organization came from the additional belief that they would all be eaten alive within thirty days of graduation if they didn't stick together. Their motto and perpetual toast was *You are only as good as the company you keep. God help us all.*

These weren't the best students in the school, but they were certainly the most ambitious. Buddy knew they would be excellent cronies to call upon someday, and he'd wrangled an invitation to their meeting even though he was just beginning his second year at the school.

Blind ambition creates some sort of pheromone that is easily sensed by others with a similar chemistry. Buddy gave off a strong odor of selfish enthusiasm and he was recognized for it. Getting invited to sit with the Pessimists was easy; it was keeping up with them that proved tricky.

The first thing they'd done by way of welcoming Buddy to their auspicious gathering was to buy him a half-dozen shots of bourbon and propose six toasts in a row to friendship, loyalty, alliance, obligation, honor, and one for the Seahawks just because the group's attention span was narrowing.

Buddy gamely plugged along with the ritual, proud of his ability to handle his liquor and eager to prove it. Unfortunately, that was just the first round. As they drank and toasted through the dinner hour the shots began to pile up in front of Buddy. He felt his forehead getting heavy and his face seemed to hang on his skull like a rubber mask. He said little and what he did say came out thick and clouded.

Nothing that was said at the gathering was of any importance. It was being there that was important. Buddy knew it was essential to keep pace with these guys and earn their trust. These young men took care of each other. They would take care of him.

Buddy let his knees fold under him and he slid down the wall of the bank. He thought if he could just sit down for a minute or two, he would be alright.

"Pull it together, Bedinger," Buddy spoke out loud wrestling with the confusion in his head. Trying to hold it still so he could get a look at it. He started with the easy stuff.

I'm in Seattle, he thought. *I'm downtown—I think.*

Buddy heard some more shouts from out of the wet night. *The Pessimists.* He remembered. They'd been asked to leave the bar and they had, in a giant wad of puffed-up ire and sarcasm. They'd staggered into the street bouncing off one another and laughing and shouting defiant inanities at passing cars and buses.

As they wandered down the street, Buddy had slipped into a side alley to relieve himself. He didn't know how long he'd been back there, but it seemed like a long long time. Being away from the lofty spirits of the group felt like a plunge as Buddy went about his business and tried to clear his vision which fogged, spun, and stirred the liquor left in his otherwise empty stomach. By the time he'd come back out of the shadows, all wet-eyed and bile, the others were gone.

This is how people become homeless, he thought, trying to straighten himself. First they pass out on the street. Then somebody hits them in the head and robs them. Then they spend the rest of their life trying to convince everybody they're not a drunken beggar, but a law student. *I can prove it. I have cronies. These are my cronies.* Buddy blinked. *Where were they?*

He couldn't stop the world from spinning. He tried closing one eye, but then he would just want to close the other. *You can't pass out, Bedinger. You have to make it home.*

Home. God, how was he going to get home? Even if he had been sober enough to drive his car, he couldn't remember where it was. He wasn't sure where he was. He let his eyes close for a moment. He wanted to sleep so badly.

He heard the shouts again, this time closer, and he forced himself to focus up the block. There was a group of young men meandering up the street. *Cronies,* Buddy thought happily. Then he saw one of the group pull something out of his jacket and smash the window of a parked car.

An alarm barked to life and the group ambled on, delighted. *These aren't Pessimists,* Buddy thought as they passed under the next streetlight. What he saw was the glint of metal and the dull shimmer of black leather. These weren't the sauntering legs of drunken law students. This was the muscular swagger of bad boys on the prowl, a pod of misdirected youth looking for trouble. And you didn't need to be sober to see where they were going to find it.

Buddy groaned and tried to get his legs underneath him. The gang was still half a block away and couldn't see Buddy in the shadow of the building. Buddy managed to get to his feet but he couldn't pull himself away from the wall. The street rocked like a boat and Buddy knew he wouldn't be able to take a step. He closed his eyes and let himself dribble down the wall again. *Sleep. If I could only sleep.*

Buddy felt the alcohol reach up with its big warm hairy arms and he relaxed into its grip. *Sleep. Just sleep.*

.　.　.

"**Walk! Walk!** Use your legs! I can't carry you."

Buddy heard a man's voice right in his ear. His eyes rolled open and he saw his feet dragging on the ground. He felt a powerful grip under his arms and realized he was being pulled backwards down a dark passage between two buildings.

"Walk! Walk, you stupid drunk!" The man stopped and stood Buddy up on his feet. Buddy could barely raise his head to face the man, but when he did, the sight of it sobered him some. The stranger who held him by the shoulders had the intense and harried features of a maniac. Jack the Ripper eyes. His voice cut like glass. "Tango and his gang! They'll see you! Walk, you drunken jackass."

Buddy walked, leaning heavily and helplessly on the phantom maniac, into the darkness. There was nothing he could do to resist, not even lie down. The man held him up. All he could do was move his legs.

Buddy drifted in and out of consciousness. He'd come around one moment and be looking into the blinding headlights of a honking car. Then all would return to darkness. He heard a ship's whistle. A train's horn. A drunk singing in a doorway.

Buddy was aware of going downhill. The sounds, the smells, the feeling of descending—it left him confused and powerless. "Where are you taking me?"

"To a friend," was all the man said as he led Buddy around a corner and up a steep concrete embankment.

Buddy stumbled and fell to his knees several times. By the time they reached the top he was awake enough to comprehend where they were. The highway interchange was elevated over a portion of the waterfront forming a sheltered little sanctuary against one end. Above the surface streets and below the busy highway overhead, the area was easily unnoticed if you didn't know it was there.

Three people sat around some sort of bucket or tub which had a fire glowing inside, illuminating their faces from underneath. Their heads appeared to float unattended in the dark recesses of the concrete cavern.

"I don't think I have any friends here." Buddy found some strength to resist, finally, and he locked his legs to keep from being propelled any closer to the gathering. Although he had some strength, he still didn't have a shred of balance. All he accomplished was launching himself head-long into the dim circle of light and into the lap of one of the floating heads.

The head turned familiar and spoke. "Well, Buddy! What are you doing here?"

Buddy instantly recognized his friend Oliver and was about to say something when the man who'd brought Buddy stepped into the light and answered for him.

"I saved him from the jaws of death. Tango and his bunch of devils were nearly upon him. The angels of hell were cheated. You have John Doe to thank for that. That's my real name and don't you forget it!"

The man stepped out of the light again and paced erratically along the edge of the overpass—a sentry under siege. Another face around the fire produced a hand that lifted Buddy from Oliver's lap and dusted him off.

"Please forgive Mr. Doe's way with people. He's quite insane, you know, but reliable. Allow me to introduce myself." The man took Buddy's limp hand and shook it. "Arthur P. Tender III. A beggar, a drunk, and a gentleman. I gather you're the Buddy with the exquisite bread Oliver speaks of so highly."

"Yes." Buddy was desperately tired. The warmth of the slight fire on his face told him how wet and cold he was. A chill swept over him.

Oliver reacted. "Buddy, you're soaking wet. Take this blanket." He produced a thick tattered blanket with a smell of musk about it and draped it over Buddy's shoulders.

The third face at the fire, a woman's, suddenly shot up and left. "I don't like it. I don't like it one bit. We'll be found. We'll be robbed and killed." She joined the wary John Doe on the periphery and said no more.

Arthur spoke again. "And that, my good man, was Ramona Bag-gins—slightly more insane than Mr. Doe, but just as reliable. She doesn't like strangers. To be honest, she doesn't like anybody, but especially not strangers."

Oliver called after the agitated woman. "Buddy's no stranger, Ramona, Buddy is a friend. He gives me bread at the hotel. Remember the good bread?"

Ramona Baggins declined to respond, choosing instead to sulk and pace with John Doe.

"They are a comfort to each other." Arthur Tender spoke as if in apology.

Buddy sat glassy-eyed, hearing but not listening, until Oliver spoke again. "Did you really get mixed up with Tango's gang? What happened?"

"My friends left me. I don't know after that. I'm too drunk to remember."

Arthur P. Tender suddenly perked up. "Ah, yes—the wicked grape. The demon barleycorn. Indeed. Laid many a good man to waste." Arthur leaned in close to Buddy's ear. "You wouldn't perchance have a nightcap left of your evening nearabouts, would you, friend?"

Oliver intervened. "Arthur, I'm sure Buddy's had enough tonight." He adjusted Buddy's blanket. "Would you like to lie down and rest, Buddy? You look tired."

"I'm so tired." Buddy let himself collapse to one side. Oliver's hands guided him to the ground. Buddy felt his weight on the Earth and let it rest there. He closed his eyes, but his stomach swirled and he opened them again. He stared vacantly at the tongue of flame flickering over the edge of the bucket and the world held still. Buddy swallowed, lifted his head onto his folded hands, and waited for sleep to take him.

"It's the second time this summer that Tango boy has caused trouble around me." Oliver was speaking quietly, as if to himself. "Remember that young boy I found who'd been robbed? Norman Tuttle? I had a dream about him. Did I tell you my dream about Norman Tuttle?"

"No Oliver, I don't believe you did." Arthur brightened and turned to the two sentinels standing off in their gloom and suspicion. "Mr. Doe, Miss Baggins. Oliver has a dream to tell. Would you care to join us?"

None of Oliver's friends had ever considered skipping one of his dream stories and the two nervous sentries abandoned their posts to join the others.

Even Buddy had heard some of Oliver's dreams. He lay in the shadows, one eye still open, and waited with Arthur Tender. John Doe and Ramona Baggins squeezed in close around the burning pail and Oliver began.

"It was a simple dream, really. Not like the others at all. There was no fire or flying or anything like that. It was just people—a bunch of people in this wonderful quiet place that was green and warm and there were trees. Trees as far as you could see, and they were full of fruit. All kinds of fruit.

"In the middle of all these trees and all these people was this boy, Norman Tuttle, and he took my hand and led me to the people. I had never seen any of them before, but they all acted as if they knew me. A beautiful woman called me by my name, gave me a kiss, and then ran off into the trees. There were these young men, younger than Buddy even, who laughed when they saw me. They clowned around and teased me, but not in a mean way.

"An older man I'd never seen, but I seemed to know, stood off through the trees. He didn't come join the rest of us, but he wouldn't stop looking at me. And the funny part of this dream was somehow I knew these people were all called Tuttle. Every last one of them. Just like the boy. Big Tuttles, little Tuttles, boy and girl Tuttles. Tuttle–Tuttle–Tuttle.

"Tuttles and trees and trees and Tuttles and everybody looking at me and it felt good and odd, too. Odd enough that I backed out of the trees and the boy yelled after me, *Come back later. You can come back later.*"

Oliver stopped for a moment and Buddy turned his one open eye to him. The older man's rough features and graying hair softened in the fire light. Buddy watched a smile build around Oliver's bright eyes as they looked around the circle of people at the fire.

When Oliver looked to Buddy he held his attention there and Buddy felt the warmth of it shining on his face. Buddy's eyelid relaxed and drew closed, the image of his friend's face lingering behind his eyes as Oliver continued.

"The dream felt like this does sometimes, you know, when I'm coming back at the end of a day and I know the four of us will sit here out of the rain and we'll have some bread, and even if I've forgotten everything else about me, I know how to get here. That feeling like we're all going to be okay just because we're all here. Have you ever felt that way?"

Arthur Tender, John Doe, and Ramona Baggins stayed silent.

"Buddy, have you ever felt that way around your friends before?"

Buddy replied with the muffled snores of a drunk and exhausted law student. Oliver reached over, and with Arthur Tender's help, spread the ragged blanket to cover Buddy's legs and feet.

The newest member of the Pessimists wriggled his head down into the blanket and let out a long and easy breath, the way people do when they know it is okay to sleep.

One by one the heads around the fire floated down to their places. Great sighs heaved as the fire bucket glowed red in the dark like the taillights of late-night traffic thundering overhead and the sparks of cigarettes from the hands of idle boys wandering the street below. And unless somebody had told you, you never would have known they were there.

III

Still, a great deal of light falls on everything.

—Vincent van Gogh

29

Norman's bedroom door swung silently into the room. All he noticed at first was the wonderful color draining from Laura's face. Her eyes stretched so wide Norman could almost hear her eyebrows singing.

"Laura?" Norman could definitely see that something had changed. He wouldn't know that everything had changed until he turned and saw his dad standing in the doorway, his face so flushed that he was very nearly bleeding.

Norman saw his father's lips moving, but his brain was temporarily seized. He couldn't comprehend the words that filled the room like black smoke, driving away all notions of privacy and feelings of intimacy.

"What in the world is going on here, young man?"

The young man couldn't answer. Norman could only lay there holding the sheets up around his neck like a deer caught in the headlights. Laura managed to recover some motor skills and slid over to one edge of the bed smiling apologetically, like it could mend the moment.

There are some things broken that can never be repaired. Norman looked across the gulf of his bedroom to the shattered remains of his father. Norman's soul settled in his heels and his heart ground in his chest like gravel. The loneliness of manhood feels like death the first time you encounter it.

"Young lady, get dressed and go home." Frank Tuttle spoke with no emotion in his voice. He was cool. Cold, really. Robo-Dad. He kept his eyes averted from Laura by burning them into his son. "I'll see you downstairs in ten minutes, Mister."

Laura dressed silently while Norman searched through the sheets for his shorts. Half an hour ago, having Laura Magruder in his bedroom with the whole evening to themselves seemed like a most wickedly delicious adventure. Now it just felt wicked.

Maybe it was the lingering scent of his father's aftershave in the room. Maybe it was the room itself. Four walls that had known only a boy could not comprehend the young man who stood looking at the back of his mate. And maybe the trouble was about her. Norman had felt done with Laura since the summer. His time away had cooled the flames of passion just as his parents had wished.

He thought he'd grown immune to her press of big ideas, but it was only a matter of days before Laura had fanned the dying coals of their curiosity back to life. Her ideas were tantalizing and terrifying, tempting and forbidden. They were out of the question and unavoidable at the same time.

Laura checked herself in Norman's mirror, made a few adjustments to her hair, and turned to her companion, willful and aloof. "My daddy better not find out about this. That's all I have to say. He'll have our heads hung side by side in his den with the moose and the mountain goat."

The thought of the powerful and ornery Mr. Magruder pushed Norman's own father problems from his head for the moment. He spoke with a confidence he didn't feel. "Don't worry, I can handle this."

Laura fixed Norman with an icy look. "You'd better," she said. Then, recovering herself, she softened and clutched both of Norman's hands—pleading. "Norman, you just have to."

Laura pressed herself against Norman, placed a kiss on his lips, and left him standing there in his room, in charge, and in trouble.

Norman finished dressing and checked the clock. He still had seven minutes and he was going to use every last one of them.

Norman's first thoughtful emotion was fear. He was dead. He knew it. His dad would have to kill him, if for no other reason than to serve as a lesson to his younger siblings. But, he thought, that was all right; he was sixteen, almost seventeen. He'd lived a good long life.

Norman looked around his room. There was the piggy bank he'd had since he could remember with a Mega-Death decal on its pink flanks. His Twisted Sisters poster hung next to a needlepoint sampler of the Twenty-third Psalm his mother had placed there years ago. A bat and ball stood in one corner. A jockstrap hung from the closet door. This was Norman's sanctuary. This was Norman's soul.

"How dare he come barging into my room like that," Norman thought. A teenager's thought process, when left to roam freely, will almost always find its way to indignation. "This is *my* room. This is *my* life. What was Dad doing home, anyway? He wasn't supposed to be home until Thursday."

Norman's mother had taken the other kids to Anchorage for a few days. His dad had been out on a late salmon opening.

I get no respect around this house, Norman's mind raged as he threw the rumpled blankets across the bed and flopped down on top of them. *This summer the Flannigans treated me with respect. It wasn't "Norman, do this—Norman, do that." It was "Norman, would you like to do this?" or "Norman, could you please do that if you're not too busy?"*

Ed had put Norman in charge of the tractor and he'd hardly run over anything valuable. Emily gave him the car and money to take the kids to a movie. He flew all by himself from Alaska and back. He made his way into downtown Seattle and got mugged. He'd learned more in a summer than he thought most knew in a lifetime. Especially his parents.

Norman sat up on the edge of his bed and looked out the window. The rolling green meadows on the ridge gave way to the open expanse of the blue bay and the rim of white mountains around it. The little town at the end of the road, the only home Norman knew, sat at the center of it all like a great big *X* on one of those *you are here* maps.

Norman saw the trailing dust of Laura's speeding car drifting across the ridge like powdered fantasy in the fading light. It would roost on leaves and blades of grass and be washed by the rains into the bay and swept out to sea like it had never been there at all.

"This town sucks." Norman condemned all that he surveyed. His fury built around his broken heart, swollen loins, and collapsed pride the way a muscle goes into spasm around an injury, immobilizing the area to save it from further harm. Norman lowered himself into the universal untruth of adolescence: The world could never understand love and passion the way a teenager can.

Norman looked at his clock. He still had three minutes.

.   .   .

Frank Tuttle paced his kitchen. Three steps and spit in the sink—turn—three steps then stare at his reflection in the microwave oven.

"What are you going to do now?"

The man staring back with the *Toastmaster* emblem across his nose didn't have a clue. This was it. The ultimate. The big showdown. Judgment Day. *What was that stupid kid thinking about? Haven't we taught him anything? Sex!? God! He's just a child.*

Frank Tuttle spit in the sink again, then ran some water into his hands. Slapping himself in the face with it, he took a deep and careful breath.

"He's not a child anymore. At least not from his neck down." The elder of the two resident Tuttles felt older by the moment and stretched his shoulders. He could feel the weight of all creation—and procreation—descending upon him.

He'd have to tell Burt Magruder. Oh, there'd be hell to pay. If the sins of the father are visited upon the son, the sins of the son will move right in with the father. But it was the only thing to do. The right thing to do. Kids that age having sex. They'd have to be kept apart. *What in the world could they know about love and passion?*

Frank heard his son's heels clunking methodically and dramatically down the stairs. A theatrical death march. Frank rolled his eyes and straightened. It was show time.

Norman sprawled across the chair and let his eyelids drape over his eyes. His father faced him across the table. To keep from back-handing the attitude right off of Norman's face, Frank focused his attention on one overdeveloped pimple in the middle of his son's peppered forehead.

Frank began low and calm. "Listen to me, Oliver."

Norman blew air from his nose and sneered, "What did you call me?"

Frank searched quietly and desperately for a response. He knew what he'd done.

"You called me Oliver." Norman seemed to gather strength from the error.

Frank was not about to lose control of this conversation so soon—even if it meant lying. "I know what I called you. You're getting just like your Uncle Oliver was before we lost him. Headstrong. Brain dead. Wild and sneaky."

Norman slumped a little deeper into his *here comes the lecture* posture. His father continued staring at the pimples on his face to avoid murdering him.

"You know you've broken every trust we ever had, don't you?"

Norman appeared unfazed. "You never told me I couldn't sleep with my girlfriend."

Frank flared for a moment, then paused. Norman was right, of course. He'd also not explicitly told him not to dismember the cat or drive the family car into a lake.

"Norman, some things you just know are wrong."

"I didn't think it was wrong." Norman looked right into his dad's eyes as he lied. He might as well have reached out with a stick and drawn a line across the table.

Frank stayed on his side of the line. "*I* think it's wrong!"

Norman picked at the edge of the table with a lazy finger. "Sounds like a personal problem to me."

Frank Tuttle felt his heart almost give out as the blood shot into his face. The wax in his ears boiled and his big fisherman's hands squeezed the edge of the table so hard his knuckles popped. He sat stunned, beads of sweat forming on his brow, and stared at his son, who was taking great personal satisfaction from the predicament.

Frank's thoughts rifled through the dustiest recesses of his experience, throwing open trunks and tossing useless memories aside. His wedding night. His sixteenth birthday. His own father's advice on women, and matters of the heart: *Don't worry, you'll know what to do when the time comes.*

That wasn't true. It still isn't true. He continued to search, and fixed finally on a scene thirty years ago. His brother Oliver sitting slumped across the kitchen table from his father. The beads of sweat had formed on the elder Tuttle's temples. Suddenly there was an explosion of words and rage. Chairs had fallen to the floor. Voices were raised to breaking pitch.

A Bible sailed like a missile out into the night, missing its mark. The shadow of an older brother blended with the darkness in the yard and disappeared.

The Bible was recovered in the morning. The rage lives to this day in the heart of an old man who never saw his son again. There were a thousand ways to handle that long-ago crisis gracefully. There were just as many ways to bungle it. A girl was pregnant. A young man was afraid. A father was outraged. It didn't have to end the way it did.

Frank Tuttle's temper cooled. He looked at the somber face of his son in the failing light and could not see the young man across the table from him. He saw the toothless smile and the squirm of a first-born baby, the diapered waddle of an adventurous toddler, and the uncertain strides of young legs on a pitching boat deck. He'd seen it all. He could reach a hand into each of these times and offer a touch of reassurance, a hand for balance, a saving grip.

And here they were again. This was not life or death, but it was right and wrong. There were a thousand ways to handle this correctly, and he had to pick one—now.

Frank let his face relax into a calm he didn't feel and he reached for some tenderness in his throat. He had hard things to say, but he knew they needed to be softly said.

"Norman, this is serious, but let's not make it any more trouble than it has to be."

This was good news to Norman. Frank stopped and worked at the dirt under his fingernails, struggling for the rest of the words. Norman held his breath.

"You and Laura are going to have to stay apart for awhile." Frank stopped and gauged his son's reaction. There was little. A slight stiffening, maybe, but there was resignation with it. This was expected.

Disciplining a teenager is like disarming a bomb. You grit your teeth, snip the first wire, and if it doesn't blow up in your face, you go to the next. *So far, so good,* Frank thought, and continued.

"And you understand that I'm going to have to tell Laura's father about this. It happened under my roof and he has a right to know."

Frank stopped breathing as he felt the young man across the table seize. The bomb had stopped ticking. Was it disarmed, or set to explode and destroy everything?

Norman sat up in his chair, faced his father, and very calmly destroyed him. "If you tell the Magruders about this I'm out of here."

Frank fought back the urge to chuckle, and spoke evenly. "Where would you go?" He regretted the question as soon as he heard the words come out of his mouth. While trying to be reasonable he'd made the catastrophic mistake of inviting logic into a foolish notion.

Norman stood, and his dad had to look up at him. "I'd move back to Oregon with Ed Flannigan. Where I could at least get treated like an adult! I'm sick of this nowhere, do-nothing town. I'm sick of everybody butting into my life. And I'm sick of you!"

Frank rose to quell the rebellion. His hand raised in a tight fist, but it loosened as it crossed the table, reaching Norman's chest with a finger extended in grave warning. Frank tried to speak, but his hurt and his fury could find no suitable phrase.

Norman looked cynically at his father's finger and turned away. As Norman's hand grasped the knob on the back door, Frank finally found a voice. "Where do you think you're going, young man?"

Norman looked over his shoulder and addressed the floor. "Out." He continued to stand there, waiting to be challenged.

Frank stood in the dim kitchen. What little light was left outside barely penetrated the room. His son was just a dark shape in a faint doorway. The shape was as large as a man and as certain. There were a thousand ways to handle this and a thousand ways to bungle it.

The frustration left Frank a blank page. There was nothing safe to say. As so often happens when we have nothing to say for ourselves, the voices of those who taught us come leeching through. Like legends, nobody believes them anymore, but we keep repeating them for the comfort of their familiarity.

"If you leave this house tonight, don't bother coming back." Frank

Tuttle heard the voice of his father cross the dark kitchen and push his son out the door.

At the window, Frank could see Norman's vague shape making its way across the yard. With every long stride his son took, a piece of Frank's life ran down his face.

At the road Norman stopped and turned. The blurred white features of his father shone out of the dark kitchen window.

Frank saw the shadowy form of his son brighten as he turned toward him. He willed every particle of his being across the yard to Norman. The shape faded. The shadows blended with the darkness in the yard and disappeared. If there'd been any more light at all, they'd have seen each other.

30

Unlike King Arthur's Avalon, Avalon, Ohio, was not paradise. And unlike King Arthur, Lloyd Decker was not being carried in on a slab. Although humbled and a little shaken, Lloyd was alive, well, and riding shotgun as Evelyn guided their motor home on the road down the main street of the only home they'd known.

"Well, not much has changed in six months." Evelyn flipped on the blinker, reflexively anticipating the turn onto their old street.

Lloyd took in the vacant sleepy sidewalks of late-afternoon Avalon. "Not much has changed around here in six hundred months."

Evelyn gave her husband a quick sidelong look before committing to her turn, and decided not to speak the words on her mind. *Oh yes, Lloyd Decker, everything has changed. Every single thing.*

They'd pulled out of Avalon in the spring with their sights set on the western horizon. A lifetime of neglected adventures awaited them. Every sight they'd seen in half a year was new. Every experience the first. The world was a big place, and life was good.

Now, they had returned from the East, the sights, sounds, smells, and value of six months of discovery diminished by one frightening day in the life of a faltering heart. The world *was* a big place and life was short. Too short to spend aimlessly living from one RV camp to the next, perpetually searching for potable water and dumping facilities, every day another blur of strange faces and foreign terrain.

Evelyn had held Lloyd's hand that day in the hospital and said the obvious. "We should go home, Pop."

Lloyd's face, nearly as pale as his sheets and partially hidden behind his oxygen mask, moved slowly up and down. His eyes closed in resignation. It was time to go back where they belonged.

Tall oak trees lined Center Street. A thick canopy of yellowing leaves created a lighted corridor of sorts. Lloyd and Evelyn traveled down the passageway without comment. Lloyd removed his sunglasses and wearily placed them on the console. He couldn't tell if it was his medication, or the long drive back from New York, but he didn't feel up to a homecoming right now.

They wouldn't be going back to their old place, but to Ralph and Rhoda Ditweillers' across the street. The Ditweillers and the Deckers had lived together on opposites sides of Center Street for nearly forty years. They'd each bought their place new and consulted one another on every aspect of their embellishment over the years: lawns, hedges, asphalt, and yard ornaments.

They were never close friends but they were close neighbors, and that counts for something. Ralph and Rhoda had graciously offered the Deckers the use of their driveway to park the motor home until they could get themselves resettled in Avalon.

"We're so excited you're coming back," Rhoda had gushed on the phone. "The place just hasn't been the same without you."

That wasn't true, Evelyn thought as she slowed the motor home to a crawl past their old house. It was exactly the same. The lawn was freshly mowed. The hedge along the driveway was neatly clipped. A child's bicycle lay in the driveway. The garage door still needed paint. A television flickered through the living room window.

It was eerie. Another family, perhaps thirty years younger than theirs, had simply plugged themselves into their house and home. The only thing Lloyd noticed out of place at all was the little Scotch pine he'd planted in the front yard. It was sitting up out of the ground on a hump of dirt like a pitcher's mound.

What's that all about? Lloyd wondered, but had no more time to consider as Evelyn swung left into the Ditweillers' immaculate driveway. Ralph stood in front of the garage, grinning. He waved with one hand and held a garden hose with the other.

"There hasn't been a speck of dirt on that asphalt in thirty years, and he's still washing it!"

Evelyn dropped the big gear lever into *Park*. "Lloyd, you be nice now."

"I'll be nice." Lloyd forced a smile into his tired features and waved as Rhoda appeared beside Ralph, wiping her hands on a red-checked apron and making dramatic *Oh my goodness* shapes with her mouth at the presence of the huge motor home in her driveway.

Lloyd stepped slowly but steadily onto the pavement, ignoring Ralph's extended hand of assistance until he was down, then offered his own hand in greeting. "Hello, Ralph, thanks for the parking place."

Ralph took Lloyd's hand tenderly. "Our pleasure, neighbor. How are you feeling?"

"Fine. A little sluggish from my heart medicine, is all."

"Well, you just take it easy, Lloyd. You know what happened to my brother, don't you?"

Lloyd didn't know what had happened to Ralph's brother, but that was of no consequence to Ralph. "My brother had a small heart attack last year, tried to get right back to work—then dropped dead three weeks later. Heart just exploded. We had to drive over to Akron for the funeral. Probably the hottest day of the summer, too."

Lloyd stayed silent and amazed as Ralph led the way through the garage. The walls were covered with the implements of short- and long-term lawn care. Each item had a bright red silhouette of itself painted on the wall behind it. Ralph drew up short at the door as the outline of one tool caught his keen eye. "Rhoda! Where's my medium hedge shears?"

Rhoda, still out chatting with Evelyn, called in impatiently. "For the third time—they're at the sharpener's where you took them!"

"Oh—the sharpener's." Ralph looked at Lloyd. "That's Mel's Hardware over on Mortimer Street past the railroad tracks."

Lloyd nodded and tried to smile at his old neighbor. He had completely forgotten how boring the Ditweillers were.

Lloyd sat at the kitchen table and felt the burning sensation working up his throat. He took two antacids from his pocket and tried to quietly remove them from their cellophane packs. Evelyn heard the commotion and looked across the table, concerned. Lloyd had confused his first heart attack with indigestion and she wasn't about to let that happen again.

Lloyd saw her anxiety and appreciated it. "Don't worry, Evy." He spoke so that Ralph and Rhoda, at the sink washing the dinner dishes, wouldn't hear. "It's just the Tuna Surprise."

Rhoda's Tuna Surprise had been no surprise. It was her favorite dish and she'd been making it for every special occasion the Deckers had shared with the Ditweillers in the past forty years.

"In honor of your homecoming," she'd said, ceremoniously placing the dish next to a Jello mold which suspended carrots, bananas, and celery pieces in an iridescent greenish ring.

Rhoda's tuna masterpiece was a simple construction of Wonder buns with a glob of tuna salad and a slice of American cheese. The whole works was melted together in the oven and then garnished with a crinkle-cut dill pickle slice.

"I'll bet you two haven't had a home-cooked meal in ages." Rhoda returned to the table with a plate of Twinkies. Ralph was right behind her carrying four mugs and a pot of coffee.

As Ralph poured, Lloyd tried to get the conversation rolling.

"So tell me, Ralph, how have *you* been feeling?"

Ralph set the coffeepot down, sat himself down, and turned serious. "It's been a dry summer, Lloyd. Real dry. I've had to water more than I wanted."

Lloyd was alarmed for a moment, then realized that Ralph was talking about his lawn, not himself. Of course. Ralph *was* his lawn. There was no question you could ask of Ralph that wouldn't end up out in his yard within ten words. Lloyd decided to indulge his old neighbor.

"It looks like the new folks across the street are taking good care of our place."

Ralph made a sour face and shook his head. Rhoda turned to Evelyn with a knowing expression. "Oh, not like you did, Lloyd. Not like you did. You used to mow parallel with the driveway. Everybody on the block does. This new fellah likes to mow with the sidewalk. Not always, though. There's no consistency with him. Can't seem to make up his mind. Same thing with that Scotch pine."

Lloyd took a sip of coffee, reminded of his question. "I noticed that. What's that all about?"

Ralph leaned back into his chair with the air of supremacy. "Now, there was a fiasco. They dug that tree up in the spring and were going to move it out back. Well, the root ball wouldn't go through the gate and they couldn't lift it over the fence, so he decided to put it back in the same hole. Trouble is, you can't ever fit a tree back in its same hole once it's been uprooted. Forget it. So the guy just set it back on the hole and called it good. It's a disaster. Annoys me every time I look over there."

Rhoda nodded her head, certifying that yes, it did in fact annoy Ralph every time he looked over there. Lloyd stared at the end of Ralph's nose, unsure of what to say. Ralph saved him the trouble.

"I'm glad you're back, Lloyd. Do you know what tomorrow is?"

Lloyd thought it was a Tuesday, but felt pretty sure there was more to it than that. There was.

"Tomorrow's our net day. And I could use your help. We had the first leaf hit the grass today!" Ralph beamed, confident that his guests shared his enthusiasm.

Lloyd had forgotten about Ralph and Rhoda's annual fall ritual of denying Mother Nature her due. Rather than let the leaves accumulate on his lawn to be raked, bagged, burned, or mulched, Ralph rolled big monofilament nets across his yard to catch the leaves before they got into his grass. When every last leaf had fallen, he would bundle up the nets and take them to the landfill. Ralph honestly couldn't appreciate why everyone didn't do this, especially Lloyd.

"Like I've always told you, neighbor, it is a real time saver." Ralph had been bragging to Lloyd about intercepting leaves for at least twenty years, and every year Lloyd had tried to see the value in it. This time he didn't even try.

"I'd be glad to help with your nets, Ralph." Lloyd pushed back from the table and stretched into a big, animated yawn. Evelyn took the cue and looked at her watch.

"Honey, we've had a long day. Maybe we should turn in."

Ralph was already on his feet. "Yessir, big day tomorrow. You better get your rest. You know what happened to my brother, don't you? Got run down after his first one. Heart just exploded. Had to drive all the way to Akron for the funeral."

"Hottest day of the summer," Lloyd said in unison as he stepped through the door to the garage. Evelyn cringed at Lloyd's mockery and turned to her old friends with real sincerity.

"Rhoda, Ralph. Thank you so much for your hospitality. It's good to be home again."

Ralph puffed up. "The grass always looks greener on the other side, but it doesn't get any greener than it is right here on Center Street. I knew you two would come to your senses."

Lloyd and Evelyn continued to wear their pinched smiles as they walked through the garage. When they made it past the outer door and into the driveway, Evelyn noticed Lloyd massaging the base of his throat. "Lloyd, are you all right?"

Lloyd swallowed hard. He wasn't having a heart attack, but his heart definitely needed to be ventilated. "Evy—my pain has a name and it is Ralph and Rhoda. *Ralph and Rhoda.* It even sounds like something you'd do to your lawn. *We'll aerate and fertilize, then we'll Ralph and Rhoda the flower beds with the Ditweiller.*"

Evelyn patted her husband's hand. "Calm down, Lloyd Decker. You'll drop dead from a heart attack."

Lloyd would not be calmed. "Dropping dead in this neighborhood wouldn't be much of a lifestyle change."

Evelyn held the motor home door open as Lloyd stepped up. "We've had a lot of excitement in our lives lately. It's going to be difficult adjusting to a slower pace again. Just give it some time, Lloyd."

Lloyd didn't say anything for awhile. He took his medicine, brushed his teeth at the kitchen sink, then paused finally on his way back to bed.

"Evelyn, time is just like money. When you haven't got a lot of it left, you become real careful how you spend it."

Evelyn didn't sleep well that night. She lay next to her husband, and between his long weary snores, she could hear the dry autumn wind rattling the leaves in the trees outside. They sounded crisp and fragile— and she knew Ralph was right. They would all be falling any day now.

The sun broke through a crack in the window blinds and found its way across Lloyd's pillow and onto his cheek. He twitched twice and then woke with a start. He sat up, mildly alarmed for a moment. This was typical of Lloyd these past six months on the road. Waking up in the back of the RV brought with it the anxiety of not remembering where he was right away.

Lloyd separated the blinds with two fingers and peeked outside. He'd looked out these blinds a hundred different times and seen a hundred different startling vistas, but none more startling than what he saw today.

The rising sun met the changing oaks and created a divine golden light that enshrined, not a hundred feet away, the house he'd lived in most of his life. A slight and frail early frost glinted from the hedge leaves and winked on the roof shingles before vanishing into the sun with a curl of vapor.

Careful not to wake Evelyn, Lloyd climbed into his pants, found his coat, and slipped out into the day.

He stood on the sidewalk in front of their old home and took in the morning. The warm smell of fried bacon mixed with the sound of air brakes gasping on a school bus one block over. Lloyd was drawn back inside his house. *The four of them sat around the breakfast table. Evelyn made lunches. The kids fought over the last piece of bacon.*

Lloyd took a final bite of hotcake and watched his children. Their determined little faces and bold hearts—charged and ready for action. They could grow up to be anything. The world was a bright and sparkling place getting shinier by the minute. Lloyd looked around that long-ago table and admired their possibilities.

A boy on a bike wobbled by with a load of morning newspapers. It startled Lloyd back to the day. A paper bounced across his former porch and banged against the screen door. Lloyd saw the inner door open and half expected to see himself step through it.

Instead, an unfamiliar young man reached an arm out for the paper. He noticed Lloyd and fixed on him for a moment. Lloyd suddenly felt uncomfortable and out of place. He'd never met the people who'd bought their house. The realtors had handled everything while they traveled. The stranger looked at Lloyd, who didn't know where to look.

All Lloyd knew for sure was that the man on the porch was not him and that his kids were not inside fighting over the bacon. His son was in Booder, Indiana, pumping gas into people's cars. His daughter was across the continent staying as far away from her past and her parents as she could. Whatever possibilities had been in this house were long forgotten. Lloyd moved his attention away from the man in the door.

The needles on the little Scotch pine tree were starting to yellow. Lloyd could see that the roots weren't going to re-root. It looked pitiful up on top of its little mound. Lloyd wished somebody would just drag it off and be done with it.

Crossing the street again to their motor home, Lloyd smelled fresh coffee. Evelyn greeted him at the door with a steaming mug.

"How you feel this morning, Pop?"

Lloyd took his mug, leaned against the cab, and looked down the street. "I feel like I've seen enough of this place for one lifetime."

Lloyd wrinkled one eye with a sip of coffee. "I wonder what the weather's like in Oregon this time of year."

Evelyn looked cheerless, but not surprised at what she'd heard. She opened her mouth to speak, but before any words could come, Ralph and Rhoda's overhead garage door swept open with a grinding screech.

Standing against the dark interior, spotlighted by the morning sun, was Ralph Ditweiller. He had a big roll of nylon netting on each shoulder. Without a word he breathed in the perfect autumn morning and stepped out to meet it.

Lloyd grinned and shook his head. He handed his mug back to Evelyn and she watched as he crossed the driveway to help his old neighbor one more time. Two old men—one with time on his mind, one with time on his hands—working to catch the leaves before they fell.

31

Katherine Bedinger-Hoople felt herself being forced back into the comfortable recesses of the leather first-class seats. The roar of the massive turbines pushing the airplane down the runway was reserved for the coach passengers. All Katherine heard from her exclusive vantage was a distant murmur and a whisper of power.

As the nose wheel lifted from the runway, Katherine's baby shifted inside. She felt the weight of it press against the base of her spine and touch a nerve. A swell of emotion welled up from that place; it built and spread like oil splashed on water revealing itself in the corners of her eyes, and in the whites of her knuckles clutching the armrest, and in the gasp that escaped her mouth when the sensation finally built into a spasm deep inside of her.

That was not a contraction, she said firmly under her breath. A man about her age stretched his left hand out into the aisle. His white-on-white Egyptian cotton shirt sleeve slipped up his arm revealing a gold Rolex watch. He frowned at it.

"Twenty minutes late." He spoke flatly and looked to Katherine to join him in his displeasure.

Seeing the anxiety on Katherine's face and noticing her condition for the first time, he became immediately condescending. "But don't you worry. It's a routine delay. Doesn't mean anything."

Katherine winced at the man's tone and recovered herself. "I'm not worried. I do this flight at least once a month."

The man's patronizing smile remained fixed around his straight white teeth.

Yale teeth, Katherine thought to herself. *Another Ivy League MBA with two children in boarding school, a BMW, a mini-van, a three-hundred-*

thousand-dollar mortgage in Connecticut, a low six-figure salary, a high six-figure ego, and the personality of a vinyl seat cover.

The Yale teeth parted and spoke. "You have family in New York, then?"

Katherine tried to sustain a friendly smile but it turned ever so close to a snarl. She knew that a man would never ask another man if he was traveling to be with family. Men presume men are on business and that women are dithering away their time on their families. The fact that Katherine had *FAMILY* embossed across the front of her in thirty-pound high relief did not soften her disgust.

"As it happens, I do have a husband in New York. He's been keeping our Upper West Side flat while I attended to my agency's West Coast division in L.A. Now, as vice-president, I'll be moving back to New York." Katherine watched for the man's reaction. She'd managed to work in enough important details of her own status and résumé to satisfy at least herself.

The man in the white shirt seemed unfazed. "When is the baby due?"

The man would not leave this family thing alone. Katherine dismissed the subject. "Today. The first one is never on time."

"Today?" The man still would not let it go. "How did you ever get the airline to let you fly?"

Katherine smiled slyly. "I talked a doctor who lives in my building into giving me a letter in return for letting him drive my Beemer while I'm gone." Katherine looked away, pleased that she'd also managed to mention her BMW.

Let the sexist Yale Yuppie middle-management twerp chew on that with his straight white teeth, Katherine thought.

The small swell of pride in her diaphragm seemed to ignite a chain reaction that spread down through her middle and around her insides. It sat her up in her seat and she let out a gasp.

"Are you alright?" The man reached across and nearly touched Katherine's wrist before she drew away.

"Yes." Katherine recovered her breath again. "It's just kicking, I think."

The man continued leaning across the aisle toward her. "You don't look okay. Should I call an attendant?"

Katherine summoned an icy charge and flash-froze the air between them. "I don't need attending, thank you."

Katherine moved to cross her arms with finality across her chest but could not find the space. They felt ridiculous perched on top of the mound of her impending motherhood so she had to let them drop. They laid palm up at her sides as she closed her eyes, let her head fall away, and pretended to fall asleep.

The arm in the white-on-white Egyptian cotton sleeve retreated across the aisle and buried itself beneath another arm just like it. For lack of anything useful to do with themselves, they laid there barely moving as the man breathed and the color of his bewilderment worked its way up his neck, out of the white-on-white shirt collar, and crept into his face.

Katherine alternately dozed and studied the changing shapes on the backs of her eyelids. She felt her insides rearranging themselves like planets aligning. She was almost ready.

The past thirty-six weeks, three days, and sixteen hours had been all a matter of timing. The change to account supervisor. The move to L.A. The promotion to vice-president. The pregnancy. That part hadn't been planned, but the timing had worked out perfectly.

Almost perfectly. She was supposed to have moved back to New York a month ago. Richard had their Lamaze classes all arranged and she could have used the time off her feet, but she'd had some delays with the Bramble account and needed to see it through. Her promotion depended on it.

Richard had walked her through the breathing exercises on the phone over the past three weeks. She would be ready for full-blown motherhood as soon as she got settled in New York. She had six weeks' paid leave and a brand-new office waiting for her as soon as the baby was born. It was all a matter of timing.

Katherine breathed into the leather seat and allowed herself a soft smile. She felt it all the way down to her toes. Her arms found their way around her belly and she drifted again. Life was good. Life was just as it should be.

The man in the white-on-white shirt jumped nearly out of his seat and turned to the incredibly pregnant woman across the aisle from him. The incredibly pregnant woman sat up like masonry and looked around, disoriented. "I was dreaming. Did I say something?"

"Well, it sounded more like a dog barking."

"I was dreaming I was having my—HAAAAFF." Katherine clutched her stomach. Her face disappeared inside the creases of her pain.

"Yes. Sort of like that. Are you . . . ?"

"HAAAFF!" Katherine now had the attention of the flight attendant and most of the rest of the first-class cabin. The attendant came over trying to put a *can I get you another pillow and blanket* smile over her apprehension.

"Is everything alright?"

The sweat poured off Katherine's face as she fumbled in her purse. Suddenly her legs shot forward and the sleeping gentleman in front of her in seat 2B vaulted into the bulkhead. "HAAAFF!"

"I'll inform the captain." The attendant disappeared into the cockpit, her face as white as the shirt on the man across the aisle.

The man reached his arm to Katherine once more. This time she grabbed it hard at the wrist forcing his hand open. Katherine stuffed a stack of credit cards into the man's palm and talked between clenched teeth. "Call—my—husband."

The man released the phone in the seatback in front of him with Katherine's airline Visa card. Katherine noticed and was pleased that she would be getting additional frequent-flyer miles for the call. Between sporadic spasms and bursts of breathing, Katherine was able to give him Richard's phone number in New York.

"Hello, Richard? You don't know me, but your wife is with me here, and I believe she'd like to have a word with you." The cord was much too short to reach across the aisle to Katherine so he held it up to her general direction.

"HAAAFF!"

"Pumpkin, is that you?" Richard's anemic little voice barely spanned the distance. Katherine leaned farther into the aisle.

"Richard, I think I'm in labor. What do I do?" She strained to hear.

"How far apart are the contractions?"

"HAAAAFF!"

"Boy, that's close. You'd better lay down."

Katherine didn't hear the instruction but followed it all the same as the airplane tipped into a sharp bank and she let herself spill into the aisle.

Another contraction immediately overwhelmed her. Putting all thoughts of bearing and stature aside, Katherine lay on the floor. She held the legs of the seats trying to hear her husband over the pilot's announcement that the plane was diverting to Fort Wayne, Indiana, for a medical emergency.

A chorus of boo's erupted from the coach section. The first-class passengers checked their watches. The man in the white-on-white shirt was quiet. He held the phone and stared straight at Katherine with a look that said it was all her show.

The flight attendant covered Katherine's legs with a blanket. Richard coached from New York. If there was any terror in his voice it did not fit through the phone. What Katherine heard was calm and essential.

"Breathe through the contractions, and relax. Breathe and relax. Remember our Lamaze, Pumpkin. Breathe—relax"

The faces around Katherine: the attendant, the man with the phone, the man in 2B holding a towel to his nose, the co-pilot looking over his shoulder. They all seemed to drift to an outer layer the way the world seems when you stand up too fast: there, but not there. Present and out of reach at once.

Katherine tried to breathe past the pain as she'd been told. She tried to think past the pain, too, but that was impossible. She couldn't move her mind out of her body. It wouldn't budge. Her job, salary, car, insurance, IRAs, address, associates, background, age, education, upbringing, ancestry, and bottled water brand all hung out on the fuzzy perimeter with the faces on the airplane.

All that was left of Katherine was an urge and a muscle and an overpowering will to move the worlds within her. The flight attendant knelt at her feet pawing through a big blue book of emergencies. Katherine focused her attention on the bright red cross on the back of the book, and bore down with such force she nearly uprooted the seat legs in her hands.

"Focus—breathe. Relax—breathe." Richard had lost the rhythm of the events. He was dancing to his own band a long way from here. Katherine pushed the phone out of her face.

There was a stillness inside her for a moment. Katherine breathed deeply, as if for a long swim underwater or a leap from a sheer cliff. A landing strobe on the wing glanced through a window and pulsated on the slack face of the man in the white-on-white shirt. *Relax—breathe— relax—breathe.* The phone dangled by its cord from the back of the seat.

Katherine felt a bolt of might like a bucking horse grab her around the waist and seize the bottom of her backbone. The wind rushed up out of her and sang through her throat like a reed in an oboe. A single long, low note rang clear in Katherine's ears like the only sound she'd ever heard.

On the ground far below the Arabian mare whipped her head and shrieked her defiance at the mighty creature streaking overhead like falling stars and train whistles. The sound struck a chord in her genetic fiber and she leapt at the gate with every ounce of her. The white boards collapsed. She pulled back her head and screamed again as her hooves dug into the dry dust of her pen, vaulting her out into the cool grass and the wide empty fields.

Every strand of her lineage, every champion and rogue, charged with her after the powerful noise. For a quarter-mile across the beanfield she screamed and snorted and sent pieces of the Earth sailing in the air behind her. She dug deeper and a lather formed on her flanks and she had the illusion that she might catch it. And she would bite at its tail, turn it to her, and fly with it.

"It's a girl." The man in the white-on-white shirt was holding a damp cloth to Katherine's forehead.

Katherine felt the weight of her baby on her chest. Her arms found their way to it and they rested there as if they had never been anywhere else.

The passengers were silent. The faces around her searched for expressions. Katherine closed her eyes and filled her head with the smell of her daughter. She heard the man on the phone.

"It's a girl—yes—both of them seem fine. We're on our final approach for landing. We will call you from the ground. Fort Wayne. That's right. I think it's in Indiana. Near Ohio—right. Goodbye, Richard."

Katherine opened her eyes and looked to the man's face. His straight Yale teeth were concealed behind stiff lips. Anything else about him was lost behind his damp eyes. The strobe on the wing still played across his features, illuminating his admiration and his applause.

"We need to get you back in your seat." The flight attendant offered Katherine two hands. The man slipped his arms beneath her shoulders. Katherine relaxed in them and allowed herself to be moved up from the floor.

The attendant covered her with blankets. The man adjusted her seat and found her safety belt. Katherine fell back into the comfortable leather with the strength to do nothing but hold her baby.

The pilot extended the flaps and Katherine felt everything in her begin to slow with the airplane and find its way back to Earth.

A hundred pairs of curious eyes tracked the landing lights to the horizon over the chopped fields and straight wind rows surrounding Booder, Indiana. It wasn't very often that an airliner passed so low over town. They would mention it to each other the next day at Ray's Garage, and while waiting for their prescriptions at Big O Drugs, and with their cheese sandwiches on the seats of their pick-up trucks at lunch.

Dirk Miller would pull into Ray's for a fill-up and tell Anthony how his wife's nervous show horse had kicked the fence apart again. How he'd looked halfway to Fort Wayne, but finally found her back in the stable—dirty and wet, sides heaving—like she'd been running all night long.

Anthony will hang up the pump and shake his head. "Well, at least she wanted to come home. That'll be ten dollars, Dirk."

32

The whole room grew quiet. It was not the quiet of reverence or reserve, more like the awkward silence of a cast on stage when an actor drops a line.

Ed stood facing Zowat, his face pale with rage except for a bright dot of color that formed beneath his ears. Like a dog's hackles, those red spots didn't appear unless Ed Flannigan was seriously and irreversibly provoked. Emily could hear his teeth grinding from across the room and she knew her husband was using every bit of will he possessed not to punch the rotund group facilitator right in the nose.

Zowat wore the expression of the willing martyr. Her serene face said *Hit me. I understand and God will forgive you.* Emily closed her eyes and prayed for it not to happen. She knew that bringing Ed to this couples workshop had its risks, but she had never anticipated a brawl.

It was impossible to predict where events like these would go once they were set in motion. Of course, to predict anything at all, you have to understand the variables.

It began over a month ago with an innocent conversation between Emily and Zowat. They'd just finished a channeling session where Zowat had revealed that Emily and Ed were chained together as slaves in another life and that's why their marriage in this incarnation was lifeless.

Emily hadn't been noticing that her marriage was lifeless. In fact, she thought she'd been pretty satisfied with it overall. But Emily had learned to trust Zowat's vision and she soon began to see things.

At times the intimacy did seem forced. As Zowat had predicted because of their involuntary closeness those thousands of years ago. And there appeared to be unspoken anxieties. Passing moments of awkwardness between them, that Emily had not noticed before. *Age-old secrets,* Zowat had said. When people are forced together as slaves are, they must withhold some part of themselves for the sake of their private souls.

Emily began to notice some changes in Ed after the visit from his nephew Webster. Having the memories of his sister Amanda resurrected after all these years weighed on Ed. It turned him introspective and brightened him at the same time.

In many ways, Emily believed, it put a new kind of life into him. He animated easily. More like the old Ed, before the accident and the drinking. The Ed with two big arms swaggering and exaggerating.

Two big arms that could open to anyone, as his one-and-a-half arms did to Norman Tuttle when he showed up at their door seeking sanctuary. Ed never hesitated. He called Norman's dad, worked out the details, and diplomatically sold the proposition of Norman's finishing the school year in Quartz Creek. Because of Webster's being the son of Ed's sister and Norman's Uncle Oliver, Ed had come to the convoluted conclusion that Norman was darn near a Flannigan, anyway. He welcomed him into their home as such.

"He just needs some time to chill out or freeze over, or whatever the heck it is they do." Ed seemed to know exactly what was going on inside Norman and was able to explain it to a scorned and bereft father in Alaska.

But all of Ed's new grace and ease was directed to people other than Emily. She stood near his preoccupation but never in it. Emily would sit in the kitchen with her husband after dinner enjoying the family prattle when suddenly Ed would come out with a remembrance of his sister. Something Mandy had done, or said to him. And Emily would realize Ed hadn't even been in the room with her. He began telling stories of his sister to their own kids, who were mildly fascinated—just enough to indulge him.

It was very sweet in its way, Emily thought, but there was an edginess to it all. If she ever tried to press Ed for more details, or try to probe his feelings on having Amanda's ghost return after all these years, Ed would close down, not mentioning her again for days. Emily was oddly threatened by this and would take her worries to Zowat.

Emily sensed that Zowat had a deep interest and curious affection toward her husband. Ed and Zowat had an antagonistic relationship, but it was all outrage and tease, with no real malice or hatred.

Zowat's interest in Ed had swelled when Emily mentioned the visit of his mysterious nephew. Emily talked about how unsettling it was to have this young man Webster Cummings show up looking so much like a Flannigan that he and Ed could have been brothers. Zowat was typically empathic and Emily could feel all her own excitement of the event mirroring back to her from the gifted psychic.

"Where has this young man gone?" she'd asked.

"He's still trying to find the path to his mother. He knows Oliver Tuttle, his father, was killed in Vietnam. But Ed was the last clue he had to this Amanda Flannigan, or Mandy as Ed always knew her."

Mandy. Zowat said the name out loud as if summoning her spirit. It gave Emily the chills to watch. *Webster.* Emily thought she saw Webster's pain and loneliness flash in the mystic's deep blue eyes. *Oliver.* Zowat seemed to hold the word on her tongue like an exotic sorbet— melting into her pallet, absorbing its every nuance. Emily shivered again. When Zowat flexed her cosmic muscles it was a thrill to be a party to it.

It was only a few days later that Zowat had called Emily to tell her about a couples workshop she was organizing. *Secrets and Intimacy—A Spiritual Cleansing.*

Emily had brought Ed to the idea gradually. She really wanted them to do something spiritually as a couple, but there were some problems.

Most of what Ed knew of spirituality wouldn't hold up one end of a ouija board. Also, there was Ed's attitude about Zowat. He called her a grandstanding charlatan. He saw her as a flamboyant mystic, a multi-colored herb-oiled freak with a dangerous influence over her impressionable following. But Ed loved to hate her and it was that friction that kept them both coming back for more.

"Secrets and intimacy? With Pocahontas?" Ed had not been thrilled with the suggestion, but he loved the subject. "I'll allow as how she probably knows something about secrets. Anybody with a handle like *Zowat* has a bone in the trunk somewhere. But intimacy! I'll bet she hasn't been—"

"Ed, don't be a pig."

. . .

Things eventually settled down and Emily was able to lead Ed to the commitment. Spending one whole day at a Zowat seminar, as bizarre as it seemed, was only building on what Ed was already doing on his own.

Although he would never brag about it, Ed had softened his view on a lot of things since moving to Quartz Creek. Self-conscious over his own bouts of sincerity, Ed would blame it on the water, or *that rock in the mountain and those crystal twirlers*. Emily knew it was all of that and much more, but she kept her knowledge to herself for fear of spooking him.

Ed seemed to take a great peace of mind from his orchard and vegetables. After spending most of his life operating noisy and dangerous heavy machinery solely designed to rip the Earth into satisfactory shape for other machinery to travel on, making food come up from the same Earth and drop from the trees touched Ed in a quieter place.

The quiet suited him. He had never been one to sit still, unless to brood, but Emily would often find her husband propped against a tree in the orchard for the most part just to be there. She admitted to a mild jealousy over these trees. But whatever they were doing for her husband was good for them all and forgivable.

Norman's return to the farm flattered Ed. It matured him as a father to his own children, and he began to engage with them again like he hadn't since the accident with his arm. Sensing how careful he must be in rationing his attentions among the young people around him, Ed tuned himself to their moods and watched them like he did his trees.

Also, the three months of nearly nightly recovery meetings were beginning to tell on Ed. He didn't say much about them, but he'd stopped complaining about them, and Emily saw something beginning to shift in him. She had glimpses of another man peering out of her husband's eyes. Tantalizing and terrifying at once. She knew for sure she was dealing with a new and improved Ed Flannigan when he agreed to attend the seminar.

"There was a guy said something about secrets in a meeting the other night. Said, 'you're only as sick as your secrets.' I think that's true. My family got real sick when Mandy left. That's when all the lies and secrets started. I never even told you."

Emily was moved by Ed's sincerity. His suspicions about Zowat never faded, but his willingness to take part in the workshop remained steady until the moment they stepped up to Zowat's front door.

"Leave your identities on the porch. We're starting all over in here with new names!" Zowat stood in the entry excitedly peeling nametags from a big sheet. Each blue-and-white conventioneer's label read *HELLO, My Name is. . .* , and in the space provided underneath Zowat had written new names for everybody in black magic marker.

"Emily, because of your lightness of spirit, you are now *Mountain Breeze.*" The exuberant mystic pressed the tag onto Emily's sweater, then placed her hands together and bowed respectfully. Emily gamely returned the bow.

Ed was backed right up against the front door as Zowat approached with his new name.

"Ed, because of your resilience and playfulness—*Dancing Otter.*" Zowat fixed the label to the flap of Ed's shirt pocket and again bowed in genuine regard.

Ed looked down at the nametag as if Zowat had just wiped her mouth on his shirt. Looking to his wife was no comfort. Emily stared at Ed, her expression making it clear that if he didn't play along, Mountain Breeze was going to freeze his pipes for him.

Zowat turned into the living room with a self-satisfied smile lingering somewhere between Buddha and a used car dealer. Three other couples sat in varied positions on pillows around the room.

"People, I'd like to introduce you to Mountain Breeze and Dancing Otter."

The gathering received Ed and Emily with thin holistic smiles. They could have been a group of vacationing funeral directors.

"This is Playful Sparrow and Little Elk." Zowat indicated a young couple molded across their pillows in expansive yoga positions. In the middle of the room a man and woman lay side by side doing measured breathing exercises while they waited.

"That's Cool Water and Forest Wind." And pointing to the last couple by the window who were massaging each other's temples: "And over there are Bouncing Bobcat and Shadow on the Ground."

Ed followed Emily to a vacant mound of pillows and eased himself to the floor muttering the name of a well-known Messiah and a few of his apostles.

Zowat sank to the carpet like entropy. The cascading garments gathered around her in layers of colors and static electricity. "We'll begin."

Seven varieties of forest animal and natural element sat up intensely on their pillows. Dancing Otter grunted and shifted onto his good elbow. Emily stroked the hair behind his ears gently. Calming a riled dog.

Satisfied, Zowat addressed the circle. "Welcome to Secrets and Intimacy—A Spiritual Cleansing. The purpose of this workshop will reveal itself as the day unfolds, but the broader theme is to illuminate the difference between what is concealed—and what is simply not visible. How to share our secrets without losing our private selves. To help with this, I've given all of you new names for today: No history, no baggage, no secrets.

"So, to get started, let's go around the group and each of you tell us something about yourself. And let me remind you, everything that's said in this seminar should be made in the form of *I* statements."

Zowat looked around the group and settled her ardent blue gaze on Ed. "Dancing Otter, why don't you get us started."

Ed rolled up on his pillow and scratched his head. "*I* statements?"

"Yes." Zowat smiled evenly. Emily stopped breathing.

"Okay here goes one—When *I* was under my tractor one day *I* got a little ball of rust stuck in my *eye*."

Emily pinched Ed on the back of the neck. He bunched his shoulders to fend it off and looked around the circle to share and take credit for his good humor.

The combined good humor of the entire group couldn't have spun a top, and they all kept their eyes averted except for Zowat. Her look remained fixed on Ed in the superior way of any counselor or priest who sits with the assumed powers of heaven and Earth on their side. "Ed, why do you resist so much?"

"Resist what?" A bright dot of color began to form under Ed's left ear. Emily saw it and her heart fell.

Zowat spread her smile even more thinly across her face. "You don't have to live in confusion and fear. Why do you resist the lighter path?"

Ed sat up and indicated the gathering in the room with his prosthesis. "You call this a lighter path? You people are about as much fun as a train wreck. Look at yourselves!" Ed pointed directly to Playful Sparrow and Little Elk who were still gloomily bending themselves into odd shapes across the room.

"You have complexions like corpses, bags under your eyes. You're afraid of everything from power lines to sunshine. You feel guilty about being white, ashamed of being American. There's only eight different things you'll eat—they all taste the same—and your shoes look stupid."

Ed, realizing he was losing momentum, snatched at a closing statement. "You're all clinically depressed and paranoid, and you're asking me to lighten up?"

Zowat was still unfazed. "Remember, Ed, *I* statements."

"Excuse me. *I* think you're all clinically depressed and paranoid and have nothing to offer but more things to worry about."

Ed was totally up on his knees now which put him head and shoulders above Zowat, who still sat serenely on her pillows. Looking at their profiles Emily saw two monuments of self-will. Chiseled features as hard as granite stood unbending in the face of the other.

Then Zowat allowed her features to soften slightly, and her face became, for the moment, that of another woman. "There's more to the world than you can always see."

The cast on stage was locked in the lights. The audience froze in their seats staring at the player who groped for his line in a script never written.

The anger inside Ed flashed from the burning coals below his ears. There was a moment of deafening quiet before the rage flew out of Ed's eyes and mouth. "I don't know where you heard that, but don't you ever say it again. My sister said that to me and while you're twice her size, you'll never be half the person Mandy was."

Emily stood helplessly across the room, shocked and touched by her husband's words. It was appalling to witness Ed speaking so savagely to her spiritual mentor and friend. But it was oddly comforting to hear him express such genuine regard so publicly for a sister he barely knew.

Zowat's air of eminence appeared to evaporate, leaving her just a person sitting on a pillow. "Your sister wasn't everything you think she was. She still isn't."

Ed sat on his haunches staring into the woman's face, fury popping his knuckles and twisting the muscles in his neck. It was a moment between murder and flight, the hedge between the crystallization of thought and the collapse of sanity. It is the place where men can turn feral and hideous actions ensue. And it is also where grace can cement itself into a permanent setting with a man's soul. A place of utter helplessness.

The other people in the room were seized in their positions. The yoga couple were fixed in permanent pose. Bouncing Bobcat, Shadow on the Ground, and the rest tried to become part of the upholstery.

No one was looking at Ed anymore when he finally spoke. "Who are you?" The question emerged through the chill as a demand. The tone, that of an arresting officer or a provoked sentry.

The woman on the pillow raised herself up and submitted. "It's me." Amanda Margaret Flannigan reached for her brother's hand, her statically charged clothes crackling with the motion.

Ed kept his hand on his left knee, every bit as uninspired as the metal limb lying across the other leg. The space between the woman's extended hand and the man on the floor filled with the electricity. The hum of the empty space and the glare of Ed Flannigan's blank heart filled the room.

Emily sat in the hush but felt no peace. It was not the quiet of tranquility that surrounded them, but the dead quiet that comes before, and after, calamity. It was impossible to tell from this vantage which was which.

33

Two weighty problems tugged on the mind of Anthony Decker. One was stacked behind him in the truck bed. The other was back in town leaning over the counter of Big O Drugstore. The first one was three-quarters of a ton of bricks. The other one was Melinda—and they weighed on him about the same.

The front end of the truck was so light it barely steered. Anthony slowed a little and clutched the wheel, swinging it in broad arcs from side to side as he bounded down Pilkington Road. The bed was piled high with concrete blocks. Too high. Anthony smelled the rubber from the overloaded, overheated tires and tried to do the math again.

It was going to take three hundred blocks to do the foundation under his house trailer. His truck could carry about a thousand pounds at a time. A block weighed about forty pounds. So, how many trips would it take to get all the blocks out to the house and would it be enough to get his courage up to ask Melinda to the ball?

Anthony untied his eyebrows and shook his head. It was impossible. He must have been home with the flu the week they taught that in school. He caught another whiff of hot rubber and slowed down a little more. You didn't have to be a mathematician to know when there were too many bricks on the truck.

Anthony's head was muddled with a lot of things this week, not the least of them being Booder Fever Days. Booder Fever Days was the week set aside each year to commemorate the town founder, Emanual S. Booder.

Unlike most other frontier settlements which were located strategically at the confluence of rivers, or along established overland routes, Booder was settled about forty miles from anything that made sense.

As legend had it, E. S. Booder was making his way across the Indiana wilderness to seek his fortune in the West when late one day his horse fell over dead. Tenacity not being a family trait of the Booder clan, Emanual woke up in the morning, looked around, shrugged his shoulders, and planted corn.

There are no Booders left in Booder anymore, but their legend deliberately lives on. Booder Fever Days is not so much a prideful look at a community's roots as it is an excuse to hang a banner across the street, put all the back-to-school clothes and lawn and garden supplies on sale, and have a dance.

The annual Corn Ball was a combination homecoming dance, harvest moon ball, and Halloween party. It was the social event of the year and seemed every bit the chore for Anthony Decker as moving the bricks he was planning to put under his trailer.

Anthony didn't know why he was in such a hurry to get a foundation under his house trailer. And he didn't know why he was in such a steam to ask Melinda to go with him to the Corn Ball. He'd lived his whole life without them and now he couldn't get either of them out of his head.

Some things just happen in their own good time, but Anthony didn't know anything about that. He did know he was becoming obsessed with a young woman who'd been selling him toothpaste and pocket combs for five years.

He knew he wouldn't have an opportunity like this for a long time. When they say the Booder Corn Ball is the social event of the year, that doesn't mean it is the foremost social event of the year. It means it's the only social event of the year. There hasn't been much of a fire under this little burg since E. S. Booder's horse hit the dirt.

Anthony also knew that he'd selected this heady week of Booder Fever Days to take a week off to work on a place he'd been letting go for eight years. But he didn't know why.

The trailer house had been needing a foundation for some time. It had been teetering on an odd collection of wooden blocks and metal jacks for years. Anthony had always been hesitant to put too much underneath his house because he could never decide which way he wanted it to face. He regularly swung it around with the towtruck from the garage as the seasons changed, or the mood suited him.

But Anthony's humble abode seemed different to him when he got back from his trip to Oregon. He'd only been gone a few days, but the old place never felt better. It was less like an aluminum box with windows and wheels falling off its cribbing, and more like an old house settling into the landscape. Anthony lay in bed the first night back listening to that hot, heavy August wind blowing back and forth in Dirk Miller's beanfield. It lulled him to sleep as it flexed the aluminum window frames like the creaky springs of a familiar old chair.

A month later, an early fall northerly came down out of Michigan bringing a chill and a whiff of winter. The weight of the wilds of Canada whisked under Anthony's floors and howled in his drainpipes. Coyotes cried in the woods in his dreams, and bears rocked his walls in the darkness.

Anthony had seen Dirk the next day at the gas station and told him, "I think I better get a footing under that thing before it falls over."

"So you're staying, then?" Dirk fiddled with the gas nozzle trying not to sound interested. Anthony had been pretty closed-mouth about his plans since the trip to see his sister. News of his father's close call with the heart attack came right after that. Dirk hadn't wanted to pry.

"I figure I'll be staying for the winter, anyhow." Anthony closed Dirk's hood and stuffed a rag back in his coverall with a trademark Booder shrug.

"You ever laid any block, Dirk? I think I want to put cement blocks down."

Anthony swung the truck into his yard and backed up to the pile of blocks already there. He jumped from the cab and began unloading. He'd have to move fast if he was going to catch Melinda before lunch break.

Anthony hefted a block in each hand. As he grunted them up onto the stack next to the trailer he thought of what he would say to her. He couldn't just come out and *ask* her. That would be too . . . direct. He'd have to see if she was at all interested first. Because if she wasn't interested, then what was the point of asking? If he just wanted to hear somebody say "no" he could call up Demi Moore and ask her out Saturday night. No, he'd have to be much more tactful than that.

Anthony had been unsure of Melinda ever since he returned from Oregon. Before he'd gone she'd seemed awfully friendly toward him. She'd even spoken directly to him on several occasions. But she'd been a little cool since then.

Anthony had gone in and tried to strike up a conversation about what he'd seen Out West, but Melinda seemed easily distracted. He'd be telling her one thing or another about the mountains he saw, the bus station in Portland, or other things that made an impression, but Melinda would just look polite and wander off into the notions aisle to price buttons, or she'd start dusting the old foot powder cans below the cash register.

Anthony thought she felt like he was bragging, so he got pretty quiet about his trip Out West, the only interesting thing he'd done in eight years. This left gaping holes in their conversations.

Anthony climbed back in the truck and headed down the road to town. His rig seemed altogether perkier without all the blocks weighing it down and Anthony gunned the accelerator a few times to feel the surge. He could make the drugstore easily by lunchtime and he knew exactly what he had to do.

Melinda was dusting the wristwatches inside the revolving counter display. Anthony could see her tongue barely visible between her lips as she concentrated on getting her hand in and out of the case before it rotated to the next position. She didn't seem to notice him come in, so Anthony leaned in over the counter with a face full of exaggerated interest in the operation.

"That might be a whole lot easier if you pulled the plug first."

Unruffled, Melinda stood up straight and laid her dustrag down. "Yes, I know, but it would take all the sport out of it."

She took a tiny flat key from the pocket of her apron and locked the plastic case securely. "Sometimes you need to invent your own fun. Especially around this place."

It was perfect, Anthony thought. "No, not much happening around this town." Anthony backed slowly away from the counter toward the wall by the stamp machine.

"No, not much." Melinda checked the time on her watch against the watches in the case, then got distracted by a chip in her fingernail polish.

Melinda was not aware of Anthony edging his way toward the Booder Fever Days poster hung on the wall which announced the Corn Ball in big letters formed by pieces of an exploding pumpkin. Anthony leaned against the wall placing his hand directly under the explosion.

"Well, I guess every so often something happens." Anthony crossed one leg over the other and leaned harder on the poster. He didn't know what was supposed to happen next, but he felt comfortable knowing he was doing his part to move this relationship along.

Melinda remained absorbed in the ends of her fingers. She opened a travel manicure set on display next to the electric shavers next to the wristwatches. "Yes, I suppose every so often there's something different."

Anthony's arm was starting to fall asleep. "Like the time one of Dirk Miller's cows got exploded by lightning." Anthony grinned at the clever link to the drawing of the explosion at his fingertips.

"Yes, there was that." Melinda checked her watch again and started to untie her apron. "Well, it's time for my break. If you need anything, Mel is back in the pharmacy."

"Umm, no. I'm good." Anthony flushed with disappointment and pulled his hand down. *What did she need, an engraved invitation?* "I've gotta get back to work myself."

Melinda stopped on her way around the counter. "You told me yesterday you had the week off."

"I do, but Dirk and me are putting a foundation under my trailer and I gotta get the block hauled out there." Anthony turned toward the door and only glanced back to Melinda. "I guess I'll see you around."

Anthony pushed through the door with his attention on his toes.

He walked past the front windows so absorbed in his defeat he could not feel her eyes upon him.

Melinda watched Anthony's head move along the Booder Fever Days Sale display and she didn't budge until he'd disappeared behind the Aloe-puree shampoo and conditioner pyramid. She looked at the empty window and spoke as if Anthony was still there. "Yeah, I guess I'll see you around."

The truck lumbered up Pilkington Road low and deliberately—like Anthony's mood. He'd loaded too many blocks again and was worried he was going to blow a tire.

I should have stopped by Ray's and put more air in, he thought. But he didn't want to go by the garage on his week off, and he didn't want to see Ray. Ray was the only person Anthony had told about asking Melinda to the Corn Ball. That was two weeks ago, and he didn't want to explain why he hadn't done it yet.

Anthony eased the truck off the pavement and onto his rough driveway. He backed up to the growing stacks of blocks and turned off the engine. *These things take time,* he was thinking. *And delicacy. There's gotta be a way to finesse this thing.*

Anthony reached for two blocks and pinched a finger between them. The edge cracked off one of his fingernails and he stuck it in his mouth with a curse. When the pain subsided he pulled the finger out to look at. Then he looked at all his fingernails—cracked, chewed, filled with dirt—and a smile spread across his face.

Finesse, he thought, grinning and piling blocks like they were hot rocks.

Melinda was changing the numbers on the price sticker machine. Anthony stopped in the doorway and watched her for a moment. He loved the way she worked her tongue in her mouth when she was concentrating on something. He took a deep breath and pushed into the store all purpose and plot.

Melinda looked up from her work and smiled. "Well, look who's back. Who do I have to pay for this honor?"

Anthony stood limp in his dirty shirt, a little overwhelmed with the question—unsure of her meaning and caught offguard by her friendly manner. Melinda was always cordial to him, but seldom warm. Anthony fumbled in his head for something easy to say and finally recovered his plan.

He held his hands out in front of himself with a huge concern on his face. "I've been thinking I need to clear up these fingernails of mine. They don't seem fit to be in public. You got any manicure tools?"

"Well, yes." Melinda bent to her display case. "We've got this set here. It's made compact for traveling. Which would be real handy—if you're traveling, you know." Melinda looked up at Anthony with part of a quiz on her face but Anthony was already examining the case.

"I don't need to take it anywhere. I just need to get some of this gunk out from under here." Anthony picked at a finger with the end of a nailfile, then ventured a glance at Melinda. "In case I have to make myself presentable for something."

Melinda leaned on the counter with her head in one hand as Anthony poked through the rest of the kit. "So, you're getting a foundation under your house, then?"

"It's not a house really. Just a trailer. But it's the only home I got and I figure I better get it bolted down." Anthony tried to dismiss the subject by holding another finger up and peering down the end of his nose at it. "No, I don't think I should take these fingernails out in public. Not that there's anything to worry about around Booder."

Melinda continued to hold her chin and her blue gaze was locked on Anthony with a frank smile on her lips. "So, if you're fixing up your place you must be planning to stick around."

Anthony blew air up his face in frustration as if giving up on the manicure. "Yeah, I'm staying put. For now anyhow. Well, listen, I better buy this thing."

Anthony swept his hand self-consciously across the glass countertop. "I shouldn't be cleaning my fingernails on your clean counter. I can work on this at home. I guess I've got a few more days to clean them up."

Anthony looked up at Melinda and his heart sank. She just wasn't getting it. She stood there looking at him with that silly smile on her face like he'd just come in to pass the time of day. What did she expect him to do, come right out and ask her? Anthony bit his lip and closed the zipper on his manicure set while Melinda worked the buttons on the cash register.

"That's eleven dollars and forty-three cents with tax, Tony."

The sound of his nickname made it difficult for Anthony to count out the change, but he finally managed to push it across the counter and into her waiting hands.

"Well, good luck with your foundation. I'm glad you're not leaving us so soon."

Melinda let her smile widen while Anthony smiled back weakly. He couldn't figure out how he'd let her stray so far from the subject. It seemed hopeless. At least for today. He had six more loads to haul tomorrow and he'd think of something.

On that happy thought Anthony turned to the door. "Well, I'll see you around."

"Yes, I guess you will." Melinda folded her arms thoughtfully on the counter in front of her. She leaned over them and followed Anthony's back through the front doors.

When he was out of sight Melinda let out a breath and lay her head in the palm of one hand, turning her eyes to the wall. The bright blue Booder Fever Days poster with the orange exploding pumpkin caught her attention and a notion lifted one of her eyebrows.

Melinda wondered what it would take to get a guy like Anthony Decker to ask her to the ball, or if he'd even consider such a thing. Then she smiled and went back to work on the sticker machine. It looked like there'd be plenty of time to find out.

34

Webster's excitement hovered so close to terror he nearly collapsed from the intensity of it. "You have to remember where it is! Where in the hell is it?" He realized he sounded hysterical, but he didn't care. He was hysterical. He dashed ahead of his companion and faced him.

Buddy Bedinger stopped and looked apologetically to his odd and eager associate. "I was drunker than a dog that night. I can't remember, but don't worry, we'll find it. How many camps can there be along here?"

Buddy fought to conceal his own feelings about the absent Oliver. His anxiety was evenly mixed with guilt that he hadn't really noticed the man was missing until he ran into Webster.

Both young men looked up and down the Seattle waterfront scanning for any vagrant enclaves carved out of the decaying urban fringe. There couldn't be many. They would find it, Webster knew they would. He drew an even breath and tried to relax. "Maybe we should ask somebody."

Webster was referring specifically to two men on the next corner. One man was obese and seemed catatonic standing in the rain in only his shirtsleeves. The smaller man's gaunt features jutted from the three or four coats slumped on his shoulders, which appeared to hunch him even further over a shopping cart piled high with garbage bags.

Webster and Buddy walked quickly up to them and startled the man in the coats. His eyes, dotted with bloodclots and yellow with disease, revealed a vague and distant regard that withdrew further in the face of Webster's urgent stammer. "Do you know a man named Oliver Tuttle? He's my father. They call him *the dreamer*. He's about fifty years old."

Buddy, seeing the man's bewilderment, touched Webster's sleeve

294

and took over with a calmer tone. "He camps around here with some other people—Arthur Bender or Blender or something. And an old hag named Rhonda, I think, and a lunatic named John Doe. It's his father." Buddy presented Webster's arm, limp in the sleeve. "This man is looking for his father."

The thin man gathered his coats in closer. His stout friend heaved himself into focus for a moment, then receded back into the folds of his face as he helped his partner shove the cart into motion. "We don't know any fathers."

They stepped into the street behind their cart directly into the path of a delivery van. Tires hissed on the wet pavement as the horn belted out a curse. The men continued wearily in front of the stalled vehicle, not even looking up as the driver shrieked, "You stupid drunks. I could have killed you!"

The fat man moved steadily forward. The man in the coats only hunched lower, resigned to the fact that his miserable life was once again not over.

Webster shuddered and looked at Buddy. "We've got to find my father."

"We will." Buddy looked down the drizzly row of warehouses in the timeless gray November light and tried to penetrate the fog enveloping a drunken night almost two months ago. It was a night he'd hoped to forget. Now, it seemed like nothing in the world mattered more than remembering.

Webster looked after the men with the cart until they disappeared with wary looks backward. The urgency welled up again—bullying and baffling him. He couldn't figure out why it had become so pressing that his missing father be found this very moment.

Nine months ago he didn't know Oliver Tuttle had ever existed. When Webster did discover who Oliver was, the most distinguishing quality of his existence was that he was dead.

Webster had made a few stabs at determining the circumstances of his faceless father's demise, but the Army was not forthcoming with assistance. Webster had reached the edges of his patience, confidence, and finances. With no hope left of reassembling any rendition of a living, breathing family, Webster was about to turn back to his life in Boston when he discovered totally by accident that Oliver Tuttle had not been killed in action. He had not been killed at all.

Oliver had been listed missing in action after the helicopter he was flying in crashed in the jungle. The young soldier survived the crash severely injured and was evacuated to a Navy ship off the coast. The Navy got Army PFC Oliver Tuttle patched back together and returned to the States in a deep coma with the incompatible record-keeping systems of the two armed services leaving spaces on Oliver's paperwork as blank as the one between his ears.

Webster finally learned of this when he ran into a sympathetic corporal in Army Records at Fort Lewis. Webster had returned only to uncover any details that might be available on Oliver's death overseas for a final footnote in his file. After Webster was able to establish his identity, the corporal made his father's service record available to him.

"Up until a few years ago, corporals like me would never see these records. They're classified, you know."

Webster wondered why a private in the Army's activities would be classified and the corporal explained that early in the Vietnam conflict the United States was not fully engaged, and the American public still thought the military was serving primarily an advisory roll to the South Vietnamese government.

". . . and sometimes their advice called for certain things to be blown up. It's hard to tell, but it looks like your daddy was some kind of explosives whiz who was over there advising things to blow up. Something went wrong and his commander needed to cover his own *brass,* if you know what I mean. He slapped *Top Secret* on your daddy's file and forgot about it. That's my guess."

The records of the living Private Tuttle stop the day he left the ship. The next thing the Army did was send notices to next of kin that Oliver's MIA status was changed to *Missing and Presumed Dead.*

Webster could not believe what he'd read. "What happened to him?"

The stoic corporal shrugged. "The Army lost him somewhere."

"How can they lose a person?"

"The military is a huge and incredibly complex web of organizations run entirely by guys like me. It can lose anything. Believe me."

Webster was incredulous. "But *people?*"

"Truckloads of 'em."

Webster had been involved with research in general and this search in particular long enough to know this couldn't be true. There were records of everything. There is a big difference between losing somebody and just not knowing where he was.

Webster had impressed upon the soldier the gravity of his mission, moved him with an emotional diatribe on lost blood ties, tossed in a little bit of good-fashioned cash bribe, and was soon down to the facts of the matter—they'd lost him, all right.

When he'd exhausted all avenues, the soldier tried to offer an explanation. "He must have walked away—gone AWOL."

"He was in a coma."

"Maybe he woke up."

"Then where did he go?"

The corporal slammed a file down on his desk. "If I knew that, I'd tell you. And do you know why I'd tell you? I'd tell you because then you'd leave and I wouldn't have to think about Oliver Tuttle anymore. Give it up, mister. It does not appear that the U.S. Army was very interested in keeping track of this soldier."

The corporal turned and indicated his computer terminal. "I can guarantee you're not going to find him in there. Face it, your daddy's gone."

Webster had sat looking at the uniformed man knowing he was right, but not wanting to give him or the world the satisfaction.

"He had to go somewhere." Webster spoke with a certainty he didn't feel as he walked out of the building and re-entered his frustration.

Webster, having presumed his father was dead from the beginning of his quest, had never considered looking for any trace of him after 1964. With the dull hope that Oliver Tuttle survived his injuries and made his way back into the world, Webster was propelled once again into the bowels of any Seattle institutions that might have brushed against his father's life: hospitals, courts, police, utilities, unions, newspapers. Oliver Tuttle might not have stayed in the area, but it was the place to start.

Webster had spent two more months on the trail. It had been exhausting. Fruitless and exhausting. Boring, fruitless, and exhausting. And pointless. In the end he'd even lost his professional demeanor. He became surly and unpleasant. He badgered innocent clerks who had offered so much help to his helpless situation. He grew to resent them and the institutions they represented for not having the information he wanted.

It had all disintegrated to one remote possibility in a cluttered basement under City Hall that morning. The room contained the ancient records of forgotten events worth nothing to anybody except auditors and archivists. A couple of their apparent ilk sat at heavy tables in the dim light pawing through large bound portfolios of the minutia of official life in Seattle three decades ago.

Webster didn't have a lead, really—just another guess. He had the idea that *if* a man had just come out of a coma, and *if* that man managed to wander off into a city, *maybe* that man would have crossed the street wrong and gotten a ticket for jaywalking. As Webster continued to elaborate on the scenario—a dazed soldier with a bandaged head staggering through a paralyzed intersection—it became a certainty. Seattle is notorious for enforcing its jaywalking ordinances.

It was certainly an indicator of his desperation, but he'd managed to enlist the aid of a naive young intern in City Records to pore over all the pedestrian citations issued starting with July 1964. They were halfway into February 1965, feverishly thumbing flimsy carbon copies with rubber tips on their middle fingers, when the clerk suddenly snatched one from her pile.

"I have it!" She thrust the form in Webster's face, who read it and sneered.

"I said Tuttle, not Teeter. Tuttle-Tuttle-Tuttle! Oliver Tuttle!" Webster threw the page back at the clerk who responded by showing Webster her rubber-tipped finger from an evocative angle, and she stomped off.

Webster dropped the other citations on the table and left a piece of his will with them. Even if he had turned up something in these citations, what would that tell him? It would just be the beginning of another dead-end journey. Just enough of a flame to lure him deeper into the cave and farther from daylight.

Obsession must wear itself thin before you can see through it. It was time to leave this alone and go home. He had his work and he had his sort of Mom. Webster could not throw any more of his life away trying to follow the tracks of his missing, probably dead, father.

Webster had just put his shoulder to the heavy metal exit door at the bottom of the stairs when one of the other people in the room approached him and touched his sleeve.

"Excuse me." Webster took the man to be in his early twenties. Preppie looking. Probably a student. "Did I hear you say the name *Oliver Tuttle?*"

"Tell me what he's like." Webster and Buddy continued down past the moldy faces of aged loading piers and black-windowed warehouses. Buddy looked into the haze over Puget Sound. *What was Oliver like?*

This was weird. Two hours ago he was at City Hall in the middle of a routine research assignment for his Statistics final, and now here he was walking in the rain with a total stranger looking for a homeless vagrant known only as Oliver the Dreamer who happens to have dreamed about people named Tuttle.

Buddy didn't feel like he knew Oliver well at all. There wasn't that much to know, at least nothing that presented itself to him now. Buddy chewed his lip awhile before speaking to Webster's curiosity. It was awkward knowing more about a man's father than the man knew himself—and having that be so very little—but he knew it was important to Webster and that made Buddy feel important to himself.

"Well, he's a really nice guy. And reliable. He shows up to do our alley every day. And he's honest. He found a dollar bill in the milk crates one day and tried to return it to me. I couldn't believe it. The guy will work two hours for a loaf of bread and he wants to give back a buck that doesn't belong to him." Buddy glanced at Webster to see if this back-handed biography of his father was doing any good.

Webster squinted into the cracks of the broken sidewalk beneath their feet, conjuring the images. "When was the last time you saw him?"

Buddy thought for a moment. "Actually, it's been awhile. A week, at least. He doesn't stay away like this very often or for very long, but it happens. He doesn't remember much, and I figure he just forgets to come by for periods of time."

Buddy heard his own words and hesitated. He couldn't recall Oliver ever being gone this long, and he effected a more relaxed tone to conceal his own swelling alarm. "If I ask him where he's been he always smiles and says, *That's a good question, Buddy.* He's a character."

Buddy tried at first to be as flattering to Oliver as he could manage considering he spent very little time thinking about him. But the more he told about Oliver the more he realized he knew and the more he realized he cared about what happened to him. Every story of Oliver's visits to the hotel kitchen implied the absence of any more visits. Each repeated Oliverism charmed Buddy in a new and unexpected way. Before long Buddy was stepping two paces out in front of Webster, swinging his head into every potential den and quarry in the warehouse rubble they passed.

Buddy recognized his own panic and thoughtfully slowed his stride. Falling in step with Webster again, he sought something to comfort them both. "I'm sure he's okay. Oliver's attention span is pretty short but he takes good care of himself. Not like some of these dirtbags."

Webster flinched at the word and Buddy immediately regretted it. He began to sputter some retraction, but was distracted by a movement in the recess of a pillar supporting the highway interchange overhead.

Webster saw it, as well, and the two men turned into the recesses of the bridge abutment for a closer look. There, in the dryness of the underpass standing now as still as the loaded shopping cart beside him, was the large languid man from the street corner. Upon seeing them, the man moved his eyes briefly to the fading wet footprints that followed along a steep concrete bank up and out of sight.

Buddy noticed and a flash of recognition jarred him. A jumbled scene from a nearly unreachably distorted memory. A drunk and a maniac stumbling up some sort of ramp.

"This is it." Buddy pointed up the bank toward the top of the bridge abutment. "This is where Oliver lives."

The man in all the coats scampered out of reach like a dog caught in a yard when Webster's and Buddy's heads cleared the edge. Sitting around a smoldering metal can in the middle of the area were two other people, a woman and a man, who stared at the intruders menacingly.

"There ain't no Oliver here. Get away!"

Buddy recognized the woman as one of the hosts from his previous trip up the bank, and the man was the lunatic who'd dragged him off the street and brought him here. *John Doe. And that was Rhonda, no, Ramona. They're both insane.* Buddy tried to smile kindly but his voice came out condescendingly. An amateur lawyer leading naive witnesses.

"Why did this man come tell you we were looking for Oliver if he doesn't live here?" Buddy looked briefly up at the man lurking in the shadows. "I've never seen him before, but you I know. Don't you recognize me? I'm Oliver's friend Buddy from the Merrimont Hotel." The pair's hostility did not soften. "Buddy with the good bread?"

"We haven't seen Oliver. He's gone." John Doe sounded as savage as he looked, but there was an element of real distress behind the fierce eyes. Buddy knew he was hearing the truth and it stirred in him an unexpected foreboding. His face went soft and serious.

John Doe's rigid features slackened with Buddy's and Webster saw it as a way in. "I've been missing him, too. He's my father. Do you have any ideas where he might have gone?"

"Arthur. Arthur took him. He's behind it!" Ramona turned totally away and moved to join the man from the street.

Buddy turned to Webster. "Arthur is another one of them. An older guy. A drunk."

"Could they be off on a tear somewhere?" Webster looked at the condition of his father's friends and felt his own faith waning.

"No, Oliver never drank. He was always sober and healthy when I saw him." Buddy squatted down on his haunches and tried to speak sincerely to John Doe, who clearly despised the gesture. "Where do you think they went?"

John Doe looked sharply at Buddy, then at Webster, and finally settled his eyes on the smoke rising out of the can in front of him. "When they go, they're gone. I can tell when they're gone and when they're not. Arthur, Oliver—they're gone. . . ." John Doe's voice tapered to a point of clarity in his eyes. Sadness overcame madness and left him to sit there momentarily sane and devastated.

It is difficult to stand in front of a person who has lost everything in his life and watch him lose one more thing. Webster turned to the opening of the vagrant's retreat. Buddy stood and joined him, the grief in John Doe's sobs tugging dangerously at his own constitution.

Buddy did not understand his place in this anymore. At the moment he did not understand his place in anything. He'd done his part. Why didn't he feel done? This is where Oliver lived—had lived. That's all he knew. He was getting cold in the rain and wanted to get back to his studies. He looked at his watch more for the gesture than for the information, and followed Webster's gaze.

A ship went by in the murky channel. The gray skies met the gray water off in the distance where one looked just like the other. With no clear horizon to focus on, Webster felt unsteady on his legs, hardly knowing where to look.

Buddy looked into the seamless cloud and felt his head swoon like vertigo. His stomach shifted in him. Then a gull appeared out of the haze, gliding easily toward them. The only valid reference point in view, the bird rocked Webster and Buddy on their heels as it dipped and dove and disappeared.

35

Oliver stared down into the sea. From this high vantage he could make out shapes on the ocean floor—reefs and canyons, pinnacles and rocks. They would never be seen from a ship. The captain might not know they were there at all. Not until he was right on top of them.

"Dear Miss, I will have another of these." Arthur Tender, Oliver's dubious companion, held his empty glass unsteadily out in front of him to the first-class cabin attendant. "I do believe that is the finest cognac I've ever tasted."

Oliver turned his attention into the airplane. The flight attendant looked at Arthur doubtfully and Oliver became nervous again. "Arthur, don't you think you've had enough?"

Arthur Tender's inebriated face fell into a lurching and grandiose smile. "My dear people." Arthur waved his glass to the other first-class passengers who were ignoring him as they had been for over an hour. "Money. Love. Cognac. One can never have enough of these."

The flight attendant took the glass. "One more before we land." She looked from Arthur to Oliver and back again, then turned into the galley.

Oliver touched Arthur's arm. "I think we better be careful. We'll get caught."

Arthur brushed off Oliver's caution. "Piffle! We've done no wrong. We've merely taken a vacation. Is that a crime?"

Oliver winced at Arthur's inability to lower his tone. "No, but isn't it a crime to take *somebody else's* vacation?"

"Perhaps," Arthur conceded and took a deep breath, sending yet another button flying from the front of his Polynesian print shirt.

The flight attendant eyed Oliver from behind the curtain, causing him to squirm inside his over-sized polo shirt. It was more than clothes that didn't fit about these two oddballs and she knew it. Oliver avoided her continued scrutiny by looking back to the sea and trying to piece it all together again.

It had begun the day before in the rain in the alley behind the Merrimont Hotel. Oliver had been straightening up the trash containers and crates for his daily bread from the kitchen staff. Arthur had happened by, huddled in his overcoat against the drizzling afternoon, and decided to wait around until Oliver finished.

"To keep you company, good friend." Oliver knew that Arthur Tender simply wanted to get the dining room bread fresh and early. Sometimes it took Oliver awhile to make the long walk from the hotel to their encampment. Sometimes if the weather was bad he didn't go back at all if he'd earned enough from his day's labor to afford one of Milton's rooms at the Crusader Arms.

Arthur must have been particularly hungry and wasn't taking any chances. The Merrimont Hotel made the finest bread in Seattle. Even the palate of a dumpster-diving drunk could appreciate the quality and anticipate the pleasure.

"I believe I'll just browse through the merchandise while you finish up, friend."

Oliver had seen Arthur Tender's feet disappear over the edge of the big green dumpster and thought nothing of it while he returned to his work. Suddenly there was a thrashing noise inside the container. There was a sound like panic, or delight—impossible to tell—and then Arthur's head popped up, his eyes wide with wonder and reverence.

"Oliver, there is a God."

Oliver didn't get it. "In there?"

"Yes, my good friend, in here." Arthur's head vanished again into the bin.

Oliver was not much for digging in trash bins. He preferred to work for his keep—but *God?* This bore looking into. He held his broom nervously in his hands and walked over to the dumpster. "Arthur?"

Instead of his friend's face appearing, a large dark shape lobbed over the side and landed at Oliver's feet. It was a brown leather valise, quite a nice one. Its several compartments were open and the articles inside poked into view. There was the tip of a shiny shoe jutting from a side pouch. The collar of a brightly colored silk shirt squirted through the zipper of the main compartment.

Oliver was standing over the suitcase trying to make a connection between it and the Almighty, when Arthur's considerable bulk heaved itself over the lip of the dumpster. He landed gracelessly on his feet in the alley and beamed at Oliver over the top of some little folded papers in his hand.

"Oliver, it is said that in times of dire need God will give us what we require. And we require a vacation." Arthur Tender held up two first-class airline tickets and fanned five one-hundred-dollar bills. "Honolulu, my good man. Waikiki. Papayas and PuPu's on the patio. Bikinis and imbibement on the beach. Ah, yes, it is just what we need."

"But these aren't ours." Oliver backed a step away. "Somebody lost them."

"Stolen, I'd say. Someone had already searched through the case and discarded it." Arthur fanned the tickets and cash one last time before tucking them into his coat out of the steadily increasing rain. "I found these inside the security pocket. I once owned a valise like this myself. Lost in the yacht fire off Catalina in '76."

Oliver had become accustomed to Arthur's references to his alter ego of a wealthy industrialist, but it disturbed him when they were somewhat substantiated by his actions or knowledge of things. "But shouldn't we try to find the owner?"

Arthur appeared not to hear. Instead, he was bent over the suitcase taking inventory. "Ralph Lauren polos, size large. Polynesian prints on China silk, Faragamo loafers—certainly a man of taste."

Arthur held a white polo up against Oliver's slight frame. "It might be a tad loose under the wings, but perfect for the climate." He held the loudest silk print to himself. Obviously, the man with the good taste who once owned this clothing was a considerably larger man than Oliver, but still a gallon or two shy of Arthur Tender.

"I see an opportunity for a diet. Come, man, our flight leaves in a matter of hours. We must change and get to the airport."

It was moving too fast for Oliver. He snatched the fine clean shirt to save it from the ground when Arthur let go of it, but it did not feel like his.

Arthur Tender's history might be sketchy and unbelievable, but at least it was something. Oliver's past was a room full of gray smoke and an anxiety in the night. But somewhere out of the smoke there was a sense of something that percolated up from time to time, less a memory of fact than a feeling about things.

As Arthur's enthusiasm led Oliver out of the alley with his tidy shirt, he had to speak what he felt. "Arthur, don't you think that God also *tests* us with these kinds of things?"

Arthur paused next to the curb and gutter running wild with the rain pouring off the downtown streets. Morality debates took all of Arthur's concentration. He could not walk and do them. As he stood and considered, a taxicab sped down the curb behind him sending a rooster tail of water across the sidewalk.

"God gives us all what we need." Arthur repeated his original premise at about the time the wall of water reached the two men and splashed them nearly off their feet. Arthur sputtered and straightened his hat, but did not waver from the point at hand. "And *we* need a vacation."

Oliver gingerly wrung the polo shirt in his hands, beginning to grasp the meaning and wisdom of Arthur Tender's spiritual position.

"But shouldn't we go back and tell John Doe and Ramona? Shouldn't I at least tell Buddy at the hotel? Everyone will worry."

"Better to leave them worried than heartbroken and envious, dear Oliver. We'll tell them of our adventures upon our return. Now, to the airport."

Oliver followed two steps behind Arthur Tender and his fine leather valise. He had a bad feeling about this. It wasn't just the integrity of the situation; it was something else. Like so much of Oliver's life, it lurked in the smoke of his memories, just out of his reach.

. . .

The plane banked over the island of Oahu and tipped Oliver toward the ground. The deep blue of the ocean, the green hues of the islands, and the white strands of beach all leapt up at him. He pushed back from the window and startled the sleeping Arthur Tender beside him.

Arthur snuffled and stretched and gathered in his surroundings. Remembering where he was at last, he leaned over Oliver to the window. "Ah, Paradise found. Have you ever seen anything like it, Oliver?"

"Yes." Oliver spoke so softly Arthur could barely hear him. "I think I have." Arthur turned to his quiet friend and said nothing. Oliver was shrunk into his seat with his eyes closed and a pinch to his face like a man about to be slapped.

The bus from the airport to Waikiki was quiet and air conditioned. All sense of Paradise was lost to the concrete and asphalt maze of rental-car lots, strip malls, and warehouses. Oliver sat near the aisle looking over the driver's shoulder, concentrating on the road ahead.

Arthur Tender scanned the scenes going by the window and occasionally let out a private chuckle or a giggle of delight. He was clearly enjoying himself. At one point he spied a man pushing a bottle in a brown bag into his face as he lay inside the cool shadow of a metal building.

"Ah Fate, ye fickle woman, you. If only I'd chosen Honolulu to be homeless. I don't know why you'd need a home in this climate—except a place to store the family, perhaps."

Arthur looked to Oliver to share his good cheer, but Oliver's attention remained fixed on the windshield.

"Come now, my glum chum. This is a *vacation*. Are you still worried about your integrity?"

"No, I don't think it's that. I'm not sure what it is. I just don't feel like I should be here."

Arthur patted his friend on the back. "The only emotion more worthless than guilt is nostalgia. Don't allow either one to destroy your good humor, friend."

Arthur returned to his scan of the sights and sensations of the city of Honolulu as it built toward Waikiki Beach, oblivious to the notion that amnesiacs are not capable of nostalgia.

Oliver wallowed in a pool of feelings that came up from inside him in convulsions—waves of anxiety that drew a sweat around his thin hairline and gave him the urge to climb entirely inside his scavenged Ralph Lauren polo shirt—a feat that was, at least theoretically, possible.

The bus came to a halt in a cool, windswept gorge of shops and hotels. Arthur and Oliver stepped onto the street. Arthur took in a snootful of air and smacked his lips as if to taste it.

"There is something on the wind that speaks of merriment. This weather puts me in mind of some rum, don't you think?" Arthur put an arm around his edgy friend as a gesture of comfort, but used it to steer him down the street. "We must find our way to the golden sands, but first we will need an item or two."

Thirty minutes later, Arthur and Oliver came squinting out of a discount store. With their day-glo flip-flops, knee-length surfer shorts, and Hang Ten visors, they blended seamlessly into the colorful streets of Waikiki. They were more likely to be taken for aging hippies in search of one last perfect wave than a poverty-stricken self-described empire builder and his empty-headed homeless comrade searching for a view of the ocean and a bottle of rum.

"To the beach, then." Arthur adjusted his visor, caught a new grip on the valise and on Oliver, and with thongs slapping their heels, they made their way into the fray and the hot Pacific sun.

"This, my friend, is vagrancy at its finest!" Only Arthur Tender's head showed above the sand. Oliver crouched nearby and said nothing. Oliver hadn't said anything for over an hour, but Arthur was far too drunk to notice. His face was as round and red as the ball of sun that plunged toward the horizon in a perfect parody of fulfillment.

Arthur had slowly and steadily dug a hole in the beach and had drunk himself into it as the afternoon wore on. Oliver had helped cover him with sand as Arthur's alarming white hide changed to frightening pink and his ability to take care of himself diminished.

Oliver, for his part, had taken refuge inside his shirt. Not just from the sun, but from the entire world. Were it not for some canine-like devotion to his inebriated friend, Oliver certainly would have bolted and run by now. The sights, sounds, even smells of Waikiki got so far inside him it felt like someone was scraping out the insides of his bones.

The shadow of a palm tree on the sand was like a spider creeping up the beach to get him. He moved to the other side of Arthur as it passed by; the sound of its willowy fronds in the warm Pacific breeze, like snake hisses, sent chills across his skin. Goosebumps in the bright hot sun. He pulled his arms inside his shirt and looked away to the people.

Legions of tourists in all manner of costume made for a colorful distraction for a time, but of the entire throng Oliver picked out two soldiers walking by. Their dress uniforms were the bleakest sight in six hundred yards, and all the more captivating.

The young men in them ogled half-naked women with their Missouri Boy grins, gripping their hats and fanning their faces in fraudulent swoons. Oliver fixed on their black boots. Spit shines flashing in the light, each flash like a burr in Oliver's sandal. He rubbed his toes absently to ease the blisters that were not there.

When the tropical sun reached the straight blue horizon, the bottom dropped out of its shape. It collapsed into the sea with the sound of music from the sunset cruises off the beach, a smattering of applause from revelers at a nearby hotel, and the loud snores of Arthur Tender. A mound of sand below his chin heaved and fractured in step to the sound.

Oliver removed the empty bottle from Arthur's limp grip. Red ants struggled through the sticky inside and circled the neck. Other rum-crazed insects great and small scurried about the dormant head in the sand. Oliver brushed them away and stood to discard the bottle.

Only two homeless people on vacation with all of Waikiki at their disposal would lounge within four feet of a trashcan. But it did seem like the most approachable place on the beach to Arthur Tender and Oliver.

As Oliver extended himself out of his shirt to drop the bottle, a pair of flight seeing helicopters suddenly roared from behind him and streaked across the growing twilight. Oliver felt the *whop-whop-whop* of their rotors chop at the valves around his heart. His legs went out from under him, and he landed hard on the ground.

A pain rushed up his back and arched him against the sleeping Arthur Tender. Arthur only twitched, shooing an ant from his nose. Oliver's cries were gobbled up by the passing airships and dragged out to sea with the light.

In the long dark shadow of the trashcan, two men lay senseless in the sand: one drugged unconscious by distilled spirits, the other dragged down and put mercifully to sleep, clinging to his knees and pulling himself farther and farther into somebody else's shirt.

It was bound to happen eventually. Thirty years is a long time. Syzygy, too, is highly unlikely, but it happens all the time. A bombed tourist took the empty beer cans from his cooler and dropped them into the barrel one by one. *Bang-Bang-Bang.*

The conga player in the hotel bar took a solo and hit his stride. *Whop-whop-whop-whop, whop-whop-whop-whop.*

A gust of wind rattled the palm fronds and peppered sand into the face and the soul of the man sleeping in the sand in the big white shirt. His face contorted, his teeth grinding the hard sand.

Bang-bang-bang. The hot tracers bore into the belly of their chopper. They were going down. *Whop-whop-whop-whop-whop.* They skimmed the trees. He could see the ocean ahead and the ribbon of sand. They weren't going to make it. He could already smell the dense, wet jungle breaking beneath them. The instrument panel shattered and glass stung his face. He braced against the bulkhead, his arms around his head. *Oh God-oh God-oh God-oh God-oh God.* His lungs filled with fear, then let go one last long defiant bellow. A primal scream. A farewell to life. A salutation to the next world.

The tourist fumbled the cooler, let it fall, and ran. He stopped, starting back for it, then continued running when Oliver let go with a second wail.

Oliver rocked on his knees, his arms clutched tightly around his head. He screamed almost directly into the face of Arthur Tender, who was awake but paralyzed for the moment, trying desperately to remember where he was, how he got there, and why he was buried half-naked in the sand. Arthur struggled out of his hole and tried to get a grip on himself by getting a grip on Oliver.

Grabbing Oliver's thin wrists, he shook them and clapped the hands together until his delirious partner looked up at him. Oliver's eyes were wild—filled with terror and with passion—and with something else.

"My God, what's happened to you?"

"Tuttle! Private Tuttle!"

Arthur stood blinking, waiting for his own fog to clear. "What are you saying?" Arthur felt Oliver's panic soften and he relaxed his grip slightly.

"Private First Class Oliver Tuttle!" Oliver's eyes shone in the lights from the hotel like clear blue sky. The horror was replaced by stunned awareness. The passion became enlightenment and it furnished his once-vacant eyes and etched a soul across his face. The bewildered soul summoned its courage, which appeared as a scowl.

Arthur let go of his friend completely. "Oliver?"

Oliver rose from his knees. His delicate frame seemed girded. In the faint light, his presence appeared to fill out his shirt as he stood straight as a boy and raised one hand smartly to his brow. "Private First Class Oliver Francis Tuttle reporting for duty, Sir!"

As Arthur stood to face Oliver, the sand cascaded from his shoulders and poured off his round belly, gathering in a circle around his feet. Uncertain how to move, he didn't. He just stood there, shedding sand and looking deep inside the face of the man before him.

"Yes, Private Tuttle. I see that you are."

36

Deirdre could see her father's hands, strong and stained brown from work. The knuckles were thick and solid. One hand held a board—a finger feeling the smooth edge. The other hand swung the hammer and drove the nail home. *BANG.*

Deirdre pulled herself together in the peach tree and realized she'd been doing it again—fantasizing. Fantasizing that her father had built a house for her. She'd been doing this for two days and it was getting weird.

"I think that's it for today." Ed Flannigan took one more swing at the trailer hitch on the tractor. *Bang!*

"I'll have to straighten this in the barn. Why don't you go on home? It's about that time, anyhow. Norman can help me with this when he gets home from school."

Deirdre said nothing. She dropped out of the tree and set her pruning sheers on the trailer. It had been a good season, and the new growth was impressive for an orchard with such little care over the years.

Every tree was producing a trailerload of brush to be hauled and burned. Deirdre stood in the center of the scaffold branches of each tree, trimming the stickwood. Ed worked his ladder along behind her, cleaning up the rest and balancing the new wood. Deirdre taught him not to let any of the new growth get out of reach of the ladder.

"It's useless to grow fruit you can't reach."

Deirdre had learned a lot working in other people's orchards over the years. She liked this part, tending the trees. It was better than picking. Picking was just hard work. Pruning felt so much more skilled somehow. You didn't have to know a lot to do it, but you had to be careful and gentle, and you had to pay attention.

Deirdre's mind hadn't been on her work all day and she was grateful that there was a problem with the brush trailer. Her lack of initiative with the job had made her cold. The cool breeze rolling down from the fog-capped hills moved right through her wool shirt. Oregon this time of year never lets a person get completely cold, or all the way warm.

Ed watched Deirdre pull on her jacket without saying anything. Deirdre measured his look and realized she owed Ed an explanation for her silence. Typically, they would talk throughout the day—about farming, usually, or family, or Ed would get on one of his Alaska benders and tell stories of home. But these past few days Deirdre had said little. She quietly hid in the centers of the trees, doing her job and inviting no questions.

"It's my dad." Deirdre picked up her thermos and turned to leave as if that explained everything.

"Is he okay?" The concern in Ed's voice was genuine.

"Oh, he's healthy enough. It's just that they—he drives me crazy. He's an old man with too much time and not enough to do. He keeps fussing around my place wanting to fix things and *tidy up*. Mother keeps waxing my floors, which is tolerable. But *he* cleaned up my compost pile and hauled it to the dump! Thought he did me a favor. I had three years into that! Mother says to humor him. I'd like to kill him."

"No, you wouldn't." Ed Flannigan knew what was going on. He suspected it from the minute he saw Lloyd and Deirdre near each other. And he became convinced over the past couple of weeks as he watched how Deirdre had shifted from a scrappy and determined woman into an ornery, stubborn daughter.

"I've never been a daughter, but I've lived with some—enough to know you don't want to kill your dad. You're all freaked out because you're afraid he's going to die before you two can stand to be in the same room together."

Deirdre stayed still. "You don't know anything about it."

Ed climbed onto the tractor seat, pulled the throttle, and spoke with his finger on the ignition. "I know enough to know I'm right."

All Deirdre could do was sharpen her gaze and try to burn holes in the back of Ed's head as he wrapped himself in the roar of the engine and steered off toward the barn.

Deirdre walked to her truck kicking dirt with every other step. She hated it when people were right about her, even more than when they weren't.

The fantasy that was beginning to haunt Deirdre started as a dream. It was a simple dream: There was a house and her father had built it for her.

She moved through the inside of the house and could feel it around her. She marveled at the quality of it. Everything about the house was exactly as she had wished.

In her dream she was aware she'd always had a dream house. And the house in her dream was that house. The doors were precisely where they should be. Closets, the perfect size. The counter and the handles on the sink felt warm and familiar even though they were brand new.

It was her favorite time of day and the windows were placed to flatter the light perfectly. She went to one and was amazed at the size of the shadow the house made on the flat green lawn outside. Her dad stood in the sun at the edge of the shadow holding a hammer and a hopeful look. She smiled her approval out to him and sat down in a big soft chair.

The fabric on the chair smelled of her father's shirt. She breathed into it and a great weariness overcame her. It was the spent relief that comes after a long, long wait. As she drifted off into a deep sleep she heard her father nailing one last piece of wood outside. It was the perfect piece, she knew—and it went in the perfect place that would finish her house—perfectly. *Bang-bang-bang-bang*. It was done. The dreaming Deirdre let herself go and swooned awake to the sound of her mother rapping on the bedroom door with a spatula.

"Wake up, Little Mary Sunshine. Your eggs will get cold."

"I don't eat eggs." Deirdre pulled her friendly old quilts around her head.

"Your bacon will get greasy."

"Bacon *is* grease. I don't eat that, either."

Then Deirdre heard her father's voice seeming to cut across time and through the door. "C'mon now, Princess, your mother worked hard on this breakfast."

"I DON'T EAT BREAKFAST! I HAVEN'T EATEN BREAKFAST SINCE PUBERTY! CAN'T YOU GET THAT THROUGH YOUR THICK OHIO HEADS?!" Deirdre, driving the long way home, used the solitude of her truck cab to say what she couldn't say yesterday morning.

Then, she'd only made complaining sounds, dressed, and once again joined her aging parents around a congealed meal of eggs and bacon. She'd only stared at her plate, listened to the repetitive prattle of her earliest role models, and excused herself from her own house at the first available lull. She'd been arriving at work earlier each day for two weeks.

It was getting worse, having them around. It was good for a short time—twenty minutes maybe. Then it was just like it had always been—awful.

Deirdre had been excited when she first heard that her parents were coming back to Quartz Creek. Her father's heart attack had scared her a lot. When her mother had called from the hospital in New York, before the doctors knew for sure he was going to be okay, Deirdre had lain in bed crying all night long.

Her own heart pounded with dread and regret and shame, and she couldn't get the picture of her tired old dad out of her head. His sad eyes the day they'd said goodbye last summer. His big hug that she wouldn't return. She could only lay her head against his chest and wait it out. *See you later, Princess.*

That's what had gotten her through the night. He hadn't said *goodbye.* He'd said, *See you later.* She hung onto that until morning.

Deirdre's dad was right, and two days before Thanksgiving he and Evelyn had roared up her driveway in their hideous motor home with all kinds of plans, none of which included leaving.

Her dad was like a great big kid, only older, fatter, grayer, more wrinkled, and less regular. He was prone to fatigue, shortness of breath, and dizzy spells, and was apt to drop dead of a heart attack at any mo-ment. In truth, he was nothing like a kid except that he got up earlier than everybody else and didn't have a clue what to do with himself most of the time.

Evelyn seemed content to dither around the motor home all day taking things out and putting them away again. Lloyd had burned a few days looking for a level place to park on Deirdre's lot, then blocked up the frame. *Just temporary,* he'd assured her, but Deirdre had gotten a bad feeling when the wheels lifted off the ground.

The way Lloyd explained things that night in Deirdre's kitchen was simple: They were tired of chasing around the country from one scenic overlook to the next. They were far too worldly to be content in Avalon, Ohio, anymore. And so, what better place to live out their days than in the vicinity of their long-lost beloved daughter, Deirdre, and the riveting country that surrounded her?

"Besides," Lloyd said, "it doesn't snow here."

"What about Anthony?" Deirdre was suspicious as to what, exactly, she owed this honor. "You haven't seen much of your *beloved son* lately, either."

"Anthony's as boring as we are. We stopped and saw him on the way through. He's settling down there in Booder. Got himself a place to live and a steady job. I guess he doesn't need his old Mom and Dad for much anymore."

Deirdre had not missed the implication. "And I do?"

Lloyd had fumbled around for something to say, then excused him-self to go check the air in the tires. Evelyn had started sorting Deirdre's silverware, humming like a lunatic.

"That's what it is." Deirdre talked out loud to herself as she made the turn onto her road. "They've run out of things to do with their lives. They've given up on Anthony's. So they've come out here to fix mine!"

By the time Deirdre reached her driveway all traces of the beloved daughter were gone. She gripped the wheel and sped down the narrow dirt lane until within panic distance of the front porch, then she locked the brakes and let the trailing cloud of dust catch up and envelop her.

By the time the air cleared, Lloyd and Evelyn were strolling over from the motor home.

Deirdre got out of the truck, planning to escape inside as if she hadn't noticed them coming, but her legs locked when she faced the house. It seemed that her aging parents had been busy.

The flowerbeds surrounding her porch, which even at the peak of summer were little more than a rabble of wildflowers and weeds, were raked totally clean. There was nothing left, dead or alive, except her two holly bushes which had been sheared to look like canisters. They were perfectly flat on top and trimmed neatly around the sides like an architects's rendering of shrubbery. And, as if to cordon off the scene of the crime, there was a little white plastic picket fence bordering the entire area.

"The fence was on sale." Lloyd stood all puffed up with Evelyn grinning over his shoulder. "So were the lawn daisies."

Deirdre hadn't noticed the plastic lawn daisies. There were three of them spread evenly around the front, turning in the cool breeze on their metal rods, flashing yellow in the low sunlight cast across the yard.

"They keep the moles away," Lloyd offered.

Deirdre found her voice. "I don't have moles."

Lloyd was pleased. "And now you never will! C'mon, let me show you what I'm thinkin' a doin' out back."

Lloyd grabbed his daughter by the wrist, but Deirdre snatched it away. "I don't want to see what you're thinking about. Did you ever think about asking me? Did you ever think I might like my house the way it is? Did you ever think that maybe I liked my flowerbeds the way they were? And how do you know I didn't *want* moles?"

Lloyd shrank slightly, not knowing what to say. His look was not one of guilt, but of total dismay. He really didn't have a whiff of an idea what was wrong with his daughter. Evelyn stepped into the mix. "Deirdre, dear, your father is just trying to be helpful."

Her tone was infuriating. Deirdre had heard it ten thousand times.

Deirdre, your daddy thought you'd like the baby doll.

Smile for your dad in the pretty dress he bought for you.

I know you wanted to go out tonight, but your father is just doing what's best for you—go in and give him a big hug.

Deirdre looked at her tired old dad and tried not to speak the rage forming in her throat. It came anyway. "I don't need your help! You help me just like you always did—you never asked me what I wanted. You just gave me what you thought I should have!"

Deirdre ripped a two-foot section of the little plastic fence out of the ground and heaved it into the yard. She looked defiantly at her father and searched her mind for something to say. Something that would cut and tear and reveal herself finally and forever to this man who held such sway over her. But all she could come up with was, "I hate plastic lawn ornaments!"

Deirdre kicked at the grass and fled into her house. She took a moment in the kitchen. Her mother had been busy, too. The floor gleamed and she could see her honey jar and her salt and pepper shakers open and drying in the dish rack.

"Nobody washes salt and pepper shakers, Mother," she muttered to herself on the way through to her bedroom.

Once inside the comfortable disorder of her room Deirdre immediately began to relax. Her bedroom could always do that for her. Full of big soft things and the smell of her. It was impossible to stay agitated, especially at this time of day.

The light played quietly through the two windows and across her rumpled quilts. Dust caught in the sunlight sparkled in slow arcs. Deirdre felt tired and wanted to lie down.

When she drew the blind facing the sun, it left a weary light in the room. It suited her mood and she moved to the other window to close herself in completely. As she reached for the shade she saw her father come into view out in the yard. He stooped to pick up the piece of white fence which lay on the edge of the long black shadow her house made on the grass. Her father stood just beyond that on the lighter gray shadow of Quartz Mountain. Lloyd looked farther to the emerald glow of her yard still in the sun. Then he turned and faced the darkened window where his daughter stood.

Deirdre felt the sadness in her father's eyes rise up from inside herself—and then she drew the shade, not wanting to look at his confusion anymore. Not wanting to look at him at all.

37

The two long bags lay side by side on the concrete pier. One was slightly larger; the other leaked water. They were both still—excessively still. The pier did not move. Neither did the police car, the fire truck, or the coroner's van. But nothing lies more quietly or more unyielding than the dead. As much as you wish they'd move, they continue not to.

Webster looked through the blur of his window at the street one story below. A small gust of wind occasionally splattered the rain across the glass. The cars on the street and the people walking by would turn into abstracts of themselves—color and motion with no purpose—until the water cleared and they became whole again.

The phone on his desk made a sound, a fragment of a ring. Webster held his breath. His phone so rarely rang, he was uncertain if it really would. It did. The long rich peal of bells inflated Webster with hope and gloom at once. The hopeful part of him waited for a second ring to ensure the call was actually there. His dark part wished it wasn't.

"Hello?"

"Hello, this is Sergeant Hayes with the Seattle Police Department. May I please speak with a Mr. Webster Cummings."

Webster pinched his eyes shut, hope and gloom colliding. "Speaking."

"Mr. Cummings, on November 29 you filed a missing persons report on two vagrants: an Oliver Tuttle—male caucasian, approximate age fifty, small build; and an Arthur Tender—male caucasian, approximately sixty years of age, large build. Is that correct?"

Webster swallowed. "That's correct. Have you found them?"

"We think so. Two bodies matching those descriptions washed up under the pier not far from where you reported their last whereabouts. No one else has been looking for a big and a little white guy and they've been in the drink two to three weeks by the looks of them."

Webster grew numb. Thinking of Buddy, Webster heard himself talking. "I can bring someone who could identify them."

The sergeant on the other end of the line was quiet for a moment. Webster could hear phones and the crackle of a police radio in the background. "I don't know how to say this, Mr. Cummings, except to say that St. Peter himself might have to check his records to figure out who these two are. They weren't the only things in the water, if you know what I mean."

Webster's numbness intensified. It lodged in the base of his neck and rang in his ears. "I see. Do you know how they got there?"

"I'm sorry, Mr. Cummings." The policeman made an effort to sound that way. "These kind of street people have, um, accidents. It happens all the time. Did you know these men?"

"Yes." Webster felt a fracture forming in his throat and it told in his broken voice. "One of them was my father."

Webster hung up the phone and gulped for air. A howl of anguish formed deep down in his chest, pushing at all his interiors. He stretched them, sucked at the empty room, and pressed inward with all his will.

Webster sat still in his chair. His heart pounded and his hands shook. He didn't understand what was happening. He had nothing to mourn. This Oliver Tuttle was a stranger. His father, yes, but a stranger all the same. He was a theory, an abstract—a *quest*.

Webster had failed at research before. It never felt good, but it never felt like this, either. He'd been away from the office too long. That was it; he was losing his professional edge. He'd set out ten months ago to find him and he had. Oliver Francis Tuttle was lying in a morgue six blocks away. Webster could scratch this project off the list.

Webster stood and began taking down the papers on his wall. There were computer printouts of names and addresses, most of them thirty years old. There were lists of dates and sketches of family trees. He had it all: every piece of his father's life from birth to death.

Webster snatched the pages from their tacks and clips with a rhythmic precision. A methodical and tactical retreat from a winless battle.

Webster began folding the pages and odd bits of notes into bland manilla folders. As the walls cleared, the room appeared to brighten. He'd already closed the file on his mother. Was she dead, too? Webster knew he would never find out. All he knew was she was gone—a thirty-year-old dead end. Just like this one.

Webster looked at the folders fanned out on the bed and took out his labeling pen. He wrote *Oliver Francis Tuttle* across the face of the top one in large black letters. A name that represented nearly a year of research and an unidentifiable corpse across town. Nothing more. Underneath that he neatly printed the date, and under that he printed, with finality, a single word: *Dead*. Or thought he did.

Webster capped the black marker and the sound of it snapped his attention to what he'd just written in bold black letters at the bottom of the folder—*DAD*.

The smaller of the two men standing hunched at the corner below turned his head to the side. A momentary lull in the passing traffic brought the faintest strains of a disturbing sound. A wail. A howl. The cry of someone falling down a deep dark hole. He couldn't be sure if he'd heard it or imagined it. The traffic resumed, and the man on the corner shivered and pulled his arms around himself.

"Boy, Arthur, we've been away so long I'm not used to this weather anymore."

The larger man huddled under his shirt collar as they stepped into the street. "We'll be back in the bosom of our friends soon enough, dear Oliver. Soon enough."

Webster tried to blink away the veil of water across his vision. The shapes on the street moved through it like unclear memories and things he never knew. He finally wiped his hands across his eyes and pulled an enormous breath inside himself trying to expel what was left of his grief. It came out with the warm, spent air in chokes and sobs and pitiful little cries.

Webster deflated into the chair at the window and stared numbly across the street, waiting it out. A burst of rain pulled a wet curtain across his view and drops ran down the glass in thin eager lines as Webster's head fell into his hands.

Down the hill and above the docks, concealed beneath the roar and the mist of rush-hour traffic, two people stirred in the shadowy interiors of the underpass.

"The rain's never going to stop again."

"They're dead, Ramona."

"It's going to rain for a hundred years."

John Doe shook the woman, who was more coats than anything. "They're dead, Ramona! Picked em outta the harbor this morning! Two bodies! Can't you stop being crazy long enough to listen to me?"

Ramona Baggins snatched her arm out of John Doe's grimy grasp. "A hundred solid years!"

John Doe got up from the fire and paced just inside the dripping edge of the highway above. The water splashed against the slanted concrete embankment and poured down into the storm sewer at the bottom. The traffic, the rain, and the sewer all became one big sound that John Doe competed with. "We'll have to tell that boy from the hotel."

Ramona sat with her arms around her head, yelling into her skirts. "A hundred years!"

"And that other one—the one who keeps coming back. The one who sent the police here." John Doe stepped purposefully with his hands behind his back. "Yes, everyone should know about this. Laundry Patty. Old Milton. Everybody."

Ramona Baggins swayed back and forth, hunched over her heels, singing quietly to herself: "Rain, rain, go away, come again some other day."

John Doe stopped and stared at his deranged companion, his own madness dancing around the perimeters of his vision and drawing the moisture from his mouth. He walked to Ramona and sat beside her again.

After a few moments the intensity drained from John Doe's eyes as he rocked with Ramona and looked through the smoke rising from their smoldering bucket. Ramona sang to her shoes and John Doe talked quietly to no one. "I'll tell everybody. Everybody should know."

"I expected at least a lantern in the window, but then—I remembered we have no window." Arthur Tender stood just inside the fall of water silhouetted by the featureless late-afternoon light. Oliver's head appeared above the embankment, and then the rest of him with a road-weary leather valise and some shopping bags hung low in his hand.

"Hi, Ramona. Hi, John Doe. We're back, and guess what? I'm *back* back."

The two men dripped and shivered with delighted looks on their brown faces. John Doe and Ramona sat huddled together and did not move.

Arthur, thinking their stricken silence was mere puzzlement, explained. "That's right. While Oliver and I were on vacation, his memory revived. Please allow me to introduce my friend and yours, Oliver Francis Tuttle."

Arthur gestured dramatically to Oliver, who set down his bags and bowed grandly. Ramona and John Doe continued to cling to each other.

"You look as though you've seen a ghost. Come now, our tans are far too rich to be taken for dead, don't you think?"

John Doe leapt to his feet and crouched in front of Ramona with his arms wide and his eyes wary. "You *are* dead. They pulled you out of the water this morning. I saw the bodies in the bags! They said it was you!"

Arthur Tender's confounded face softened as he stepped forward. "John Doe, I have missed these psychotic episodes of yours."

Arthur put an arm across his old friend's shoulders. John Doe froze in place anticipating a horrid end, but relaxed just as quickly when it did not come. He felt the weight and warmth of Arthur's big arm and its authenticity was assured.

Oliver moved into the circle and set down the bags. He waved the smoke from the smoldering bucket out of his face and bent, automatically, to toss a fresh plank of wood on the fire. No one said anything as Oliver stirred the coals with a metal band from a shipping crate. The fire came to life again, and as the warm light of it lit their faces, it also seemed to ignite Ramona.

"So what are you gonna do, wait'll Christmas?" Her eyes shone wet in the firelight—elation almost edging out her paranoia. "Cough up what you brought for us."

The afternoon light of December, barely there in the first place, was hardly noticed as it left them. Four old friends sat, leaned, squatted, and kneeled around the fire. Their faces were streaked with dirt and the sticky juice of pineapples.

John Doe wore a straw beach hat with a colorful scarf, and tiger-striped sunglasses.

These were Arthur's idea. "Mr. Doe, I believe you look even more sinister than usual—but in a festive sort of way."

Ramona Baggins had taken off all four of her coats, forced a bright yellow sundress over her clothes, then put all her coats back on again. The hem of her new dress would sneak from under the coats and every so often she would rub it with the back of her hand, brush at it with her fingertips, and push it up out of sight again.

They all watched the fire working on the coconut shells, burning up the coarse hair like fuses as Oliver finished telling his long story. It played like one of his dreamscapes and his friends gave it the same respectful attention. Oliver described his boyhood in Alaska. He told of the fishing boat and the bays and coves that made up the landscape in so many of his dreams. He recalled his little brothers and his mother and the sanctimonious father who drove him away with Amanda—Amanda Flannigan, the love of his life, and the star goddess who appeared to him a thousand times in his sleep since then.

Oliver gravely told of his time with the Army, the letter from Mandy telling him he had a son, the day of the adventure that ended in such colorful lasting tragedy in the jungle. The calamity that had stolen his life and memories and replaced them with scars and aching bones and nightmares.

Oliver looked up from the smoke and smiled apologetically to the others. "And that's all I've remembered so far. I have no idea how I got back from the war or what happened after that until I met all of you."

"And that is the best thing that's ever happened to any of us." Arthur was trying to put a conclusion on Oliver's narrative. He got uncomfortable with where Oliver took it from this point. He'd been listening to it for two weeks and he still didn't like it.

Arthur could see by the wandering eyes of Ramona and John Doe that they were also growing uneasy with this new Oliver—this rounder, fuller Oliver. The Oliver of the dim eyes and vacant smile had become a man of experience and hidden longing. A type of knowledge, almost wisdom, bridged his nose and a hint of worry creased his forehead.

Oliver was oblivious to his friends' discomfort. "I thought I would try to get in touch with my family again, but I'm not sure they'll be too eager to see me." A thought of his father brought a passing flash of hostility to Oliver's eyes. "Some of them might like to know I'm alive, though."

Oliver looked at his friends and then at himself and back to the fire bucket. "Or maybe not."

He shifted uncomfortably in the gravel. So did everyone. "And Mandy—I'm sure she's long forgotten. The baby would be a full-grown man by now. Grown up without me. They must have stopped thinking about me a long time ago."

"Don't!" Ramona Baggins jumped to her feet and went to the dim recesses of their covey, where she often did, to get away from any unpleasantness, real or imagined. John Doe looked from Oliver to Arthur, all his intensity returned, and he joined Ramona.

Oliver and Arthur could still hear their biting whispers. "Don't! Don't tell them!"

Oliver was vexed over his two troubled friends' behavior. He was about to move and go to them when Arthur touched his shoulder.

"I think what they're trying to express in their deranged way is a fear of losing you to these old alliances of yours, Oliver. Apparently our unexplained absence these past weeks has intensified their feelings about you. They see you as their family, you know." Arthur paused and looked timidly away to the fire. "Many of us do."

Oliver turned to Arthur, whose familiar old features drew his attention to the thin warm light coming from the bucket. The faint forms of John Doe and Ramona lurked just at the edges of the fire glow. Their pale faces magnified the light and Oliver saw their frightened and disturbed eyes clearly through his own confusion.

"I guess you're right. If any of those people had really wanted to find me, they would have by now." The words caught in his throat, but Oliver felt lighter for having said them. He allowed the fire to charm him and quiet his thoughts. The yellow tongues of flame licked over the metal edges. The base of the bucket blushed red hot and Oliver shifted his legs toward it.

Ramona and John Doe could not sustain their distance any longer. They crept in close and settled themselves in the circle again. No one said anything. No one had to.

The fire snapped and sizzled and spoke for each of them as it sent waves of warmth and rays of assurance into their hearts and their skeletons. A fire makes its own kin and knows no strangers. Any who come within range belong to it.

Webster stood in the evening mist looking up at the ill-defined light at the top of the highway abutment. *Why was he doing this? Going to tell two deranged derelicts that their friends were dead? What did it matter?*

Webster had visited Ramona Baggins and John Doe several times in the past weeks, hoping for some news of Oliver Tuttle. He had told the police about them and then worried that they'd be chased from the convenient shelter they'd made their home. He was glad to see the signs of a fire.

Webster looked up for a long time, deciding whether to go any farther. The darkness and the wet turned the faint light almost enchanting. A rivulet of rain found its way around his tilted hat brim and into his jacket. It sent a shiver down his spine and an incentive to his legs.

Webster stepped across the storm drain and looked up the steep embankment. The glow of the fire played across the rivulets of water washing down the concrete face. The tiny streams appeared like hot lava flows in the red glare leading up to the summit and out of sight. Webster took a breath, placed his hands in the red floes, and clambered up the slope on all fours.

He called ahead of himself as he went. "Hello, there. Hello the fire! It's just me—Webster Cummings!" Webster felt the water running between his fingers.

"Hello the fire!" he said again as he cleared the top. "Do you remember me?"

38

Zowat closed her eyes and listened again to the sound of her son's voice. Thirty years of imagining and wondering, fashioning and fantasizing what his voice would sound like. Reality will always win over fantasy once they face each other.

Hello Ed and Emily, this is—um—your nephew Webster. Sorry I missed you. Listen—uh—I'm driving down from Seattle today and I've got somebody with me. You won't believe it. I'm just going to have to surprise you, though, because I'm not going to say on this answering machine. We'll be there around six and I hope you are, too. Bye.

Zowat stared at the flashing red light on the Flannigans' answering machine and cringed again at the sound of the shrieking beep at the end of the message. "Can you play it one more time?"

Emily got up from the kitchen table to rewind the tape for the fifteenth time. Ed's metal-and-latex arm lay unattached on the table in front of him. He adjusted the tensions and oiled the joints and stayed quiet. The kids evaporated into distant corners of the house, wary of the somber mood the adults had been in since Aunt Zo had come over. Norman borrowed the car with a nod to Ed. He'd be back when things were a little less intense.

Zowat looked across the table to her brother. "And he looks like you?"

Ed looked up from his work, growing annoyed with this ritual. "Sort of—only smaller. Kinda scrawny looking."

Zowat ignored Ed's attitude. Emily did not. She knocked the wrist of the limb on the table as if that should teach him. Ed's screwdriver slipped from its fitting. He opened his mouth to complain, but Zowat interrupted.

"His father was a small man. Not scrawny, though, not by any means. Oliver was a strong, hard little man. A real scrapper."

Ed watched his sister drifting, staring at the tape machine. The beep ended the tape and she didn't ask for another replay. "He sounds nervous. Who do you think he's bringing here?"

Ed had had enough. "Everybody sounds nervous on an answering machine. Why don't you just wait awhile and we'll see who he's with? He's probably in love and is comin' down to show off his girlfriend. We're the only family he's got."

Emily didn't like Ed's tone, but she approved of the scenario. "I'm sure that's it, Zo. Webster seemed to get attached to Ed during the two days he was here. I'd guess he's looking to be near his family for Christmas and he's bringing a new friend."

Zowat folded her hands on the table with some sort of finality. "I don't think I should be here when they arrive. Webster's not expecting to see me. I don't want to shock him, or interfere."

Ed slapped down his screwdriver in exasperation and waved an empty sleeve at his sister. "You don't want to shock *him?* That's a lotta crap, Mandy! You just want to go hide from your life the same way you've been doing for thirty years."

Mandy Flannigan sat inside of Zowat sitting inside of Mandy. The layers curved out of sight like facing mirrors getting closer and dimmer and never touching. They both felt the pain and the truth of what Ed said, but only the stronger one answered. "My name is Zowat. And you don't know what you're talking about."

"Don't I?" Ed tried to fasten his synthetic appendage back into position. "You've known about Webster for over a month. You've had his addresses in Boston and at the hotel in Seattle. You know he's spent the better part of a year and most of his money looking for you, and you still didn't call him. Now he's coming right to your doorstep and you want to run away."

Too distracted with his harangue to make the connection on his arm, Ed tossed the prosthesis back on the table and let his stump fall to his side. "You can't hide forever. Sooner or later, *Mandy Flannigan,* you've gotta face who you are!"

Mandy's attention was pulled again to the red light flashing on the answering machine. It was true. The man who belonged to the voice on the tape was her baby—the most precious thing she'd ever held in her life and she'd failed to hold onto him.

She'd been only seventeen years old. Amanda didn't know anything about babies. If it hadn't been for her neighbors Judy and Bill Cummings, she probably wouldn't have even made it to term. They shared two halves of a duplex out in that damp and horrible tract housing by the Army base. Bill was going to school; Judy worked with Mandy at the commissary on the base. Judy and Bill didn't have much between the two of them except a future.

Mandy had been so jealous of her neighbors' plans. Once Bill got his engineering degree he was going to MIT for his master's. He would teach, or join the space program, or design a motor that ran on nuclear fallout.

Judy would raise the family they were working on. They'd had no success to date, but that didn't keep Judy from acting more maternal than the six-months-pregnant Mandy. She talked about it constantly. She told Mandy what she should be eating and helped her scavenge the Goodwill for clothes, diapers, and bedding.

Mandy would watch their bright faces and listen to their happy talk, then she'd sit in her dark room and try to fashion a future for herself. It was impossible. Seventeen-year-olds are able to sustain mountains of idealism, but optimism alludes them.

Mandy and Oliver were too young to marry without her parents' consent, but they endured that knowing they were righteous in their love. Change was in the air at every turn. Old ideas were being challenged and America belonged to a new generation. *Ask not what your country can do for you, but what you can do for your country*. They were young and in love and Americans and on their own.

Oliver joined the Army because it was a steady job with good benefits and there were no wars to speak of. The recruiting officer assured Oliver of the president's intention to keep the United States out of the escalating conflict in Vietnam. Oliver rationalized that the Army could teach him a trade, and then they'd be set to raise their baby in peace without the meddling judgments of their families in Alaska.

Oliver reported for duty on a drizzly day in November, heavy with the news of John F. Kennedy's death, more committed to his decision than ever. Learning that his military benefits would not extend to his unmarried partner only made Oliver throw himself at his responsibilities even harder. Hard work equals advancement equals money. Unfortunately, throwing yourself at your responsibilities in the Army did not necessarily ensure you a better job. Quite the opposite.

After basic, Oliver's specialized training in the Army concentrated on a fundamental education in blowing things up. The harder Private Oliver Tuttle worked at learning how to blow things up, the better he got at it, and the more difficult they made it for him. The more difficult it became, the more dangerous it got. The more dangerous it got, the harder he tried, and the harder Oliver tried, the better he became. The advanced training consumed the young soldier, who saw nothing but hope in every make-believe bridge and powerhouse he destroyed.

Mandy, swelled with the new life inside her, became divided between the joy and the desperation of her circumstances. She saw Oliver during his scant weekend furloughs and irregular glimpses through fences and windows at the base.

Meanwhile, political events in a tiny divided land across the Pacific swelled to include a hopeful and reluctant nation and the stalwart army that served her.

Mandy was eight months pregnant when Oliver left. He couldn't tell her where he was going or when he'd be back. None of Mandy's letters were answered. The only thing that ever came back was a series of official telegrams with some muddled explanations and classified dead-ends from the Department of Defense.

Mandy had the baby with Judy at her side. When the doctor placed the newborn Webster at her breast, he would not suckle. He just lay there with those sad and unseeing eyes and made pathetic little noises. He didn't even have the passion to cry, and neither did his mother.

Mandy's own child-like heart grew hard beneath her little son. It was Judy Cummings who finally lifted the child away to bathe him and dress him and talk him into staying in the world—a routine that lasted for weeks.

Mandy would sit in the stark light of her kitchen and listen to the radio and her baby. News reports, hit parades, gurgles, sports on the half-hour, and lonely piercing wails. Judy would come over from next door, turn down the radio, and sing softly while Mandy watched and Webster nursed on a clear glass bottle.

Judy and Bill Cummings received confirmation of their infertility the same hot July week that Mandy received confirmation that her husband's status had changed from *Missing* to *Missing and Presumed Dead.*

Amanda Flannigan sat in the window that muggy night sucking on the ends of her hair and watching the red tail lights flashing in traffic. She released the hold on her baby and let it lie on her lap. Webster slept with his wrinkled hands curled up tight beside his face. The young mother felt the weight of him upon her and stared after the cars moving deliberately south along the highway. Some part of her moved with them. It would not be long before the rest of her followed.

The first time she saw the bus was in the shade of oak trees at a wayside along the highway. The mottled day-glo paint was camouflaged by the sunlight playing through the tree limbs. A woman leaned on the bumper playing a wooden flute while a tall dark man pounded a bongo and looked at Mandy with a smile as if he'd been expecting her.

"We're going to see the shaman." A big-eyed man in blond curls and little else had handed her a cup of orange juice and swept Mandy and her duffle into the bus before reason could prevent her. There was no reason not to. There was no reason for anything.

The last time she saw the bus it was shining like a fire ship against dark hills behind the tall man's head. He was pushing her and screaming in her face, *So What—So What—So What,* the smile in his eyes gone sinister and meanness in his hands.

She'd tried to tell them her story. She'd tried to get them to make it all stop. The man stomped away as she fell on the dirt shoulder.

The fire ship left in a cloud of bus dust leaving Amanda Flannigan beside the road confused and alone with the chemical electricity they'd hidden in her orange juice. Laughing maniacally, she saw the silhouette of a mountain against the stars. It appeared solid in a world made of paste and it called to her. She felt it and heard it and tasted it on the far back of her parched tongue.

She turned toward the mountain and was calmed. She walked into the weeds beside the road and climbed a wire fence and crossed through a black orchard with demons dodging in and out of the trees and she never took her eyes off the mountain. Somewhere in the night she forded a creek. She fell and remembered water.

As Mandy drank, she'd cried and piled rocks on her legs and they'd made the shape of a pyramid. A vision came to her that lasted for what seemed to be days and nights and months of rocks and pyramids and pain and dark, damp, cold stones.

She'd cried on the river gravel and the water poured over her like anesthesia. Her baby came down the stream and floated past in her tears. She watched him drift out of sight. The weight of the stones held her down and she'd called for Oliver to save him. When she heard the emptiness of his name and saw how alone she was in the black woods, Mandy had laid her face toward the mountain and tried to die.

A white-haired man with brilliant blue-green eyes she'd never forget touched her on the forehead as she woke up.

"What's your name? Can you remember your name? You're about froze to death, young lady!"

Mandy had pulled her head away from his touch and the bright sun and spoke with the viciousness that a night in the creek couldn't dampen. "So what."

The little man straightened and yanked her to the dry warm grass with incredible ease. "Welcome to Quartz Creek, Zowat. Tell me about yourself."

.   .   .

Mandy sat next to Emily on the Flannigans' back porch swing. Mandy looked out at Ed's orchard and a chill went through her. Emily reached over and held one of her hands.

Mandy pulled her afghan closer and patted Emily's hand to dismiss it. "It's just the cool air. This is as cold as I've ever seen it here."

Emily let her hand remain. She doubted it. "You've been through a lot these past few weeks, Zo, or Amanda, or—what *do* I call you now?"

"*Mandy* seems to be gaining in popularity around here." Mandy smiled the half-tolerant half-smile Emily had grown accustomed to seeing whenever Ed's sister was referring to him.

It was true. From the minute he learned who Zowat was, Ed would not acknowledge her as anything but Amanda Flannigan. And he could not muster even the slightest regard for the spiritual practices she'd pursued and taught over the past three decades. How she'd grown in touch with her past lives and channeled the wisdom of the ages to countless paying disciples over the years. How she'd led a life of chastity and meditation and counseled at the college and ran a thriving audiotape business with *Zowat* musings being mail-ordered from every part of the country except maybe Indiana.

Ed would talk about it only in terms of her *religious addiction* and the *New Age hocus pocus* she used to hide from her loss of Webster and Oliver. Emily conceded to Mandy that Ed was becoming a real pain in the pants since he started to actually understand what was going on in his twelve-step group.

"I think I liked him better as a meathead." The two women shared a smile at Ed's expense and looked off into the orchard together.

Ed pushed through the back door impervious to the sentiment on the porch. "If they don't get here pretty soon you'll freeze out here." He held his artificial limb by the wrist with his left hand and made a face and a little snort as he turned it into place.

"There, I think that's got it." Ed swung the arm up and around his head to test the connection. Satisfied, he leaned against a post and cocked an eye toward the road. "They oughta be showin' up any time now, Mandy. How you doin'?"

Mandy shifted her weight on the swing as if to stand. "Frankly, I feel like running screaming into your orchard, little brother."

Ed smiled at the good humor of his sister and offered his limb to brace herself against as she rose. "Oh, there's nothin' to fret about. It's all just family, ain't it?"

Mandy heaved herself to her feet, nearly staggering through the screen door as the plastic arm came loose in her hand. Ed was there to steady her before Emily could even react and he retrieved his accessory from Mandy's wary grasp.

"Sorry." He gestured uselessly to the two appalled women with his empty sleeve. "If I screw around with this thing too much, sometimes it doesn't wanna go back together."

39

Webster paid an undue amount of attention to his driving. So did his passenger. It kept them from looking at each other too much. Oliver leaned heavily on his door and listened while Webster filled him in on what he knew.

"My mother—Judy, my mother in Boston—said that after Mandy signed the adoption papers she just took off. They moved to Boston without ever knowing where Mandy went. I've been trying to turn up a trace of her all year. There's nothing. Wherever she went, she went all the way there."

"That's just like her." Oliver spoke as if he'd seen her the day before. "When Mandy was up she was way up, and when she was down she was flat on the bottom. There never was an in-between with her. On or off. Black or white. Mandy detested compromise. She was stubborn as a rock. *Flannigans*. Her father was the same way."

Oliver's voice drifted off as he looked at the young man driving. The sight of Webster enchanted and confounded him at the same time. The Flannigan and the Tuttle blended into one person like an aberration from one of his dreams. Faces on faces, and voices out of the trees. "She was beautiful."

Webster heard the emotion in his father's voice and shrank from it, distracting himself by adjusting the mirror and checking his speed. "You remember what she looked like?"

Oliver focused on nothing and smiled. "I do now. I've been dreaming her for years. I just didn't know it was her. She had long black shiny hair that felt like chenille to touch it. Her eyes would look out of that round white face and see right inside of me. I've looked in her face alot of times in my sleep. When I'd reach for her she'd dance away and toss her hair and be gone. She used to do that when she was real, tease me and run off." Oliver blinked and concentrated on the road again. "I would follow her anywhere."

Webster glanced at the man across the car and tried to summon the elation again. The staggering exhilaration he'd felt those few days ago when he'd found his father alive after twice giving him up for dead. The bodies the police had dredged up belonged to two other men. Webster remembered them and was not surprised or distressed. None of them were.

My father, he thought. *I've found my father.* But the thrill of it hadn't lasted long.

He'd found his father generally, but specifically he'd found a dream-prone recovering amnesiac who was hopelessly and homelessly bonded to two mentally disturbed derelicts and a pompous drunk who thought he used to be an industrial tycoon. It had taken Webster an entire day to convince Oliver to leave the camp and join him at the hotel.

"You don't have to sleep under a bridge anymore. I've *found* you." Webster did not understand Oliver's resistance.

Oliver didn't understand exactly what being found meant. His life was still much more centered under the highway than around this stiff young stranger who happened to also be his son. Webster had finally pried him away from his friends with promises to return and a little guided imagery along the lines of soft beds, hot baths, and three-over-easy for breakfast.

Oliver had promptly disappeared the next day. After trekking all the way back to the waterfront and back twice, Webster finally found him straightening the crates behind the Merrimont Hotel with Buddy.

"But it's my job," Oliver had protested when Webster came to get him. "It's how I earn our bread."

Buddy took a crate from Oliver and heaved it up to the top of the stack. "Hey, Oliver, maybe you can get a real job here, now that you've got an actual name to put on your application."

Buddy teased, but the offer was genuine. "I could put in a word for you with Carlos. We're losing one of our night dishwashers after Christmas."

Webster stood helplessly aside. He had never considered what he would do with either one of his parents once he found them. In his deepest fantasies he supposed he'd featured himself as the one being taken in. Certainly he couldn't support Oliver. His savings were gone and his position at Bittner, as prestigious as it seemed, was no goldmine. This only meant that Oliver would have to support himself.

Oliver looked at his son absently and then handed Buddy another crate. "You know, Buddy, that's a good idea. If I worked here I could afford a room every night and Arthur and Ramona and John Doe could visit me all the time and Arthur would come by and then I would give *him* bread."

Oliver's face went from mere pleasure to near smugness as he thought it all through. "It's just perfect, isn't it, Buddy?"

"Too perfect." Buddy was teasing again. "Washing dishes all night. Living at the Crusader Arms with three bums. It don't get any better than that, Oliver."

Oliver smiled at his young friend. "I might get to work with you sometimes, Buddy. I'd like that."

Buddy stood quietly for a moment looking from Webster back to Oliver. "Yeah, I'd like that too."

As Oliver and Webster turned to go, Buddy hollered after them. "Hey, Tuttle!" Oliver turned to capture a loaf of bread tossed squarely at his chest. "Don't run off like that again without telling somebody, okay?"

Oliver held the warm bread to his nose and breathed in the familiar smell.

"I won't," he said and turned to go. "I have to take this down the hill. Would you like to walk with me, Webster?"

Webster needed to get his father out of Seattle. Oliver was far too comfortable in his desperate routine. Taking him back to Massachusetts was out of the question. Quartz Creek was the only reasonable alternative until Oliver could be reconstituted from the streets.

Webster reasoned there must be some disability money owed him by the government. Until that could be researched and claimed, Oliver needed to be in healthier surroundings. He'd convinced Oliver to come down to the farm for Christmas if only to offer Ed some comfort.

Oliver was distressed that Mandy had also disappeared without ever contacting her family. "They must have been just sick about it."

Webster told Oliver of his visit with the Flannigans in the summer and the impressions his sister had left on Ed.

"Little Eddie." Oliver only knew Ed as a child. "Gone and lost an arm, did he? Poor boy—maybe we should go see him."

Shut up together in a rented compact, it was painfully evident that there was no chemistry between Oliver and Webster. They'd shaken hands when they first introduced themselves, and that was the only touch they'd shared. Oliver was intimidated by Webster's clear ideas about things and his crisp manner.

Webster was dismayed by Oliver's obvious misgivings about his arrival and this caused him to be even more thoughtful and precise with what he said and did, which intimidated Oliver even further, and the awkwardness continued to bind them nearly to the point of paralysis.

Webster was apt to fill the long silences by probing Oliver for details about specific events. Oliver did not remember everything yet. He recalled being in some kind of hospital for a long time, and then one day being put out on the streets with twenty dollars and his first name.

"The hospital years are still a fog. Not much has come back to me between the crash and when they let me go."

Webster wanted to know why the Army thought he was dead. Oliver didn't know. All he remembered was that he was part of an advance demolition unit and they were on classified assignment. "I didn't ask questions; I just blew things up."

Webster quietly figured the military had been going into areas they didn't think Congress or the public at large needed to know about. Oliver had too many screws rattled loose to be debriefed properly and was too much of a wildcard to send home to the family—so it was best to keep him institutionalized until he could be handled.

In the meantime the bureaucracy had trudged on without him. Webster assumed that the traumatized veteran had been put on the street with the thousands of other ambulatory mental patients cut loose during the Reagan years. It made sense.

Oliver was more inclined to fill the silences with random sentiment, or read slogans from billboards. *Best Chicken in the Valley Two Miles Ahead. Motel 6, We'll Leave the Light on for You, Twenty-Five Dollars.* "Boy, I have been gone for awhile," he said to himself.

As they grew closer to the Quartz Creek area, the broad valley the highway followed narrowed and rolled up into wooded hills cradling farms and horse pastures. Oliver sat up, entranced by the passing orchards—the long straight rows clipping past and teasing his eyes.

"I've dreamed these orchards, lots of times." Oliver spoke precisely, never questioning what he saw. "There were always these trees in long straight rows—but they were full of fruit mostly. Once I saw all my brothers and my mother and father in an orchard. I didn't know who they were. Sometimes I saw the trees from above. These were in my helicopter dreams. We would be crashing and off in the distance I would see the trees and they would look cool and white—and peaceful. I always felt like I would be alright if I could just land in the white trees."

Webster dismissed the image out of hand. It was highly unlikely that Oliver had ever seen his family in an orchard in Alaska. Surely not in Vietnam, either. It didn't make any sense. The orchards must have just been a dream.

Ed's Fruits and Vegetables. Oliver read the sign at the end of the driveway before Webster could point out the farm.

"This is the place." Webster swung the car off the road and was happy to see the windows in the house were lit. He slowed the car until it hardly moved. The gravel crunched and popped under the tires. "Well, are you ready to meet the relatives?"

Oliver paused a moment before answering. "No." He spoke it quietly, like the truth, and Webster believed him.

"I know. I've just met them myself. Don't worry, they're nice people."

The car came around behind the house and Webster was a bit startled by the three figures on the porch. "Oh, there's Ed and Emily right there. I don't know the other woman."

Webster switched off the key. "I guess this is it." He turned to offer

Oliver one more word of encouragement but Oliver was already pushing his door away. By the time Webster got out of his seat Oliver was halfway to the porch. He walked to within a few yards of her and faced the unfamiliar large woman who had come to the top of the stairs.

"It's you." They both spoke at once.

Webster looked to Ed who looked to Emily who looked to Webster who could only stand dumb in the face of the intensity that radiated from these two people. Hot with the plasma of absolute incredulity, their eyes were locked for what seemed a dangerous amount of time. But it passed with the words of the woman: "You look thin."

Oliver swallowed and finally released his face. "You don't."

Nearly one eye at a time, the woman forced her attention away from Oliver to Webster. The power of her gaze remained unchecked. It only seemed to switch direction. Webster felt himself being taken in by it. Gone over. Touched. He crossed his arms uncomfortably and looked away.

"Ed and Emily." Webster tried to find an appropriate expression, but in his discomfort he ended up only sounding joyless. "I'd like you to meet Oliver Tuttle, my father."

The Flannigans each started to say something, but Oliver's voice rose above them. "And Webster," Oliver turned to the young man behind him, "I'd like you to meet Amanda Flannigan, your mother."

The group in the back of the Flannigans' house seized like a machine. Webster put a foot forward then veered over to lean against the hood of the car. His eyes darted randomly around the yard, searching for logic. Mandy vacated altogether, pulling her shawl around herself, closing her eyes and swaying on her heels. Oliver, too, let himself drift away. His eyes found their way into Ed's orchard to the cool quiet light beneath the trees. Ed and Emily had their heads bowed like praying, waiting respectfully.

They might have stayed that way until they dropped had not Norman suddenly arrived with a glare of headlights and a cocky power slide through the gravel. He climbed through his door into everyone's rapt attention.

"Norman Tuttle." Oliver spoke as if expecting him.

"Aw, man." Norman looked from face to face, recognizing nothing but the fervor of the moment, then fixed pleadingly on the Flannigans. "Can I come back when this is all over?"

Ed stepped deliberately off the porch toward Oliver as he spoke. "I don't think we're going to live that long, Norman. You might as well stay."

40

The poetry of it, especially coming from his Katherine, had intrigued Richard, and he'd readily accepted the idea. He'd continued to think it was a great idea right up until about the moment they slid into the ditch.

It had begun as a notable nod to maternal whimsy on the part of Katherine. The Bedinger-Hooples had been planning to go to Chicago to spend the holidays with Richard's parents. His father was in poor health, and with the new baby to highlight his own mortality, Richard felt an urgency to spend some time with his dad. Katherine was warm to the idea and thought that as long as they were headed into the hinterlands they should stop and visit their daughter's birthplace on the way out.

The odd fact that little Anita Hillary Bedinger-Hoople was born in-flight on a Boeing 727 stretch while on an emergency approach to the Fort Wayne Airport did not confuse the mission. At the hospital in Fort Wayne the flight crew had presented the baby with an aviation map of the area. The navigator had circled the geographic point of the birth, whose dead center was a little black dot called Booder.

"We could stop over in Fort Wayne for a few hours, rent a car, and drive out to this Booder just to take a look around and snap a few pictures. It'll be the perfect introduction to her *My First Christmas* scrapbook."

The enthusiasm his wife had displayed over the adventure was suspiciously absent when the road whited out and Richard drove into the ditch. He stood beside the little red rental car lurched to one side and made a tent out of his cashmere coat. Katherine's cellular phone wouldn't work inside the car, so he had to stand out in the blizzard to place the call to their travel club. He dialed the toll-free number and waited for the holiday switchboard to clear.

His call was answered by a mechanical operator who assured him his membership was important to them, wished him a Merry Christmas and Happy Motoring, and then placed him on hold to the anemic musical strains of the Ten Thousand Strings playing "Holly Jolly Christmas." Richard was not entertained and he checked his watch. If they didn't get out of here soon, they would miss their connecting flight to Chicago.

Richard finally got through to a dispatcher and gave their location as well as he could. "Yes, that's Bedinger-hyphen-Hoople. We're about thirty miles south of Fort Wayne just off Highway 1 on the way into Booder."

"I can't hear you over the static, did you say Booger?"

"No, Booder, Boo-der, der, like in *der*-matologist. And that's not static, that's a blizzard you hear." Richard squinted an eye out of his coat and was alarmed to see that even the vaguest shapes of trees and fence lines had disappeared from view. It unnerved him and he tried to sound as pathetic as possible. "Listen, my wife and two-month-old daughter are in the car and we have to get to Chicago to be with my father, who is ill."

The dispatcher waited patiently for Richard to finish his whine, told him that was the best story he'd heard in an hour, then put him on hold. When the man came back on the line he sounded pleased with himself. "You're in luck, Mr. Hyphenhoople. We have a contractor in Booder, and they'll be dispatched to your location. Please stay with your car and be sure to allow yourself plenty of fresh air—and Happy Motorin'."

Richard fell back into the car gasping fresh air and wiping the ice crystals off his eyebrows. "Good news. They've got someone on the way, and it looks like if they hurry, we'll still make the plane. If it doesn't get any worse."

Richard flipped the wipers on to take a look and suddenly Katherine grabbed at his arm in horror. Richard himself froze for a moment, trying to make sense of the massive shape peering through the windshield with wild eyes.

Katherine was the first to nail down an identification and speak. "It's a horse!"

Richard put the wipers on high speed thinking that might clear the horse as if its image were a stain on the window. "It's a wild horse. It must have been out there with me! It's a wonder I wasn't mauled."

Katherine held her baby close to her neck. "Horses don't maul people, do they?"

"I don't know what they do to people." Richard honked the horn and flashed the lights. The tall dark horse stood rigid. Even the baby seemed to stare transfixed at the one big shining eye turned to the car, and the long powerful neck that seemed to fade away into snow. Then, as if it had never been there at all, the horse stepped back into the obscurity of the storm and was gone.

"Yeah, Dirk. Okay. I'll keep an eye out for her. Merry Christmas to you, too." Anthony hung up the phone and turned to Melinda, who was on her knees in front of the open oven, basting the turkey.

"Dirk's horse got spooked by the storm and kicked her stall down again. I ain't goin' after it. Only an idiot would be out in this stuff."

Before Melinda could say anything, the phone rang again. Anthony picked it up and covered the receiver, speaking, as if to apologize, to Melinda. "Prob'ly my folks in Oregon."

"I'm okay. Do what you have to do." Melinda smiled, closed the oven, and stood. Anthony grinned like a dog wagging its tail and just looked at her for a moment. The green-and-red Christmas dress she'd made specially for the occasion flattered her so thoroughly and revealed just enough leg to make Anthony wonder if she was real and actually standing in his kitchen cooking dinner. The fact that she'd arrived ahead of the storm and might not be able to leave had so filled him with joy that he'd started believing in Santa Claus again. He returned to the phone in his hand, absently.

"Hello, Mom? Oh, sorry. Yes. What? He told you to call me? Well, yes, I do have the truck, but it's Christmas! I know, we've got the contract, but geez, Louise, what kind of idiot would be out in this blizzard anyway? New York? That figures."

Anthony looked at Melinda like he'd cry. Melinda busied herself shaking the cranberry sauce out of a can, pretending not to listen.

"Where are they? Oh good, that's just up the road. Sure, I can get there. Ray's towtruck will go through anything. Right, Happy Motoring to you, too." Anthony hung up the phone and sat down heavily at the kitchen table.

"Some dermatologist from New York is stuck in the ditch out past the Millers'. Ray's the area contractor for their travel club, and it's my weekend with the truck." Anthony slapped the table with his open hand and stood again. "Well, there's nothin' to do about it, might as well just do it."

Anthony moved to his coveralls hanging by the door and Melinda untied her apron. "I'll go along for the ride. I don't want you out alone in this storm."

Anthony resisted. "What about the turkey?"

Melinda turned to allow Anthony to help with her coat. "The turkey doesn't mind."

Anthony pulled the coat up over Melinda's shoulders and that settled the matter. "At least let me go warm up the truck."

"I'll wait." Melinda smiled her commanding smile—sweet and powerful like a ton of sugar. Heavy. Mostly indigestible.

"I'll honk when I'm ready."

Anthony's smile turned into a grimace and a squint as he stepped through the door into the weather. The towtruck was a mound of snow with a derrick sticking out of it in the growing darkness. Anthony shoveled and felt warmed by his labors and by thoughts of Melinda.

She wanted to be with him, really wanted to be with him. It was almost too much for Anthony to believe sometimes. It had been nearly two months since their first dance and the band was still playing their song. They'd spent every weekend together since then.

Although she was twenty-five, Melinda lived with her mom and dad for the sake of economy. Melinda's father rarely acknowledged Anthony, even when they were in the same room together. Her mom always looked hard at Anthony's shoes when he arrived, terrified he would track something from the gas station across her linoleum.

Melinda's parents were jealous of her and made it difficult for her to be comfortable alone with Anthony. They used little things: dubious glances, parting shots, waiting up. It was a rare evening on Anthony's couch that Melinda didn't end with, "I should go now. My folks will worry about me."

Having her parents go to a Christian Holiday retreat in Sarasota, Florida, was the best thing to happen to Anthony and Melinda's relationship since Booder Fever Days. The second-best thing was this snowstorm.

Anthony slapped the snow off his coveralls and laid on the horn. Melinda moved unsteadily from the door trying to hold her too-short coat around her bare legs as she trudged through the drifting snow in a pair of Anthony's extra boots.

Anthony let her in on the driver's side and slid in beside her. The sight of her uncovered knees made him shiver with a combination of cold and heat. "Those boots are a little big on you."

"They feel just right," Melinda giggled, and nestled close beside Anthony as he pulled the gear lever past her knee.

"Ray's Full Service to the rescue!" Anthony hooted as they burst through the drift at the edge of the drive and turned onto the vague outline of the road. The shringing sound of the tire chains and the carnival of emergency lights playing around the truck so overwhelmed Anthony and Melinda with Christmas cheer that they burst into song.

They were on their second time through "Jingle Bells" when the ditched rental car came into view and Anthony reluctantly slowed the towtruck.

Melinda moved across the seat to give Anthony elbow room as he expertly maneuvered the big truck around and backed up to the stranded car.

"Wait here." Anthony closed the door with an air of good-natured command.

When Anthony approached the car the driver's window rolled

partly down, and just a voice came out. "That was fast. Thank God, you're here. Be careful, there is a wild horse out there somewhere."

"You saw a horse?" Anthony tried to peer past the commotion of lights into the distance.

"Yes, about twenty minutes ago. It threatened us through the window and then disappeared. It may be close by."

"Good. That's my neighbor's horse. He'll be glad she's still around." Anthony stepped back and squatted to look under the car.

"This isn't bad. I'll just jerk you out with the haywire and you'll be on your way."

The window rolled down a little further. Anthony could now see the man's frightened eyes and the head of a humorless woman beside him. "On our way? You can't leave us out in this blizzard. We'll die!"

Anthony said nothing. He hadn't thought of this. Of course he couldn't leave these people to drive on these roads. They were nearly impassable and the storm seemed to be gathering a second wind.

As Anthony rubbed his big gloves together pondering what to do, the woman in the car spoke. "We have a two-month-old infant with us and my husband's father is waiting ill in Chicago. You'll have to take us back to Fort Wayne."

Anthony laughed before he could stop himself. "Fort Wayne? That would take two hours in this weather, and two hours back! We've got a turkey in the oven. I'll just have to take you into Booder."

"What's in Booder?" The woman's tone answered her own question and Anthony could only agree.

"Nothing. Even the Quick Trip closes on Christmas. Well, sorry about your dad, but I guess I'll have to bring you to my place until the snowplows come through."

"That's unacceptable. We'll miss our plane! I'm going to report you to the travel club."

Anthony was unfazed by the threat and not listening to the ensuing string of whines, complaints, and pitiful invention coming from the car. His concern was totally focused on the cab of the towtruck. Melinda peered through a little round hole she'd made on the window and waved with her fingers. Anthony waved back and cursed under his breath as he jerked the towbar from its mount.

There were no Christmas carols sung on the trip back to Anthony's. Melinda sat heaped next to Anthony moving her legs with the gear pattern. Richard and Katherine huddled against the far door, cradling the wailing baby between them.

Melinda couldn't stand the tension any longer. "Is the baby okay?"

"She's hungry and she's afraid and she is *not* on the way to her grandparents' house for Christmas." If there was any sense of Katherine's poetic pilgrimage to Booder left in her, it was not evident in her voice.

Melinda hoped the husband was more cordial. "So, you're a dermatologist?"

"What?" Richard sounded no more gracious than his wife, but Melinda pressed on.

"They said you were a dermatologist. My brother had real bad acne. Went to see a specialist in Indianapolis. It didn't help, though. He had zits all the time."

Richard was totally dismayed. "I'm not a dermatologist. I'm a book editor, and my wife is in advertising. Where did you get your information?"

Melinda brightened. "Advertising? I love doing advertising. Mel has me do all the specials in the *Thrifty Shopper*. I love cutting out the little pictures of shampoo and stationery and stuff and pasting them altogether into our full pager. What kind of advertising do you do?"

Katherine shifted rigidly in her seat. "How far is this *home* of yours, anyway?"

Anthony answered as he shoved past Melinda's knees into first gear. "Right here she is. Home, sweet home."

Anthony's transparent cheer meant even less to his guests as the headlights swept across the side of his house trailer. The dim kitchen light pushing through the frosted window in the door offered no invitation, as it also presented no options.

"Oh, my God." Katherine held her bundled baby to her chest and looked at her husband desperately.

Richard thought that humor was his wisest choice. "Merry Christmas, Pumpkin." And he tried to hold his smile as the lights went dark and Anthony opened the door to the snow.

"Mmm, smells good in here." Anthony stood in the middle of the kitchen breathing the air with his head back while he unzipped his coveralls. Melinda dropped her coat and went straight to the oven, still clodding along in Anthony's boots.

The Bedinger-Hooples, despite their reluctance to be here, wanted to be outside even less. They quickly piled through the door, closed it behind them, and backed up against it. The air was heavy with the smell of the roasting bird—and hot. Melinda had splattered some drippings onto the oven door and the smoke formed an even haze across the ceiling.

Richard and Katherine scanned the interior of Anthony's trailer. Katherine's eyes fixed on a sagging ceiling tile. Anthony self-consciously pushed it back into position, then let it slouch again.

Anthony's guests tried on their polite faces, but gave up on them when Melinda turned in her boots and held the turkey pan in front of her. "Well, this bird's cooked. I guess you folks are staying for dinner."

Katherine brushed off an area on the couch and sat to attend to her baby. "Maybe you should call your dad."

Richard sat on the corner of a kitchen chair like he was waiting for a bus to come. "Let's call when we know for sure what's happening."

Anthony pulled himself out of his coveralls while Melinda peeled potatoes at the sink. She was determined to keep it friendly. "So, what's your baby's name?"

Katherine spoke to the baby's bottom. "Anita Hillary. She's named after Anita Hill and Hillary Rodham Clinton."

Melinda was delighted. "Anita Hill! She's the lady who used to sing about the orange juice. She's pretty. Hillary Clinton's pretty, too, but I liked her hair better the old way."

Katherine sniffed, bored and weary. "I believe you're thinking of Anita Bryant, and we did not name her after the first lady because she is *pretty*."

Melinda was losing patience with this New York snob and grew peevish herself. "Well, she is pretty. There's worse things than being pretty."

Katherine rolled her eyes and turned to say something, but Richard cut her off. He stood and spoke to Anthony as he moved to the couch. "Listen, I'm very sorry that we're intruding on your holiday. If we could be anywhere else we would. Katherine and I will sit over here and wait until the roads are cleared. You people act as if we aren't here."

The insult was so complete that Anthony and Melinda had no reaction at all. Melinda stood in her pretty dress and big boots with a half-peeled potato in her hands. Anthony hung up his coveralls and looked at his own boots.

The room was ten by fourteen feet and it was filled to the corners with furniture, people, smells, and attitudes. The delicious golden turkey smell had turned into a greasy pall when mixed with the aroma of Anita Hillary's diapers. When the phone rang, although a welcome distraction, it took whatever available space was left and consumed it.

"That reminds me, I gotta call Dirk about his horse. Maybe this is him." Anthony sat down to the phone. "Hello—Deirdre?!" Anthony cupped the receiver and spoke to the Bedinger-Hooples, as if they cared. "It's my sister in Oregon."

Katherine had her arms folded across her baby. Richard had his arms folded across himself. Their faces were flat and their feet were flat on the floor. They listened absently to Anthony's end of the conversation.

"Oh, no—When?"

Everyone's attention was drawn to the effort in Anthony's voice. He dropped in his chair as if someone had removed some shims from underneath it. Anthony put a hand through his hair and looked intently at the formica tabletop. Nobody breathed.

"How's Mom?" As Anthony listened in silence, his form seemed to turn to stone. Any who looked turned with it, and the entire assemblage hardened in their places. A pot of water on the stove began squeaking and snapping as it built to a boil. A gust of wind bonked against the aluminum sides of the trailer.

"I have to go now, Deirdre. Take care of Mom. I'll be there as soon as I can." Anthony hung up the phone and summoned a new voice for the room.

"My dad was shoveling snow from my sister's porch this morning." Anthony looked at Melinda and then, feeling uncomfortable with her penetrating gaze, turned and spoke directly to Richard and Katherine. "He had a heart attack. He's dead."

Anthony was trying to sound level and informative, but a wrinkle in his voice caused Richard to clear his own throat. Katherine looked evenly at the young towtruck driver and then had to look away. Melinda fumbled the potato in her hand and dropped it on the floor.

The silence in the room screamed with the boiling water on the stove and covered the sounds of Melinda's boots as she went to Anthony at the table and took his hands. The baby gurgled and gave a little fuss at the bottle in her face. Richard smoothed his rumpled slacks and watched the water drying on the tips of his shoes.

Anthony felt the room crowd to the breaking point with the weight of the news. The bits and pieces of implication, loss, and helplessness trickled down from his head like hot sand onto his icy interior. And each place they touched turned to pain—in his knees and his groin and up through his guts. It gripped his throat and took his breath, and all he could do was turn to the window and wish himself away from there.

To see out the window he had to look past his own reflection and that of everyone else in the room. Every face was reproduced in the window glass equally dumb and useless. Anthony shifted his focus with some effort to look beyond his own face and into the currents of the storm as it whipped by the lights of the kitchen.

When he did, he jerked in his chair at the sight of a big eye glowing out of the snow and the dark silhouette of a horse.

"It's Dirk's mare!" Anthony pressed his face to the window and watched the animal wheel into the murk again. Anthony swung himself away from the window and his face was suddenly full of purpose, his voice under control. "I've got to catch her. She'll break a leg roaming around in these drifts."

Anthony talked with the breathlessness of panic and was out the door before anyone could move. Melinda stood up, looked at Richard and Katherine, then at the boiling pot. Her own eyes boiled with uncertainty and she seized her coat, but then she dropped it and bent to retrieve her potato.

She went to the stove and moved the pot from the flame. Melinda huddled over the sink as she washed the potato and noticed the turkey losing its luster as it congealed on the counter.

Richard stood up and went to the window. There was nothing in view but a swirling collection of ice and chaos. He listened and heard nothing but the wind and the random reply of the loose siding. "That horse is dangerous!"

Katherine held the bottle for her baby and sat with the same wide eyes she'd worn into the ditch. "Isn't there somebody we can call?"

Richard leaned closer to the window, trying to see Anthony through his own reflection. "No." Richard cleared his breath from the glass with his hand. "I don't think there is."

Anthony came around the corner of the trailer and had to shield his face from the driving snow. Looking from underneath his raised arm he saw the mare standing at the fringe of light cast from the kitchen. With no rope or bribe, there was little Anthony could do with the horse even if he did get close to it. But none of this occurred to him as he bounded after the impertinent animal and galloped himself straight into a waist-deep drift of snow.

He leaned over it helplessly as the mare stretched her lips in sinister joy and disappeared for good. Anthony felt the strength pouring out of his legs and his spirit as he sank deeper in the snow and called into the storm.

"I've been chasing you for years! I'm sick of chasing you and I'm not going to do it anymore! You're not even my horse!"

Anthony turned to the trailer and fell back into the drift like an easy chair. He didn't know how to move. He didn't know where to move.

He just sat looking at the man in the window looking out and felt the numbness coming in from all around him.

Richard leaned harder on the window and cleared the glass one more time with his shirtsleeve. He couldn't tell what that was out there. It could be a horse. It could be almost anything.

41

The white-and-black world was barely interrupted by the bright yellow pick-up truck working carefully down the road. The farm stood like a ham-handed painting of itself done in blues and whites. Clotheslines fat as cables. Tall hats on fenceposts. All the hard lines of the house and barn and cars made soft and obscure.

Ed stepped out into the snow and let the smell of it fill his head. There is something rare about the day after Christmas. Like the eye of a hurricane, a pause in the confused and wearisome events of life. Everything has been given and received; there is a millisecond of contentment in this day somewhere.

Ed's heart soared with memories of his Alaska home. He bundled his thin Oregon jacket around himself and stepped toward the orchard, rows of patient trees made lazy with the weight on their branches.

As he walked, Ed felt the snow touch his face like the ends of a baby's fingers and he listened to it swell around his farm. He didn't hear the sound the snow made, but the sound missing. Ed had forgotten how much noise there is in the world until it snows.

It was good to be out of the house. Too many things happening with too many people for too many days. Inside the orchard there was only the cool air and the drip of melting snow which described a circle around every tree. It was warming up and Ed knew this snow would not be snow for long.

He dragged a wooden peach box inside the dry canopy of a tree and sat down. The damp, the peace, his boots on the ground. It took him back to Alaska and his life gone by up there. These were the boots he hunted in. This was the quiet of a duck blind and the seeping sound of a September snow in the woods. Suddenly Ed breathed deep and thought of a drink.

He hadn't had one in almost six months. Probably the longest he'd gone since he was sixteen. Maybe fourteen. Ed looked up into the tree and let the sensation come; the friendly memory of a taste of Schnapps rolling back on his brainstem and down his throat.

A wad of snow fell free from a dangling peach leaf and landed square in Ed's right eye. As he bolted forward on the box and tried to blink it clear, he had to laugh. "Alright, alright. I hear ya'."

"Sorry to bother you."

Ed had talked to his orchard before, but it rarely spoke back. He wiped his eye clean and opened it to see Deirdre standing nearly in front of him.

"I followed your tracks." Deirdre stepped into the circle of the tree and leaned awkwardly against a scaffold branch. "Mother and I stopped to borrow Emily's car. Anthony's coming in and I don't think my bald tires will make it to the airport on these roads. Anyway, I didn't want to leave without saying hello."

Ed blushed, apologetic. "I needed to get some fresh air."

Deirdre forced a tired smile. "There's alot going on in there." Deirdre indicated the house, but Ed didn't see.

He made a ridge of dirt with the inside of his boot heel. "Sorry about your dad."

"Thanks. And thanks for your help yesterday."

"How's your mom?"

"Fine. Tired. Still in shock, I think." Deirdre looked at her watch but made no move to leave.

Ed looked up at her. "How are you?"

"Fine. Tired." Deirdre clamped her arms hard around herself and jostled the branch at her back. Shards of snow rained down and filled her collar. The chill seemed to remind her.

"I've never seen a snow last more than twelve hours here. I told him that. But he had to shovel the damn porch anyway. I told him not to do it. I told him to stop helping me so much!"

Deirdre stopped and Ed watched her will her eyes dry. She swallowed the anger and hid it behind her fatigue. "Why do old people always die on Christmas?"

"People die all the time; we just really notice it on Christmas." Ed regretted his glibness. It was the first emotion Deirdre had let show over her father's sudden death.

Ed thought of her cool and efficient call the day before. *We're at the hospital. . . . The doctor said he was probably dead before he hit the ground . . . we rode in the ambulance . . . could you come take us home?*

Ed asked what he already knew. "You never got your chance to talk to him, did you?"

The plain sad truth of it heaved in Deirdre. "I was going to wait until after Christmas."

"Yeah."

"It'll be good to see Anthony."

"Yeah."

Deirdre held out her left hand and Ed shook it like a man's. "If you ever want to dump about it . . ."

"Yeah, I know." Deirdre pressed hard, then turned to the house. She took two steps and stopped again. She looked up at the snow-burdened tree and indicated all the others. "Is this hurting them?"

Ed looked one way up the row, then the other, and then straight at Deirdre. "Probably."

Ed watched Deirdre's back disappear through the huge falling snow-flakes as she followed their tracks out between the peach trees weeping snow all around her. The peach box complained under Ed's weight as he shifted back against the treetrunk. He settled himself and rubbed his hands on his legs and studied the falling snow. When the flakes got this big, he knew it would stop snowing soon, and rain.

"Mom and Dad say *Hi.*"

Ed made a barking sound and groped for balance on the box again. "For cryin' out loud, Norman, don't sneak up on me like that!"

Norman ducked under the branches and shook the snow from his hair. "Sorry, I thought you heard me coming."

"It's alright." Ed slid over and perched himself on one end of the peach box and Norman dropped onto the empty corner.

Over the summer, and in the two months since Norman's return, Ed and Norman had developed a quiet but distinct friendship. For Ed it held an easiness that he couldn't quite feel with his own children. There were none of the compulsions to control or admonish. And he was listened to without resentment.

For Norman it was even easier. Plain and simply, he wanted to grow up to be Ed Flannigan—no more, no less. Ed personified all the qualities a young man envied: charm, strength, irreverence. And he could fix cars.

Ed dug a trench in the dirt with his boot and spit in it. Norman spit between his Reeboks and studied it with his elbows on his knees.

Ed spoke without turning his head. "So, you talked to your dad, then."

"Yeah." Norman's nervous system ignited. He picked at something on his neck and made sucking noises through his teeth. Ed waited.

"Yeah, I talked to Dad, and we decided I should come home. He's fishing black cod and Mom needs help with the family, and you know how it is—Mom really misses me."

"And your old man?" Ed held his breath. He knew Norman's feelings about his father were barely under control even after two months away from him.

Norman wasn't aware that his escape to the Flannigan farm was sanctioned and partly arranged by his dad. Frank Tuttle saw the wisdom in lowering Norman's fences a little bit. If they're determined to jump them anyway, you can at least minimize the risk.

"The ol' man's still an ass, but ya know, it sounds like he's trying." Norman's voice turned low and important. "I think he's learned his lesson."

Ed coughed and looked away. "That's good. When you heading up?"

Norman paused at the slam of the back door and turned with Ed to see Webster shuffling through the soggy snow toward them.

"I'll be going up next weekend along with Oliver and maybe even Mandy. She can't decide. Oliver talked to Dad and Uncle Stu for a long time. But nobody said much about it to me. Everybody sure is freaked about Oliver being back. Grandpa won't even talk to him."

"Your grandfather's a hard man. He lets his religion take the heart out of him. You ever think you've got it tough at home, look at what your dad was raised with." Ed stood up to shake the chill off and bumped his head on a sagging limb. The loose snow hit the ground with a wet thud. "Boy! That snow's getting heavy."

The branch, eased of its load, raised and presented an entry for Webster. "Am I interrupting?"

Ed brushed the wet snow from his head and shoulders. "Heck no, Web. Step into my office."

Webster ducked in under the tree. "Norman, Eddie and Missy were looking for you. They want to play monopoly and they need three."

Norman blushed and dug his hands into his jacket, feeling dismissed by his older cousin. Ed reached over and pulled Norman's hood up for him, a gesture no one else on Earth could have gotten away with. "We'll be right in, Norm. It's starting to get wet out here."

Norman slouched out from under the tree and left. Webster looked after him. "Is he upset about something?"

"He's sixteen years old. It's his job to be upset." Ed found a drip-safe place to locate his box and sat down again as casually as possible. He was getting cold and wanted to go back into the house, but was too flattered by his sudden popularity to give it up. "How's with you, Web?"

"I don't know." Webster looked for a dry place to stand. "I'm not saying that to be evasive; I really don't know how I am."

"Heading back to Boston soon?" Ed knew that Webster's leave of absence expired at the end of the year.

"Yes." Webster squatted beside Ed in the only dry spot left. "I talked to Mother—my other mother, Judy—today. She'd like to have me home. Back home there. Her home, you know. I feel like I belong, well I mean, I don't belong here and Boston is where I, well . . . like I said, I don't know."

The screen door clattered and Oliver and Mandy stood on the porch looking for them. Webster looked away and Ed sat thinking of Webster's last couple of days. His reunited parents had not exactly fallen into each other's arms. They talked to each other politely, like strangers do. Both of them talked to Webster that way. The fact that they were all strangers couldn't take away Webster's disappointment with the grand reunion. He'd allowed himself the most meager of expectations during his forlorn year of searching. This fell even below those low marks.

Ed knew. "Looking for your mom and dad is a whole lot better than looking at them, isn't it, Web?"

Webster couldn't smile about it, but he tried. "They are pretty weird, but what's weirder is how I found them. I mean, I didn't. They found me just when I'd stopped looking. It doesn't make sense."

"Things happen when they happen. Best thing to do is give up and let it. You know what they say, *Good things come to good people.*"

Webster shook his head. "That doesn't seem to apply."

"Give it some time, Web. You're just getting to know each other. Oliver just figured out who he was a few weeks ago. He's got brothers he hasn't seen in thirty years, a bastard of a father who still won't talk to him, and thinks he wants to live under a bridge.

"Mandy—Hell, she's just getting around to admitting who she is to herself. Once you all get used to being in your own skins, I bet you'll find they're not any weirder than you are." Ed stroked Webster's shoulder warmly, thinking that hadn't come out just right.

Ed stood before Webster could dwell on it. "It's cold! I gotta move my bones back to the heat."

Ed and Webster ducked under the tree and walked toward the house. Oliver and Mandy stood waiting on the porch. Webster spoke quietly and quickly.

"Whatever happens, I just wanted to thank you and Emily for all the help you've given me and for welcoming me into your house and home."

"It was God brought you into the family, and I just rent the house, but you're welcome any time, Webster."

Ed's voice carried to the porch and Mandy smiled as the men approached. "You two sure do look alike."

Ed grimaced and shook his head. "If you say that to me one more time I'm gonna grow a beard."

Webster rubbed his chin. "*I* was thinking of growing a beard."

Ed shoved Webster playfully up the stairs and Mandy grabbed Ed's hand. She held it for a moment like a stolen kiss, then let it go uncertainly and went to the door. "I'm making hot rice milk and carob, or echinecea tea for anybody who wants it."

Webster followed his mother through the door. "Do you have any coffee?"

The door closed on the beginning of Mandy's lecture on the effects caffeine has on various chakras in the body. Ed held back for Oliver, but the older man made no move to go. He leaned on the porch post with the vacant little grin that hadn't left his face since he'd arrived. Oliver seemed less interested in his immediate surroundings than by what he saw in the orchard.

Ed glanced into his trees. "Umm, is everything okay, Oliver?"

Oliver blinked and drew himself into focus. "I've dreamed these trees a bunch of times. White like this, too."

Ed smiled patiently, having learned to indulge Oliver's eccentricity over the past few days. "Yeah, you keep saying that. Pretty nice, these dreams of yours. You and my sister have a lot in common. You have visions, she speaks for dead people. You oughta get along just fine. Maybe go into business together."

This was the nine-hundredth time Ed had tried sarcasm on Oliver and it still was going nowhere. Oliver just stood there pleasant and barren. Everyone else in the family was a little unsettled by Oliver's manner, but Ed liked him immediately.

Mandy allowed privately to Ed that it was as though Oliver had had a lobotomy. *He's nothing like the man I ran away with.*

Ed had been defensive on Oliver's behalf. *You're not much like the woman he ran off with, either. And if being quiet and nice means you had a lobotomy, then maybe we all should get one.*

A creaking noise came from the orchard and Ed turned to where Oliver was already looking.

"There he is again."

Ed didn't see anything. "Who?"

"That little old man. Me and Mandy saw him when we first came out. He's behind those trees."

"Mandy saw him?"

"Yes, she said she knew him. There." Oliver pointed with a bare arm that was quaking. Ed realized he wasn't wearing a coat.

"Geez, Oliver, stop acting like a homeless person. Get in the house. I'll go find out who this guy in the orchard is."

Ed knew exactly who was in his orchard and he was up on his toes waiting for Oliver to leave them alone.

"It is a little chilly. I think I'll have some of that coffee now."

"Good luck." Ed didn't even wait for the door to close before he charged toward the trees.

"Ed? . . . Ed—zat you?"

"Who'd you think it was, Santy Claus?"

Ed swung around to face his little friend Ed who squinted up at him through those impossibly thick, white, and damp eyebrows. "Well, now I know you're not a hallucination I've been having all year."

The little man was, as always, underwhelmed with anything Ed had to say. "How do ya know that, bigshot?"

"Because Oliver saw you and so did Mandy." Ed held a satisfied face.

The other Ed shook his head, as if talking to a fool. "Everybody sees me. You're just the only one around here who does anything about it. Which is more than you're doing for your trees!"

"What's to do with the trees?" Ed looked around at the snow-canopied peach trees and shrugged.

The little man became indignant. "Don't tell me you sat out here this long and didn't notice what was happening to your trees!"

Ed was at a loss. "Well, I noticed they were getting heavy, but I didn't think much about it. People kept coming out to talk to me."

"Well, ain't you special. Everybody wants to talk to a man who lets his trees fall down." The little man walked over and pushed on the lowest hanging branch. There was a creak and a snap, and then the limb dipped to the ground.

"Hey!" Ed pounced to the rescue of the branch. He looked at the trunk of the tree and the bare white wood where the branch had separated. "You little fruitcake! You broke it!"

The man looked a full two heads up to Ed Flannigan with his hands on his hips. "That's just the first one. Listen!"

Ed listened. Through the muffled sound of random tufts of snow falling from branches and the incessant drip of the thaw and rain, there was a distant squeal. It turned into a long, low wail and then ended abruptly with a muted pop.

"Yer whole orchard's comin' down, mister. You gotta get this snow off 'em." The man made no move to do anything.

Ed shook one branch near him and the snow plopped to the ground. He shook another, then another. His flesh hand quickly went numb with cold. He put it in his pocket and worked solely with his clamp. Working under the tree, he soon became coated with snow and after just a dozen or so branches he stopped.

Already breathless with a combination of panic and effort, Ed considered the four acres of trees around him and spoke helplessly to the old man. "Aren't you going to help?"

The man didn't budge. "It ain't my orchard, I ain't doin' your work for you."

Ed protested, "It would take me days to clear all these trees like this!"

"It'll be too late," he told him. "You can't do this yourself."

Ed scowled. "Every farmer in the county must have the same problem. Where am I gonna get any good help today?"

The little man laughed. "You don't need good help. You just need help. And you got a houseful of that."

Ed turned to the house. "My family?"

"They all came to you, Buster. Why do you suppose that is?" The man's eyes stood still as stones.

Ed felt a peculiar sense of assurance for that moment. Pure unentitled grace. But the feeling left as quickly as it arrived with the sound of another cracking limb.

"I'll be back with the whole damn menagerie," he shouted to the empty orchard over his shoulder on the way to the porch.

It isn't very often a person gets the opportunity to announce an out-and-out disaster. *Fire! Flood! Incoming!* The words roll off our tongues with divine license. And it was with this latitude that Ed Flannigan rushed through his own backdoor and announced that his orchard was breaking down.

The natural command in his voice coupled with the urgency in the message and the fact that nobody had a clue what he was talking about mobilized the household in a blur of buns and bluejeans.

Monopoly pieces lay stranded on undeveloped real estate. Steam rose from lonely mugs of tea. A television's cartoon clowns played tricks to an empty room.

Out in the back, an army was marshaling itself to battle. Ed described the crisis as they dressed. "If we don't get the snow off these trees I'm going to lose them. No trees, no peaches. No peaches, no farm. Come on, people!"

The extended Flannigan family were throwing on as many clothes as they could fit over their Oregon hides while Ed handed out weapons.

"Short people, get the long sticks. Tall people, use your hands. Oliver, you're on your own. Norman, you too. Corey, use this broom. Missy, take the leaf rake. Don't poke anybody's eye out. Webster, you use that piece of irrigation pipe to get the very highest branches. Let's go, let's go, let's go."

The children were having great fun with the excitement. Mandy and Emily refused to hurry in mild protest over Ed's domineering tone, but they moved toward the work all the same.

There was not a slacker in the bunch. They hit the orchard like Samurai and cowboys—faces set. Jabbing, swinging, prodding, hooting, and hollering.

Ed staggered through the slush trying to watch them all at once. "Easy, easy. Shake 'em, don't break 'em."

He stood still a moment to watch. It was working. The clean trees were standing up, their green leaves sharp against the snow and gray sky. There was real progress. The end row was clear and they were moving inside the outer boundaries.

The family spread out naturally, avoiding the fallout from each other's branches. One by one the trees cleared. Ed ran ahead and searched for the worst of them—pulling the heaviest branches gently and releasing them from the load they were never meant to carry.

The foot tracks in the snow are small and evenly spaced, leading out of the orchard and through the field across the highway toward Quartz Mountain. They rise up the base of the slope and disappear step by step, closing behind themselves, into the white face. White on white with a gash of blue sky across it where the weather breaks behind the peak.

From this vantage you can look down on the valley and the fields and the town laid low with uninvited snow and crisscrossed with the black lines of roads and fences. In the middle of it all is one small farm not unlike the others, except that trees begin to flourish from within its dreary borders. The pattern is ragged and the pace unpredictable, but if you watch long enough, an orchard begins to take shape.

It would be the only thing stirring at all in the listless scene except the impervious and orderly traffic along the highway. Cars full of strangers going north and strangers going south, and all of them heading the same way. All of them heading home.